JOHN'S STORY
THE LAST EYEWITNESS

**Center Point
Large Print**

**This Large Print Book carries the
Seal of Approval of N.A.V.H.**

THE JESUS CHRONICLES

Book One

JOHN'S STORY
THE LAST EYEWITNESS

TIM LAHAYE *and* JERRY B. JENKINS

CENTER POINT PUBLISHING
THORNDIKE, MAINE

This Center Point Large Print edition
is published in the year 2007 by arrangement with
G. P. Putnam's Sons, a member of Penguin Group (USA) Inc.

The text of this Large Print edition is unabridged. In other
aspects, this book may vary from the original edition.
Printed in the United States of America.
Set in 16-point Times New Roman type.

ISBN-10: 1-58547-867-9
ISBN-13: 978-1-58547-867-5

Library of Congress Cataloging-in-Publication Data

LaHaye, Tim F.
   John's story : the last eyewitness / Tim LaHaye and Jerry B. Jenkins.--Center Point large print ed.
   p. cm.
   ISBN-13: 978-1-58547-867-5 (lib. bdg. : alk. paper)
   1. John, the Apostle, Saint--Fiction. 2. Bible. N.T.--History of Biblical events--Fiction.
3. Large type books. I. Jenkins, Jerry B. II. Title.

PS3562.A315J64 2006
813'.54--dc22

2006026336

To the memory of
DR. KENNETH N. TAYLOR,
a lover of the Word

Thanks to
John Perrodin
for research assistance,
and to D. Michael Hostetler
for advance exposure to
the invaluable reference work,
The Nazareth Jesus Knew
© 2005 by Nazareth Village
www.NazarethVillage.com

PART ONE

THE
HERETIC

ONE

Rome, A.D. 95

Bright sunlight interrupted the old evangelist's reverie, and when dust invaded his stone chamber, John was spurred to stand and peek out. He had been extradited the night before in chains from Ephesus to Rome, the capital of the empire, where he was to stand trial before Caesar Domitian.

Once Jesus' youngest disciple, John was nearing his ninetieth year, and his long, lanky frame bore a massive crown of white hair and a full, long beard that framed his leathery face. Thick brows hooded dark eyes his friends had always described as piercing, at times accusatory. Robust for his age, especially considering the long, arduous journey, he had been unbound and imprisoned in a dungeon cell beneath the Colosseum. Now, at dawn, he discovered that by standing on tiptoe he could peer out a tiny barred opening at ground level to the vast stadium's athletic fields. It was much too early for festivities, and yet men, women, and animals had begun to fill the grounds. Large, powerful women practiced wrestling holds in the rising dust, and brightly costumed dwarves ran in place and stretched. Ferocious animals, prodded and agitated by their handlers, were led snarling to cages. John had only heard of such bizarre acts, confirming reports of the emperor's fascination with the macabre. Clearly all these participants were preparing for some spectacle. John could assume only that it was his own execution. His stomach growling, he retreated to sit with his back to the wall and pray silently.

Having long outlived all the other disciples of Jesus the Christ, John had known this day would come. He had invested his life in telling the world of the Man he believed rose from the dead more than half a century before and held the power of eternal life. All his compatriots, every one, had been martyred for the cause. He expected no less for himself. And yet, despite his years, it seemed too soon. No, he didn't anticipate living another decade to reach a hundred years, but it struck him that there remained so much to do. The flock he led in Ephesus was growing in number and in maturity. And what of all the other churches in Asia? His frequent journeys had endeared him to all of them. Perhaps it had been all that traveling that had spared him from the Romans for so long.

Others—the younger, the more robust—could accomplish the work. But John took what he believed was a justified pride in his station as the only remaining disciple of the very Messiah Himself. John neither feared nor dreaded death. He did not welcome it; who would? And yet the privilege of dying for his faith, for his Lord . . .

With his bony shoulder blades pressed against the cold stone, John lowered his chin to his chest and prayed silently. "Father, my life has been rich and full, and if I am to perish in Your service, then I willingly commend my spirit into Your hands and consider it an unspeakable privilege to follow my Lord. But there seems so much more to accomplish in Your name. Nevertheless, not my will . . ."

John jerked to attention at the sound of a sniff and saw a guard leaning against the bars of his cell. "I can douse the torch if the oil bothers you," the man said, his beard greasy from the fowl flesh he'd been gnawing. He appeared a civilian, unarmed, glassy-eyed, perhaps from drink. And yet those were the first kind words John had heard since his capture.

"If it's not too dark for you, sir," John said.

"I need no more light than the sun this time of the day," the guard said, reaching for the torch with his free hand and plunging it into a bucket of water. He smiled at the hissing and the steam, nodded at John's thanks, then reached a grimy hand through the bars, offering the rest of his meal.

John hesitated, hoping not to offend but reluctant to eat that which had touched the man's mouth, his hands. Even as he fashioned a courteous response, he

11

was inwardly bemused by his own concern just hours before his certain death. "I am obliged," he said. "But I prefer only a bit of bread if I have a choice."

The man's countenance fell and he withdrew. "Another hour, then," he said, "and you'll share a stale chunk covered with creatures you won't want to eat."

"Forgive me," John said. "I—"

The guard waved him off and settled against the wall, appearing to doze between bites.

"What's happening here today?" John said.

The man raised a brow. "Oh, my meat is no good for you but my conversation is?"

"I'm sorry. I—"

"No need to apologize to me, sir. You'll get your chance to plead your case before our master and god this evening."

"This evening? Not today?"

The man shook his head. "Today the event is for the citizens, not for the emperor. He won't be back from Alban until late in the day, they tell me. The preparations for you are being made at the Latin Gate."

John's shambling, wood-cart transport had rumbled through the Latin Gate just hours before.

"Preparations?"

The scruffy guard's eyes livened and he struggled to his feet. "Oh, his lordship excels at pageantry. Were you here for the Capitolines last summer?"

"The games? No."

"Spectacular," the guard said, moving closer. "Domitian hosted chariot races, sports of all kinds, music, and poetry too. Some were held at night! Imagine. Great torches lining the field. Gifts of food dropped from ropes stretched across the Colosseum. The people loved it!"

"They admire the emperor, then?" John said.

"When he does that they do, yes sir. We don't see much of him, though. You know the rumors."

"Rumors?"

"What a solitary man does with his time."

"No," John said, though he had heard of Domitian's dalliances with women, his having forced a divorce so he could marry his lover, his new wife's later adultery and banishment and eventual return to the palace to marry him yet again.

The guard smiled. "You never know who to believe, but people say they've seen him torturing."

"Torturing? He handles the torturing himself?"

"No! Not of people, man! Flies. Catches them alive and tortures them to death."

John was eager to change the subject. "You've been to the nighttime spectacles?"

"A gladiator bout, yes sir. Don't know how they did it in the low light, but they did. Today's show features jesters and all. You should be able to watch. They won't move you until it's over and the emperor is back."

"Move me to the Latin Gate?"

"For the hearing, yes. And the inevitable sentence."

John squinted.

"They have told you what happens if—when—you're found guilty, no?"

13

John let his eyes close and shook his head.

The man, who seemed at least cordial, now laughed. "I am not permitted to say, but I can tell you this: I will be there. I wouldn't miss it."

Domitian's penchant for cruelty was legend. *God, grant me grace. Allow me to endure without crying out.* Dying for the most righteous cause imaginable was one thing; departing this life ignominiously was another. If the eyewitness accounts could be believed, all John's colleagues had faced their ends with dignity. He longed to do the same.

"What was it you did, sir?" the guard said.

John sighed. Was it what his gospel had accomplished, as he had with his preaching in Jerusalem years before, urging citizens to follow the Man Rome considered a false god? Or was it what he would not do?

"I do not worship the emperor as God," he said.

The guard blanched and stepped back. "Oh! You can remedy that by bowing to him tonight, and all will be well."

John shook his head and stood. "He is not God. I serve the one true God and His Son, Jesus the Christ."

Shuddering, the guard tossed the remains of his meal into the water bucket. "Please tell no one you have said this in my presence! I do not wish to testify. I have nothing against you."

"Be at ease, my friend," John said. "I am the one the emperor wants. Jesus did not call me a Son of Thunder for nothing."

The guard shook his head. "You speak with the bravado of one who has never been arrested before."

John smiled. "On the contrary. Being apprehended by the proconsul of Asia and held in prison in Ephesus reminded me of decades ago when my friend Peter and I were arrested in Jerusalem."

"Jerusalem! Before the destruction . . ."

"Of course. This was nearly forty years prior."

"And the charge there?"

"Preaching in the name of Christ following His resurrection."

"Following His crucifixion, you mean. There's no evidence He actually—"

"Now, young man, do not start down that road with me. You're talking to one who knew Jesus, before and after His death. And let me tell you further, I resolve to answer any Roman charges as I did in Jerusalem all those years ago."

The guard ran his filthy hands through his hair and pressed his lips together. "I'm surprised you weren't put to death, then."

"Such matters are in God's hands," John said. "I spent more than a dozen years after the resurrection taking care of Jesus' mother. And with my friends, Peter and James—Jesus' brother—I served the fledgling Christian church in Jerusalem."

"So you really are the only one remaining," the guard said.

"The only one. I have seen no end of danger. All my fellow disciples—save Judas, the traitor, who committed suicide—perished as martyrs. My own older brother—also called James—was the first, accused of leading citizens to worship false gods. He was beheaded by authority of Herod Agrippa I."

"Were you chased from Jerusalem by the attack?"

"No, I left after Jesus' mother's death some twenty years before that. I believed God wanted me to spread the truth to the rest of the world. How I loved encouraging new churches and founding several others! But while it seemed I was revered and even loved for my bold proclaiming of the faith, which thousands found fascinating because of my eyewitness accounts of Jesus Himself, naturally Rome considered me an enemy."

John had heard not another sound in the underground, yet the guard looked about, as if to be sure they were alone. He whispered, "You ought to be proud of yourself, eluding capture until you were too old to run anymore."

"Run? I never ran, young man. Believe me, Rome knew where I was. If I was not leading the church at Ephesus, I was in Asia Minor visiting the other believers. They did not find me cowering somewhere. I was taken right from my own church."

"Sit, sit," the guard said, and John lowered himself to the floor as the younger man did the same.

"I'm no child myself," the guard said. "I was just becoming an adult when Jerusalem began revolting against Roman rule. You remind me of those rebels."

"You flatter me. Within four years they had pushed

Rome's patience to the breaking point."

The guard leaned closer. "I've always believed that Titus leading the army to the northern wall during Passover when those hundreds of thousands of pilgrims were visiting is what made him emperor eventually."

"No question," John said. "As you can imagine, I am hardly an admirer of his."

"*I* am! Within five months Jerusalem lay in ruins and the great Temple had been destroyed. More than a million Jews were killed and a hundred thousand captured. Titus had so many of your people crucified that he exhausted the area's supply of wood. I was among the crowds right here when exiled captives were attacked and killed by wild beasts."

"You enjoyed that, did you?" John said, bile rising in his throat. He stood. "That was a quarter century ago. Now it is I who have finally pushed the emperor past his tolerance threshold. I have been traveling, preaching, teaching, and discipling young men for the cause of the church of Christ all these years, but it was my writing that landed me here. The proconsul of Asia called my crime 'adding to the literature of a seditious religion by penning your own account,' and for that I find myself locked in the bowels of a killing field by an empire bent on destroying me and everything I stand for."

WHEN A SOLDIER ARRIVED late in the afternoon with John's only meal, the guard wobbled to attention, wiping his hands on his grimy toga. But the soldier ignored him and slid a metal platter under the bars. It bore a handful of dried corn kernels, brown from age, a small chunk of bread crawling with tiny insects, and a wooden cup half full of water.

As the soldier left and the guard watched wide-eyed, John crossed his legs beneath him and placed the platter in his lap. He bowed his head. "Thank You, Father. Bless this gift in the name of Your Son, the Bread of Life."

"Wise of you not to have prayed to your own God in the presence of the soldier," the guard said. "I need say nothing, but he is duty-bound to report blasphemy."

"I will proclaim my loyalties tonight for all to hear," John said.

The guard shook his head. "Then I will not see you on the morrow."

"Probably you will not. But you have already expressed your glee at the executions of Christians. My absence should cause you no concern."

John found the bread hard and stale and the water brackish. He crunched the kernels gingerly with fragile teeth, then sopped the bread in the water, ignoring the creatures. *This is merely fuel,* he told himself, *for what I must endure.* His enjoyment of a meal as repast was over.

John slid the platter back out of his cell, and the guard gathered it up and sniffed the cup. "That cannot have been good for you," he said. "Listen, you can at least delay your fate by denying their charges. Make them bring witnesses. That would take time, unless you have spread this heresy close by here in Rome."

"Tonight such will be my privilege."

"Then there will be no trial. If you confess your offenses, there is no need."

"I plan to proudly confess."

"You do not protest your guilt?"

"I proclaim my freedom."

"You will never be free again."

"I will never be freer than when I meet again my Lord Christ."

The guard shook his head and moved away. "You Jews . . ."

Knowing his fate and eager to exploit it for the cause, John stretched prostrate on the dirt floor, fatigue washing over him as he silently prayed for his brothers and sisters in Christ all over the world. His aim had been more than to merely gain converts; it had been also to produce others like himself so the truth might go forth regardless what became of him. If only the younger men—those like Polycarp, who so ably assisted him in Ephesus and on his many journeys, and Ignatius, the bold bishop at Antioch who regularly risked his own life by thumbing his nose at the threats of the emperor—would be even further emboldened by John's demise, imagine what could come of it. John had long fought pride when others credited him with the wide expansion of the church in Asia. It was the work of Christ, he knew, and yet the Lord worked through His people. If John's death would cause others to rise up, he would run to his demise.

LATE IN THE DAY John roused to the sound of thousands of spectators filling the Colosseum. He stood to watch as the vast crowd exulted at several acts commencing simultaneously. The muscled women wrestled each other while the dwarves frolicked just beyond the reach of the tethered animals. Jesters preened and danced and mimed as the crowd laughed. But the greatest outbursts were reserved for the mayhem that ensued whenever something went wrong. Or did it only appear that way? Clearly someone intentionally prodded the ferocious beasts and freed them before the players could escape.

"The animals were fed less than you were," the guard said, his face lit with excitement.

"But the performers," John said, "why is this their fate?"

"They have been told that if they amuse the crowd, they will be spared. But it is their lot to entertain this way."

"To be ripped apart?"

"If they escape, they are free and their misdeeds forgiven."

"Misdeeds earned them this?"

"If their offenses were more severe, they would have no chance at escape," the guard said. "The criminals come next."

"There's more?"

The guard nodded. "And their only hope is to kill all the animals."

"That's not possible! Lions and elephants?"

"Watch."

"I choose not to."

John's hunger returned and he considered asking the guard to see about even a small piece of fruit. But a roar caught his attention, and before he could turn away he saw a diminutive man torn to pieces, and his appetite was gone. He was left to await his own fate on an empty stomach.

By the end of the carnage, the infield was pooled with blood, and slaves spread sawdust to sop it. The sun was setting as the spectators noisily exited. John looked expectantly at the guard.

"They will not all leave the city," the man said. "The news of your trial has spread. Many will remain to view that as well."

"My trial or my sentence?"

"The latter, of course," the man said. "If you persist in making the decision for the emperor, the sentence will follow soon enough."

When the Colosseum was empty, the dungeon seemed to come alive, soldiers clambering up and down the steps, armor clanging. Several whispered with the guard, who seemed to revel in the attention. When they were gone he approached John's cell.

"The emperor has returned," he said, "in time to enjoy the final act. He now dines in anticipation of meeting you."

John prayed for peace, but he was human. His heart galloped and he fought to maintain composure. He told himself that if this was to be his last day on earth, he would look forward to being with his Lord in paradise. And yet he dreaded an excruciating end.

John hated himself for his fear. Why should he be spared the fate of his compatriots? He had resolved to be a worthy spokesman for the cause. No amount of dread, no intimidation could make him deny his allegiance to the living God. Exhibiting peace at his own end would be a powerful testimony. Most, like this guard, would think him a fool to hasten his own demise, but he could do no other.

"They will be here for you soon," the guard said. "Will you fall limp and force them to carry you? Or will you struggle against men much bigger and stronger and younger?"

"I go willingly."

"You are a strange man."

"I am a believer."

"As am I, sir," the guard said, smiling broadly. "I believe my master and god will sentence you to a slow, horrible death."

The guard's look appeared anticipatory, as if for mere sport the man was hoping for an angry retort, a curse.

Rather, John raised a palm. "I wish you peace in the name of Jesus Christ," he said.

The guard's eyes grew cold. "Still you deny the deity of the emperor."

Two soldiers noisily descended the stairs and ordered the guard to open the cell. "No trouble now, ancient one," the first said.

John shook his head and extended his arms, wrists crossed.

"No," the soldier said, "behind you."

They bound him with manacles, but when the other guard knelt to apply ankle restraints, the first waved him off. "He is no risk."

John was strangely grateful for their strength, propelling him up the steps with a hand on each arm. Unable to reach for balance, he knew he would have otherwise tumbled over the side. Outside in the courtyard, a milling crowd awaited, jeering and slapping the sides of the horse-drawn wagon that carried him through narrow streets toward the Latin Gate. The soldiers scared them off, and John was soon delivered to the scene of his final examination.

It was dark now, and the sky starless. A semicircle of soldiers and their centurions held back the crowd of thousands. Blazing lampstands outlined the boundaries of a makeshift court. Beautiful draperies hung over two-story wood frames, and long benches bore musicians, senators, and other dignitaries John did not recognize. On an elevated platform sat what he assumed constituted the emperor's inner circle—his wife and perhaps advisers. These looked out over the mass of spectators jostling for better views.

John saw no gallows, no stake with kindling. Might his execution, should it be prescribed, be delayed? He was prepared either way. Yet there was a huge drapery covering . . . what? Soldiers and slaves entered and exited, clearly busy at something behind it.

All rose when the musicians stood. Trumpets blared, and courtiers led in the emperor himself. Domitian was tall and handsome enough, in his mid-forties, with a thick neck, full face, hooked nose, and protruding upper lip. He wore a purple robe and a gold crown, which, though large enough to exhibit images of Jupiter, Minerva, and Juno, could not mask his baldness.

The crowd erupted in cheers, and all in the assembly—save John—knelt or bowed or saluted. The soldier who had kindly eschewed the massive ankle bracelets for him now barked in his ear, "Bow to your ruler!"

John raised his chin and gazed heavenward, whereupon the soldier hammered him between the shoulder blades, driving him to his knees. The old man pitched forward, turning his face at the last instant to take the brunt of his weight on his cheekbone.

The crowd was quieted.

Domitian spoke. "Present the accused!"

Soldiers on either side of John yanked him to his feet.

"Are you John bar-Zebedee, born at Bethsaida, northeast of Syria Palestine, and currently of Ephesus?"

"I am he, but I reject the renaming of Judea to Syria Palestine."

"Regardless, are you aware of the charges against you?"

"I am not."

The emperor reddened and glanced at his advisers. His wife appeared amused. The others nodded, as if to urge him on.

"It has been brought to my attention that despite your status as a resident of the Roman Empire, you deny the deity of your god and have deigned to do so in writing."

"On the contrary," John said. "My written record proves that I serve the true and living God and His Son, Jesus the Christ, whom I believe is divine."

The crowd seemed to gasp as one, and the soldiers who held John glared at him. The emperor appeared speechless, and two advisers rushed to him, conferring quietly. As one returned to his seat, Domitian nodded to the other, who faced John and spoke. "You have the freedom to renounce your loyalty to this false god," he said, "destroy your written record to the contrary, and pledge your fealty to your master and lord, the emperor, the censor for life, the pontifex maximus, the father of his country, and the erector of fifty new buildings, including the Temple of Jupiter on the Capitol and the palace on the Palatine."

"Thank you for that freedom," John said, "which I choose not to exercise. Whether it is right in the sight of the God of Abraham, Isaac, and Jacob to listen to you more than to His resurrected Son is for you to judge."

At that all on the dais rose, and the throng behind John began to shout.

"Kill him!"

"Crucify him!"

"Feed him to the lions!"

The advisers and the emperor conferred again, and Domitian raised his arms to quiet the crowd. "My friend and trusted consul, Senator Marcus Nerva, shall pronounce the sentence."

Nerva, a full-haired man in his sixties with a long, thin nose and a cleft chin, announced that "for the crime of heresy and for serving false gods, the guilty is to be boiled in oil."

With a sweep of his hand, Nerva signaled slaves to sweep back the curtain to reveal a colossal black iron cauldron suspended over a grate covering kindling and logs drenched with pitch. Additional wood stood in neat piles. Slaves filled the pot with oil from tall earthen jars. The crowd roared anew.

Emperor Domitian thanked Nerva and said, "John bar-Zebedee, do you understand the charges brought against you and their consequences?"

John did not respond, imitating his Lord when He faced His accusers. Trembling as much with anticipation as fear, John reminded himself of the Scriptures, of the prophecy of Isaiah, who had written:

He was oppressed and He was afflicted,
Yet He opened not His mouth;
He was led as a lamb to the slaughter,

And as a sheep before its shearers is silent,
So He opened not his mouth.

John could see his silence enraged Domitian, though that had not been his aim.

"Ignite the flames!" the emperor bellowed, and the crowd cheered. Domitian took his seat beside his wife, and slaves tossed torches beneath the gigantic pot. As the flames licked the sides of the vessel, soldiers lowered John to his stomach on the ground, and drew his feet up behind him and manacled them, attaching them with chains to his bound hands. They hoisted him over the pot and slowly lowered him until he was kneeling, the slowly warming liquid reaching just above his shoulders.

Unable to steady himself, John drifted forward until his chin caught the edge of the pot and he perched there to gaze upon the frenzied, delirious multitude. Were such radiant faces what Jesus saw from the cross? John's attention had been on the Master and on the Master's mother that day. How the gleefulness of the mockers must have crushed Him, as it now did John.

Buoyancy kept John's knees from pressing too heavily on the bottom, and while that relieved him from pain, he assumed that once the heat of the oil forced his body to respond, he would topple and his head would plunge beneath the surface. The people, and the emperor, would have what they so desired. And so would John. For what appeared to them as his end was merely the beginning of his eternity with God.

He was struck that while his mind raced, his heart had calmed and he exhibited no panic. Is this grace, he wondered, or the prospect of paradise so soon after torment? If he could somehow endure this without thrashing, without cries of pain, how much better would be his testimony to the goodness of God.

Long minutes passed as the crowd murmured, then began to move and leap with excitement. Water would have been near boiling by now, but it was too precious a commodity. Oil takes more than twice as long and will smoke well before it reaches a boil, though John could already feel the heat. The first bubbles traversed to the surface from near his feet and splashed near his head. He closed his eyes. *Grant me grace until I am with You, my God and my Redeemer.*

The crowd clapped rhythmically and chanted, "Death to the infidel! Death to the heretic!"

And as the din increased, the flames shot higher and smoke rose from the hot oil. John had not moved, and he kept his eyes closed, feeling the steam on his face and the warmth of the heavy metal under his chin, certain he would soon find the flesh separated from his bones by the heat. The acrid vapor attacked his nostrils, and he imagined the blanket of black fog that enshrouded him, obliterating him from the view of the crowd. He was grateful they would not see when he inevitably slid from view and was boiled to a crisp in the cauldron of death.

But what? Warmth was all he felt on the sensitive skin under his jaw. And with the crackling of the wood below and the coursing of the steam and smoke, should not that alone have heated him past tolerance, past consciousness? Could it be that God had granted him some immunity to the awful pain that should accompany this death?

John frantically searched his mind for a favorite passage, a Psalm that had provided so much comfort and courage over the decades. Silently he recited:

He who dwells in the secret place of the Most
  High
Shall abide under the shadow of the Almighty.
I will say of the Lord, "He is my refuge and my
  fortress;
My God, in Him I will trust."

Surely He shall deliver you from the snare of the
  fowler and from the perilous pestilence.
He shall cover you with His feathers,
And under His wings you shall take refuge;
His truth shall be your shield and buckler.
You shall not be afraid of the terror by night,
Nor of the arrow that flies by day,
Nor of the pestilence that walks in darkness,
Nor of the destruction that lays waste at
  noonday.

A thousand may fall at your side,

And ten thousand at your right hand;
But it shall not come near you.
Only with your eyes shall you look,
And see the reward of the wicked.

Because you have made the Lord, who is my
  refuge,
Even the Most High, your dwelling place,
No evil shall befall you,
Nor shall any plague come near your dwelling;
For He shall give His angels charge over you,
To keep you in all your ways.
In their hands they shall bear you up,
Lest you dash your foot against a stone.
You shall tread upon the lion and the cobra,
The young lion and the serpent you shall trample
  underfoot.

"Because he has set his love upon Me, therefore I
  will deliver him;
I will let him on high, because he has known My
  name.
He shall call upon Me, and I will answer him;
I will be with him in trouble;
I will deliver him and honor him.
With long life I will satisfy him,
And show him My salvation."

John slowly opened his eyes and through the smoke
became aware of activity all about him. The soldiers

had moved away from the pot. The slaves assigned to keep the fire stoked advanced quickly, shielding themselves with heavy tarpaulins, tossed in more wood, and rushed back to safety. John managed to twist enough to see in his peripheral vision the regal spectators behind him move so their benches could be slid farther from the heat.

The bubbling of the oil had begun in earnest now, and as the air pockets exploded, sizzling oil splashed onto John's head and the sides of his face. Yet it felt only tepid! Soon the giant pot was fully aboil, the liquid in an angry rage, steam roaring even from the sides of the vessel.

"Move! Move!" a centurion cried, sweeping the curtains back. "The draperies are about to catch fire!"

No one could stand within thirty feet of the inferno now, and John could tell his manacles had softened in the heat. With barely any effort he pulled them apart and could now support himself with hands and feet, but he remained in position lest anyone notice he was free.

Everything was being moved now—benches, platform, backdrop, all of it. The crowd cheered and applauded, leaping for a better view, obviously hoping to see when the clouded head of the heretic finally dropped out of sight.

The oil boiled over now and dripped into the flames, sending them higher. The pot glowed orange, and yet the apostle lived. In fact, he was no more aware of the heat than if he were frolicking in the Gennesaret on a hot summer day with his brother as a child.

John once thrilled to the Pentateuch's story of Shadrach, Meshach, and Abed-Nego surviving the fiery furnace. They had not even felt the heat, but enduring that would be worth it to wake up in paradise. But this seemed to be taking so long. Was he dreaming, suspended in some lull between earth and heaven?

As the soldiers protected the royal entourage and forced the crowd back, John stood, a pale specter in an impossible scenario. The man of God was not only alive, but he was also unharmed. Musicians fell faint. The emperor's wife ran screaming, followed by soldiers. The crowd began to riot, many to flee. Others stood apoplectic as Domitian and his advisers cowered just past the reach of the flames and steam.

"Spear him!" the emperor shrieked. "Run him through!"

But dozens of soldiers and centurions merely watched agape, seemingly frozen.

"Kill him!" Domitian shouted now. "Death to him!"

But no one moved.

Suddenly the crowd burst into a new shout. "We would believe!" they ranted. "Praise to the Most High God of Abraham, Isaac, and Jacob! Praise to the God who spares His own! Blessed is the God who saves His servant from the fire!"

John carefully placed his hands on the lip of the pot and hoisted himself over the side, sliding to the ground next to the source of heat that had driven everyone else away. He lifted his hands in thanks to God.

"We would believe!" the crowd yelled.

"Kill him!" Domitian snarled.

As the people pressed against the soldiers, John walked slowly toward the emperor, his simple tunic strangely already dry, bleached pure white by the oil.

"I want him beheaded," Domitian said, his voice quavery.

"His sentence has been carried out, Augustus," Nerva said quietly.

"What are you saying, man? I want him dead!"

"He was boiled in oil. That was his sentence. The law does not allow you to attempt to put him to death twice."

"Nonsense! He survived! He must be executed."

"What will kill him, if not the oil?"

"He cannot die!" the crowd shouted. "Blessed is the immortal, the servant of the Most High God!"

"To Patmos with him then," the emperor said. "He is banished to toil in the mines for the rest of his days."

Nerva leaned close to Domitian, but John heard him. "I am not certain you are free to sentence him twice for the same offense, regardless whether the second sentence is death or not."

"I have spoken! Patmos!"

John turned toward the crowd. "Would you believe?" he said.

Many fell to their knees. "We would! Tell us of the one true God."

"I will tell you of Him and His Son," John said.

"No, you shall not!" Domitian raged. "Seize him!"

Soldiers warily approached as John urged the assembled, "Seek out the people of The Way. They will tell you the truth. They will lead you to the living God."

This time John was not bound, not chained, not manacled. And while he was bound for a sentence that might destroy a man even half his age, his very spirit felt as free as if he could fly. God had shown Himself! Surely no one would mistake this miracle for some human accomplishment.

John was led to a cart that would transport him all the way to the harbor at Three Taverns. Throughout the long journey he prayed aloud and sang, praising God and confounding his guards. Finally he was led aboard a ship that several days later would deliver him to the island of Patmos, where he had been assigned hard labor in the marble mines.

Punishing as this would be on his old bones, worse to John was the torment of spending the rest of his days just fifty miles southwest of beloved Ephesus. On clear days he would be able to see it across the Aegean Sea, the beautiful port city that had been his home and his base for so long.

Over the next several days at sea, he was eager for even one glimpse of the harbor that rivaled Egypt's Alexandria and Syria's Antioch. It was known by merchants as the most strategic harbor on the route from Rome to the East, but to John it represented his home church and the dear brothers and sisters he had served as bishop and to whom he had always returned after long missionary journeys.

Persecuted, fearful, they met throughout the city in homes, primarily in one left by the dear departed martyrs Aquila and Priscilla. There, in an upper corner of the large three-winged dwelling, John had resided for years between journeys. It was a humble abode, plain, with a latticed window that looked out to the sea, a sleeping mat, a chair, and a wood table he had used both for simple meals and for crafting his messages. The very thought of a piece of fruit, a slice of cheese, and a cup of wine delivered by one of the believers made him smile. Others had praised John's austerity, but that chamber and those delights now seemed to him extravagant.

It was from those humble quarters that John had traveled the world, helping to found and then to visit and encourage churches throughout Asia Minor. He had discovered a gift for preaching and teaching, but also for making disciples of young men, much as the Master Himself had done with John.

John had left the work at Ephesus with the young, impetuous Polycarp, who would even now be seeking any information he could share with the others about John's fate. Had he heard of the miracle, or would all be assuming John dead? If they learned of his sentencing to Patmos, they might abandon all hope.

And yet Polycarp reminded John of himself as a

young man, when he and his brother had earned the nickname the Sons of Thunder. Might God spare him yet again to one day rejoin the beloved in Ephesus? Or had his secret work with Polycarp and Ignatius—which had quickly become public and led to his arrest—rendered him forever banished from those he cherished? If that was true, he wondered why God had spared him from the oil. What had been the purpose behind the enemy on his own doorstep who had exposed him to Roman authorities not so long before?

TWO

Ephesus, A.D. 94

As John walked through the bustling port city, now boasting nearly a quarter million residents, his most trusted young disciple, a redhead in his early twenties, had been trying to talk the old man into taking a break from leadership of the Ephesian church.

John had already acceded to Polycarp's insistence that he invite a surprise guest to take over the teaching and preaching for two weeks. That was not easy for the bishop. "It shows how much I trust you, young man. And I cannot persuade you to tell me who it is?"

"No. I wish to see the look on your face when he arrives. Of course, you have so many friends from afar and have had such influence that it could be any of hundreds, and you would be glad."

"I am trying to guess."

"I will not say."

"Very well."

"You will be pleased by my choice, teacher. You must get some rest. And you must visit the new Roman Varius Baths too."

"A bathhouse? Now that I would rather not do. How easily that could become a place of debauchery, especially considering its source."

"The Lord gave me the liberty to try it, sir, and I found it most enjoyable, and appropriate. Men and women bathe separately, of course, and patrons may choose not to disrobe completely. It is so refreshing and relaxing, I know it would do wonders for you."

"But, dear one, I have heard the stories out of Rome, how ostentatious men bathe in wine and their wives in milk. Rumors say Nero's wife's bath was supplied with the milk of five hundred donkeys. And aren't these bathhouse buildings akin to temples erected for Roman gods?"

"Master, you yourself taught me not to concern myself with lesser gods. We know the futility of allegiance to anyone but the one true God. Paul tells us we are free from the law and that the world, even other religions, have no sway over us. Every day we have walked past the state agora and the temple deifying Julius Caesar, not to mention the divine personification of the Roman Empire itself."

John shook his head. "This is hardly persuading me. It's bad enough I have to endure the Temple of Isis even before I reach Domitian Square. And when we are at the baths, how far would we be from that brothel with the ridiculous name?"

"The House of Love?" Polycarp said. "Look past it to the great theater where Paul was accosted. We can pray there and thank God for all the rich teaching that beloved man bestowed upon us and the entire church."

John stopped. "Perhaps. But please don't refer to the brothel as a house of anything but decadence. Sometimes I wonder what we are even doing in this city."

"Respected teacher, I mean no disrespect, but Ephesus has for more than five hundred years been a shrine to the Goddess Artemis, and yet you—as did Paul—chose it as a base for telling the world of the only true path to God. Didn't you tell me that the Master Himself dined with publicans and sinners? We are here because it is where we must be, among the people who need our message as much as or more than anyone else in the world."

John sighed. "I fear we had best begin heading back. And Polycarp, I know you are right. Sometimes it is true that the teacher needs to be taught."

"Or at least to be reminded. I would not presume to teach you, sir."

"But you do. You do. The greater church has need of you, son. Pray to keep yourself pure for the broader ministry to which God may call you. I foresee you as an angel to one of the very churches I recently visited."

"An angel? I consider you such, master, as I do

many of the other church leaders, but the term has always sounded so alien, so foreign to my mind."

"I mean bishop, of course."

"I cannot think of myself in those terms either, sir," Polycarp said, as they ambled back toward Aquila and Priscilla's estate. "I feel privileged, of course, to have sat under your teaching and counsel. Who else knew the Master personally?"

"No one I know anymore."

"Indeed," Polycarp said. "But past your mentoring, I am not an educated man."

"And you are still young."

"So you remind me daily."

"I'm sorry, Polycarp, but I have admitted that I learn from you as well. And your energy and enthusiasm inspire me, as they will another church someday."

"If that is true, rabbi—and I confess it still does not reach the core of my soul—forgive me and indulge me further to plead with you to imagine the healing powers of the Varius Baths! It is very inexpensive. And interesting. Full of unique chambers that are entered in order. I started in the cold room, where I disrobed to my inner tunic and was issued wood sandals."

"Sandals for a bath?"

"Yes! The Romans have an ingenious heating plan, and by the time you have worked up a sweat in the warm room and move to the hot room, the floors are steaming from wood-burning furnaces below. And they have even devised a way to pipe this heat into the walls! After you have bathed, you return to the cold room where you plunge into cool water. It's so invigorating!"

John made a face. "Is it not on the same street as the public latrines I find so revolting?"

"Yes, and I know you find them distasteful because both men and women use them and there is no privacy, but we need not even go near those. We'll go only to the baths, and from there straight to the theater."

"Perhaps next week, after the Lord's Day."

SATURDAY EVENING John was enjoying a leisurely meal in the courtyard with several dozen of the saints when he realized Polycarp had left his place. Before John could ask about the young man, others began interesting discussions with him. A woman wanted to know whether John thought Sunday would ever be recognized as a religious holiday, the way the Romans allowed the Jews to observe Shabbat.

"I'm afraid it's unlikely," John said. "We must enjoy our day of rest on Saturday as we always have and celebrate Resurrection Day while we work."

"It's difficult to have to wait until the end of the workday for all of us to assemble on Sunday," she said.

John nodded as he munched grapes. "And yet that is the nature of what the Romans consider an insurrectionist sect. We dare not even make too widely known our evening Lord's Day worship. That is also why

Paul's letters and the correspondence between churches must be kept so private."

An older man asked John to tell a story of Jesus. "Something He said in your hearing."

John laid a hand on the man's shoulder. "Nothing would give me greater joy," he said. "But this is something I have planned for the next time I address the saints here."

Yet another man asked John if he was aware Cerinthus was in Ephesus, and the old man shuddered. "The heretic?" he said. "What is his business here?"

"I don't know," the man said, "but he has been busy. Twice I have heard him speaking to large crowds on the street. He sounds highly educated, and frankly he puzzles me."

"You should pay him no mind," John said. "You have been here long enough to recall Paul's admonition to your bishop Timothy to beware of false doctrines within the church. Cerinthus propagates heresy from without. Cross to the other side when you see him. Don't listen to a word of his blasphemy."

"Begging your pardon, teacher, but that is what troubles me. We should not be afraid of ideas, should we, if we know the truth? What he is saying has not struck me as blasphemous."

John sat back and rubbed his eyes. Where was Polycarp? He could help here. He could explain Gnosticism, which amounted to nothing less than the worship of knowledge and the danger of counting on "knowing" for one's salvation.

41

"It is more complicated than I can get into at this moment," John said, "but I pledge to speak on this sometime soon as well. In the meantime, you would do well to close your ears to such an enemy of the truth as Cerinthus. Fortunately for him, I have not run into him yet. I fear I would be compelled to challenge him publicly."

"I would relish seeing that," the man said.

"Do you recall," John said, "when we recently read aloud those last two epistles of Paul?"

"I do, yes, but I confess I don't remember them in their entirety."

"That's understandable, but let me remind you: In the first he cautioned against becoming enamored of philosophy and vain deceit. In essence, he was saying that those who enjoy considering every new wave of doctrine run the risk of being blown about by the wind."

Seeing the man's response on his face, John added, "I say this not to scold you, sir. Please just take my counsel as a caution."

And suddenly there stood Polycarp with a wide grin, and next to him one of John's dearest friends and former disciples, a tall man, reed-thin, with a black beard and piercing dark eyes.

"Rabbi," Polycarp said, "I believe you know Ignatius?"

John was struck dumb. Ignatius. All the way from Syria. What a perfect choice for his temporary substitute. Now John could truly relax. Years ago Ignatius had been John's Polycarp, learning at his feet, traveling with him, and becoming one of the boldest defenders of the faith John had ever known. John had joined Peter and other disciples of Jesus in selecting Ignatius for his role as bishop at Antioch. All the reports in the years since bore witness to a man, now about half John's age, who had become a beloved and courageous pastor in the midst of a hostile Roman Empire.

John greeted his dear old colleague and protégé with a kiss and insisted on personally ushering Ignatius to the guest parlor and washing his feet.

"This is too much, teacher!" Ignatius said, eyes full. "How wonderful to see you again and to be able to praise God with you."

"In spite of my age, you mean to say," John said, covering the younger man's feet with water. "I can see it in your eyes. I am grateful for a little more time to serve my Master, and I wish the same for you, though reports of your recklessness worry me."

"You need not invest a moment's concern for me, kind sir. You are as willing as I to be martyred for the cause of Christ."

"Willing, but not eager, Ignatius. I have heard from more than one source that you consider martyrdom a thing to be grasped, a crowning achievement to a life of service to God."

"I have heard the same," Polycarp said.

Ignatius smiled. "Does this game have no rules?" he said. "Am I to be attacked by more than one at once?"

As John wiped dry Ignatius's feet, the Antiochan added, "At least let the youngster fetch my drink so I am required to answer to only one inquisitor at a time."

"With pleasure," Polycarp said, and as he headed for the water he threw back over his shoulder, "Youngster indeed."

"Verily," John said, allowing Ignatius to help him up so he could sit next to him, "may I exhort you as an elder, if you don't consider me too much an old fool by now?"

"Don't even whisper such a thing," Ignatius said. "I yearn for your wisdom as always."

Polycarp returned with the cup and asked if he could sit at the men's feet.

Ignatius grabbed the young man's wrist and tugged him down. "As long as I see open ears and a closed mouth. From what John tells me, by the end of my visit I will have learned more from you than you from me."

As the visiting bishop seemed to ponder his reply to the charge that he elevated martyrdom over a life of service, John had to smile. He was encouraged that Ignatius had learned not to answer immediately, as he used to, and as Polycarp often did. John remembered his own impetuousness as a young man. Not much older than Polycarp, John twice humiliated himself before the Master Himself, who responded with such grace that John was even more humbled.

First, he and his brother James went to Jesus and

said, "Teacher, we want You to do for us whatever we ask."

John felt his face flush even remembering the incident. Why had he not been able to detect from Jesus' amused look the gaffe they had committed? Jesus said, "What do you want Me to do for you?"

John said, "Grant us that we may sit, one on Your right hand and the other on Your left, in Your glory."

Jesus' look had turned to sadness. "You do not know what you ask. Are you able to drink the cup that I drink, and be baptized with the baptism that I am baptized with?"

John had said, "We are able."

Jesus motioned to them to sit, and he joined them on the ground. He shook his head slowly and spoke softly. "You will indeed drink the cup that I drink, and with the baptism I am baptized with you will be baptized; but to sit on My right hand and on My left is not Mine to give, but it is for those for whom it is prepared."

The other disciples soon became aware of what John and James had asked, and they cast glares at the brothers and rebuked them. But Jesus called them all together and said, "You know that those who are considered rulers over the Gentiles lord it over them, and their great ones exercise authority over them. Yet it shall not be so among you; but whoever desires to become great among you shall be your servant. And whoever of you desires to be first shall be slave of all. For even the Son of Man did not come to be served, but to serve, and to give His life a ransom for many."

It had not been the first, nor would it be the last time Jesus had taught with paradoxes. Sadly, neither was that the last time John had humiliated himself before Jesus. Not long after, he said, "Master, we saw someone casting out demons in Your name, and we forbade him because he does not follow with us."

But Jesus said, "Do not forbid him, for he who is not against us is on our side."

Later, while they were steadily on their way to Jerusalem, a village of the Samaritans did not receive Him. James and John said, "Lord, do You want us to command fire to come down from heaven and consume them, just as Elijah did?"

But He rebuked them. "You do not know what manner of spirit you are of. For the Son of Man did not come to destroy men's lives but to save them."

John had borne that shame for days, and yet he learned. Perhaps if he was kind and not contentious with Ignatius, this brother would learn too, even from a mild rebuke.

"It is one thing to be willing to die for Christ, Ignatius, and yes, the martyrdom of so many of our beloved brethren crowned their lives. But should we not desire even more to present ourselves as living servants?"

"I know you are correct, rabbi," Ignatius said. "But our Lord has given me such boldness to speak publicly for His name's sake and against this world's system that there is little doubt I will one day push Rome past its breaking point. Caesar Domitian has proven anything but tolerant and moderate, but even if I should outlast him, there is no telling the tenor of those who might follow him. Some say there is a plot afoot to again unify the empire by forcing everyone, even the Jews, to bow before Roman gods."

"I pray it never becomes so."

"I pray the same, loved one, but I am a realist. And you know, because you taught me to be this way, our message and the way I proclaim it does not change with the winds that blow from Rome. Regardless of the emperor or his degree of tolerance for us infidels, I will, as our dear departed Paul so eloquently put it, preach Christ and Him crucified."

John shook his head. "And the Master called my brother and me the Sons of Thunder. What would He call you?"

"To martyrdom, I hope," Ignatius said.

"I too can imagine no greater honor, friend, but I confess I pray He spares you as He has me so the saints may continue to prosper under your wisdom."

"The courage is of the Lord, father. Any wisdom is from you."

THAT EVENING, Ignatius explained that when Polycarp's confidential invitation had arrived, he was already planning a tour of the Asian churches. "This fit perfectly into my plans, and my colleagues and congregation graciously permitted me to come."

Polycarp said, "He has agreed to speak at special nightly meetings for the entire fortnight. And, rabbi, beginning first thing tomorrow, you and I will take a refreshing break. A warm, steaming break."

John sighed. "Please, Polycarp, don't begin with the—"

"But you should walk every day anyway, sir."

"Granted. But we do not need—"

"Yes," Ignatius said. "Yes, we do."

"*You* know of this already?" John said. "You two have been conspiring?"

"We have," Ignatius said. "And I think it will be just the tonic for you."

John shook his head. "Surely you know the Roman baths are mere fronts for temples to false gods, filled with idols, and— Well, if you are both determined to frequent them, I should resign as your mentor."

"It is too late for that," Ignatius said. "I beseech you give it a try. Allow us to teach you something this once. You walk with the Holy Spirit and you are immune to pagan gods. Allow the heat of the water to refresh your ancient bones."

"You are both unbending and unrepentant, are you not?"

Ignatius and Polycarp caught each other's eye and laughed.

"Get your rest, rabbi," Polycarp said. "Enjoy a late breakfast. We shall leave mid-morning."

"Good night, rebellious youngsters," John said, waving them off. And as they left he slipped beneath his blanket, thanking God for young men who seemed to love him so much.

And he actually looked forward to the healing power of the hot water, Roman or not.

THREE

C an you not just walk?" John said the next morning as he struggled to keep up with Ignatius. "It seems you march everywhere. By the time we get there, I will need whatever repairs the waters offer." Polycarp hung back with John, but it was obvious he would have rather broken free and rushed to the Varius Baths too.

John slowed even more than he needed to as they approached the colossal building. He had a bad feeling about it all, and while he had decided that his young friends were right—that it was harmless and spiritually neutral—he was repulsed by the extravagance and the homage clearly paid to pagan gods and to Rome. He was not blind to the beauty and magnificence of the architecture, but the very idea of paying—though the amount would be minuscule—to traffic in a Roman establishment bothered him more than he could say. But Ignatius had already pledged the stipend for all three from personal funds.

"I accept with gratitude," the old man said. "But we both know your resources come from the Lord's work and the Lord's people."

"Then do not think about it."

But John could think of little else. He felt conspicuous and was grateful the baths were busy but not terribly crowded. When the men had paid and were directed to the cold room to shed their outer garments and slip into the wood sandals, John was ready to be done with this. But Ignatius and Polycarp's enthusiasm was hard to ignore. The taller Ignatius had changed in an instant and was ready to go. Polycarp helped John put on his sandals. As if knowing their elder was self-conscious, the other two allowed him to fall in between them as they moved to the warm room.

"Ahh!" Ignatius roared. "This is where you work up a sweat and prepare for the hot water in the next chamber." He strode about, slapping Polycarp on the shoulder, sweeping his arms here and there, and stretching. John wished Ignatius would settle down, but he had to admit, if only to himself, that the warmth from the floor and the walls felt wonderful on his skin and already seemed to be seeping into his bones and joints.

While Ignatius and Polycarp moved about, working up a sweat, John sat and crossed his legs and arms, feeling the moisture begin to pour from him. He immediately grew drowsy.

"Come, come," Ignatius said. "Get yourself good and warm so the hot water will not be such a shock. Then prepare for the plunge into the cold."

"I feel well," John said. "Allow me to just sit here and enjoy this."

"But we're going into the next room and the spring-fed bath soon," Polycarp said. "Will you be ready?"

John tucked his chin to his chest, and his breathing quickly became even and deep. He couldn't keep his eyes open. "You go when you're ready. I'll be along."

"Let us go," Ignatius said.

"Are you sure, master?" Polycarp said. "You will join us, will you not?"

"I will. In time."

Steam poured through the door as the two left, and John heard vendors from the pool room offering refreshments—wine, cheese, and sausages—for sale. He found himself dozing in the soothing heat but planned to follow through on his promise to join his young friends.

John opened one eye as other parties moved into the warm room, and most took no notice of him, moving on as soon as they were ready. Soon a party of a half dozen entered, and all seemed to be listening to the obvious leader, a thick, stocky, athletic man of full face and thin lips who seemed to speak with authority. Through the steam John squinted to watch the man, who clearly had the attention of the rest.

"Many conclusions can be drawn from the life and teachings of Jesus," he said. And John had to wonder if the man had any idea that he shared a room with someone who had been a personal friend of the Christ. "My Egyptian teachers and angelic muses confirm that the world we live in, as well as the one we will go to upon death, were not created by the Supreme Being but by the Demiurge. Jehovah has not given us the world and the law, but rather the angels have."

Heresy! Who is this?

"Is Jesus the Christ?" one of the young men said.

"No, no. Jesus was the son of earthly parents, and the Christ descended upon Him at His baptism but left Him again at His crucifixion."

"Let me ask you this, Cerinthus," a young man said, and John shivered despite the heat.

Cerinthus!

The small group headed into the baths, and the old man leapt to his feet. He pushed through the door and called out, "Polycarp! Ignatius! Come now! We must leave!"

Ignatius stopped and turned in the shallow water. Polycarp rushed from the pool. "What is it, master? Are you ill?"

"We must leave this place now! An enemy of the truth is here, and we must flee lest the roof cave in on him and crush us too!"

The men splashed from the water and leaned in to John. "What is it, rabbi?" Ignatius said. "Who is here?"

John pointed. "That is Cerinthus!"

"Verily? The Gnostic? I'll debate him right here!"

But John pulled him away. "If you still consider me your mentor, you will come with me now. I do not want to meet my end in a Roman bath. Now, please!"

"Do we have time to rinse in the cold pool?" Polycarp said, but John's look alone was his answer. The two hurried back to the cold room, drying and dressing while kicking off their wood sandals and replacing them with their own leather ones. With his young charges on either side, John rushed toward the exit, eager to breathe freely again in the open air.

"Do you really believe God will strike him dead in there?" Ignatius said.

"I don't know," John said. "But I'd rather die a martyr's death than be taken in the judgment meted out to an enemy of the truth." But he slowed. Something was niggling at him.

"I remain in a mood to counter him," Ignatius said. "Are you sure it is he?"

"No doubt," John said, stopping. Had he grown so old that he was now a coward? Where was the Son of Thunder his own Master had christened? "Am I wrong? Shall we take him on, right here, right now? Oppose him before he draws yet a larger crowd on the street?"

"Nothing would give me more pleasure," Ignatius said. "I long to see you face him and tell them the truth."

FOUR

Y ou're flushed," Polycarp said, bending close to John, who had dropped onto a wood bench in the changing room. "And breathing heavily. Isn't he breathing heavily, Ignatius? It seems to me he's—"

"Breathing heavily, yes, I can see that. *Panting* is the word you're looking for there, Polycarp. Let him catch his breath."

"I am angry, that's all," John said. "You young pups can't wait to debate the man. I prefer tearing him limb from limb."

"My, my," Polycarp said.

John stood. "You don't understand, Polycarp. You weren't with the Master when He—"

But the blood rushed from John's head and he teetered, then plopped to the bench again.

"Whoa there, old-timer," Ignatius said. "Steady. Deep breaths."

"I didn't mean to agitate you, rabbi," Polycarp said.

"Well, you did! You think scolding me will ease my fury? It doesn't. And all this does is make me chastise myself. What am I thinking? A believer all these years and still no control over my emotions."

Ignatius massaged John's back. "Settle now. You have reason to be indignant. But think, man. You are no match for the young Cerinthus. If he is the one you pointed out, I should be the one to take him on."

"I would that you not fight him either, Ignatius. Though I would love to see that. But for a man who never saw Jesus, let alone walked by His side for three years, to speak as with authority . . ."

"I know," Ignatius said. "I know. Let's gather our wits about us."

"I don't know how long we should let him sit

without eating, Ignatius," Polycarp said. "The noon hour approaches."

"I'm fine," John said.

"No, he's right," the Bishop of Antioch said. "Why don't we head toward the theater. You wanted to pray and remember Paul there, did you not?"

"I did."

"Unless you are not up to it."

"Don't play the fool," John said. "I am up to anything, but I'll not forgive myself if I let that heretic out of here without facing him." He rose but allowed his young consorts to each take an arm. "I'm all right."

As they moved again into the steaming baths, John recognized one of the young men in Cerinthus's entourage, lounging by the door.

"Excuse me, sir," he said. "Are you not a disciple of Cerinthus?"

"I certainly am!" the young man said, grinning. "He is in the water and about to speak. Would you care to meet him?"

"I would very much, but I should inform you that I plan to—"

It was all John could do to restrain himself. He wanted to follow the young man, to shout, challenge, start the argument himself as soon as he saw Cerinthus. But he knew he must not. He prayed silently that God would give him the patience, the fortitude, to hear the man out. Paul had been so good at this, listening and then picking apart a man's arguments logically and forthrightly. Soon enough the double-talker would be seen for what he was—a blasphemer, a cultist, an antichrist.

Who had allowed this man to address the bathers? Would the Romans allow a true Christian the same privilege? Of course not. Worse, another young man, who had assumed the role of master of ceremonies, introduced Cerinthus as a Christian!

And why did this crowd, certainly largely unaware of who the man was and what he was about, applaud him before he began? Would they worship any man who appeared worthy, even before hearing him?

Cerinthus looked to the tile floor and raised a hand for silence, and John was sickened by that obvious fake humility. "I am but a poor man," he began, "not of any rank or privilege that should lend me credence. I consider myself a believer, though I will be swift to say you will not find me among the worshipers of Jesus who turn their backs on the Sabbath and try to institute a new day, a so-called Lord's Day. It is the Christ I worship, not the man Jesus."

John felt on his arms the grips of both his friends, as if they knew instinctively that such heresy might make him bolt. He shuddered. *Jesus* is *the Christ! I know it! I know it! I knew Him! I know Him still.*

"I do not come to tickle your ears," Cerinthus continued. "I speak plainly so you may understand. Though I have studied long under divine instruction and may be considered an educated man, I do not set myself above you. I will not mislead you. I tell you clearly that I deny the claims of the divinity of Jesus

56

made by many of His followers. He never said He was the Christ. He never claimed Godship for Himself."

Liar! Jesus told me Himself that He and His Father were one!

Someone from the crowd called out, "But what of the teachings of the missionary Paul?" And John was proud of whoever that was, while yet hoping it was not a member of his church. Oh, that true followers of Jesus would ignore this man!

"Again," Cerinthus said, "I speak not to gain popularity but to tell the truth. I regard Paul as apostate. He clearly taught that Christ existed before the foundation of the world, but I say that only matter is eternal and a product of the Deity. Material things constitute the body of the Creator God. Creation, the world, is then the transformation of what preexisted, and that does not include the Man Jesus.

"God created the universe by His wisdom, a demiurgic hand, not through another entity, another being, another person."

Not true! Jesus was with God from the beginning, and it was Jesus Himself who created all things!

"What is he saying, master?" Polycarp said. "I thought a demiurge was a Greek magistrate."

"No, no," John said. "The Gnostics believe the Demiurge is a deity who created the world out of chaos and originated evil."

Cerinthus said, "I can see the puzzlement on your faces. Let me explain. Our universe is made up of two realms, the good and the evil. The Son of God, the

Christ, rules over the realm of the good, and to Him is given the world to come. But the Prince of Evil is the prince of this world. The Christ resides between God and His creation, thus He is not a creature, but still not equal to or even comparable to the Father."

John quivered and moaned, clenching his teeth to keep from crying out.

"The union of Christ with Jesus is a mystery," Cerinthus intoned.

It is not! They are one and the same!

Ignatius leaned in and whispered to John. "No wonder people's ears are tickled by this nonsense: people do not want to accept that they cannot save themselves. They do not want their salvation to rest in the grace of God. They'd rather believe this and play a role in their own destinies."

Someone else spoke up, and John turned to try to see him because the voice was familiar. Polycarp did the same and whispered to Ignatius, "He's one of ours!"

"How, then," the man said, "is a man saved from his sins? For Jesus to die for our sins, He had to be the Christ."

"No, no," Cerinthus said. "You see, man is saved by knowledge, by believing in the Teacher, God, and by being baptized for the forgiveness of sins. Thus he receives knowledge and strength to be able to obey the law. I am telling you a revelation of Christ and His apostles."

John could contain himself no longer. "I *am* one of those apostles," he shouted, "and you, sir, are misinformed! Gaining the knowledge and strength to obey the law will leave one still under the bondage of his sin! You cannot work to save yourself!"

The crowd stirred, but Cerinthus quieted them, squinted through the mist, and smiled condescendingly. "You are one of the apostles?"

"A disciple! I knew Jesus personally."

"Indeed? If that is true, you are the only one who remains, and that would make you John."

"I am he."

Cerinthus bowed. "I greet you with humble respect, if you are to be believed."

"It is true," Polycarp said, "and I vouch for him."

"And who might you be? Mary of Magdala?"

The crowd roared. Cerinthus continued, "Unless you too were an eyewitness to Jesus—and you are clearly too young for that—you can vouch for no one who said he has seen the Man."

Voice shaking, John said, "Let me tell you, sir, you have it all wrong."

"And let me beseech you, honored associated of Jesus, to act as He would wish and hold your tongue while I have the ears of these people."

"But you do not deserve their attention, man! You are lying, making bold claims from thin evidence, confusing truth with—"

"I assure you, John—if that's who you are—that when I am finished here I will urge any who wish to to stay and listen to you."

He turned back to the people. "The salvation I

preach and believe has nothing to do with the redemption of every human soul. It is a grand, cosmic process. It is the return of all things to their state before a flaw in the realm of the good brought matter into existence and entrapped some of the divine light. The Christ was sent as a savior who united Himself with Jesus, the son of Mary, at His baptism."

"You must not continue with this!" John cried, but Cerinthus ignored him.

"The human is a creation of the Demiurge, a composite of soul, body, and spirit. Your salvation rests in the return of your spirit to God."

"No!" John yelled. "Men of Ephesus, hear me! Your salvation lies in your resurrection, based on the work of Jesus the Christ on the cross and *His* resurrection!"

Cerinthus plunged ahead. "There is no resurrection of the body! God revealed Himself in Jesus and appeared as a man in Judea; to know him, and to become free of the angry, vengeful Creator God of the Old Testament, this is salvation."

"Your savior, then," John said, "is not my Savior! Your savior does not save. Where is the atonement for your sins? You recognize no sin to be atoned for, except ignorance. How does your savior suffer for you? How does he draw you to God or grant you grace? To you Jesus was merely a teacher who brought truth, which you believe alone can save. You know nothing of the real Savior, who said He came to seek and to save all who were lost."

"It is true that we differ," Cerinthus said. "I do not

debate that. My savior has no human nature; He is not a man. He only seemed to be a man."

"He was both God and man!" John said. "I knew Him! I know Him!"

Cerinthus smiled patiently again and addressed the crowd. "Ephesians, if you would believe this man is truly the disciple John, ask him about the magic language."

"The what?" John said, as people whispered. "I do not know of what you speak."

"Of course you do! You say you were there! My angel muses tell me that Jesus and His disciples often broke into a gibberish of only vowels. Spells have been cast made up of vowels in sets of twenty. Tell us, O great one who was there, what did it all mean?"

"It means your muses cannot be angels, but rather demons! This never happened! I was His friend. He knew me by name. He called me beloved."

"If that is true, sir, if you are truly one of His, you know that we obey God by abstaining from flesh, meat, and marriage, and by leading an austere life. In this way we earn our salvation."

"Such a life is well and good and may be profitable," John said, "but in Christ we are free from such strictures."

"Now who is the blasphemer?" Cerinthus said. "If you knew the truth, you would worship the Father, the Son, and Hyle, which is matter."

"I worship God the Father," John said, "and His Son Jesus the Christ, and the Holy Spirit."

"That is where you are wrong, sir! The Son is the cosmic serpent who freed Eve from the power of Hyle. We represent the universe by a triangle enclosed in a circle, because the number three is the key to all mysteries. There are three supreme principles: the not-generated, the self-generated, and the generated. As we study these mysteries, we exercise our God-given intellects, and knowledge frees us."

"Vain philosophy and deceit!" John yelled. "Paul calls these 'profane and idle babblings and contradictions of what is falsely called knowledge—by professing it some have strayed concerning the faith.'"

It appeared to John that Cerinthus had lost patience with him. He addressed the crowd: "Men of Ephesus, whom would you rather hear, this deluded old man who claims to have been a friend of Jesus, or one who has been mentored by angels into a new revelation?"

"You! You!" the crowd cried, and John was stunned. "We know the old man and his old ideas! Tell more of the new!"

John tried to regain a hearing, but the crowd shouted him down. Cerinthus continued to harangue, and Ignatius said, "Polycarp, this is no good. Let us go."

"No!" John said. "Stay and fight! When he is gone, the crowd will remain."

"No," Ignatius said. "The crowd has spoken. Desist in trying to cast your pearls before swine."

FIVE

The men made their way out onto Curetes Street and headed northwest past the Latrines toward Marble Road. Polycarp slowed as they neared the Mazaeus and Mithridates Gates into the Agora on their left. "We must enter and find some refreshment," he said.

"At least some shade," Ignatius said, and John was grateful for their concern.

A few minutes later they sat under a canopy, sipping wine, and John was soon rejuvenated. "To the theater," he said, eager to pray.

The three exited the gates again and turned left to head north. Soon they stood under the covered portico of the massive twenty-five-thousand-seat theater. John put a hand on each man's shoulder, closed his eyes, and lifted his face toward heaven. "Lord," he said, "I am nearly overcome with the privilege of standing here where your servant Paul bravely faced angry accusers, lo, many years past. How I have thrilled to the accounts of his traveling companions being seized and dragged here before thousands, and Demetrius the silversmith raging against Paul and his teaching that men are to worship Christ, not idols made with hands. Oh, I pray You would grant us such courage in the face of opposition and heresy. . . ."

John was startled by a commotion when Cerinthus

and his party hurried past.

"We must not let one more word of his heresy go unchecked," John said. And as they followed Cerinthus and his people from a distance, excited crowds passed them. People were shouting. "Hurry! Cerinthus! Outside the stadium!"

The stadium farther north covered more ground than the theater but held only about half as many spectators. John assumed this impromptu event outside the place would probably draw no more than a hundred, but he was mistaken. As he and Polycarp and Ignatius rushed along as fast as old bones would carry him, more and more people passed them.

John turned to the bishop. "Ignatius, send Polycarp ahead to reserve us places near where Cerinthus will speak. Otherwise we will be futile in our efforts to challenge him again."

Polycarp gathered his hem and sprinted on. "Look for me near the front!" he called over his shoulder. By the time John and Ignatius arrived, John was stunned to see people crowding the street, pushing close to surround Cerinthus and his huddled disciples. "There must be more than two hundred men and women here, Ignatius. How did they know of this?"

"Cerinthus is eloquent and has become popular, preaching on street corners. And he has many volunteers who spread the word of where he will be. I tell you, John, his intellectual approach to pleasing God by doing good works resonates with the people."

The two picked their way through the murmuring

assemblage to find the waving Polycarp about six deep from the head of the crowd. John could see Cerinthus's head above those of the disciples who surrounded him, all eager young men appearing proud to be there and desperate to please him.

For his part, Cerinthus appeared preoccupied, and while he seemed to be chatting with his charges, he peered over and around them at the growing crowd. Finally he gave the nod to one who called for attention.

"Men of Ephesus!" he cried out. "Welcome to a brief treatise by the brilliant man of intellect, Cerinthus, a follower of the Christ!"

Again John was repulsed by the blasphemer claiming the name of Christ. But as they approached, Cerinthus nodded to a couple of his own young disciples, and they quickly descended upon John and Ignatius. "You have had your say, old man. Now why not leave Cerinthus alone? He does not come to your church and counter you."

"This is his church?" John sputtered. "This is public property, and I have every bit as much right to be heard here as he does! As for the heretic—"

But Ignatius quickly stepped between John and the young men and was soon joined by Polycarp. The two urgently tugged their teacher out of the crowd and away, back to the streets that led to his home. "Please, master, this is clearly not the place or time. Cerinthus owns this crowd and they will not hear you."

More than once John stiffened and turned, nearly

unable to keep from heading back to the stadium. "Something must be done!" Burning deep within him was the need to somehow defy this new form of blasphemy that sounded so erudite and yet flew in the face of all he knew to be true.

Worse, he knew such slick-tongued men had the power to sway the weak-minded, yea, even many within his own congregation. John wept with fury, desperate to plan a rebuttal before this false teaching swept the city.

All the way back to the memorial home of Aquila and Priscilla, John spoke earnestly to Ignatius and Polycarp. "You see, gentlemen, this is important. It is doctrine. It is teaching. The life of Jesus is dramatic enough, and He must have known that opportunists would run away with all the stories and create their own systems, their own interpretations. That is why He spent so much time with us. You have no idea how much time the Master invested in simply telling us the mysteries of His kingdom. I feel a tremendous weight of responsibility as the last of His confidants. If in just sixty years men like Cerinthus—with what motive I would not venture to guess—can get it so wrong, how urgent it is that I set the record straight for as long as I have breath."

The young men kept trying to slow John, urging him to calm down and preserve his strength. And yet he did not stop talking.

Finally Ignatius led him to a bench and made him sit. "Now, hear me, master," the bishop said, squatting before him. "You are allowing yourself to grow so agitated that it cannot be good for you. Let us not jeopardize your health when you have so much to tell us. You're no longer a young man."

John sighed and took a deep breath. "I need not be reminded of that, friend. What troubles me is the effect Cerinthus and his kind might have on true believers, even those from our own gathering. Rumor has it he is founding his own school, which could impact the world. But my immediate concern is Ephesus and the believers here—not to mention the lost. Might he not leave behind some of those eager young disciples? We must counter them, counter him, at every turn."

Polycarp's concern was worn into his young face. He paced, his countenance clouded. "I don't know what more you can do, rabbi. It is too much to ask that you follow this man about and debate him in public. Perhaps you should—when you have fully regained your health—plan to speak every Lord's Day on these matters. Tell the people what Jesus Himself told you, and soon we will not have room for everyone."

"Believe me," John said, rising, "this is that important. Perhaps I should teach with Luke's or Mark's or Matthew's accounts in hand, adding what the Master taught us in private. But Matthew and Mark wrote their accounts with different purposes and audiences, and Dr. Luke helped complete the full story. They did not write in the face of all this opposition. They saw the Lord die, saw Him buried, saw Him alive again.

Nothing could make them doubt. But what might my colleagues have written had they known the minds of the Greeks and the Romans?"

By the time the men reached John's small quarters, he was exhausted and acceded to their urging that he try napping. One of the women delivered fruit and a cup of water, and when his stomach was sated and his thirst slaked, John stretched out on his pallet. But weary as he was, his mind continued to race.

The old apostle rolled up on his side and let the breeze from the window fan his face. And he felt a deep urgency in his spirit. "What is it, Lord?" he whispered. "What would you have me do?"

John rose and knelt by his mat, knees aching. "Father, I am at Your mercy. I will do whatever You give me the strength to do. Preach? Teach? Do the work of the evangelist? Tell me. Please."

He laid his head on his mat and found himself dozing, pierced with a recollection of falling asleep when Jesus had asked him to stay up with Him.

Of all times, it had been the night Jesus would be betrayed. All evening the Master had seemed, to John, to be acting out of character. Yet as he reflected, he realized that Jesus was entirely Himself. He had spoken plainly, had loved and served His men, had prayed with them, prayed for them, seen to their nourishment, talked of His future, predicted His own end, washed their feet. That last had caught everyone off guard, just as had His averring that He would be betrayed. To a man they had pledged their loyalty, Peter the most vociferous, but Jesus foretold that he was the one who would deny Him thrice before the cock crowed twice.

Peter had responded in anger, "If I have to die with You, I will not deny You."

The pain of having been singled out was etched on Peter's face, and John not only believed his friend, but he also joined the others in chorusing, "Yes, yes, I would die first."

And yet it had been just after this that Jesus went to His favorite place to pray, and John and the rest had followed, as was their custom. John had always loved to hear Jesus pray. It was one thing to be taught by Him and to try to approach God in the manner the Master had instructed. But to come to believe that your teacher was the Son of God Himself and then to hear Him speak to His Father directly . . .

Jesus told John and the others to pray so they would not enter into temptation. It was not unusual for them to be puzzled by such comments, but it was unusual that no one asked for clarification. What form of temptation had He meant? What were they to avoid? It was clear Jesus was deeply distracted and troubled in spirit, yet He had not asked that they pray for Him, but rather for themselves.

As they made a show of huddling near the trunk of a large olive tree, Jesus moved away from them about a stone's throw and knelt. John listened carefully as the teacher prayed, "Father, if it is Your will, take this cup away from Me; nevertheless not My will, but Yours, be done."

John squinted in the darkness as his dearest friend seemed to recoil and then open His eyes, as if something or someone had interrupted Him. He soon returned to His reverie, praying earnestly, but John could no longer make out the words. Anyway, John himself was to be praying against falling into temptation. He turned and bowed his head, but almost immediately fatigue washed over him.

His mates were not praying aloud, and one—he wasn't sure which—had drifted into deep, rhythmic breathing, as if about to snore. John had to smile. Perhaps the temptation to sleep was what they were to pray to avoid! They had been fed, washed, had ventured out into the cool evening air—and now they sat. Perhaps on another evening they would have been content, but for himself, sorrow consumed John. Jesus had spoken elusively at first, but soon He clarified that His end was near. John could only hope and pray it wasn't so. Sadness at that prospect only made him sleepier. He was not aware of drifting off, but suddenly Jesus stood in their midst, and John jerked awake when sweat from Jesus' chin dripped onto his head.

Jesus said, "Why do you sleep? Rise and pray, lest you enter into temptation. Peter, James, John, come with Me." He told the others, "Sit here while I go and pray over there."

John and his brother and Peter rose and followed to

where He had been praying. "My soul is exceedingly sorrowful," He said, "even to death. Stay here and watch with Me." He went a little farther and fell on His face, saying, "O My Father, if it is possible, let this cup pass from Me; nevertheless, not as I will, but as You will."

John felt great waves of pity for his friend, but as he sat there with his brother and Peter, he dozed yet again. Here he had only so recently pledged his loyalty unto death, yet he could not even stay awake as Jesus had asked. He roused when Jesus returned and spoke harshly to Peter: "What! Could you not watch with Me one hour? Watch and pray, lest you enter into temptation. The spirit indeed is willing, but the flesh is weak."

Again He went away and prayed. "O My Father, if this cup cannot pass away from Me unless I drink it, Your will be done."

When He returned, John was yet again humiliated to find that he had drifted off. Jesus said, "Are you still sleeping and resting? Behold, the hour is at hand, and the Son of Man is being betrayed into the hands of sinners. Rise, let us be going. See, My betrayer is at hand."

Some sixty years later John found himself unwilling to allow what happened next to pass his mind's eye. It remained the most painful night of his life. "Lord, forgive me," he prayed, ashamed anew that he dozed then and now. "Some things are not learned in a lifetime. But I feel compelled to clarify Your teaching, to set straight the heretics. Yet my time is limited. How can this be done? Make it plain to me."

Unable to stand the pain and cramping in his legs, John climbed again atop his cot. But as he lay back with his hands behind his head, he heard excited voices from the courtyard. He could not make out individual words, but he recognized the enthusiastic tone and heard Polycarp and Ignatius in the middle of it. He crept out of bed and stopped halfway down the stairs. No one noticed him, but he could hear and understand now.

Ignatius was speaking to a dozen or so, about a third of them women. "But I understand that your bishop and his aide have made clear that you are not to go near that man, let alone listen to him."

A woman responded, "Begging your pardon Rabbi Ignatius, but we, my husband and I, found Cerinthus most humble. And his story of having been counseled by spiritual muses—"

"Angels," her husband said.

"Yes, angels. Why is this necessarily untrue?"

Others chimed in, nodding. "What reason would he have for misleading?"

"He might be a tool of the evil one," Ignatius said. "And the reason we know what he said is untrue? Because we have the witness of a friend of Jesus, the disciple He loved."

"But John is an old man! How can we trust his memory? Has he been taught by angels?"

"How can you ask that?" Ignatius said. "He was

taught by Christ Himself! How quickly you forget!"

John began to make his way down the steps, but his legs gave out and he had to grab the wall to catch himself. Polycarp cried out, "Teacher!" and ran to him, grabbing him as he sat heavily on the stairs.

But as the young man tried to help him up and steer him back to his room, John said, "Indulge me, Polycarp. Allow me to address them."

Polycarp turned and called for attention, but the small assemblage had already fallen silent at the collapse of their old leader.

His heart still racing, John announced with hoarse voice, "Beloved, truth and time walk hand in hand. In eternity you will know the truth, and Jesus Himself said the truth will set you free—free from the bondage of vanity, of empty philosophy and deceit. Yes, I am old, and perhaps my memory is not what it once was. But when you have walked with the Messiah, the chosen One, the Lamb slain for the sins of the world, you cannot forget. You must not forget. I have been praying for what God would have me do about the erosion of veracity when it comes to the facts about Jesus. And as I stand here and listen to my own flock, led to distraction, to confusion, to pretense and treachery, it comes to me what must be done. Pray with me that this is of God the Father, that it is He who has laid this on my heart and soul. If it is, He will confirm it.

"Now, Ignatius, if you would do the teaching tonight, I must retire to pray anew. Polycarp will stand with me, will you not?"

"Of course," the young redhead said, as Ignatius herded the others toward the makeshift chapel in the main rooms. And as he helped John back up the steps, Polycarp whispered, "Master, I too have been praying, and I believe God has impressed something upon me also. Perhaps this is His way of confirming what He has put in your heart."

"If it agrees with my spirit, I will consider it so."

Polycarp helped John onto his bed once more and sat in the chair opposite him. "Do you believe what was going on down there? You made it clear that our people were not to give any credence to Cerinthus."

"People are people," John said, shaking his head. "They are like children, wanting to go where you tell them not to. Perchance our deep instruction has been too much for them. It could be that it was too much meat, as Paul would have put it, and not enough milk."

"Cerinthus is not offering them milk either, master. And these people are *not* babies. You are the reason for that."

"Not I alone, surely."

"But largely, sir. You have taught them patiently for years, and when you were away, others were steadfast."

"Regardless," John said, "the time has come to face this attack from the enemy. What is God telling you?"

"That you should write."

John became aware of his own breathing. That was indeed what the Lord had impressed upon him, but he needed this validation. "Write?" he said. "The state of my scribbling alone is evidence enough that I should not put my hand to papyrus."

"I will be your scribe!" Polycarp said. "I wrestled with this in prayer, rabbi. I truly did. I feared this is what I *wanted* to hear from God, because I long to be the one who hears again all the stories you've told about Jesus."

"I would tell those stories, Polycarp, but I sense what is needed is something deeper, something with teaching, something with a purpose beyond rehashing the things He did and the places He went."

"Then you will do it?"

"I am fearful, young one. In spite of all you have done to bring me back to health, I am fading. Every day I feel more fragile. I am following your orders, believe me, but it becomes more difficult all the time. Would you pray and fast more about this? If we are to do this, much of the work of the church will fall to Ignatius, beyond his preparation to continue his journey to the other churches, as you will be occupied with this, with me."

Polycarp stood and paced. "I cannot wait to begin, sir. I will pray and fast as you instruct, but then I will set about marshaling supplies. We would do it right here, would we not?"

"I would be most comfortable here, yes."

"I will obtain more lamps and oil for the dark days . . ."

"And for when we might work into the night."

"Yes, and I will gather papyrus scrolls and new quills, and plenty of ink."

John pressed his lips together. "I hesitate to broach this, but you are not the most artistic of hand yourself and have expressed concern over your own hand-writing."

"I will devote myself to the task, master. I'll write as slowly and as neatly as I can, and I will copy it over whenever necessary."

John reached for Polycarp's hand, if for no other reason than to slow the man and keep him from walking about the room. "Let us contract to not eat and to give ourselves to prayer until dawn. If we agree then that we believe this is of God, bring me all the supplies, arrange for our meals to be delivered, and let us begin when the sun is bright."

"I will!"

"Before you go, son, you need to know that for many years people here and there have pleaded with me to write my own account of the ministry of Jesus. Until now I thought it would be redundant. I did not know what I could add to all the good work that has already been done. And much of what I enjoyed with the Master was private and personal, as He taught me and just one or two of the others some of the deep mysteries of God. Much is still perplexing to me, of course, and more of what He tried to tell us we will not understand until we are with Him in paradise. Be that as it may, if He leads me by His Spirit and gives me the words, I am willing to tell all for this higher, overarching purpose. Polycarp, we may have the unspeakable privilege of revealing to any and all who read our words that Jesus is the Christ, the Son of the living God, and that by believing, they might have life through His name."

Polycarp stopped in the doorway. "I'll not sleep, sir."

"You had better not. We're fasting and praying, remember?"

"I couldn't sleep anyway. And please don't refer to this task as *ours*. It is yours. The words will be yours, from God, of course. I will be just your secretary."

Much of the day still remained, and as John lay prone on the floor and cried out to God, he soon became aware of his empty belly and the smell of baking bread wafting from the courtyard. He prayed that the Lord would help him use that hunger to focus his attention on the cosmic matter at hand.

"If I am not the one," he prayed, "I surrender to Your will." But even as he said that it seemed God impressed upon him that no one else was left who could bring such authority to the project.

"I pray You will give me utterance that can be understood both by those educated only enough to be read to, and by the learned men from the great city-states."

John believed the Lord impressed upon his heart, "Trust Me. Listen to Me."

"I pray this account unmistakably exalts Your Son as God in human flesh. May this be a treatise of belief for all who come under its hearing."

John heard the soothing baritone of Ignatius from

below as he read to the people from an epistle Paul had written to the church at Corinth. How refreshing to know that his former protégé had become so mindful of lost souls that even in a service of worship and instruction, he insisted on a straightforward presentation of the reason God came to earth in the form of His only Son. John thrilled especially to the passage, ". . . that Christ died for our sins according to the Scriptures, and that He was buried, and that He rose again the third day."

Ignatius concluded with Paul's admonition, "But if there is no resurrection of the dead, then Christ is not risen. And if Christ is not risen, then our preaching is empty and your faith is also empty. . . . But now Christ is risen from the dead."

John was nearly lulled to sleep as Ignatius then read portions of the Pentateuch and led the assembled in prayer. John hummed along as they sang psalms and hymns and spiritual songs. Ignatius led them in a corporate confession of their faith, then they broke bread for communion.

John closed his shutters so his prayer and devotion would not be distracted. As the sun dropped from the sky, John found himself renewed, energetic. Any fear that a sleepless night would hamper his efforts the next morning disappeared as he communed with his God.

"I was the youngest of the twelve," he reminded his Lord. "Where shall I begin?"

It was as if God Himself said within John's soul, "In the beginning . . ."

John had long loved the beautiful simplicity of the first paragraph of Moses' five scrolls, "In the beginning God created . . ." The plain assumption that God existed eternally from before time rang loud and clear from that adored text. As John continued in prayer, it came to him that fundamental to his belief in Jesus was that Christ is God, that He and the Father were one, and, thus, Jesus was also there in eternity past.

John wished he could begin his work immediately.

SIX

By the wee hours of the morning, John had begun to repent of his instruction to Polycarp to fast and pray alone and considered venturing out to find the lad. His own fasting and prayer had suddenly led John to a most unusual state of mind that began with a deep, mournful view of his own sin. He had been reminded of his anger at Cerinthus, and righteous though it may have been, it triggered in John emotions and intentions he thought had been long buried with what his friend, the late Paul, referred to as "the old man." And that "old man" did not refer to John's age, but rather his personality and character before the Spirit of Christ took up residence in him.

The more John pondered his anger and vitriol and the near murderous hatred he had felt for a fellow human, the lower he felt. It was as if God had thrust a lantern into his inner self and searched him for every weakness, frailty, and sin.

John was soon at his lowest, persuaded that perhaps God was telling him he had been mistaken, that he of all men was least equipped to write the message that so burned in him. It was as if the Spirit of God was revealing that John had forfeited the privilege because of his lack of self-control. Rather than the eagerness he had at first encountered—with the setting of the sun, the departure of the church members, and the quietness of the chapel—John now faced the ugliness of his own humanity and was brought to tears.

Is this the enemy, trying to rob me of my joy? Distracting me from a grand assignment?

He only wished that so. Reminded of his pettiness, jealousy, pride, covetousness, John dropped into his chair, sobs invading his throat. "Do You want me broken, Lord? Is that it? For I see myself as an intruder in Your kingdom, an interloper, a foreigner. Forgive my sins and grant me peace!"

And with that came a gentle knock on his door. Polycarp? That would be so refreshing.

"It is I," came the voice of Ignatius.

John swept open the door. "Oh, welcome guest!" he said. "Please, please do come in. I cannot stand to be alone in my own presence another instant. But why are you not asleep, friend?"

"John, you've been crying. What is it?"

John told him of the events that had occurred from the end of the impromptu meeting in the courtyard, all the way through to his feeling as if his very soul had been exposed to God.

"This is monumental, teacher. I envy the experience you and Polycarp will enjoy. But you should not be put off by the Lord's cleansing of your heart in advance of such a task. Did you not warn me of the same when you and the other apostles commissioned me to the work of God?"

"I did, didn't I?"

"Of course you did. This should be seen only as further confirmation that God is in this. I don't want to speak for the Lord, but—"

"That has never stopped you before."

"I suppose I deserve that," Ignatius said. "I was about to question your judgment about fasting and praying all night, especially now that the Father has brought you through this ordeal to a place of peace. You do have peace, do you not?"

"I do! It came with your knock."

"The way I heard you tell it, master, it came with your repentance and plea for forgiveness. It is clear God has something very special in mind for you, and He wants you wholly prepared."

John pointed to the chair and sat on his bed. When Ignatius sat, John said, "If you are not too exhausted, perhaps you should invite Polycarp to join us. Surely he is as lonely as I was, and if God took him through what I endured, he is probably longing for company now as well."

Within minutes Ignatius had fetched the young disciple, and John was immediately struck by Polycarp's paleness. "The Lord has been speaking to you too?"

"More than I wanted to hear, frankly. But I feel more prepared for the chore than ever. Before I was merely eager to get started for my own selfish purposes. Now I believe He has corrected my thinking, put me on the right path."

Ignatius appeared to have been thoughtfully taking this all in. "Allow me to posit an opinion, then," he said. "I propose that you end your fast, continue in prayer, but do not run from sleep. Perhaps I am speaking in the flesh, but it seems to me God was after your heart's attitude, and you were willing to spend the night hungry and on your knees. That He has worked in both your souls should tell you that He has brought you to the place He wants you."

Polycarp smiled. "That falls comfortably on my ears, rabbi. But am I being selfish again?"

"Let us not be too introspective," John said. "Let us accept our brother's wise counsel as from the Lord. Enthusiastic as I am about our undertaking, I believe I could sleep soundly now."

"I know I could," Polycarp said.

"And I need to," Ignatius said. "Good night, gentlemen."

JOHN AWAKENED at first light with such a sense of anticipation that he barely remembered sleeping and was certain he had not dreamed. He felt more refreshed than he had been in a long time, but he was hungry. The plate on the floor outside his door was a godsend. As he ate he wished he had a quill and papyrus. It's not that he would have attempted to record this account on his own, but already it seemed God was pouring into him the thoughts and very words He wanted communicated.

As John put out his empty plate, Ignatius accosted him. "Polycarp is back from the markets," the Antiochan reported. "Are we about ready to commence?"

"We?"

"You and Polycarp, I mean."

"Yes, and as much as I know you want to be involved, Ignatius, have we not agreed that someone, someone we all know and love—you, in fact—must take over our duties here until the time you set sail?"

"In fact," Ignatius said, "do you not find it providential that the Lord sent me here for what I thought was mere filling in so you could get some rest, but had no doubt ordained this very work before even putting the thought in my head to come?"

"I do indeed," John said, his eyes shining. "We serve a good God."

Polycarp rushed in, laden with supplies. "What?" he said, his gaze alternating between the men. He smiled at Ignatius. "I do not know what your business is here, sir, but if you would kindly move on, we have important duties."

"Let me help you," Ignatius said, and when Polycarp hesitated, Ignatius added, "help you arrange everything. Then I'll be on my way."

Ignatius and Polycarp spread the papyrus on the desk, filled the inkwell, and arranged the quills. "I will need to be able to move, to walk, to see out the window," John said. And so they cleared a path for him in the tiny chamber. Polycarp situated the chair to give himself plenty of room to work while staying out of John's way.

Once everything was set, the three looked at one another awkwardly. Ignatius broke the silence. "I have a meeting with the deacons and deaconesses in a few moments. Lord's Day preparations. But first, may I make a request? You both have to know how difficult it is for me to remain on the periphery of this great effort. You must promise that at the end of the day, after I have been faithful in filling in for you both here the best I know how, that you, Polycarp, will tell me all you can remember. Will you do that?"

"With John's permission," Polycarp said.

"Of course!" John said. "I covet your evaluation of each day's work, my friend. Feel free to pore over the manuscript with Polycarp."

"Thank you, John. Thank you from my heart. And now, dear brethren, I believe the Lord would have me pray for you."

Ignatius had John sit in the chair and Polycarp kneel beside him. He placed his hands atop their heads and lifted his eyes to heaven. "Our great God and Father of our Lord and Savior Jesus Christ, hallowed be Your name. I beseech You this day on behalf of these two, my friend and my mentor, believing that You have called them and set them apart for an enterprise sacred and holy. You confirmed within both their hearts that this mission is of You, and You brought them through valleys of purging to make of them pure vessels for Your use.

"I pray You would quicken John and fill him with Your Spirit, flooding his heart and mind and soul with what You would have him record. And I pray that the result of this divine work will settle any question of the deity of Your Son, refuting heresies that blaspheme the truth of His identity. We offer our thanks for the privilege of having a part in this, and may we never be the same because of it. I pray in the holy and matchless name of Your dear Son, Jesus the Christ. Amen."

SEVEN

Unaware until he opened his eyes that Ignatius had left and quietly pulled the door shut behind him, John silently rose and moved to the other end of the room. Polycarp slipped into the chair and took quill in hand, dipping it into the ink until the liquid was drawn into the stem. John was aware of Polycarp's eyes, showing his readiness, but John was also determined not to utter one word he was not entirely convinced was from the mouth of God Himself.

John steepled his index fingers and pressed them

against his lips as he slowly walked to the window and back, thinking, open to the leading of the Spirit, listening for that still, small voice. And as John painstakingly began to softly speak, Polycarp applied the ink to the page.

According to John
In the beginning was the Word, and the Word was with God, and the Word was God. He was in the beginning with God. All things were made through Him, and without Him nothing was made that was made.

Polycarp looked up, trembling. "Master, it is as if I am in the presence of the Almighty. You are speaking with His authority."

"I too feel it, son.

"In Him was life, and the life was the light of men. And the light shines in the darkness, and the darkness did not comprehend it."

John sat on the bed, folding his arms and hanging his head as if exhausted. Finally he whispered, "I need tell of the baptizer. Bear with me as I ponder this, Polycarp." He sat another moment, then lifted his head. "All right," he said. "Thank you, Lord.

"There was a man sent from God, whose name was John. This man came for a witness, to bear witness of the Light, that all through Him might believe."

"Pardon me, rabbi," Polycarp said. "Just so I understand. 'That all through *John* might believe'?"

The old man nodded.

"He was not that Light, but was sent to bear witness of that Light. That was the true Light which gives light to every man coming into the world.

"He was in the world, and the world was made through Him, and the world did not know Him. He came to His own, and His own did not receive Him. But as many as received Him, to them He gave the right to become children of God, to those who believe in His name: who were born, not of blood, nor of the will of the flesh, nor of the will of man, but of God."

"Give me a moment, master," Polycarp said. "This is overwhelming. I have never heard anything like it."

"Nor have I. Tell me when you are ready."

"Ready."

"And the Word became flesh and dwelt among us, and we beheld His glory, the glory as of the only begotten of the Father, full of grace and truth.

"John bore witness of Him and cried out, saying, 'This was He of whom I said, "He who comes after me is preferred before me, for He was before me." '

"And of His fullness we have all received, and grace for grace. For the law was given through Moses, but grace and truth came through Jesus Christ. No one has seen God at any time. The only begotten Son, who is in the bosom of the Father, He has declared Him.

"You know, Polycarp, I was a disciple of the baptizer before I met Jesus."

"So you heard him say these things yourself?"

John nodded. "I recall well when the Jews sent

priests and Levites from Jerusalem to ask him, 'Who are you?'

"He told them boldly and forthrightly, 'I am not the Christ.'

"And they asked him, 'What then? Are you Elijah?'

"He said, 'I am not.'

" 'Are you the Prophet?' they wanted to know.

"And he answered, 'No.'

"Polycarp, they were most frustrated. They said, 'Who are you, that we may give an answer to those who sent us? What do you say about yourself?'

"He said: 'I am *The voice of one crying in the wilderness: 'Make straight the way of the Lord,' "* as the prophet Isaiah said.' "

"Pardon me, rabbi," Polycarp said, "but who were these who questioned him?"

"They had been sent from the Pharisees. And they asked him, 'Why then do you baptize if you are not the Christ, nor Elijah, nor the Prophet?'

"The baptizer answered, 'I baptize with water, but there stands One among you whom you do not know. It is He who, coming after me, is preferred before me, whose sandal strap I am not worthy to loose.' "

"Where was this, sir?" Polycarp said.

"In Bethabara beyond the Jordan, where John was baptizing. Now listen, because this next marks the first time I saw the Lord."

"What must that have been like?"

"You cannot imagine. The next day the baptizer saw a man coming toward him, and said, 'Behold! The

Lamb of God who takes away the sin of the world! This is He of whom I said, "After me comes a Man who is preferred before me, for He was before me." I did not know Him; but that He should be revealed to Israel, therefore I came baptizing with water.'

"Now, Polycarp, James and I stood there, mouths agape. The baptizer had been preaching about the Messiah in our presence for so long that we had begun to wonder if we would ever see Him. And suddenly there He was. I was well aware of the Scriptures that foretold that He would have 'no form nor comeliness; and when we see Him, there is no beauty that we should desire Him,' so I was not surprised that He was not handsome. But as for me, I confess I was surprised at how plain He at first appeared. I am speaking now only of his features, the cut of his face. He merely looked like one of us, but James and I both agreed later that there was something about his bearing, his carriage. Perhaps it was because John the Baptist immediately identified Him, I don't know. But there seemed such a peace and serenity about this Man, it was as if I imagined all the knowledge of the universe resided in Him.

"The baptizer had said that God Himself, the one who had sent him to baptize with water, had told him, 'Upon whom you see the Spirit descending, and remaining on Him, this is He who baptizes with the Holy Spirit.' And Polycarp, that is what I saw, the Spirit descending from heaven like a dove and remaining on that Man. Even the baptizer admitted that he did not know this Man—surprising when you realize that they were cousins—but the Spirit descending on Him made it plain to all of us who He was. John said, 'I have seen and testified that this is the Son of God.'

"This remains with me as if it were yesterday. When John baptized Him and He rose up out of that water, the heavens opened and a voice said, 'This is my beloved Son, in whom I am well pleased.' You can imagine, then, why it so infuriated me when Cerinthus represented as fact that Jesus was not the Son of God."

Polycarp nodded.

"The next day, I was standing with my friend Andrew—another of John's disciples—as Jesus approached again. John said, 'Behold the Lamb of God!'"

"This is Peter's brother, Andrew?"

John nodded. "Polycarp, I was so drawn to Jesus that I could barely tear my eyes away. I looked to the baptizer—for permission, I suppose. We were his disciples, after all. And I noticed that Andrew was doing the same, merely looking to John for the freedom to follow Jesus. The baptizer smiled knowingly and nodded, and we moved quickly to fall in step with the Lord.

"Jesus turned, and seeing us following, said, 'What do you seek?'"

John laughed and shook his head. "Polycarp, I didn't know what to say. And Andrew was clearly at a loss. I said, 'Rabbi, where are You staying?'"

Polycarp dropped his quill and roared. "You asked Him that?"

"I didn't know what else to say."

"And how did He answer?"

John nodded to Polycarp to signal him to keep writing.

"He said, 'Come and see.' We went and saw where He was staying, and remained with Him that day.

"Then Andrew ran to find his brother and said, 'Peter, we have found the Messiah.' And he brought Peter to Jesus.

"As soon as Jesus saw Peter, He said, 'You are Simon the son of Jonah. You shall be called Cephas,' which, as you know, means 'stone.'"

"Jesus knew who he was?"

John nodded. "He was God, son. He knew everything."

"And how were the others called?"

"The next day we followed Jesus to Galilee, and He found Philip and said, 'Follow Me.' Philip was from Bethsaida, the city of Andrew and Peter. Philip found Nathanael and said, 'We have found Him of whom Moses in the law, and also the prophets, wrote—Jesus of Nazareth, the son of Joseph.'

"Nathanael was skeptical. He said, 'Can anything good come out of Nazareth?'"

"He actually *said* that?" Polycarp said.

John smiled. "This would be the wrong place to be making up stories, would it not? Philip said to him, 'Come and see.'

"When Jesus saw Nathanael coming toward Him, He said, 'Behold, an Israelite indeed, in whom is no deceit!'"

"He knew Nathanael too?"

"I told you, Polycarp. He knew all. Nathanael was as astounded as you are. He said, 'How do You know me?'

"And Jesus said, 'Before Philip called you, when you were under the fig tree, I saw you.'"

"You never told me this before, master," Polycarp said. "If Jesus had said something like that to me, I would have known without question that—"

"You're getting ahead of me."

"Sorry."

"Nathanael immediately said, 'Rabbi, You are the Son of God! You are the King of Israel!'

"Jesus said, 'Because I said to you, "I saw you under the fig tree," do you believe? You will see greater things than these. Most assuredly, I say to you, hereafter you shall see heaven open, and the angels of God ascending and descending upon the Son of Man.'"

EIGHT

Following a brief rest, John and Polycarp decided to get some air and exercise and venture out onto the stone streets of Ephesus. John was growing concerned about pressure in his chest and a dull ache behind his breastbone, but he chose not to mention this to his young friend.

"John the Baptizer must have been a fascinating man," Polycarp said. "What drew you to him?"

"Well, he was a man of nature, not unlike my brother and me. But he was not a fisherman—he spent his time in the wilderness, eating off the land."

"Locusts and honey."

John smiled. "Matthew writes of the baptizer as I remember him, wandering the hills of Judea wearing a covering made from the skin of a camel, hair and all. He also wore a thick leather belt. Not a city man."

"Yet he became known. How did people find him out there?"

"Frankly, Polycarp, the man was a curiosity. He would venture close to the highways and byways, and whenever a crowd, or even a small group, passed, he would begin to preach. I daresay that early on most considered him a madman, ranting and raving in the wilds."

"But you did not see him that way."

"At first we did. In fact, James and I were on our way to deliver some fish and had to move out of the road as an entourage passed coming from the other way. It was obviously some dignitary, his curtained carriage surrounded by servants and slaves and animals. They were kicking up quite the dust storm.

"Well, just before they reached us, James nudged me and nodded in the direction of the strange man on the hillside, crouching by a rock and watching the road. In James's eyes I read mischief. He probably thought the man a lunatic and considered making sport of him.

"But when that caravan drew near us, the man began to shout and gesture. 'Beware!' he cried, 'the kingdom of heaven is at hand!'

"James raised his eyebrows and looked at me, on the verge of laughter. He whispered, 'Oh, it is, is it?' And as if the man had heard James, he shouted, 'Yes, it is!'

"James froze and stared as the man ventured down from the hillside and commanded the caravan to stop. The dignitary, I still know not who he was, demanded to know what was the holdup. Well, the man we eventually came to know as John the Baptizer took command. He stood at the side of the road proclaiming the imminent coming of the promised one, the Deliverer of Israel. And when the official commanded his people to move again, the baptizer roared, 'You ignore the signs at your peril, for surely the day is coming when you will fall on your knees before the King!'

"The master swept back the veil of his traveling chamber and glared out at John, demanding, 'Are you a bandit? If you are, show your weapon so I may instruct my guards to kill you.'

"John fired back, 'You threaten the anointed one of God, the forerunner of the Messiah? You are a snake, a viper, a fornicator, a liar!'

"'Kill him!' the diplomat yelled, but as his men drew their swords, John rushed forward, clearly unarmed.

"'Beware, for I come to you under the authority of the Most High God. You shall bring no harm to me.

Examine yourself, O representative of Rome, and woe to you if you are found wanting at that great and terrible day!'

"That must have scared even the official, because the caravan soon rumbled from sight. I was young, about the age you are now, and this wild man frightened me. I urged James that we should be about our business, but he was plainly curious. 'You are anointed of God?' he said.

" 'Call me John,' the baptizer said.

" 'That is my name too,' I managed.

" 'And you are brothers,' he said, 'fishermen, on your way to market.'

"Polycarp, I was taken aback. I said, 'Surely you must be of God to know that.' And with that the crazy man threw his head back and laughed loud and long.

"He said, 'It takes no otherworldly ability to divine this! You look alike, you smell of fish, you are carrying salted fish containers, and you are headed toward town in the middle of the day.'

"I felt foolish, but I could not be angry, as he said this with such good humor. James had lost his mischief, and while the man looked all the more uncivilized the closer we got to him—uncut hair and unshaved beard—the more we sensed something in his eyes and in his voice. While he had rasped and growled while chastising the public official, his natural tone of voice was low and soothing. He was so earnest. He told James and me that he would be glad to tell us of the coming Messiah. We had heard of this for years in our synagogue school, and I confess that we did not believe him at first. But it didn't take long being around him to know that he was no madman.

"Word spread throughout the region that he was preaching in the wilderness and baptizing people, and they began to come from all over.

"We spent many days with John, learning from him and witnessing his bold approach to announcing the coming of the Lord.

"When my brother James left the baptizer, he urged John to be careful about so brazenly calling down government and religious leaders. 'You could get yourself killed.'

"'That is why I am here,' John told us. But we had no idea what he meant."

"I suppose we had best start heading back," Polycarp said, but as they turned around John became aware of a commotion on Curetes Street.

"Not again," the old man said. "Cerinthus."

"Ignore him," Polycarp said. "Your best effort against him is what we are doing at the house."

"I cannot pull myself away," John said, and he moved to stand at the back of the crowd, heart pounding and chest tightening even more. As soon as John positioned himself, Cerinthus noticed him.

"Is it not John, the last of Jesus' disciples? Are you beginning to see the light, old man? Seeing the wisdom of youth, of a fresh perspective? Would that you would become a disciple of mine."

John wanted to shout, "Never!" as rage overtook

him again. The crowd was growing and would soon be larger than the one that had gathered outside the stadium. All these people being led astray! John had spent his life teaching of salvation by grace through faith, and in a matter of a few months this blasphemer could ruin everything. People *wanted* to play a part in their own salvation by weighing their good deeds against their bad, somehow earning heaven. But John knew that was futile. As Paul had said, "There is none righteous, no not one."

John allowed Polycarp to pull him away before he said anything, but it took the entire walk back to the house church before his pulse returned to normal and he stopped panting.

As they reached his chamber, John motioned Polycarp to the desk. "Not that I needed it," he said, "but God has provided even more impetus to carry on. Let's begin immediately."

"What comes next?" Polycarp said. "How long were you with Jesus before you witnessed a miracle?"

"Only a few days. He had been invited, we all had, to the wedding of a friend of Jesus' best friend, Lazarus. You should have seen those two together. They could talk seriously, of course. Often they would get away to pray together. But the good humor too! How they laughed. They would wrestle, tease each other, and they even tricked each other just for fun."

"Jesus did this too?"

"Of course! Oh, He was a serious Man, yes. A Man of sorrows, the Scriptures say, and acquainted with grief. But he was also able to find joy and laughter. Lazarus was with us the night we sat around a fire on the shore in Galilee and Jesus slapped at something on His neck, then slowly pulled His hand away and toward the light of the flames to reveal that He had crushed a biting insect.

"No one thought anything of it until He studied the tiny creature in his palm, then carefully rolled it over with His thumb. As He sat there, seeming amused at our reactions, He held out his palm for all to see that the bug had been restored to life. It soon flew away."

"You must put that in your account."

"Only if the Spirit leads. Later, before James and I retired, we talked long into the night about what we had seen. Finally my brother concluded, 'It only makes sense, John. If He is who the baptizer said He is, and if He is who He said He is, He created the world and everything in it. That gives Him power over life and death."

"And so then He began healing people all over the area?"

"Not yet. He often said His time had not yet come. We never knew what to make of that. He even said that to His mother at the wedding when she asked Him to act. That shocked me. It sounded disrespectful at first, but she plainly did not take it that way. It was almost as if she hadn't heard it. Perhaps she understood Him at some deeper level."

"We must get all this down, teacher," Polycarp said, quill in hand.

"Not all of it. Just the important things. Let readers glean from it what they will. The wedding at Cana was on our third day there. Jesus and all His disciples were invited. Mary, Jesus' mother, came and whispered to Him—in my hearing, as I sat on one side of Him and Lazarus on the other—'They have no wine.'

"Now, I thought it strange that she would tell Him that, and apparently so did Jesus. He said, 'Woman, what does your concern have to do with Me? My hour has not yet come.'

"But Mary, without another word, said to the servants, 'Whatever He says to you, do it.'

"There were set there six waterpots of stone, according to the manner of purification of the Jews, containing twenty or thirty gallons apiece. Jesus said to the servants, 'Fill the waterpots with water.' And they filled them up to the brim. And He said to them, 'Draw some out now, and take it to the master of the feast.'

"When the master of the feast had tasted the water that was made wine, and did not know where it came from (but the servants who had drawn the water knew), the master of the feast called the bridegroom. And he said, 'Every man at the beginning sets out the good wine, and when the guests have well drunk, then the inferior. You have kept the good wine until now!'

"Polycarp, if any of us had had any doubts about who Jesus was, they were gone. He had manifested His glory, and we all believed in Him."

"I can only imagine," Polycarp said quietly. "Who

could not have believed after that? Seeing it must have seemed like a dream to you."

"It did, and yet it was so real. And do not forget, we did not only tell this tale and some of us write it, but we also were among those who tasted the wine. Do you have an inkling what such must have tasted like? I have not had its like since. It was as if the grapes had been plucked plump, directly from vines in the sun, and pressed just before pouring, and yet the nectar hit our tongues as if it had been aged not only to the perfect season, but also to the perfect day, yea the perfect hour. You know, Polycarp, that the Greeks believe wine is the life-giving drink of the gods. Well, in this case, it is no myth. Little wonder that Jesus would later use the cup to represent His life-giving blood.

"I hope without my being overly didactic I am making clear the point of all this. Do you see the import of Jesus' actions here, and why I include this?"

"Tell me."

"This was clearly a miracle, but it did not save a life, did not still a storm. It merely saved a host from embarrassment. On the other hand, it did so much more. It established Jesus as divine. He was a miracle worker and showed Himself as the very source of life. That's why I conclude that it was the beginning of signs.

"After this He, His mother, His brothers, and we disciples went down to Capernaum, and we stayed in Peter's home. But we were soon on our way. Passover was at hand, and Jesus told us it had been His custom since childhood to spend it in Jerusalem. I daresay, Polycarp, while this was early in our time with Him, it quickly became one of the most momentous. To be frank, we wondered if He could be pushed to anger. He was a man's man, don't get me wrong. He had the muscle and sinew and skin of a man who had worked all His life with His hands. But He was so soft-spoken, so kind, we talked among ourselves about whether He would be a good mate should trouble ever break out. He appeared strong and agile enough, but that is not what struck you when you looked at Him."

"What struck you?"

"His eyes. As I've said, He was not a particularly handsome man, but there was something in his countenance, in his eyes, that seemed able to bore into your soul, your heart, your mind. He asked each of us about ourselves frequently, but we never once had the impression He was asking questions to which He did not already know the answers. And whenever any of us embellished our own backgrounds, not lying—certainly not that, but, you know, shading a story to make ourselves look more godly or devout—a look of amusement came over Him and we were forced, without a word from Him, to correct our account right then.

"But nothing seemed to bother Him. When things went wrong, as they often did with that many men traveling here and there, He never seemed to trouble Himself over His own comfort. But, I mean, He was the man! The leader. We were His followers. And yet

He worried more about us and our comfort.

"Well, I must say, whatever image we had formed of Him changed soon after we arrived in Jerusalem. Being fishermen, James and I preferred solitude to the bustling crowds at the feast, but they seemed to invigorate the Lord. His eyes lit up and He was reminded of stories of Passovers past, especially the now famous one when He was twelve and His parents lost track of him shortly after their departure. He was pointing out the broad streets where He and his brothers had run and played, and as we neared the great temple He appeared deep in thought before telling us of how He had found it so fascinating to talk with the elders. In truth, of course, He had taught them and astounded them.

"But as we reached the outer courts His demeanor changed. His face flushed, His jaw was set. There were no more stories as His eyes flashed this way and that, taking in all the commerce being conducted in the stalls where men were selling oxen and sheep and doves. The money changers were doing a brisk business.

"As we watched, transfixed, Jesus made a whip of cords and drove them all out of the temple, with their sheep and the oxen, and poured out the changers' money and overturned their tables.

"And He said to those who sold doves, 'Take these things away! Do not make My Father's house a house of merchandise!'

"That's when James grabbed my garment and pulled

me close, whispering the old Scripture, *'Zeal for Your house has eaten Me up.'*"

"Where was that written, teacher?" Polycarp said. "And what does it mean?"

"Jesus had read it to us Himself from the Psalms and explained that at the time of the writing, David was being attacked from all sides because of his zeal toward the house of God and his defense of the Lord. You know Paul wrote of this to the believers in Rome, quoting David further, 'The reproaches of those who reproached You fell on Me.' Well, I tell you, Polycarp, that's what we feared would happen, that the Roman soldiers would intercede on behalf of the money changers and make an example of Jesus. But the Lord had somehow succeeded in not making a scene. He was simply determined and forthright, and the offenders were alarmed that He spoke to them as if they reported to Him."

"That must have been amazing."

"As I say, we had not seen Him angry. He had been so kind and friendly and engaging, carrying himself as a much older, wiser man than one of about age thirty. He was but five years older than I, and yet I always felt I was in the presence of a sage."

"But when something irritated him . . ."

John nodded. "Yes, His blood could boil. But it was always over the reputation of His Father."

"How did the merchants respond?"

"Why, of course they wanted to know who He thought He was. They said, 'What sign do You show to us, since You do these things?'

"Jesus said, 'Destroy this temple, and in three days I will raise it up.'

"And the Jewish leaders said, 'It has taken forty-six years to build this temple, and will You raise it up in three days?'"

"That's what I would have said," Polycarp said. "What did He mean?"

"He was speaking of the temple of His body. And while I hesitate to get ahead of myself, later, when He had risen from the dead, we remembered that He had said this to us, and we believed the Scripture and the words He had spoken."

"This all came back to you at His resurrection?"

John nodded. "Indeed, and it was of great comfort to us. Gradually all these memories came to us, and we marveled at the truths He had scattered in our paths every day of those three years. He often said that those who had ears would hear—meaning they would understand, of course. But we later recognized that we must not have had ears. He tried to tell us many times that He had been sent only to do the will of His Father, and He even made clear that this would mean His own death. But we heard only what we wanted to hear."

"Now, you said that the authorities were not aware of what He had done at Passover, but with the city teeming, word must have spread to the people."

"Oh, yes! And many believed in His name when they saw the signs He did. But Jesus did not commit

Himself to them, because He knew all men, and had no need that anyone should testify of man, for He knew what was in man."

"I am not following, teacher. What are you saying?"

"You rightly question this, son, as I did at the time. I recall being perplexed that Jesus did not seem to revel in the adoration of the crowds. He was already healing people and speaking such profound mysteries that people began flocking to hear and see Him wherever He went. I could only put myself in His place and imagine how fulfilling it would have been to have people gaze with such wonder and devotion. Yet it was clear He did not go out of His way to endear Himself to any. He seemed above it, not with any air of conceit, but rather as if He distrusted mere humans. We disciples had already proven less than worthy companions, and if we who were beginning to know Him so well could not be thoroughly trusted, He certainly wasn't about to cater to the whims of the public."

"But you say"—Polycarp referred back to his writing—"that 'He knew all men, and had no need that anyone should testify of man, for He knew what was in man.' I realize that means He didn't need their applause or their affirmation, but what was it that He 'knew' was 'in man'?"

"Oh, I believe we know, do we not, son? Were we not both reminded of what is truly in us, at our core, when we presented ourselves to the living God for His service? I hate to see myself in His light. And if we who have given our lives for His service can be brought so low by such a peering into our souls, imagine what must be in the hearts of people who had just been introduced to Him.

"All they knew of Him were His impressive speeches and His miracles. No one I know had witnessed a miracle in our lifetime. These people did not know the Man. And any lauding of His person or character would have sprung from their own, frail, human perspectives. No, the Messiah was not looking for the approval of men."

"That must have frustrated them," Polycarp said. "I can envision them, as I can see myself, hoping to get near Him, to speak a word or hear one directed solely at me. I would have wanted to be able to say I had interacted with the Man who had become the spectacle at Passover in Jerusalem."

John nodded. "Yes. I confess I myself was proud to be seen in His very presence and recognized as one of His. As I reflect on it, however, I doubt anyone really looked at the men surrounding Him. He alone was the object of the crowd's desire."

NINE

That Tuesday evening, John excused Polycarp to join Ignatius for the teaching of the people. The crowd the night before had been larger than the Lord's Day gathering, and the deaconate felt Polycarp was needed in case even more arrived for this meeting.

John took his dinner alone in his quarters and found himself strangely melancholy. He tried to put out of his mind the discomfort in his chest and blamed his mood on the fact that he was used to having his young disciple with him. Polycarp, always a bright student, had proved an ideal companion for this difficult work, asking just the right questions and exhibiting a contagious enthusiasm for every anecdote. John looked forward to getting together with him and with Ignatius again before bedtime.

John had been told that some had asked for him the evening before, so he was not surprised when a small boy was dispatched to seek him out again now. "Oh, please tell them that I appreciate their kind invitation but that I am in the middle of a complex project and must beg their pardon. Perhaps one evening later this week I will feel up to joining them."

John lit another small lamp on the desk and reviewed Polycarp's careful handwriting. He reminded himself to encourage the young man. The script was clear and legible, and as John read it over he was again transported to Galilee and the most remarkable season of his life. And he knew what story must come next, one that only he was privy to, and thus one that had not appeared on papyrus before. Fortunately, John believed he remembered every detail, and short of that, he trusted the Holy Spirit to remind him.

Hearing no music from below, John realized that Ignatius and Polycarp had eschewed the singing that evening in the interest of immediately digging in to the text of one of Paul's epistles. The old man was grateful for Ignatius and his willingness to devote this time to John's own flock. Ignatius had come to faith and to a calling to serve God from a place almost as unusual as that of the missionary Paul. He had not been religiously devout, however, as Paul had. That zealousness had led to Paul—then known as Saul—persecuting and even killing Christians. Ignatius had been thoroughly pagan, but he too had been a reviler of believers.

That he had come to faith in Christ from such a background, and the obvious change in his behavior, allowed John to trust him implicitly to render Paul's writings understandable for the believers. If only the three of them—John, Ignatius, and Polycarp—could make the Ephesian saints as interested in shunning the heresies of Cerinthus!

JOHN NODDED OFF and roused two hours later when sounds reached him of people chatting and milling about on their way out of the house. Many still had questions for the leaders, and John was pleased to hear both Ignatius and Polycarp promise to get to those another night. Soon their welcome footsteps mounted the stairs.

"Ah, Ignatius," John said, as the bishop set a plate of fruit and cheese on his table and laid a small knife beside it, "you always seem to anticipate my needs."

Polycarp smiled and Ignatius said, "Truth be told, I am merely the bearer of the vittles. The idea was the redhead's here."

"My thanks to you then, Polycarp," John said. "Please, gentlemen, sit. I want to tell you a story neither of you has heard before. Indeed, I do not believe I have shared it with anyone but my brother so many years ago. Are you up to it?"

"Up to it?" Ignatius said. "Teacher, after what Polycarp has related to me already, I feel as if I will burst if I cannot sit here whilst you dictate some of this. Please. My ears are yours until you have run out of things to say."

"Or until I collapse onto my bed."

"Shall I record this?" Polycarp said.

"Oh, I don't know. My intention was to simply tell you both what happened, and then we can cover it tomorrow. Let me begin without having to slow for the quill, and you tell me whether it's worth recording."

Ignatius sat at the desk, slicing the fruit and cheese, eating some and handing pieces to the other two. Polycarp sat on John's bed. The old man, as was his custom, paced as he spoke, sometimes with a chunk of food tucked in his cheek.

"Often Jesus would ask one or more of us to stay with Him for an evening when He had to be out after dark. More than once He hinted that the night would come when He would be taken from us, but we did not want to hear that and told ourselves—at least James and I did—that He was speaking symbolically, trying to tell us something about the coming kingdom that we did not understand. Of course, it eventually became clear that what we did not understand was the simple truth of what He was saying. And as you know, the night did come when He was arrested and led away away before our eyes.

"But one late afternoon after He had spent a few hours telling us of the Father, we enjoyed a hot meal, cooked by Peter." John smiled at the memory. "He could cook on an open fire as well as any man I ever knew, but I suspect the Lord frequently chose him just to give him something to do to keep him quiet. Curious? Peter had more questions than the rest of us combined.

"Jesus had a way of moving about during a meal, getting a bit of time with each of us. Sometimes He merely asked how we were, whether we were under-standing His teaching, that kind of thing. I cannot speak for the others, but He always made me feel cherished. When He was speaking with me I felt as if I were the only person in the world to Him.

"He had spent a few moments with Thomas, and then Nathanael, before I saw Him whispering to my brother. I didn't mean to stare, but I noticed James shake his head and shrug, then nod toward me. I looked away, but soon Jesus joined me and asked that I walk with Him.

"I hate to admit this, gentlemen, but I was filled with

pride whenever He did that. You would have thought that our spending that much time with a Man we knew was the Son of God would cure us of jealousies, but anytime Jesus spoke privately with one of us, the others wondered what was going on and why someone had been singled out. As I moved away from the group with Him, I knew all eyes were on us.

"He said, 'John, I have been asked to meet in secret after dark with a member of the Sanhedrin, and I need someone to accompany Me.'

" 'Well!' I said. 'I would be honored. But the Sanhedrin?'

" 'Verily,' He said, 'I must tell you I asked others first, as I prefer an older man. But they are otherwise occupied, and—'

"I know. James has promised our father that he will—"

" 'And so I must ask if you are available to serve Me in this way.'

" 'Certainly, Lord.'

" 'My wish is that it not be obvious I have brought anyone along. You will stay out of sight, within earshot, and come to my aid only if I call for you.'

" 'I understand. You do not suspect this man, do you?'

" 'On the contrary, beloved . . .'

"I know I have told you this, Polycarp, but it was not at all uncommon for Him to call me that. And forgive me if still more than a half century later I fight this pervasive conceit, but I do not recall His calling

111

another of the twelve the same. Sometimes He addressed crowds as 'beloved,' but I was the only individual. . . .

"Anyway, He assured me He believed this member of the Sanhedrin was a sincere seeker after the things of God."

Ignatius stopped in mid-bite. "Who was this?"

"Nicodemus."

Polycarp perked up. "Wasn't he the Pharisee who spoke up for the Lord before his colleagues?"

"And privately helped bury Him?" Ignatius added.

"The same."

John noticed that the eating had stopped, the rest of the food remained on the plate, and Ignatius, apparently unaware the knife was still in his hand, appeared rapt. "So Nicodemus had a private meeting with Jesus . . ."

"Yes, and I was close by and heard every word."

"Tell us!"

"Trade places with me, Ignatius," Polycarp said. "Do you not agree I should get this down?"

"I do indeed. John, are you willing? Or should it wait until the morrow when your strength has been renewed?"

"Let me cover it this night. It is all coming back to me. Nicodemus proved an elderly man, dressed formally in his religious garb, and sporting a long, pure-white beard. He was articulate and thoughtful, respectful in his conversation. He said, 'Rabbi, we know that You are a teacher come from God; for no one can do these signs that You do unless God is with him.'

"Jesus said, 'Most assuredly, I say to you, unless one is born again, he cannot see the kingdom of God.'

"Nicodemus said, 'How can a man be born when he is old? Can he enter a second time into his mother's womb and be born?'

"Jesus said, 'Most assuredly, I say to you, unless one is born of water and the Spirit, he cannot enter the kingdom of God. That which is born of the flesh is flesh, and that which is born of the Spirit is spirit. Do not marvel that I said to you, "You must be born again." The wind blows where it wishes, and you hear the sound of it, but cannot tell where it comes from and where it goes. So is everyone who is born of the Spirit.'

"Nicodemus said, 'How can these things be?'

"You see, gentlemen, though Nicodemus was a sincerely religious man and devout in his own way, he didn't understand that Jesus was talking about entering the *spiritual* kingdom. Christ had come to make it possible for people to enter into this kingdom by putting their faith in Him. You can plainly see what He was saying: that just as we must be born physically into this world, it is essential that we be born spiritually to get into God's spiritual kingdom. In turn we are then guaranteed entrance someday into the physical kingdom God is preparing for those who love and receive Him by faith.

"Jesus said to Nicodemus, 'Are you the teacher of

Israel, and do not know these things? Most assuredly, I say to you, We speak what We know and testify what We have seen, and you do not receive Our witness. If I have told you earthly things and you do not believe, how will you believe if I tell you heavenly things? No one has ascended to heaven but He who came down from heaven, that is, the Son of Man who is in heaven. And as Moses lifted up the serpent in the wilderness, even so must the Son of Man be lifted up, that whoever believes in Him should not perish but have eternal life.' "

"Excuse me, teacher," Ignatius said, clearly moved, "but Jesus was speaking of Himself, was He not?"

"Of course, but at that time I had no idea what He meant about being lifted up, though I understood that men were required to believe in Him to inherit eternal life. And what He said next tells His entire story in merely a few words, and I have quoted it to thousands in the years hence. 'For God so loved the world that He gave His only begotten Son, that whoever believes in Him should not perish but have everlasting life. For God did not send His Son into the world to condemn the world, but that the world through Him might be saved.

" 'He who believes in Him is not condemned; but he who does not believe is condemned already, because he has not believed in the name of the only begotten Son of God. And this is the condemnation, that the light has come into the world, and men loved darkness rather than light, because their deeds were evil. For everyone practicing evil hates the light and does not come to the light, lest his deeds should be exposed. But he who does the truth comes to the light, that his deeds may be clearly seen, that they have been done in God.' "

John moved near Polycarp and steadied himself against the desk. Ignatius immediately rose. "Here, sir. Take to your bed. That had better be enough for one day."

It took John longer than usual to fall asleep that night, his memories having transported him so far into the past.

TEN

Immediately after breakfast the next morning, Wednesday, Polycarp told John, "I am beginning to see how you are shaping this manuscript."

"How *I* am shaping it? I am trying to stay out of the way of the Spirit, son."

"Yes, but it is clear that, as you have said, your purpose in this account is different from that of those who came before you, in light of the heresies of the day."

"True."

"I was intrigued as I read over what you had dictated last night, where Jesus tells Nicodemus that no one but the Son of Man has ascended into heaven. That counters the claims of Cerinthus and his ilk, that they have some sort of supernatural knowledge that could come from only God and the angels."

"I included it because I remembered it, Polycarp. But you may be right that the Lord reminded me of it for this purpose."

"It reminds me, teacher, of the Proverb you are so fond of, the one that has become my favorite."

John nodded and smiled.

"Surely I am more stupid than any man,
And do not have the understanding of a man.
I neither learned wisdom
Nor have knowledge of the Holy One.

Who has ascended into heaven, or descended?
Who has gathered the wind in His fists?
Who has bound the waters in a garment?
Who has established all the ends of the earth?
What is His name, and what is His Son's name,
If you know?

Every word of God is pure;
He is a shield to those who put their trust in Him.
Do not add to His words,
Lest He rebuke you, and you be found a liar."

"Cerinthus had best beware," Polycarp said. "What a waste of intellect he has become."

"And yet people flock to him," John said. "So we must press on. Now, I had intimate knowledge of this next event, because I had been a disciple of the baptizer. When we came into the region where he was still preaching and baptizing, James and I spoke with him and with old friends who still traveled with him. They told us of some ruckus caused by religious Jews seeking the baptizer's opinion on whether Jesus had apparently now rendered their purification rituals unnecessary."

"Why did they think that?"

"That was never clear, but even the baptizer's disciples wondered if viewing Jesus as the Christ, the Messiah, meant they were departing from their faith, falling away from Judaism. And they had to wonder if this revealed a disagreement with John's own teaching, that a person was baptized for the remission of sins.

"Jesus was saying that outward cleansing—such as the purification rites of the Jews—does not makes a person clean. As He told Nicodemus, purity comes from being born of the Spirit from above. The dispute, at its core, was really whether this Man from Galilee had any standing that gave Him the right to even question, let alone overturn, a Jewish ritual. The baptizer himself answered that clearly, stating that heaven has ordained the Son of God. Let's get this into the scroll.

"After these things Jesus and His disciples came into the land of Judea, and there He remained with them and baptized. Now John also was baptizing in Aenon near Salim, because there was much water there. And they came and were baptized. For John had not yet been thrown into prison.

"Then there arose a dispute between some of John's disciples and the Jews about purification. And they came to John and said to him, 'Rabbi, He who was with you beyond the Jordan, to whom you have testified—behold, He is baptizing, and all are coming to Him!'

"John answered and said, 'A man can receive nothing unless it has been given to him from heaven. You yourselves bear me witness, that I said, "I am not the Christ," but, "I have been sent before Him." He who has the bride is the bridegroom; but the friend of the bridegroom, who stands and hears him, rejoices greatly because of the bridegroom's voice. Therefore this joy of mine is fulfilled. He must increase, but I must decrease. He who comes from above is above all; he who is of the earth is earthly and speaks of the earth. He who comes from heaven is above all. And what He has seen and heard, that He testifies; and no one receives His testimony. He who has received His testimony has certified that God is true. For He whom God has sent speaks the words of God, for God does not give the Spirit by measure. The Father loves the Son, and has given all things into His hand. He who believes in the Son has everlasting life; and he who does not believe the Son shall not see life, but the wrath of God abides on him.'

"Do you see the danger of what we encountered there, Polycarp?"

The young man finished and looked up. "No, I am afraid I don't."

"Word was getting around about Jesus and what He was supposedly doing. The last thing He needed was for the Pharisees to take notice of Him, because, as He continually told us, His time had not yet come. And anyway, it was not He who was baptizing. In truth, we were doing that work at His behest. And, you know, by now there were many more than twelve of us, as the winnowing process had not yet begun. But let me continue, as I have another story that has never before been published.

"Jesus knew that the Pharisees had heard that He made and baptized more disciples than John, so we left Judea and departed again to Galilee. But He needed to go through Samaria."

"That could not have been good," Polycarp said. "Didn't the Jews try to avoid Samaria?"

"Oh, Polycarp, that is a vast understatement. We Jews considered the Samaritans such enemies of our religion and way of life that we used the very term 'Samaritan' for anything or anyone we found morally contemptible. Samaritans were not even allowed inside our temples. Keep that in mind as I recount this incident.

"So Jesus came to a city of Samaria which is called Sychar, near the plot of ground that Jacob gave to his son Joseph. Now Jacob's well was there. It was about the sixth hour, and Jesus, being wearied from the journey, sat down by the well and sent us to find food.

"Upon our return He told us that a woman of Samaria had come to draw water. Jesus said to her, 'Give Me a drink.'

"The woman said, 'How is it that You, being a Jew, ask a drink from me, a Samaritan woman?' For Jews have no dealings with Samaritans.

"Jesus answered, 'If you knew the gift of God, and who it is who says to you, "Give Me a drink," you would have asked Him, and He would have given you living water.'

"The woman said, 'Sir, You have nothing to draw with, and the well is deep. Where then do You get that living water? Are You greater than our father Jacob, who gave us the well, and drank from it himself, as well as his sons and his livestock?'

"Jesus said, 'Whoever drinks of this water will thirst again, but whoever drinks of the water that I shall give him will never thirst. But the water that I shall give him will become in him a fountain of water springing up into everlasting life.' "

Polycarp held up a hand as he finished writing. "What a beautiful image!"

"No one has ever spoken like the Master, son. But the woman did not understand. She said, 'Sir, give me this water, that I may not thirst, nor come here to draw.'

"Jesus said, 'Go, call your husband, and come here.' When she responded that she had no husband, Jesus told her, 'You have well said, "I have no husband," for you have had five husbands, and the one whom you now have is not your husband; in that you spoke truly.' "

"She must have been astonished!" Polycarp said.

"No doubt. The woman said to Him, 'Sir, I perceive that You are a prophet. Our fathers worshiped on this mountain, and you Jews say that in Jerusalem is the place where one ought to worship.'

"Jesus said, 'Woman, believe Me, the hour is coming when you will neither on this mountain, nor in Jerusalem, worship the Father. You worship what you do not know; we know what we worship, for salvation is of the Jews. But the hour is coming, and now is, when the true worshipers will worship the Father in spirit and truth; for the Father is seeking such to worship Him. God is Spirit, and those who worship Him must worship in spirit and truth.'

"The woman said, 'I know that Messiah is coming. When He comes, He will tell us all things.'

"Jesus said, 'I who speak to you am He.' "

Polycarp finished and set down his quill, sitting back and staring at John. "That alone makes Cerinthus a liar!"

"Along with *any* who say Jesus never claimed to be the Christ. At this point we returned from buying bread and marveled that He was talking with a woman, let alone a Samaritan. She then left her waterpot, went her way into the city, and said to the men, 'Come, see a Man who told me all things that I ever did. Could this be the Christ?' Then they went out of the city and came to Him."

"You heard her say these things, master?"

"No, no. Jesus told us. And I do not question the One who knows men's names, as He did Peter's, and can see them under trees, as He did Nathanael. Anyway, while she was gone, I said, 'Rabbi, eat.'

"But He said, 'I have food to eat of which you do not know.'

"I looked at the others. We murmured, 'Has anyone brought Him anything to eat?'

"As we shook our heads, Jesus said, 'My food is to do the will of Him who sent Me, and to finish His work. Do you not say, "There are still four months and then comes the harvest"? Behold, I say to you, lift up your eyes and look at the fields, for they are already white for harvest! And he who reaps receives wages, and gathers fruit for eternal life, that both he who sows and he who reaps may rejoice together. For in this the saying is true: "One sows and another reaps." I sent you to reap that for which you have not labored; others have labored, and you have entered into their labors.' "

"Did you know whereof He spoke, teacher?"

"Not fully at that time, no. But of course it is clear to me now and, I pray, to any who read or hear this. I have seen this truth borne out in the decades since. Followers of the Christ feel compelled to draw others into His kingdom, and yet few do all the work themselves. Some plant the seed of salvation, telling someone of the gift of forgiveness of sins and eternal life through the work Christ accomplished on the cross. Someone else may till that soil by explaining the Scriptures or living an exemplary life before that person. And finally yet someone else may harvest the crop by leading that one to become a believer.

"Many of the Samaritans of that city believed in Jesus because of the woman saying, 'He told me all that I ever did.' Many of those who came to hear Him urged Him to stay, and He did, two days. And many more believed. They said to the woman, 'Now we believe, not because of what you said, for we ourselves have heard Him and we know that this is indeed the Christ, the Savior of the world.'"

"My mentor, you must feel so privileged. Oh, that I had been born in your generation and could have witnessed this firsthand."

"Is it any wonder that I speak of the Lord with such confidence? Well, we soon left that place and headed to His homeland. Galilee. Jesus Himself testified that a prophet was not without honor, except in his own country. But this time the Galileans welcomed Him, having seen all the things He did in Jerusalem at the feast.

"We were again in Cana, where He had turned the water to wine, when we were met by a nobleman. He fell at Jesus' feet, nearly in tears. 'I heard that You had come out of Judea into Galilee,' he said, 'and so I walked an entire day's journey from Capernaum to find You and implore You to come back with me and heal my son. He is at the point of death.'

"Capernaum, of course, is where we had spent a few

days at Peter's home. It was a long, long walk. I felt deeply for the man and his problem, but Jesus at first seemed irritated. He said, 'Unless you people see signs and wonders, you will by no means believe.'

"But the nobleman would not be dissuaded. He said, 'Sir, come down before my child dies!'

"Jesus said to him, 'Go your way; your son lives.'

"Just like that, Polycarp. If any one of us had a lingering doubt about Jesus, even after the turning of the water to wine and His speaking with such authority to the money changers in the temple, such was erased now. It was plain that the man believed the word that Jesus had spoken to him, and he sprang to his feet and went his way. The next day Jesus told us that the man's servants had just met him on the road to tell him, 'Your son lives!'

"Oh, Polycarp, Jesus' eyes shone as He said, 'The man had inquired of them the hour the boy got better, and they said to him, "Yesterday at the seventh hour the fever left him."' That had been the very hour in which Jesus said to him, 'Your son lives.' Jesus told us, 'The man himself believes, and his whole household.'

"So that was the second sign Jesus performed when He had come out of Judea into Galilee."

"Teacher," Polycarp said, "I am curious. Do you mean to say this was the second sign? Had Jesus not performed many miracles by now?"

"True, but this was the second in Galilee."

"The first being at the wedding."

"Correct. And I emphasize it because it was yet another significant sign of His deity. Can you tell what I mean by that? What was the sign and what did it mean?"

"I feared you were about to ask that."

"Ponder it. His turning of the water to wine was so pervasive that not one of us disciples ever doubted again that He was who He said He was. And I explained that this was the first sign that He was the Son of God, the very provider of life. What sign can you glean from His healing of the nobleman's son?"

"That He has victory over death?"

John cocked his head. "I can see how you might arrive at that, but there is no evidence in this episode that the boy had died. Jesus did not raise him from the dead but rather healed him. And what is unusual about how that took place?"

"Jesus was not even there."

"Yes! The man met us on the road and told us his son was dying in Capernaum. We were twenty miles away! For all he knew, his son had already died. I have long admired that man for his devotion to his family, that he would make a forty-mile walk to us and back for the sake of his son. And while the Master at first chided the crowd, through the man, because it seemed they needed to see miracles in order to believe, in truth the man's faith made his son whole, and Jesus accomplished this from that far away. This is a sign that Jesus is God, because He is not bound by distance. He is the Master of distance and time."

ELEVEN

John believed he was too old, past the time when he could be shocked or even amazed by anything temporal. Hardly anything surprised him anymore. Even encountering Cerinthus, while agitating him to no end, did not surprise. Some news that Wednesday evening did, however, and he felt it where he wanted to feel it the least. In his chest.

This concern over his health was new to John, despite that he had outlived most of his contemporaries. Men and women in their seventies were considered ancient, and yet he still felt like a Son of Thunder at nearly ninety. He suffered the expected aches and pains, but other than expecting that one day Rome would come calling—as it had to nearly every other bold proclaimer of the gospel of Christ—John rarely allowed himself to dwell upon his own mortality. But chest pains—even he could not ignore those. And there was so much more to do.

Again Polycarp joined the evening teaching session, and again John had to decline. He admitted to exhaustion and fatigue, but he was determined not to reveal his growing concern over his health. Polycarp would tell Ignatius, Ignatius would tell the elders and deacons, and surely someone would urge the ceasing of his work. That must not happen.

But the task became all the more urgent when Polycarp returned from the meeting to report that Ignatius would not be able to join them that evening but wished to review the day's work if Polycarp could deliver it.

"Certainly," John said. "In time I will wish even more eyes on the project."

"Well, rabbi," Polycarp said, refusing to sit, "we have discovered Cerinthus's purpose in Ephesus."

"And?"

"He is founding a Gnostic church."

John swallowed a sharp retort as pain stabbed behind his ribs and made him sit to catch his breath. The news surprised and angered him, but John was more concerned about hiding his pain from Polycarp. The deep throbbing had been with him longer than he cared to remember. John had never been a complainer, and for years he had labored despite all sorts of illnesses, diseases, and ailments. But this, he feared, would eventually be the end of him. It was not getting better. And it was not remaining the same. It was growing worse, and alarm was the last thing his ailing body needed.

"We simply must not allow this," John said finally. "We must marshal our resources, our people, and fight it to the death. This city is already replete with evidences of the enemy, from the worship of Greek and Roman gods to the celebration of the sensual and the profane and the pagan. Do you see why this would be even worse, son?"

"I do, because this false doctrine has already proven

attractive to believers. It would deny God and Christ the power of salvation and make the sinner believe he could accomplish it on his own."

"Exactly. Our flock knows to stay away from the pagan idols, but look how they respond to a poison that tastes so refreshing at first. Polycarp, we must finish our work and publicize it far and wide before this so-called church is able to gain purchase. Let us work day and night."

"I am at your service, sir, as you know. I have the endurance for it. Do you?"

"I have no choice."

Polycarp leaned close and moved his head out of the way of the oil lamp so it illuminated the old man. "You do not look well, if you don't mind my saying so."

John turned his face away. "I do mind! You are not my physician, and I do not appreciate being examined like an animal."

Polycarp's face fell and John felt immediately repentant.

"Forgive me, lad. I did not mean to lash out at you."

"No, forgive *me,* rabbi. You know how I revere you. I had no right to treat you as a patient. Would you like me to send for your physician?"

"I am fine, Polycarp. I will tell you when I need to rest, and if I need medical care, you will be the first to know."

"First I must have your forgiveness."

"Of course you have it. And I would like yours."

The men embraced, then set about to work in the low light of the lamp during a starless night. During this session John recalled a miracle that made him wish he were back in the Holy City of David with the Master and could come under that healing touch himself.

And yet it was the day of that very miracle that finally touched off the firestorm among religious leaders concerning Jesus. He could no longer minister without coming under their watchful and condemning eyes. Starkest to John as he reflected was how bold Jesus had been in speaking of Himself and about His Father to the men who believed they were the only authorities on the subject of God. He risked His life speaking to them in that manner, and yet no one without true authority could have said what He did.

"We were at the Pool of Siloam near the Sheep Gate in the north wall. Springs fed this vast pool, causing the waters to move at random and become colored with minerals. Many believed there was some medicinal value in it, and legend said that the first to immerse himself when the water stirred would be cured. We arrived there on a Saturday, and the five great porches at the edges of the water were crowded with people bearing all sorts of afflictions—the sick, the blind, the lame, the paralyzed, waiting for the moving of the water.

"When Jesus saw a certain man there, He knew the man had borne an infirmity thirty-eight years, thus afflicted since before Jesus was born. You should have seen how wasted were his muscles as he lay there. Jesus said to the man, 'Do you want to be made well?'

"The man said, 'Sir, I have no man to put me into the pool when the water is stirred up; but while I am coming, another steps down before me.'"

John closed his eyes and turned his face toward the ceiling. He could not stifle a shudder at this memory. "Jesus said to him, 'Rise, take up your bed and walk.' And immediately the man was made well, took up his bed, and walked. I believe the Master purposely chose a man so debilitated that there would be no doubt in the mind of anyone who had ever seen him that a miracle had occurred and that he had indeed been fully healed."

John fell silent and wished he could sleep. Yet it was stories like these he had to recount to put to shame the blasphemy of men like Cerinthus. How the common man loved to believe that in himself, in his intellect, lay salvation. And what a dangerous belief!

"That happened on the Sabbath, Polycarp. The Jews said to the cured man, 'It is not lawful for you to carry your bed today.'

"The man said, 'He who made me well said to me, "Take up your bed and walk."'

"They asked him, 'Who is the Man who said this to you?' But the one who was healed did not know who it was, for Jesus had withdrawn, because of the crowds.

"Later we came upon the same man in the temple, and Jesus said, 'See, you have been made well. Sin no more, lest a worse thing come upon you.'

"The man departed and told the Jews that it was Jesus who had made him well. This was why the Jewish leaders persecuted Jesus, and sought to kill Him, because He had done these things on the Sabbath. But Jesus answered them, 'My Father has been working until now, and I have been working.'

"What He was saying here, Polycarp, was that He and His Father are One, and that just as God works constantly, so does He as the Son. There is no real day of rest for God, and certainly no law against doing good on the Sabbath. Even the laws the Pharisees cited were not in the Scripture but were rather oral traditions that seemed to grow and become more complex with the years. But, oh, this infuriated the religious leaders! Listen to what Jesus tells them about Himself and see if you can detect all the ways He compares Himself to the Father. The Gnostics would never be able to even begin to refute the claims of Christ.

"The Jewish leaders sought all the more to kill Him, because He not only broke the Sabbath, but also said that God was His Father, making Himself equal with God. Jesus said, 'Most assuredly, I say to you, the Son can do nothing of Himself, but what He sees the Father do; for whatever He does, the Son also does in like manner. For the Father loves the Son, and shows Him all things that He Himself does; and He will show Him greater works than these, that you may marvel. For as the Father raises the dead and gives life to them, even so the Son gives life to whom He will. For the Father judges no one, but has committed all judgment to the Son, that all should honor the Son just as they honor the Father. He who does not honor the Son does not honor the Father who sent Him.

" 'Most assuredly, I say to you, he who hears My word and believes in Him who sent Me has everlasting life, and shall not come into judgment, but has passed from death into life. Most assuredly, I say to you, the hour is coming, and now is, when the dead will hear the voice of the Son of God; and those who hear will live. For as the Father has life in Himself, so He has granted the Son to have life in Himself, and has given Him authority to execute judgment also, because He is the Son of Man. Do not marvel at this; for the hour is coming in which all who are in the graves will hear His voice and come forth—those who have done good, to the resurrection of life, and those who have done evil, to the resurrection of condemnation. I can of Myself do nothing. As I hear, I judge; and My judgment is righteous, because I do not seek My own will but the will of the Father who sent Me.

" 'If I bear witness of Myself, My witness is not true. There is another who bears witness of Me, and I know that the witness which He witnesses of Me is true. You have sent to John, and he has borne witness to the truth. Yet I do not receive testimony from man, but I say these things that you may be saved. He was the burning and shining lamp, and you were willing for a time to rejoice in his light. But I have a greater witness than John's; for the works which the Father has given Me to finish—the very works that I do—bear witness of Me, that the Father has sent Me. And the Father Himself, who sent Me, has testified of Me. You have neither heard His voice at any time, nor seen His form. But you do not have His word abiding in you, because whom He sent, Him you do not believe. You search the Scriptures, for in them you think you have eternal life; and these are they which testify of Me. But you are not willing to come to Me that you may have life.

" 'I do not receive honor from men. But I know you, that you do not have the love of God in you. I have come in My Father's name, and you do not receive Me; if another comes in his own name, him you will receive. How can you believe, who receive honor from one another, and do not seek the honor that comes from the only God? Do not think that I shall accuse you to the Father; there is one who accuses you—Moses, in whom you trust. For if you believed Moses, you would believe Me; for he wrote about Me. But if you do not believe his writings, how will you believe My words?' "

"It is hard to fathom," Polycarp said, "Jesus saying anything more offensive to Jewish leaders than to accuse them of not believing what Moses had written."

"Everyone who heard this exchange was astonished. But a careful reading of the ancient texts shows that they all point to the coming Messiah. And yet these men rejected Him when He appeared."

TWELVE

J ohn woke before dawn Thursday, clutching his chest and desperately thirsty. Not wanting to awaken and alarm anyone, he forced himself out of bed and painfully made his way down the stairs to a waterpot, where he poured himself a cup. While it satisfied his thirst, the trip down and then up the stairs made his pain only worse.

He tried to sleep, but the fear of death overtook him and he prayed, pleading for healing. He longed to be with Christ in heaven, but the thought of not finishing this sacred task tormented him. "Lord, I am desperate to believe you will spare me long enough to finish what You have given me to do. Forgive my lack of faith. Cure my unbelief."

All the while God was putting on John's heart that he should confide in his protégés and seek treatment, but John's mind whirled with the task at hand. There was so much more he had to tell Polycarp. He wanted his entire treatise penned before he dared take any time away. A week from the Monday following the coming Lord's Day, Ignatius would embark on the rest of his trip to each of the other six churches in Asia. John and Polycarp had to finish their work before that or risk leaving their fellow believers without a shepherd.

John needed Polycarp to also start copying his

account of the miracles of Jesus. The message had to be circulated to the churches, but even more important, it had to be made public right there in Ephesus—first in the church and then in the city itself. John believed he could cut the heretical cult's beliefs off at the knees if he could document Jesus' claims of His own deity.

The problem was that he was simply not well enough to work that day. He told Polycarp that he had not slept well and had to rest. While this was not the entire truth, it was true, and John pacified his conscience by telling himself that he merely didn't want to be a nuisance.

By late afternoon, John had slept the better part of the day, and the pain in his chest had subsided enough to make working bearable. He summoned his young charge and they continued, leaving with Ignatius the whole responsibility of running the meeting that night, despite the largest attendance so far.

"People have so benefited from the writings of Paul," Polycarp said. "And Ignatius is a gifted teacher. I hope only they are as receptive to this history."

"History sometimes seems more interesting than doctrine," John said. "But I would be at a loss to say which is more crucial and timely."

Polycarp seemed to be studying John, and the old man sighed. "What is it now, young friend?"

"At least you call me friend. I am only concerned about you, master. I left you to rest for the entire day and yet you appear no more refreshed than when I saw you this morning. Now, don't look at me that way and do not be vexed with me. You are God's gift to this church, and I would not want to be responsible for sending you to heaven before your time."

"Nothing happens outside of God's timing." Even as he said it John realized how shallow this platitude sounded. There was no question he had spoken the truth, but should he have admitted that while he pined for heaven, he dreaded the passage from one life to the next?

"It was just a figure of speech, teacher. How can you be annoyed with me when my concern is earnest?"

"I appreciate it and you, Polycarp, truly I do. But we must not waste time discussing me. You know the urgency of the matter at hand and the few days we have to finish the task. Let us get on with it. I want to pick up the story a year later, again near the time of Passover. Are you ready?"

"Of course."

"This is a story you have read or heard from the accounts of my colleagues, one of the most thrilling episodes in the life of our Lord."

"The feeding of the multitudes?"

"That is the one. And while there may not seem a need for me to repeat it, I feel compelled to, as it again supports my thesis. If the healing of the paralyzed man at the Pool of Bethesda was yet another sign of Jesus' deity, what did it portray?"

"Ah, I am now the student again, and not just the secretary?"

"Consider yourself studying with me every day."

"That is how it feels. Well, Jesus was not subject to the law. Specifically the law of the Sabbath."

"Excellent. By now we have shown that He is the provider of life, the master over distance, and now the master over time. With what He accomplishes here we will have to acknowledge that He is, as He said, the Bread of Life. Do you not find it interesting that two of His signs have to do with wine and bread, the very elements He would eventually use to symbolize his body and blood?"

"Interesting? Rabbi, sitting under your teaching all these years and now being privileged to record your account have been the apexes of my life. I cannot imagine anything that could hope to compare."

"I just pray these have been laying for you a foundation for your ministry, because, as I have said, the greater church has need of you. Pray that you will remain pure of heart and close to Christ."

"I will."

John scrutinized the young man. "You love children, do you not?"

Polycarp nodded, clearly puzzled.

"I ask only because they are the lifeblood, the future, of the church. The Master Himself was particularly fond of youngsters. Everywhere we went He sought them out, but usually He didn't have to. They were drawn to Him. They could see in His eyes, in His smile, that He loved them. They would gather about Him and climb into His lap as He spoke. And though

He was speaking to their parents of things far beyond their comprehension, they seemed settled and quiet in His presence. They sensed His care, perhaps sensed His importance. And when He was finished telling the mysteries of heaven and the kingdom and often parables confusing even to those of us who knew Him best, He would then turn His attention to the children. He told them stories from the Scriptures, stories of the heroes and miraculous events of generations past.

"That affected me, Polycarp, and while I had long since lost touch with people less than half my age, I found myself drawn to them anew. That is what happened the day of the miraculous feeding. It was near the time of Passover again, and we had gone with Jesus across the Sea of Galilee, which is the Sea of Tiberias. By now huge crowds were trying to follow Him everywhere He went, because they had seen the miracles He had performed on those who were diseased. We tried to give Him some peace away from the people and so we led Him up on the mountain where He sat to rest.

"Well, it wasn't long before we began to hear voices and the sound of many people milling about. Thousands of them. I'll never forget Jesus looking up and seeing a great multitude coming toward Him. He said to Philip, 'Where shall we buy bread, that these may eat?' I know now, of course, that Jesus was only testing Philip, for He Himself knew what He would do.

"Philip said, 'Two hundred denarii worth of bread is

not sufficient for them, that every one of them may have a little.'"

"A denarius is a whole day's wage now," Polycarp said.

"It was nearly the same then. Yes, Philip was right. Seven months' wages would not have bought enough bread. Jesus had assigned us—and by now we disciples were many—to see that the people were directed to areas where they could hear Him. Imagine His speaking to such a throng. He was soft-spoken with us, but when need be, His voice would ring out clear and powerful.

"Well, Andrew and I spied a young lad carrying a leather bag. I was intrigued with him because he appeared to be alone. 'Have you lost your parents?' I said.

"'No,' he replied, shaking my hand. 'My name is Nathanael. You may call me Nathan. I came to hear and see the miracle worker.'

"Andrew said, 'You know we have one among us with your name?'

"'Truly?' the boy said, scowling playfully as if he thought Andrew was teasing.

"'Verily,' Andrew said. 'Perhaps later you can meet him. For now we are all busy.'

"And the engaging boy said, 'Well, if you get hungry, I have plenty of food. I believe my mother feared I would be gone the entire day. Look.'

"He opened the leather bag slung over his shoulder, and we could smell immediately that the fish was local and fresh. I peered in. He had two undersized but meaty beauties. I told him I was a fisherman and asked if he had caught these himself. He shook his head. 'But I caught these, right out of my mother's oven this morning.' He showed five small loaves of golden brown bread.

"'A veritable feast!' I teased him. 'At least for me. But what would you eat?'

"'You couldn't eat all of this,' he said, laughing. 'But if you or your friends or the Teacher need it, you can have it.'

"Later, when Jesus was asking how we would possibly feed nearly twenty thousand people—there were about five thousand men alone, and nearly all had their families with them—Andrew went looking for the boy again. When Andrew returned, he reported that the boy gladly gave his entire lunch, 'of five barley loaves and two small fish, but what are they among so many?'

"Then Jesus said, 'Make the people sit down.' So the people sat in the grass. And Jesus took the loaves, and when He had given thanks He distributed them to the disciples, and the disciples to those sitting down; and likewise of the fish, as much as they wanted. You can only imagine, I had never seen anything like it. No one had. My mates and I kept giving one another wondering looks as people ate and ate and ate. And when they were filled, Jesus told us, 'Gather up the fragments that remain, so that nothing is lost.' Polycarp, we filled twelve baskets with the fragments of the five barley loaves that were left over by those who had eaten.

"I went looking for the lad Nathan, but I never saw him again and so was never able to ask if he realized that it was his gift the Lord had miraculously multiplied to feed that whole crowd and leave leftovers for us disciples to enjoy later that evening. No doubt the boy ate his fill that afternoon as well."

"What must the people have thought?" Polycarp said.

"I am not certain all knew what had happened. But many did, and the word spread quickly. Some said, 'This is truly the Prophet who is to come into the world.'

"Jesus told us He perceived they were about to come and take Him by force to make Him king, so He departed again to the mountain by Himself alone. When we were certain He was safe, we headed down to the sea. By the dark of the evening, He still had not joined us. We knew better than to wait for Him. He did not report to us, after all. We crowded into the boat and went over the sea toward Capernaum. Suddenly the sea arose with great waves under a huge wind. We must have rowed three or four miles. I wondered if we would ever reach the shore at Capernaum.

"Squinting into the darkness, I fell back, grabbing Peter's shoulder and pointing. What was that on the water? A ghost? It was the form of a man! He was walking on the sea and drawing near the boat! We were terrified.

"Jesus said, 'It is I; do not be afraid.' I nearly wept from relief as we eagerly helped Him into the boat. Instantly we were at the shore."

"What? But you said you had rowed a few miles in the storm."

"I'm telling you," John said, "that we were there just like that," and he snapped his fingers. "In an instant."

"A miracle in itself."

"True, but it was His walking on the water that was the fifth major sign proving His deity."

"He was master over nature."

"Every day we were with Him, Polycarp, we witnessed such things. He knew the hearts of the multitude and that they were actually of a mind to make Him their king. Imagine if He had not known that. His hour had not yet come, and so He was able to steal away alone until they had left. He told us later He was disappointed that despite what they had seen and heard that day—and despite that they had been fed both physically and spiritually—it seemed all they cared about was themselves. They wanted Him to be their victorious leader, delivering them from the tyranny of the Romans. That's what they thought the Messiah was all about."

"Teacher, did you ever wake up wondering if you had dreamt all this?"

"More than once. Every morning I found it reassuring to look about me and see my brother and old and new friends, but especially to see Jesus. Not a day passed in which He did not tell me that He loved me.

I knew it. He showed it in so many ways, not just to me, but to all of us, of course. And all this might still seem like a dream had it not been for His resurrection. That so burned itself into my mind and soul that I recall every detail of it, and it brings back to me all the events of the previous three years too."

THIRTEEN

Friday morning broke unusually hot for autumn in Ephesus, and John despaired to realize he was feeling no better. He did not look forward to the frowns of concern—which always looked like pity—on the faces of Ignatius and Polycarp. Yet today he feared he must break down and ask for help. Not for a doctor. No, it was much too early for that and would create more alarm than he cared to, in light of the task at hand. But he needed a bath, and he could not manage the stairs.

The sad fact was, he had to ask to move to a room on the first floor. That way he might be able to care for himself somewhat and not have to depend so much on others for his simple needs. If only he could count on his protégés not to make a fuss. Trading rooms with Ignatius would be ideal, but John simply wanted this without fanfare. He and Polycarp had much to cover. And if the move could be effected early, he might enjoy cooler air throughout the day.

To John's amazement, Ignatius and Polycarp had

apparently lost interest in how he looked in the morning. They arrived with something else on their minds.

"Late in the afternoon yesterday," Ignatius said, "I got word in the city that a disciple of Cerinthus was making the rounds, telling people of a church that would soon be formed."

"Old news," John said.

"But that they are spreading the word, that's news. I wanted to talk to the young man. I had something I wanted communicated to Cerinthus, not knowing whether he was still in the city."

"To Cerinthus?" John said. "What?"

"I wanted to invite him to church."

John scowled at Ignatius. "You're mad."

"That's what I said," Polycarp said. "In fact, if I had seen Cerinthus I would have told him I believe he is a child of the devil."

"Well," Ignatius said, "he may be what you say, but consider the effect on him should he sit under the teaching of true doctrine, inspired by the living God. Besides, it would give us a chance to engage him once more."

"Forgive my lack of faith," John said, "but surely you don't expect to be able to reason with the man, to make sense to him."

"I thought you would welcome the opportunity to try."

John sat on the edge of his bed. "And so? Did you find him, or did you send word with his man?"

"The latter," Ignatius said. "Of course he laughed in my face."

"The impudence! Even if the invitation sounds ludicrous, with which I must agree, how dare a young man respond to his elder that way?"

"I too was offended, John," Ignatius said, "but I did not remain so. And I was quite clear in telling him where and when Cerinthus should come."

John camouflaged his physical discomfort with concern. "Bishop! Was that wise? It is already difficult enough to hide the largest Christian church in all of Asia."

Ignatius paused. "We need not worry about Cerinthus turning us in to the Romans. While *we* know he is apostate, *they* would consider him in league with us. Exposing us would merely leave him vulnerable to the same."

John pondered this. "Perhaps. I am not so sure he wouldn't jump at the chance to expose us to Rome. I don't know whether to hope he arrives or not."

"I hope he does!" Polycarp said.

"I'm sure you do. Ah, the naïveté of youth."

Polycarp looked crestfallen.

"Oh, son, I didn't intend that to be mean. In truth I envy your idealism. Certainly I would love to face the man again too, but I wish I were your age again, or even Ignatius's. Yet I fear we would be allowing the nose of the camel under our tent."

John was relieved that his health had not become the topic of conversation, but that reprieve was short-lived. Presently Ignatius said, "So how are you this summer day anyway?"

"It does feel like summer, doesn't it? I need to ask, Ignatius, if there would be any chance we could trade quarters."

"Too hot for you up here?"

"Yes."

"That is an aberration, as I'm sure you know, and within a fortnight the guest room might prove too cold for you."

"If you wouldn't mind, I would like to work down there, especially today, but it would be of great help if I could permanently move."

In less than an hour the switch was made, and John was so delighted with his new chambers that he wished he had made the request days earlier. He had much more room, another window on yet another wall, and a bigger desk for Polycarp too. They dove directly into their work.

"Well, the next day, the people on the other side of the sea had to be astonished that Jesus was not there. They had seen us leave, so they knew He had to still be in the area. When they could not find Him, they sailed to Capernaum. And when they found Him on the other side of the sea, they said, 'Rabbi, when did You come here?'

"Jesus said, 'Most assuredly, I say to you, you seek Me, not because you saw the signs, but because you ate of the loaves and were filled. Do not labor for the food which perishes, but for the food which endures to everlasting life, which the Son of Man will give you, because God the Father has set His seal on Him.'

"So He's changing the subject, teacher? Evading their question?"

"Clearly. And by turning the lamp onto them, He makes them forget that He seemed to have no way to get across the lake. They said, 'What shall we do, that we may work the works of God?'

"Jesus said, 'This is the work of God, that you believe in Him whom He sent.'

"Of course they still did not understand and said, 'What sign will You perform then, that we may see it and believe You? What work will You do? Our fathers ate the manna in the desert; as it is written, "He gave them bread from heaven to eat."'

"Jesus said, 'Most assuredly, I say to you, Moses did not give you the bread from heaven, but My Father gives you the true bread from heaven. For the bread of God is He who comes down from heaven and gives life to the world.'

"They said, 'Lord, give us this bread always.'

"Now, listen carefully, Polycarp. This is such a wonderful saying. Jesus said, 'I am the bread of life. He who comes to Me shall never hunger, and he who believes in Me shall never thirst. But I said to you that you have seen Me and yet do not believe. All that the Father gives Me will come to Me, and the one who comes to Me I will by no means cast out. For I have come down from heaven, not to do My own will, but the will of Him who sent Me. This is the will of the Father who sent Me, that of all He has given Me I should lose nothing, but should raise it up at the last day. And this is the will of Him who sent Me, that everyone who sees the Son and believes in Him may have everlasting life; and I will raise him up at the last day.' "

John took a deep breath and sat. As encouraged as he was with his new room, he found himself sitting more and even lying down occasionally as he dictated, which naturally caused Polycarp alarm. The young man continually entreated him to break, to take refreshment, to nap, to see a doctor.

"Verily, lad, you must stop this. Can we not establish that if I have need of anything, anything at all, I will admit it?"

Again it was plain he had offended Polycarp. "I am only trying to—"

"I know, son, I know! Please! I do not know how else to say this. You know how uncomfortable it makes me when one is so solicitous of me."

The young man shrugged, and John was content that he had kept Polycarp at bay yet again. But in truth, he knew he should take a break and gather himself. While he feared he was not being a worthy steward of his own resources, John's greater dread was that they would run out of days. If despite all the Lord had brought him through, he expended his life over what might seem to some a menial task, so be it. He would consider it a worthy investment. Unlike Ignatius, he did not desire, nor did he see as necessary or gallant, a martyr's death any more dramatic than that.

FOURTEEN

It had been John's custom to eat only morning and evening meals, but as his strength waned, he lay down and asked Polycarp to fetch him some midday sustenance. The young man hurried off, leaving John to regret how he had seemed so frequently to brush aside the lad's obvious concern for him and his welfare.

It was his wish only to encourage as fine a young disciple as Polycarp. John had not once over the years been disingenuous in his proclamations regarding Polycarp's future in ministry. As it was, even in his mid-twenties, Polycarp played a respected leadership role in that important church. And surely he was destined for a bishopric—if not here, then in one of the other churches under John's care.

John told himself that his point had been made, and that if Polycarp fell into any more doting, he would accept it gratefully as a sign of the young man's love and concern. He would merely thank him. And ignore him.

The young man had gifts, of that there was no question, not the least of which was knowing just the right refresher for his mentor. John sat up as Polycarp returned and set before him a small bowl of grapes and olives. Such an unusual combination, and yet perfect for that moment. The sharp saltiness of the olives proved delicious, and the sweetness of the grapes energized him.

Oh, the pain in his chest was still there, and John resigned himself to the fact that if he was for some reason forced to exert himself, it would surely result in his demise. Fortunately, the work he was doing and the insightful questions of his helper proved to somehow take his mind off his ailments—at least temporarily.

"I am amazed," Polycarp said, "at how often Jesus refers to His mission, who He is and what He is about. I do not see how anyone who studies His life and message could come to any other conclusion than that He claimed to be the Son of God, sent from Heaven to do the will of His Father. I am not so deluded as to think that everyone will agree and believe in Him. But they cannot say He was about anything else or that He did not claim this identity. And the beautiful imagery. I live for water and for bread, so He reaches me when He uses that language. Let me predict that your account will find an enthusiastic hearing among the brethren."

"Let us pray it will also be received by those who are not yet with us," John said. "The pagan, the apostate, the unbeliever, they need it even more than we do. And so we must resume. You know, the religious leaders complained about Him, because He said, 'I am the bread which came down from heaven.' And remember, He is saying this in the synagogue in Capernaum."

"They must have been outraged."

"They said, 'Is not this Jesus, the son of Joseph, whose father and mother we know? How is it then that He says, "I have come down from heaven?"'

"Jesus answered them, 'Do not murmur among yourselves. No one can come to Me unless the Father who sent Me draws him; and I will raise him up at the last day. It is written in the prophets, "And they shall all be taught by God." Therefore everyone who has heard and learned from the Father comes to Me. Not that anyone has seen the Father, except He who is from God; He has seen the Father. Most assuredly, I say to you, he who believes in Me has everlasting life. I am the bread of life. Your fathers ate the manna in the wilderness, and are dead. This is the bread which comes down from heaven, that one may eat of it and not die. I am the living bread which came down from heaven. If anyone eats of this bread, he will live forever; and the bread that I shall give is My flesh, which I shall give for the life of the world.'"

"How did the Jewish leaders react to that?" Polycarp said.

"As you can imagine, they quarreled among themselves, saying, 'How can this Man give us His flesh to eat?'

"Jesus said, 'Most assuredly, I say to you, unless you eat the flesh of the Son of Man and drink His blood, you have no life in you. Whoever eats My flesh and drinks My blood has eternal life, and I will raise him up at the last day. For My flesh is food indeed, and My blood is drink indeed. He who eats My flesh and drinks My blood abides in Me, and I in him. As the living Father sent Me, and I live because of the Father, so he who feeds on Me will live because of Me. This is the bread which came down from heaven—not as your fathers ate the manna, and are dead. He who eats this bread will live forever.'"

Polycarp sat back. "The religious leaders must have been speechless."

"We all were. It was a complicated treatise, and I, for one, did not understand it. Later He told us He had, of course, been speaking symbolically. His point was that just as food and drink are necessary to sustain life, people could live spiritually only by His offering His body and His blood as a sacrifice for their sins. We did not know that this giving meant His literal death, though that eventually became clear. It would take days of conversation with the Master to gain some understanding. Some among us, in fact the broader group of disciples, grew so frustrated that they gave up trying to decipher His meaning and left us."

"That was when the winnowing began?"

"Oh, He still had those of us closest to Him, the twelve. But, yes, the rest left Him at that point."

"Will you be explaining Him here, master, making it easier for those who hear or read this to understand?"

John shook his head. "Christ Himself made it clear to us. I sense I need to let His Holy Spirit do the same for readers and hearers. People often responded to

Him by declaring, 'This is a hard saying; who can understand it?'

"When Jesus knew in Himself that His disciples complained about this, He said to us, 'Does this offend you? What then if you should see the Son of Man ascend where He was before? It is the Spirit who gives life; the flesh profits nothing. The words that I speak to you are spirit, and they are life. But there are some of you who do not believe.' "

"What did He mean by that, teacher?"

"Oh, Jesus knew from the beginning who did not believe and who would betray Him. And He said, 'Therefore I have said to you that no one can come to Me unless it has been granted to him by My Father.' That was when many of His disciples went back and walked with Him no more. Then Jesus said to us twelve, 'Do you also want to go away?'

"Simon Peter spoke for all of us when he said, 'Lord, to whom shall we go? You have the words of eternal life. Also we have come to believe and know that You are the Christ, the Son of the living God.' "

FIFTEEN

By the middle of that Friday afternoon, John had become aware of the workers in the household making preparations for Shabbat. There had been much controversy among believers over whether Jewish Christians should still observe Jewish rites.

John had come down on the side of freedom, that they were certainly free to, but not bound to. He himself still felt compelled to pray three times a day, as in the tradition under which he had been raised, but he also frequently prayed much more often.

Ignatius came by, speculating on whether the crowd this evening, during the Sabbath, would be larger or smaller. The three were divided, Ignatius predicting fewer, Polycarp more, and John opining that there would be little difference from the night before.

"Of one thing I am certain, however," he said. "Cerinthus will not be here."

"Of course not," Ignatius said. "His type of Gnostic remains imprisoned by the laws and will surely observe Shabbat. By the way, teacher, if ever there was an evening when you should try to join us, it is tonight. Many have asked after you, and I promise not to make you read or speak or even pray."

"Perhaps."

The bishop had read the previous day's output of John's account and continued to rave about the far-reaching potential of it. "My favorite part," he said, "is where you recount the people asking Jesus for this eternal, life-giving bread—clearly assuming He is talking about the bread that never runs out, as they had eaten the day before. But He responds, '*I* am the bread of life.' That is beautiful! He was talking about Himself, and they had not understood it, so He simply tells them."

As the sun set, the Sabbath was an hour old and the house was quiet until the crowd started to arrive for

Ignatius's teaching session. John felt little better than when he had risen, but he forced himself to make his way to the chapel. Not having to mount or descend stairs was a great help, but as soon as he took his place, he regretted having come.

People crowded around to greet him, to touch him, to smile at him, to study him. John felt he had become a spectacle, yet he had no choice other than to be cordial. Once Ignatius got into his teaching, John leaned close to Polycarp and whispered, "You were correct. This has to be the biggest crowd."

The young man nodded. "Do you need anything, rabbi?"

"I need you to take me out of here."

Without hesitation, Polycarp helped him up and escorted him back to his new room. John could tell the young man wanted to ask if he was all right, but apparently he had been chastised enough about this. "I'm fine," John told him. "Just tired. And I didn't want to have to fight the crowd later. You may go back, if you wish."

"I would like to," Polycarp said. "But I am at your service, should you care to work more. I do not recommend it and, as you know, wish you would get your rest. But you have convinced me the time is short."

"No, please. Return. Then you and Ignatius come back and report how the evening goes."

"Only if you are still awake."

NOT ONLY was John awake later, but he was also ready

to take Polycarp up on his suggestion that they keep working. It wasn't that he felt better. In fact, John felt worse. That was the point. He didn't want to worry unnecessarily, but he was becoming convinced of his own mortality. And the timing must have been all right with God, because He was not answering John's pleas for relief and healing. Perhaps, he decided, he should stop banging on heaven's door. Clearly the work was more important than his own life, and John had long ago learned not to question the mind of God. There had to be some purpose in his own demise, and much as he longed to stay at the task, he would not fight his fate. John would, however, work for as long as he had breath.

What the men reported from the meeting settled in John's mind that he would work that evening until he fell asleep.

"There are often faces we don't recognize in these meetings," Ignatius said. "And we are always on the lookout for people who would intend evil upon us. But tonight we saw some who might have been Gnostics."

"But would not they be observing the Sabbath?"

"No one said they were devout or consistent. Perhaps Cerinthus is able to be personally observant by sending them in his stead."

"Keep an eye on them, should they return," John said. "And get your rest. Polycarp and I shall continue awhile."

"I would love to sit in," Ignatius said.

"Suit yourself. I am jumping ahead now about half a

year, when Jesus walked in Galilee. He no longer wanted to walk in Judea, because the Jews sought to kill Him. It always touched me deeply that while He spent a few days here and there with great multitudes, He spent days and weeks and months at a time with us, teaching us, preparing us for our duties when He would no longer be with us. We did not comprehend that, of course, not wanting to believe He would not be with us for years to come.

"But it was during this period, when He was continuing to preach and teach and heal, that the discomfort with Him on the part of the religious leaders grew into true hatred. You see, once Jesus had taught, He also healed, but He did not just heal the worst cases. He did not heal a representative portion of each crowd. He healed them all.

"The Jews' Feast of Tabernacles was at hand. Jesus' brothers therefore said to Him, 'Depart from here and go into Judea, that Your disciples also may see the works that You are doing. For no one does anything in secret while he himself seeks to be known openly. If You do these things, show Yourself to the world.' You know, at this time even His brothers did not believe in Him. They did not become His followers until after the resurrection. His brother James became head of the church at Jerusalem, and his brother Jude wrote a treatise against apostates that it would serve us well to study as we face the Gnostics.

"Jesus said again that His time had not yet come and so He would remain in Galilee and not go to Judea. He added that the world hated Him 'because I testify of it that its works are evil.'

"But once His brothers had left, He also went up to the feast, not openly, but in secret. The Jews looked for Him there, asking everyone, 'Where is He?' And there was much talk among the people concerning Him. Some said, 'He is good'; others said, 'No, on the contrary, He deceives the people.' However, no one spoke openly of Him for fear of the Jews.

"Now about the middle of the feast Jesus went up into the temple and taught. And the Jews marveled, saying, 'How does this Man know letters, having never studied?'

"Jesus said, 'My doctrine is not Mine, but His who sent Me. If anyone wills to do His will, he shall know concerning the doctrine, whether it is from God or whether I speak on My own authority. He who speaks from himself seeks his own glory; but He who seeks the glory of the One who sent Him is true, and no unrighteousness is in Him. Did not Moses give you the law, yet none of you keeps the law? Why do you seek to kill Me?'

"They said, 'You have a demon. Who is seeking to kill You?'

"Well, Polycarp, it was a most unusual day. Jesus boldly challenged them. He said, 'I did one work, and you all marvel. . . . Are you angry with Me because I made a man completely well on the Sabbath? Do not judge according to appearance, but judge with right-eous judgment.'

"Some from Jerusalem said, 'Is this not He whom they seek to kill? But look! He speaks boldly, and they say nothing to Him. Do the rulers know indeed that this is truly the Christ? However, we know where this Man is from; but when the Christ comes, no one knows where He is from.'

"Suddenly Jesus cried out with a loud voice in the temple, saying, 'You both know Me, and you know where I am from; and I have not come of Myself, but He who sent Me is true, whom you do not know. But I know Him, for I am from Him, and He sent Me.'

"Why, Polycarp, I was afraid they would overtake Him. They rushed forward to seize Him, but again no one was able to lay a hand on Him. And why?"

Polycarp looked up. "Because His hour had not yet come?"

John nodded. "Many witnessed this and believed in Him, and said, 'When the Christ comes, will He do more signs than these which this Man has done?' The Pharisees heard the crowd discussing Him, and they and the chief priests sent officers to take Him.

"Jesus told them, 'I shall be with you a little while longer, and then I go to Him who sent Me. You will seek Me and not find Me, and where I am you cannot come.'

"When I reflected on this I could hardly believe I had missed it and wondered what else I could have concluded from such a prophecy. The Jews said among themselves, 'Where does He intend to go that we shall not find Him? Does He intend to go to the

Dispersion among the Greeks and teach the Greeks? What is this thing that He said, "You will seek Me and not find Me, and where I am you cannot come"?'

"On the last day, that great day of the feast, Jesus stood and cried out, saying, 'If anyone thirsts, let him come to Me and drink. He who believes in Me, as the Scripture has said, out of his heart will flow rivers of living water.' I know now, of course, that He was referring to the Holy Spirit, whom those believing in Him would receive; but the Spirit had not yet been given, because Jesus had not yet been glorified.

"Therefore many from the crowd said, 'Truly this is the Prophet.'

"Others said, 'This is the Christ.'

"But some said, 'Will the Christ come out of Galilee? Has not the Scripture said that the Christ comes from the seed of David and from the town of Bethlehem, where David was?' So there was a division among the people because of Him. Now some of them wanted to take Him, but no one laid hands on Him.

"As you can imagine, Polycarp, the chief priests and Pharisees lost patience with the officers and demanded, 'Why have you not brought Him?'

"The officers said, 'No man ever spoke like this Man!'

"The Pharisees said, 'Are you also deceived?' and said, in essence, that none of the rulers or the Pharisees believed in Him. 'But this crowd that does not know the law,' they said, 'is accursed.'

"As the Pharisees stood heatedly discussing this, I recognized the snow-white beard and regal bearing of the one who had come to Jesus by night. Nicodemus asked his colleagues, 'Does our law judge a man before it hears him and knows what he is doing?'

"The rest grew infuriated with Nicodemus and said, 'Are you also from Galilee? Search and look, for no prophet has arisen out of Galilee.'"

In his mind, John was still talking, images swirling, memories cascading. And yet now this felt like a dream. He was vaguely aware that he was stretched out fully on his back, and he wondered if Polycarp remained able to hear and understand him.

John's breathing was labored, his chest was tight, and he tried to roll up onto his side so the young man would have no trouble deciphering his words. And yet he felt confused. Was he dreaming, or was he still working? He forced open an eye and squinted against even the low light of the two lamps illuminating Polycarp's writing area.

"You wanted to continue until you slept, sir," the young man said. "I believe that time has come."

"No. No. I am all right. We can continue."

Yet several minutes later John roused and realized he had said nothing more. The room was dark. Polycarp was gone. And John's blanket had been pulled up to just under his chin. Though he felt miserable, the old man reached for the elusive comfort of sleep, grateful for friends.

SIXTEEN

By Saturday morning John was seriously ill. And with much of the house staff still observing the Sabbath, only Ignatius and Polycarp and a few others were able to attend him. Though he still kept from them the truth about the pain in his chest, John could not deny that he had lost his appetite, his bones and muscles ached, and he was short of breath. His voice was but a whisper, and he had trouble keeping his eyes open.

Against John's wishes, Ignatius agreed with Polycarp and sent for a member of the church who was a physician. The doctor prescribed bed rest and warm food whenever John could tolerate it. John accepted fresh-baked bread and wine, yet ate and drank only a little.

Ignatius took charge and told everyone to leave John, except a young boy who would sit outside his door and call for Ignatius or Polycarp should an emergency arise. John shook his head, but no one paid any attention, and soon the room was empty and quiet. He tried to sleep but could not get comfortable, worrying that each breath would be his last. Suddenly he was desperate. There was so much more to do, so much more to tell. What if the interlopers in the previous evening were, in fact, sent by Cerinthus? Might they advance their cause by harming the true church, exposing it to authorities? John's gospel account could be the sole opponent of the Gnostics in Ephesus. The work must continue.

"Son?" John rasped. "Lad?"

The boy crept in, looking fearful. "Did you call, rabbi? Are you well?"

"Come closer, boy. I am all right. I have need of Ignatius, if you would be so kind."

"Shall I tell him it is urgent?"

"Just tell him to come. Thank you."

Ignatius arrived almost instantly, rushing to John's bed and kneeling to hear him.

"Dismiss the boy, please."

"What? Was there a problem?"

"No. He was very attentive, but I do not have further need of him. Now do not quarrel with me, Ignatius. I remain your elder and expect you to do what I ask."

"Of course," Ignatius said, thanking the boy and pressing a coin into his hand before waving him off. "And now what? You would like to attend a sporting event? Run a marathon?"

John was not amused. "Closer," he managed. And when Ignatius bent farther, John clutched at his garment and held as tight as he could. "I would have merely sent for Polycarp, because I am determined to get back to work."

"Oh, but you must not now, teacher. You—"

John tugged harder. "Ignatius, I sent for you because I knew Polycarp would never do what I'm asking without consulting you anyway. I am telling you that I am going to lie here, and even if delirium overtakes me, I am going to continue with my account. You tell Polycarp this and inform him that if he shirks his duty, he will miss some of the heart of the story. I will have neither the time nor the strength to repeat myself."

Ignatius whined, "Master, I do not know what to do. I am only thinking of you. . . ."

"Stop!" John said, coughing. "You will make me only worse if you do not accede to my wishes. Now, remember who is the mentor and who is the student, and do as I say! I absolve you from all responsibility, should this exercise finish me. I fear I am soon finished anyway."

Ignatius gently removed John's hand from his garment. "You will not be dissuaded, I see."

"I will not."

"You are a stubborn man, you know."

"The Lord Himself called me a Son of Thunder when I was but half your age. What do you expect?"

"I expect I'll do as you ask."

JOHN WAS NEARLY ASLEEP when Polycarp arrived. His eyes were shut and he was not moving, and he could tell the young man was arranging his materials as quietly as possible, so as not to interrupt the old man's nap. John heard the squeak of the chair and Polycarp's sigh as he settled. Ignatius whispered, "I am going into the city. If he does not rouse in a few moments, leave him to sleep."

164

"I am awake," John said, still not moving and eyes shut. "I am about to begin."

"Well, there you are," Ignatius said, and he took his leave.

Polycarp settled in, and John began again.

"We soon followed Jesus to the Mount of Olives. Early the next morning He came again to the temple, and a huge crowd gathered. He sat and taught them. Right in the middle of all that, the scribes and Pharisees brought to Him a woman. They said, 'Teacher, this woman was caught in adultery, in the very act. Now Moses, in the law, commanded us that such should be stoned. But what do You say?'

"They were testing Him, of course, trying to find something over which they could accuse Him. But Jesus stooped and wrote on the ground with His finger, as though He did not hear."

"What did He write?" Polycarp said.

"Why, He was not really writing anything. I believe He was simply pretending to be preoccupied, as if He did not care what they were saying. If I were to guess, I would say He was forcing them to say their piece again, so it might sound as foolish to them as it did to Him."

"When they continued pressing Him, He rose and said, 'He who is without sin among you, let him throw a stone at her first.'

"Profound," Polycarp said.

"More than you know, son. Think it through. Do you realize what He was saying?"

"I think so."

"I think not, not if you hear only what is on the surface. Do you not realize that He was referring to Himself yet again?"

"To Himself?"

"Yes! You see, there *was* One among them who was without sin, wasn't there?"

Polycarp was silent a moment. Then, "You are correct, rabbi. It *is* more profound than I knew. He was giving Himself permission to be her judge and executioner, yet choosing not to act. But I do not suppose the scribes and Pharisees understood this any more than I did."

"No, but they got His larger point. When He stooped again and wrote on the ground it was obvious those who heard Him were convicted by their consciences, and out they went one by one, beginning with the oldest, even to the last. And Jesus was left alone with the synagogue crowd, the woman before Him. He said, 'Woman, where are those accusers of yours? Has no one condemned you?'

"She said, 'No one, Lord.'

"And Jesus said, 'Neither do I condemn you; go and sin no more.'

"Then Jesus began teaching again, saying, 'I am the light of the world. He who follows Me shall not walk in darkness, but have the light of life.' "

"The light of life," Polycarp said. "So He is the bread, the water, and the light."

"And much more, but all in good time. Other Pharisees said, 'You bear witness of Yourself; Your witness is not true.'

"Jesus said, 'Even if I bear witness of Myself, My witness is true, for I know where I came from and where I am going; but you do not know where I come from and where I am going. You judge according to the flesh; I judge no one. And yet if I do judge, My judgment is true; for I am not alone, but I am with the Father who sent Me. It is also written in your law that the testimony of two men is true. I am One who bears witness of Myself, and the Father who sent Me bears witness of Me.'

"One of them said, 'Where is Your Father?'

"Jesus said, 'You know neither Me nor My Father. If you had known Me, you would have known My Father also.'"

"So bold," Polycarp said. "He must have had an aura of authority to get away with talking to them in such a manner."

"Oh, Polycarp, you should have seen their faces. Flushed, snarling. And he was in *their* territory. But you know what is coming."

Polycarp nodded.

"No one laid hands on Him . . . ," John said.

And Polycarp said, ". . . for His hour had not yet come."

"But Jesus pushed further. He said, 'I am going away, and you will seek Me, and you will die in your sin. Where I go you cannot come.'

"So the Jews wondered aloud what He meant. 'Will

He kill Himself?' they said.

"But He told them, 'You are from beneath; I am from above. You are of this world; I am not of this world. Therefore I said to you that you will die in your sins; for if you do not believe that I am He, you will die in your sins.'

"They stared at Him, obviously incredulous. And one said, 'Who are You?'

"And Jesus said, 'Just what I have been saying to you from the beginning. I have many things to say and to judge concerning you, but He who sent Me is true; and I speak to the world those things which I heard from Him.'

"Did they understand that He was speaking to them of His Father?"

"No. That much is clear. Jesus said, 'When you lift up the Son of Man, then you will know that I am He, and that I do nothing of Myself; but as My Father taught Me, I speak these things.'"

"Again He talks of being lifted up," Polycarp said. "Did you know what He meant?"

"None of us did. Not until later, of course. Then we realized He had been quite plain. Those who had ears could have heard. And then He spoke again about Who He was, Who had sent Him, and what His mission was. He said, 'And He who sent Me is with Me. The Father has not left Me alone, for I always do those things that please Him.' As He spoke these words, many believed in Him.

"Then Jesus said to those Jews who believed Him,

'If you abide in My word, you are My disciples indeed. And you shall know the truth, and the truth shall make you free.'

"Then He turns His attention back to His accusers, for they have overheard this and still try to counter, saying, 'We are Abraham's descendants, and have never been in bondage to anyone. How can You say, "You will be made free"?'

"Jesus said, 'Most assuredly, I say to you, whoever commits sin is a slave of sin. And a slave does not abide in the house forever, but a son abides forever. Therefore if the Son makes you free, you shall be free indeed.

" 'I know that you are Abraham's descendants, but you seek to kill Me, because My word has no place in you. I speak what I have seen with My Father, and you do what you have seen with your father.'

"They said, 'Abraham is our father.'

"Jesus said, 'If you were Abraham's children, you would do the works of Abraham. But now you seek to kill Me, a Man who has told you the truth which I heard from God. Abraham did not do this. You do the deeds of your father.' "

"Who is He saying is their father, if not Abraham?"

"He makes that clear soon. They said, 'We were not born of fornication; we have one Father—God.'

"Jesus said, 'If God were your Father, you would love Me, for I proceeded forth and came from God; nor have I come of Myself, but He sent Me. Why do you not understand My speech? Because you are not able to listen to My word. You are of your father the devil, and the desires of your father you want to do. He was a murderer from the beginning, and does not stand in the truth, because there is no truth in him. When he speaks a lie, he speaks from his own resources, for he is a liar and the father of it. But because I tell the truth, you do not believe Me. Which of you convicts Me of sin? And if I tell the truth, why do you not believe Me? He who is of God hears God's words; therefore you do not hear, because you are not of God.'

"The Jews said, 'Do we not say rightly that You are a Samaritan and have a demon?'

"Jesus said, 'I do not have a demon; but I honor My Father, and you dishonor Me. And I do not seek My own glory; there is One who seeks and judges. Most assuredly, I say to you, if anyone keeps My word he shall never see death.'

"Polycarp, the Jews were furious. They said, 'Now we know that You have a demon! Abraham is dead, and the prophets; and You say, "If anyone keeps My word he shall never taste death." Are You greater than our father Abraham, who is dead? And the prophets are dead. Who do You make Yourself out to be?'

"Jesus answered, 'If I honor Myself, My honor is nothing. It is My Father who honors Me, of whom you say that He is your God. Yet you have not known Him, but I know Him. And if I say, "I do not know Him," I shall be a liar like you; but I do know Him and keep His word. Your father Abraham rejoiced to see My day, and he saw it and was glad.'

"The Jews said, 'You are not yet fifty years old, and have You seen Abraham?'

"Jesus said, 'Most assuredly, I say to you, before Abraham was, I AM.'"

"They must have wanted to kill him!" Polycarp said.

"Oh, they did indeed! They picked up stones to throw at Him, but Jesus hid Himself and went out through the midst of them, and so passed by."

"He went through the midst of them? He hid in plain sight?"

"Polycarp, I was there, and I could not see Him. It was as if He had vanished into thin air."

"Another miracle."

"Of course, but not a sign. This I believe He did merely because His time had not yet come and He could not allow Himself to be taken by them. His next sign, the sixth, would come next."

John still had neither moved nor opened his eyes, but he heard Polycarp set down his quill. "Oh," John said, "we are not stopping. This next is most dramatic."

"Of that I have no doubt, rabbi, but is this not a natural point to rest?"

"How could I rest more than to lie here as dead? If you must rest, rest, but I will remain here working. You would not want to miss any of this, would you?"

Polycarp sighed. "No, sir."

"That's a good lad."

"I am nothing if not a good lad," Polycarp said, and

John opened an eye to see him dip the quill again.

"Oh, but you are so much more. Now let me proceed."

SEVENTEEN

Help me sit up, would you, friend?"

Polycarp moved to the bed. "You're not comfortable?"

"I just want to be as clearheaded as possible now, because we are coming to the sixth sign of Jesus' divinity. Of course, it's more important that I remain open to what I believe the Spirit is saying through me, but the last thing I want is to be an impediment. If Jesus were not divine, how could He do these things that He does, as Nicodemus said, 'unless God is with Him'? While I fear Ignatius is wasting his time trying to engage Cerinthus, I also wish the heretic were here to hear this."

"Be careful what you wish for, teacher. Ignatius would like nothing more than to deliver the man to you."

John waved off his young friend. "Ach! It is too late for me. My record here will have to do the work, along with you two young men."

"We're not both young, master. Ignatius is older than my father!"

"Remember whom you're addressing, lad. You're both children to one of my vintage. Now, let us carry on, keeping men like Cerinthus at the forefront of our minds. We will pick up on that Sabbath where Jesus disappeared from the crowd that meant him ill. He reappeared on a crowded street.

"Now as Jesus passed by, He saw a man who was blind from birth. And we disciples asked Him, saying, 'Rabbi, who sinned, this man or his parents, that he was born blind?'

"Jesus said, 'Neither this man nor his parents sinned, but that the works of God should be revealed in him. I must work the works of Him who sent Me while it is day; the night is coming when no one can work. As long as I am in the world, I am the light of the world.'

"He then knelt and spat on the ground and made clay with the saliva; and He anointed the eyes of the blind man with the clay. And He said to him, 'Go, wash in the pool of Siloam.' Now this pool, Polycarp, was a magnificent basin stretching some hundred and fifty feet, and—"

"Begging your pardon, teacher, but I care less about the pool than what happened to the man blind from birth."

John smiled weakly. "Well, you are right, of course. The man went and washed, and when he came back, he was seeing. And certainly it was not the pool that held the healing power. It was the Lord Himself and the man's faith."

"Many must have seen him begging there for years. What did they think?"

"They said, 'Is not this he who sat and begged?' Some said, 'This is he.' Others said, 'He is like him.'

"But the man himself said, 'I am he.'

"People said, 'How were your eyes opened?'

"He said, 'A Man called Jesus made clay and anointed my eyes and said to me, "Go to the pool of Siloam and wash." So I went and washed, and I received sight.'

"So the people said, 'Where is He?'

"He said, 'I do not know.'

"Some brought him to the Pharisees, who also asked him how he had received his sight. When he told them, they said, 'This Man is not from God, because He does not keep the Sabbath.'

"But others among them said, 'How can a man who is a sinner do such signs?' So there was division among them. They asked the formerly blind man what he had to say about Jesus after what He had done.

"He said, 'He is a prophet.'

"But, Polycarp, most of the Pharisees did not believe the man had been blind and received his sight. They sent for his parents and said, 'Is this your son, who you say was born blind? How then does he now see?'

"You can imagine how his parents responded. They were awestruck and yet also terrified at having been dragged before the religious leaders. They said, 'We know that this is our son, and that he was born blind; but by what means he now sees we do not know, or who opened his eyes we do not know. He is of age;

ask him. He will speak for himself.'

"I believe his parents said these things because the Jews had agreed already that anyone who confessed that Jesus was Christ would be put out of the synagogue. The Jewish leaders again called the man who had been blind, and told him they knew Jesus was a sinner. I have never forgotten his response.

"He said, 'Whether He is a sinner or not I do not know. One thing I know: that though I was blind, now I see.'

"They said, 'What did He do to you? How did He open your eyes?'

"He said, 'I told you already, and you did not listen. Why do you want to hear it again? Do you also want to become His disciples?'

Polycarp laughed aloud. "I like this man! How discerning he was for one seeing for the first time."

"Yes, and the authorities did not appreciate that. They tried to bully him, saying, 'You are His disciple, but we are Moses' disciples. We know that God spoke to Moses; as for this fellow, we do not know where He is from.'

"The newly seeing man was brilliant. He said, 'Why, this is a marvelous thing, that you do not know where He is from; yet He has opened my eyes! Now we know that God does not hear sinners; but if anyone is a worshiper of God and does His will, He hears him. Since the world began it has been unheard of that anyone opened the eyes of one who was born blind. If this Man were not from God, He could do nothing.'

"Imagine how the Pharisees took that. One said, 'You were completely born in sins, and are you teaching us?' And they cast him out of the synagogue.

"When Jesus heard about that, He found the man again and said, 'Do you believe in the Son of God?'

"The man said, 'Who is He, Lord, that I may believe in Him?'

"And Jesus said, 'You have both seen Him and it is He who is talking with you.'

"The man fell to his knees, worshiping Jesus and saying, 'Lord, I believe!'

"So much for those who say Jesus made no claim to His own deity. Jesus told the man, 'For judgment I have come into this world, that those who do not see may see, and that those who see may be made blind.'

"Some of the Pharisees who heard these words said to Him, 'Are we blind also?'

"Jesus said, 'If you were blind, you would have no sin; but now you say, "We see." Therefore your sin remains.' "

"What was He saying, rabbi?" Polycarp said, as he helped John lie back down.

"That they remained in their sins because though they were not physically blind, yet they *chose* not to see. Now, Polycarp, you know what comes next."

"In the text?"

"No."

"Ah, it is time for me once again to play the student. Let me review a moment." He was poring over the document when Ignatius arrived.

John had briefly closed his eyes, but now he peeked at the big man. "You appear to have news."

"Indeed," the bishop said. "Cerinthus, and not only he but his retinue, have agreed to join us tomorrow for the Lord's Day."

John fell silent.

"You do not approve, master? What can be the harm in their sitting under sound doctrine and teaching, being exposed to true faith?"

John shook his head and rolled onto his side with his back to the men. "I must ponder this. Are you prepared to withdraw the invitation if I so decide?"

"Of course, master, I would defer to your wishes. But I pray you would fairly hear me out, as I earnestly and respectfully disagree on this. I too abhor our members being swayed by this man in the open air of the marketplace, but here he would be in our camp, as it were, and we would have sway over him."

"I need time to think and pray about it."

"Jesus calls Himself the light of the world," Polycarp announced. "Is that it, teacher? Is that His sixth sign, revealed in giving sight to the blind?"

John merely nodded, knowing Polycarp undoubtedly was looking for, and deserved, higher praise for having discerned this. But Ignatius had troubled John beyond his ability to maintain his composure. John had planned to move directly into the telling of what he considered Jesus' most dramatic miracle and the resounding proof of His deity, but this potential confrontation with Cerinthus himself reminded the aged disciple of something that should perhaps come first.

"Ignatius," he whispered, his back still turned, "are you still here?"

"At your service."

"Are you free to stay?"

"It would be my privilege."

"Then sit and listen, for this pertains, even if you may not at first see the connection. I begin with the words of Jesus as He addresses yet more multitudes."

And as John began to dictate again, knowing he was making Polycarp strain to hear him, as John had still not moved, he was lulled into a steady cadence by the soft scratching of the quill tip on the papyrus.

"Jesus said, 'Most assuredly, I say to you, he who does not enter the sheepfold by the door, but climbs up some other way, the same is a thief and a robber. But he who enters by the door is the shepherd of the sheep. To him the doorkeeper opens, and the sheep hear his voice; and he calls his own sheep by name and leads them out. And when he brings out his own sheep, he goes before them; and the sheep follow him, for they know his voice. Yet they will by no means follow a stranger, but will flee from him, for they do not know the voice of strangers.'

"Jesus could tell, as we could, that His listeners did not understand. He said, 'I am the door of the sheep. All who ever came before Me are thieves and robbers, but the sheep did not hear them. I am the door. If anyone enters by Me, he will be saved, and will go in and out and find pasture. The thief does not come except to steal, and to kill, and to destroy. I have come that they may have life, and that they may have it more abundantly.

" 'I am the good shepherd. The good shepherd gives His life for the sheep. But a hireling, he who is not the shepherd, one who does not own the sheep, sees the wolf coming and leaves the sheep and flees; and the wolf catches the sheep and scatters them. The hireling flees because he is a hireling and does not care about the sheep. I am the good shepherd; and I know My sheep, and am known by My own. As the Father knows Me, even so I know the Father; and I lay down My life for the sheep. And other sheep I have which are not of this fold; them also I must bring, and they will hear My voice; and there will be one flock and one shepherd.

" 'Therefore My Father loves Me, because I lay down My life that I may take it again. No one takes it from Me, but I lay it down of Myself. I have power to lay it down, and I have power to take it again. This command I have received from My Father.'

"There was a division again among the Jews. Many of them said, 'He has a demon and is mad. Why do you listen to Him?'

"Others said, 'These are not the words of one who has a demon. Can a demon open the eyes of the blind?'

"Now it was the Feast of Dedication in Jerusalem, and it was winter. And Jesus walked in the temple, in Solomon's porch. Then the Jews surrounded Him and said to Him, 'How long do You keep us in doubt? If You are the Christ, tell us plainly.'

"Jesus said, 'I told you, and you do not believe. The works that I do in My Father's name, they bear witness of Me. But you do not believe, because you are not of My sheep, as I said to you. My sheep hear My voice, and I know them, and they follow Me. And I give them eternal life, and they shall never perish; neither shall anyone snatch them out of My hand. My Father, who has given them to Me, is greater than all; and no one is able to snatch them out of My Father's hand. I and My Father are one.'

"When the Jews took up stones again to stone Him, Jesus said, 'Many good works I have shown you from My Father. For which of those works do you stone Me?'

"The Jews said, 'For a good work we do not stone You, but for blasphemy, and because You, being a Man, make Yourself God.' Don't you find it interesting, gentlemen, that Jesus was nearly stoned for making Himself God, and yet people still say He never claimed deity?

"Jesus said, 'Is it not written in your law, "I said, 'You are gods' "? If He called them gods, to whom the word of God came (and the Scripture cannot be broken), do you say of Him whom the Father sanctified and sent into the world, "You are blaspheming," because I said, "I am the Son of God"? If I do not do the works of My Father, do not believe Me; but if I do, though you do not believe Me, believe the works, that you may know and believe that the Father is in Me, and I in Him.' Therefore they sought again to seize Him, but He escaped out of their hand."

"By now they must have been convinced he was invincible," Polycarp said.

"I don't know what they thought," John said, "but we disciples were certainly convinced. It was becoming quite clear that until His time came, no one could touch Him. He went away again beyond the Jordan to the place where John was baptizing at first, and there He stayed.

"There, many came to Him and said, 'John performed no sign, but all the things that John spoke about this Man were true.' And many believed in Him there."

John fell silent again and waited for some indication from Polycarp that he comprehended Jesus' message, or from Ignatius that he understood why he was to listen to this. The two must have thought him asleep, John decided, so he rolled over to face them. "Well?"

"Profound again," Polycarp said. "To have sat under the teaching of such a Man . . ."

"For three years," John said. "And pardon me, but to call the Christ profound strikes me as both obvious and understated."

"I have no better word for it, rabbi."

"I found this fascinating, of course," Ignatius said. "But I confess I am deliberating over why you felt this was specific to me just now. Tell me."

"It is encouraging to know you remain teachable,

despite your station. This discourse on Jesus being the Good Shepherd can easily be applied to our roles as bishops and pastors. We are the gatekeepers, the guardians of our flocks. Need I say more?"

Ignatius stood and paced. "You wish me to use this analogy with Cerinthus."

"Precisely."

"That I am to protect the flock against one such as he."

"No. *I* am to protect this flock, even against *your* best intentions."

"I stand corrected, master."

"Understand, bishop, that should you disinvite him, the man will label us close-minded and exclusive, and he will, no doubt, assure you that we are most welcome at their gatherings. His intention will be to make you seem small and petty."

"And while I am your hireling, I must not run from the wolf and leave the sheep unprotected."

"Precisely."

EIGHTEEN

All indications were that Ignatius's Saturday-evening teaching service would be overrun with people. Despite that the Sabbath had ended and that the regular weekly worship service was scheduled for the next evening, the Lord's Day, the house vibrated with anticipation.

John sensed Polycarp's discomfort.

"What is it, son? You need to be of service to Ignatius this evening?"

"Yes, but you are my chief concern. I will make arrangements if you would like to continue, as tomorrow will probably be wholly lost to us. I cannot imagine the throng we should expect then."

"Are you suggesting we break from now until Monday morning?"

"I am at your service, rabbi. A week from then, Ignatius is off."

John could not bring himself to tell Polycarp his true fear: that he would not last until Ignatius departed. "In the interest of time," he said, "I need you. And while I prefer treating the Lord's Day as our Sabbath, we must redeem that time too, do you not agree?"

"I concur that time is a factor."

"Then let us work through the evening or until my strength gives out. We will have Ignatius's report to look forward to."

"I more look forward to the seventh sign."

"And well you should. Let me begin.

"You recall the Master's dear friend, Lazarus of Bethany. He had two sisters, Mary and Martha. It was Mary who anointed the Lord with fragrant oil and wiped His feet with her hair. I'll get to that story in due time. Others have written of it, so it is well known already throughout the church.

"The sisters sent word to Jesus, saying, 'Lord, behold, he whom You love is sick.' Because of where we were, Polycarp, this message would have taken at least a whole day to reach Him. Lazarus was probably already dead.

"When Jesus heard the news, He had an interesting response. He said, 'This sickness is not unto death, but for the glory of God, that the Son of God may be glorified through it.'

"My brother James and I and a few of the others were confused. We knew and admired Mary and Martha. Besides being friends of Jesus, they were believers, very devout and serious. We were certain they would not go to the trouble to send word to Jesus about their brother's illness, unless it was very serious and likely to be 'unto death.'

"Jesus loved the sisters and Lazarus, but even after receiving the message, He stayed two more days where He was. I was frankly glad, because if He went back, He would be going again where His life was in danger. But finally He said to us, 'Let us go to Judea again.'

"I said, 'Rabbi, lately the Jews sought to stone You, and are You going there again?'

"Jesus said, 'Are there not twelve hours in the day? If anyone walks in the day, he does not stumble, because he sees the light of this world. But if one walks in the night, he stumbles, because the light is not in him.'"

"I'm confused, teacher," Polycarp said.

"As I was. Only later did I realize what He was saying in His unique way. I believe He considered His time on earth the daylight, when He could safely do the work His Father had assigned Him. But the 'night' was coming, when He would be betrayed and sentenced to death. So He wanted to redeem the time while there was still the light of day. Finally He said, 'Our friend Lazarus sleeps, but I go that I may wake him up.'

"My brother James said, 'Lord, if he sleeps he will get well.'

"But Jesus shook His head. 'Lazarus is dead,' He said. 'And I am glad for your sakes that I was not there, because now you may believe. Nevertheless let us go to him.'

"Then Thomas said to us fellow disciples, 'Let us also go, that we may die with Him.' He was certain the trip into the lair of the religious leaders was suicide for all of us, and while he was being rueful, he was also loyal. He did not want Jesus to face this peril alone."

"This," Polycarp said, "from the one who would question Jesus' resurrection until he saw His scars?"

"The same. Well, when we approached Bethany, about two miles from Jerusalem, we heard that Lazarus had already been in the tomb four days. Many of the Jews had joined the other women around Martha and Mary to comfort them concerning their brother.

"Martha heard Jesus was coming and actually met us on the road. She was very distressed and said, 'Lord, if You had been here, my brother would not have died. But even now I know that whatever You ask of God, God will give You.'

"Polycarp, by now I should not have been surprised at anything the Master said or did. But I shuddered when He said simply, 'Your brother will rise again.'

"Martha said what I was thinking. 'I know that he will rise again in the resurrection at the last day.'

"But Jesus said, 'I am the resurrection and the life. He who believes in Me, though he may die, he shall live. And whoever lives and believes in Me shall never die. Do you believe this?'

"Now hear me, Polycarp, I have gently chastised you and Ignatius for describing the Lord as profound, as that seems such an understatement. Yet, like you, I must say that nothing as profound as this has ever been uttered, before or since. And His question to her is the question of the ages, for therein lies eternal life: 'Do you believe this?'

"She said, 'Yes, Lord, I believe that You are the Christ, the Son of God, who is to come into the world.'

"Then she ran and found Mary and sent her to Jesus. We still had not reached Bethany. Mary came, followed by several Jewish women mourners, and fell at Jesus' feet, saying the same thing Martha had said: 'Lord, if You had been here, my brother would not have died.'

"Polycarp, it was as if seeing her distress finally made Jesus realize fully what had happened, though of course He knew all along. But when He saw her and the mourners weeping, His countenance fell and

He groaned. And He said, 'Where have you laid him?'

"She said, 'Lord, come and see.'

"Jesus cried, and some of the mourners said, 'See how He loved him!' But others said, 'Could not this Man, who opened the eyes of the blind, also have kept this man from dying?'

"When we arrived at the tomb, Jesus appeared extremely troubled in His spirit, and I was close enough to hear that He was still groaning. The tomb was a cave with a stone lying against it. Jesus said, 'Take away the stone.'

"Martha said, 'Lord, by this time there is a stench, for he has been dead four days.'

"Jesus said, 'Did I not say to you that if you would believe you would see the glory of God?' They took away the stone, and Jesus lifted His eyes and said, 'Father, I thank You that You have heard Me. And I know that You always hear Me, but because of the people who are standing by I said this, that they may believe that You sent Me.' Then He cried out with a loud voice, 'Lazarus, come forth!'

"Polycarp, this was nearly sixty years ago, but I shall never forget, nor would I want to, seeing Lazarus appear in the mouth of that cave, still bound hand and foot in graveclothes and his face wrapped with a cloth. Jesus said, 'Loose him, and let him go.' "

John, shuddering, grew quiet. Polycarp whispered, "Jesus proved His power over death. The seventh sign."

John nodded. "Yes, and while He had proved this at

least twice before, both times He had raised people who had just died, so some conjectured that they had not really died. But here He raises a man who has been dead four days, wrapped in graveclothes, and lying in his tomb. Now there could be no question. Many of the Jews who had come to comfort Mary now believed in Him.

"But some went to the Pharisees and told them what had happened. Then the chief priests and the Pharisees gathered a council and said, 'What shall we do? For this Man works many signs. If we let Him alone like this, everyone will believe in Him, and the Romans will come and take away both our place and nation.'

"And one of them, Caiaphas, the high priest that year, said, 'You know nothing at all, nor do you consider that it is expedient for us that one man should die for the people, and not that the whole nation should perish.'"

"What did he mean?" Polycarp said.

"He was merely saying that it was better that one man should die than that the entire nation be slain for living counter to Rome. Yet God used this as a prophetic statement, as He had with the high priests of old. From that day forward, the religious leaders plotted to put Jesus to death. Things had been growing worse, and He was hated by many, but after this, nothing was ever again the same. We all lived in danger and in fear for our lives, but He was their main target.

"He could no longer walk openly among the Jews,

so we went from there into the country near the wilderness, to a city called Ephraim, and there remained. Passover was near, and many came from the country up to Jerusalem to purify themselves in advance of the feast. They sought Jesus and spoke among themselves as they stood in the temple, wondering aloud whether He would come. Both the chief priests and the Pharisees had announced that if anyone knew where He was, he should report it, that they might seize Him.

"Polycarp, are you weeping?"

The young man wiped his tears. "I know where this is going, of course. But to record a firsthand account simply makes me feel as if I were there."

NINETEEN

John believed he had rallied somewhat physically by dawn of the Lord's Day. The air was crisp again and John thought it would make for a more comfortable day of work, but still he had to pray continually to avoid panic. While he believed he could actually try pacing again intermittently while dictating—which allowed him to think more clearly and feel more attuned to the Spirit of God—he was more convinced than ever that his days were numbered. He wanted to finish the account, and he had more epistles—at least three—he wished to write to the churches, and for those he had further need of Polycarp.

While John and the young man worked, much noise emanated from the courtyard, where the house staff prepared for the evening service. They expected record attendance, and without John's or Polycarp's assistance, the work fell more heavily on Ignatius and many others.

John raced through more incidents from the earthly ministry of the Christ, eager to get to one more miracle. "Not a sign," he assured Polycarp. "Your examinations are over. And, of course, nothing could be greater evidence of His Godship than the resurrection. Still, there is the story of the miracle while fishing, yet we have so much more to cover first."

Pacing gingerly, John told of Mary anointing Jesus' feet with expensive perfume that permeated the air. "Lazarus was there, and Martha, but also Judas, who demanded to know why such an expensive item was wasted. He suggested selling it and giving the money to the poor, but we all know now he had no interest in the poor. Such income would have simply given him more to embezzle.

"Lazarus soon became a target for murder as well, because the religious leaders pointed to his resurrection as the impetus for many turning to belief in Jesus. Several people, including all of us disciples, urged Jesus to flee Judea, especially Jerusalem during the Passover feast. But He knew better. He was on assignment from His Father and knew what He was about. Not only did He not avoid Jerusalem, but He also went there with a purpose. He taught everywhere He went, even in the lair of His enemies. The crowds welcomed Him as a conquering king, and He spoke again of being lifted up, prophesying what manner of death He would endure. But we were still not listening."

"I'm sorry to interrupt you, master."

"By all means."

"You say Jesus taught everywhere, even in the lair of his enemies."

"Yes."

"What is worse, or shall I say, more dangerous? Teaching in the lair of the enemy, or having the enemy in your lair while you are teaching?"

John squinted at the young man. "I need not ask what you are implying. If you believe I am wrong in my exhortation to Ignatius, simply say so."

"I think you are wrong."

"Well! And does Ignatius agree?"

"It matters not, rabbi. We will, as we have always done, defer to you and your wisdom."

"Even if I am wrong."

"You seldom are, teacher."

"But a teacher is all I am," John said. "I am not the Christ. I am not divine. I am far from perfect and certainly not all-knowing."

"Far be it from me to counsel you, rabbi. But I urge you to consider our views on this."

John fell silent. Then, "I will. Prayerfully. You know my fear though, do you not?"

"Of course. That Cerinthus would not be content to sit under our teaching. He would be compelled to debate us in front of our own flock."

"If you two are to sway me on this, you must find a remedy for that possibility. Now, while we are thinking about that, let me proceed and speak of something that has not before been recorded.

"Before the Feast of the Passover, when Jesus knew that His hour had come that He should depart from this world to the Father, having loved His own who were in the world, He loved them to the end. He took us to an upper room where we enjoyed a meal with Him. And supper being ended, the devil having already put it into the heart of Judas Iscariot, Simon's son, to betray Him, Jesus, knowing that the Father had given all things into His hands, and that He had come from God and was going to God, rose from supper and laid aside His garments, took a towel and girded Himself. After that, He poured water into a basin and began to wash our feet, and to wipe them with the towel with which He was girded.

"When He came to Simon Peter, Peter said, 'Lord, are You washing my feet?'

"Jesus said, 'What I am doing you do not understand now, but you will know after this.'

"Peter said, 'You shall never wash my feet!'

"Jesus said, 'If I do not wash you, you have no part with Me.'

"Simon Peter said, 'Lord, not my feet only, but also my hands and my head!'

"Jesus said, 'He who is bathed needs only to wash his feet, but is completely clean; and you are clean, but not all of you.' For He knew who would betray Him.

"So when He had washed our feet, taken His garments, and sat again, He said, 'Do you know what I have done to you? You call Me Teacher and Lord, and you say well, for so I am. If I then, your Lord and Teacher, have washed your feet, you also ought to wash one another's feet. For I have given you an example, that you should do as I have done to you. Most assuredly, I say to you, a servant is not greater than his master; nor is he who is sent greater than he who sent him. If you know these things, blessed are you if you do them.'

"I was sitting close to Jesus, my head leaning against His chest after the humbling experience of His washing our feet. I could hear His heart beating when He predicted that one of us would betray Him. Peter motioned to me and mouthed, 'Ask Him who it is.'

"And so I did. And Jesus whispered, 'It is he to whom I shall give a piece of bread when I have dipped it.' No one else heard this, but when Jesus dipped a piece of bread and handed it to Judas, I saw the man's face cloud over. Jesus looked directly into his eyes and said, 'What you do, do quickly.'

"Judas rushed out into the night, causing some of the others to wonder aloud where he was going. Someone said they assumed he was purchasing things we would need for the feast or was giving money to the poor, as he was our treasurer.

"So, when Judas had gone, Jesus said, 'Now the Son

of Man is glorified, and God is glorified in Him. If God is glorified in Him, God will also glorify Him in Himself, and glorify Him immediately. Little children, I shall be with you a little while longer. You will seek Me; and as I said to the Jews, 'Where I am going, you cannot come,' so now I say to you. A new commandment I give to you, that you love one another; as I have loved you, that you also love one another. By this all will know that you are My disciples, if you have love for one another.'

"Simon Peter said, 'Lord, where are You going?'

"Jesus said, 'Where I am going you cannot follow Me now, but you shall follow Me afterward.'

"Peter said, 'Lord, why can I not follow You now? I will lay down my life for Your sake.'

"Jesus said, 'Will you lay down your life for My sake? Most assuredly, I say to you, the rooster shall not crow till you have denied Me three times.

"'Let not your heart be troubled; you believe in God, believe also in Me. In My Father's house are many mansions; if it were not so, I would have told you. I go to prepare a place for you. And if I go and prepare a place for you, I will come again and receive you to Myself; that where I am, there you may be also. And where I go you know, and the way you know.'

"Thomas said, 'Lord, we do not know where You are going, and how can we know the way?'

"Jesus said, 'I am the way, the truth, and the life. No one comes to the Father except through Me. If you had known Me, you would have known My Father also;

and from now on you know Him and have seen Him.'

"Philip said, 'Lord, show us the Father, and it is sufficient for us.'

"Jesus said, 'Have I been with you so long, and yet you have not known Me, Philip? He who has seen Me has seen the Father; so how can you say, "Show us the Father"? Do you not believe that I am in the Father, and the Father in Me? The words that I speak to you I do not speak on My own authority; but the Father who dwells in Me does the works. Believe Me that I am in the Father and the Father in Me, or else believe Me for the sake of the works themselves.

" 'Most assuredly, I say to you, he who believes in Me, the works that I do he will do also; and greater works than these he will do, because I go to My Father. And whatever you ask in My name, that I will do, that the Father may be glorified in the Son. If you ask anything in My name, I will do it.'

"Oh, Polycarp, it was a sad and melancholy time because we were finally, slowly realizing that He was saying goodbye. He taught of our relationship to Him, of our relationship to one another, and our relationship to the world. And it was clear He was talking about not only us, but about all who believe. He promised His Holy Spirit would comfort us after He was gone.

"Then He told us what was to come, but we did not understand, and further, we did not want to hear it or believe it. He said, 'A little while, and you will not see Me; and again a little while, and you will see Me, because I go to the Father.'

"We did not understand and whispered to one another that we did not know what He was saying. It was, as usual, as if He had heard us. He said, 'Are you inquiring among yourselves about what I said . . . ? Most assuredly, I say to you that you will weep and lament, but the world will rejoice; and you will be sorrowful, but your sorrow will be turned into joy. A woman, when she is in labor, has sorrow because her hour has come; but as soon as she has given birth to the child, she no longer remembers the anguish, for joy that a human being has been born into the world. Therefore you now have sorrow; but I will see you again and your heart will rejoice, and your joy no one will take from you.

"'And in that day you will ask Me nothing. Most assuredly, I say to you, whatever you ask the Father in My name He will give you. Until now you have asked nothing in My name. Ask, and you will receive, that your joy may be full.

"'These things I have spoken to you in figurative language; but the time is coming when I will no longer speak to you in figurative language, but I will tell you plainly about the Father. In that day you will ask in My name, and I do not say to you that I shall pray the Father for you; for the Father Himself loves you, because you have loved Me, and have believed that I came forth from God. I came forth from the Father and have come into the world. Again, I leave the world and go to the Father.'

"Finally we said, 'See, now You are speaking

plainly, and using no figure of speech! Now we are sure that You know all things, and have no need that anyone should question You. By this we believe that You came forth from God.'

"Jesus said, 'Do you now believe? Indeed the hour is coming, yes, has now come, that you will be scattered, each to his own, and will leave Me alone. And yet I am not alone, because the Father is with Me. These things I have spoken to you, that in Me you may have peace. In the world you will have tribulation; but be of good cheer, I have overcome the world.'

"He prayed for Himself, then for us, then for all believers. Not long after came all those horrible events others have written so much about: His betrayal, His arrest, His trial, His crucifixion, and His burial."

John knew he would have to recite these horrible events yet again, adding his perspective to the accounts already written. Though he dreaded calling to mind such heart-wrenching memories, he was comforted to know he would soon finish his account with triumph. And none too soon, as even what was left of his feeble strength was waning.

TWENTY

It pained John to tell of the awful last week of Jesus, but he forced himself to recount the story that had been made so familiar by his colleagues' writings and his teaching and preaching over the previous six decades. He wept as he told Polycarp that while, yes, Jesus' prophecy of Peter's denial came true, "I too was among all the rest who ran away during the worst of it before His crucifixion. Though I knew one of the men on the high court—because my family had done business with his—and thus I could have appeared there without fear, it was only when Jesus was finally forced to carry His cross that I mustered the courage to accompany His mother to Golgotha. Oh, the horror of that day!

"No one can know unless he experienced it himself the depths the soul endures watching One you have loved, admired, learned from, and pledged your life to, now reviled, scorned, and mutilated beyond recognition while being put to death. With my eyes I pleaded with Jesus to forgive me for not standing with Him in the Garden of Gethsemane when they led Him away. Judas had betrayed Him with a kiss. Peter, as if to prove he would never waver, attacked one of the guards—only to falter later and deny our Lord.

"I can't blame him. I mustn't judge. We hoped and prayed and could not imagine the worst to come for

Someone who proved His power over nature and time and distance. But He had told us and told us that this was necessary. Still, the agony of having to witness it firsthand, to stand there with His mother and see the pain on her face . . .

"But then my Savior, His precious face bruised and bloated to where it could have been mistaken for that of an animal, wrenched Himself up enough to draw breath. He looked at His mother—who stood there with me, with Mary of Magdala, another Mary, and James's and my own mother—and said, 'Woman, behold your son.'

"Well, at first I thought He meant that she should see what her Son had come to. But then He slowly, clearly painfully, turned to look into my eyes. He said, 'Son, behold your mother.' Had I not been directly beneath Him and seen His look and heard His inflection, I might have thought He was somehow referring to my own mother. But His intention was clear. He was asking that I take Mary in and be her son in His absence, for His brothers were still not believers. I nodded, resolving to treat her as He would have until the day she died."

The very telling of the account took John back all those years to every emotion. He sat on his cot and hung his head, speaking softly, knowing Polycarp had to strain to hear. "You can only imagine how devastated we were. All of us. Nothing looked or smelled or tasted or felt the same. It was as if with His death, God had taken our lives too. We stuck together, commiserating, remembering, reminiscing. But we had lost the spark of life. What was the point of going on?

"We didn't doubt Him. By now we knew who He was. No one would ever be able to shake that conviction. But we had missed all the signs that He would return to us. That was not on one of our minds, as far as I could tell. We wondered how and why God would bestow upon the earth such a gift and then snatch Him away again.

"Wise men since before I was born have said that time is the great healer, but this wound was going to require eons. On the following Sunday my grief was as sharp as it had been when Jesus finally lowered that precious head and breathed His last. I did not know how I would survive it. I could not eat or sleep. Even talking about Him was nearly impossible, for we would tear up and break into sobs.

"I was forcing myself to take a few bites of something Peter had cooked for breakfast that morning of the first day of the week, when Mary Magdalene came running to us. 'I went to the tomb early,' she said, gasping, 'while it was still dark. The stone has been taken away! They have taken away the Lord out of the tomb, and we do not know where they have laid Him.'

"We were infuriated! Peter said, 'Roman guards were assigned! How could grave robbers have gotten past them?'

"I had to see for myself. I sprinted toward the tomb, with Peter lumbering alongside me. I wanted to be the first there, so I ran ahead. When I got to the tomb and saw that Mary of Magdala was right and the stone had indeed been rolled away from the opening, I stooped and looked in and saw the linen cloths lying there. I could not move! Peter went right past me into the tomb. 'The linen is still here,' he said. 'And the hand-kerchief that had been around His head is folded over there.' Then I went in also, and I believed. We ran back even faster than we had come, to tell His mother and the other disciples.

"Mary told me that she had followed us and stayed behind, and as she wept she too stooped and looked into the tomb. She saw two angels in white sitting where the body of Jesus had lain, one at the head and the other at the feet. They said, 'Woman, why are you weeping?'

"She said, 'Because they have taken away my Lord, and I do not know where they have laid Him.' Then she turned around and saw a man standing there. He too said, 'Woman, why are you weeping? Whom are you seeking?'

"She told me she assumed He was the gardener and said, 'Sir, if You have carried Him away, tell me where You have laid Him, and I will take Him away.'

"The Man said, 'Mary!' and she knew.

"She turned and said, 'Rabboni!' (which is to say, Teacher).

"Jesus told her not to touch Him because He had not yet ascended to His Father but to go to the disciples and tell us He said He was 'ascending to My Father and your Father, and to My God and your God.'

"That evening we—all but Thomas—met behind closed doors, still fearing the religious leaders, and as you can imagine, excitedly discussing what we had discovered. All of a sudden Jesus appeared in our midst, and said, 'Peace be with you.' He showed us His hands and His side where He had been pierced. I am at a loss to describe our joy. It was as if we were dreaming, but we knew we were not.

"Jesus said again, 'Peace to you! As the Father has sent Me, I also send you.' And then, Polycarp, He breathed on us and said, 'Receive the Holy Spirit. If you forgive the sins of any, they are forgiven them; if you retain the sins of any, they are retained.'

"When Jesus was gone, Thomas returned, and of course we told Him we had seen the Lord. Can you blame Him for not believing us? He said, 'Unless I see in His hands the print of the nails, and put my finger into the print of the nails, and put my hand into His side, I will not believe.'

"Eight days later we were again meeting privately, but this time Thomas was with us. Jesus came, again without the door opening, and stood in our midst saying, 'Peace to you!' He said, 'Reach your finger here, and look at My hands; and reach your hand here, and put it into My side. Do not be unbelieving, but believing.'

"We could only smile as Thomas said, 'My Lord and my God!'

"Jesus said, 'Thomas, because you have seen Me, you have believed. Blessed are those who have not seen and yet have believed.' "

John lay back on his bed and sighed.

"More stories!" Polycarp exulted. "There must be many more."

"Oh, there are," John said softly. "Many have already been written. But for my purpose, I have told almost all I want to tell."

"Almost?"

"Yes, I will get to one more. But first, I want you to write this:

"And truly Jesus did many other signs in the presence of His disciples, which are not written in this book; but these are written that you may believe that Jesus is the Christ, the Son of God, and that believing you may have life in His name."

"I pray many will," Polycarp said, his voice thick.

"I too," John said. "Now, after these things several of us were together at the Sea of Tiberias. Peter, Thomas, Nathanael, my brother James and I, and a couple of other disciples were there. Peter wanted to go fishing.

"I said, 'We are going with you also.' We went out and immediately got into the boat, but that whole night we caught nothing, not one fish. In the morning a stranger on the shore called out to us, 'Children, have you any food?'

"We apologized and said we did not. We would have been happy to share if we had. He shouted, 'Cast the net on the right side of the boat, and you will find some!' We were amused. We had been fishing all night from both sides of the boat. But what was the harm? We cast the net on the other side, and we were not able to draw it in because of the multitude of fish.

"I said, 'Peter! It is the Lord!'

"Peter threw on his outer garment and plunged into the sea. The rest of us rowed the boat about two hundred cubits to shore, dragging the net full of fish. Jesus already had a fire of coals going, cooking bread and some other fish. He said, 'Bring some of which you have just caught.'

"Peter dragged the net to land, full of large fish, one hundred and fifty-three; and although there were so many, the net was not broken. Jesus said, 'Come and eat breakfast.' Yet none of us dared ask Him, 'Who are You?' We knew it was the Lord. We sat with Him and He served us the bread and fish. This was the third time Jesus showed Himself to us after He was raised from the dead.

"After we had eaten, Jesus said, 'Simon, son of Jonah, do you love Me more than these?'

"Peter said, 'Yes, Lord; You know that I love You.'

"Jesus said, 'Feed My lambs.' And He said a second time, 'Simon, son of Jonah, do you love Me?'

"Peter said, 'Yes, Lord; You know that I love You.'

"And Jesus said, 'Tend My sheep.' And He said a third time, 'Simon, son of Jonah, do you love Me?'

"It was clear Peter was grieved because Jesus had asked him this yet again. He said, 'Lord, You know all things; You know that I love You.'

"Jesus said, 'Feed My sheep. Most assuredly, I say

to you, when you were younger, you girded yourself and walked where you wished; but when you are old, you will stretch out your hands, and another will gird you and carry you where you do not wish.' "

"What was He saying, rabbi?" Polycarp said.

"I believe He was signifying by what death Peter would glorify God. And when He had spoken this, He said to Peter, 'Follow Me.' Polycarp, I will always believe that the Lord asked Peter three times whether he loved Him to allow the man to make up for the three times he had denied Jesus. Peter turned around and saw me and said, 'But Lord, what about this man?'

"Jesus said, 'If I will that he remain till I come, what is that to you? You follow Me.'

"You know, young friend, the word somehow went out among the disciples that Jesus had told Peter that I would not die. But of course that is not what He said.

"Now finish it this way:

"This is the disciple who testifies of these things, and wrote these things; and we know that his testimony is true.

"And there are also many other things that Jesus did, which if they were written one by one, I suppose that even the world itself could not contain the books that would be written. Amen."

TWENTY-ONE

The Lord's Day dawn broke chilly and windy, the wood latticework covering John's window tapping rhythmically and allowing in brief bursts of pink and orange. He pulled his blanket to his neck, then tested his appendages, contracting and stretching arms and legs, hands and feet. Carefully pushing himself to sit up, he left the bed and knelt on the cold floor, beginning his day the way he had more than twenty thousand times since the departure from earth of his risen Lord.

"Our Father in heaven, hallowed be Your name. Your kingdom come. Your will be done on earth as it is in heaven. Give us this day our daily bread. And forgive us our debts, as we forgive our debtors. And do not lead us into temptation, but deliver us from the evil one. For Yours is the kingdom and the power and the glory forever. Amen."

He added his own refrain: "Father, I am wholly yours today, as always. Use me as You see fit."

Rising, John found himself already sturdier than the day before. His stomach had settled, while he knew it would take the heat of the day to temper his muscle and bone. He pulled the window fully open and saw women streaming to the local wells, pitchers balanced on their heads, shoulders, or hips. And he was struck to realize that his gospel account was finished. God had spared him long enough and favored him with compatriots as loyal and faithful as Polycarp and Ignatius so that the task would be completed. Now if he could only see it copied enough times before Ignatius's departure that it could be circulated to the other churches.

As important as that, of course, was getting more copies into the hands of people right here in Ephesus. While the evil serpent of vain philosophy and deceit threatened the truth around the world, its very head now resided in John's own adopted city. It had been the blasphemous teaching of the Gnostics that had spurred—yea, necessitated—his version of the gospel, and now he prayed God would use it to thwart both the fledgling Gnostic church and the institution of higher learning that Cerinthus also planned. John believed with all his heart that the truth of Christ need fear no man-made religion, but he was also persuaded that he himself had been called to stand and fight.

Today was the day Cerinthus was expected at the house church. John remained troubled in his spirit over whether allowing the enemy in was the right thing. But he trusted the wisdom of his young friends and prayed they had the mind of God about this.

Would Cerinthus even show up? John's first visitor brought the answer. Polycarp knocked quickly and swept in, as invigorated as John had seen him in weeks. "Oh! You're awake! Good. Good. And how did we sleep?"

"*I* slept well, son. How did *we* sleep?"

"I hardly slept at all, of course. You finished the hard work. I finished the easy. Well, are you ready for news?"

"And if I am not, will I not hear it?"

"Of course you will," Polycarp said, smiling. "I have news."

"What a surprise."

"He's here. Cerinthus is here. Along with a few of his disciples. They are dressed in finery, and already they are talking with Ignatius. You must come."

Polycarp pulled him to the window and pointed through the shrubbery to where Cerinthus, with a couple of young men earnestly listening behind him, spoke animatedly with Ignatius.

"Do you really think I should be there?" John said.

"One of us must spell Ignatius. He must prepare for the gathering. People are beginning to arrive already."

"Very well."

"Are you up to it, teacher? I don't want to tax your strength."

John's very looked silenced Polycarp, and they made their way out. John prayed silently the whole way, not knowing what to expect. The stocky Cerinthus greeted him with a hearty smile and introduced him to his disciples.

"Your man Ignatius here has been very kind, sir, and I appreciate the warm welcome."

John was not smiling. "He has a way of being kinder than I," John said. "It was his idea, not mine, that you be invited. And while I can be civil, having allowed

208

myself to be overruled by a protégé, let me make clear to you how I feel about your presence here today."

"Oh, I think I know," Cerinthus said, more loudly than John expected and making the old man suspect the Gnostic was not as comfortable as he tried to seem. "I realize that it can be disconcerting to have someone who disagrees—"

"Pardon me, sir," John said. "But you need to know that I take seriously my calling as shepherd of this flock. I cannot, nor will I, allow anyone to attempt to have sway over the hearts and minds of those under my charge."

"You fear ideas."

"I fear nothing, sir, but you will not be allowed to speak. And if you make a display of your disagreement over what I teach and preach today, I will ask that you be removed from—"

"So you're saying that you fear nothing but me and my views. Plainly you give those under your 'charge' no credit for being able to think for themselves. Why not let them hear both sides of the argument and exercise their own brainpower?"

"There are not two sides to this argument, sir. I walked and talked with the Master Himself, and—"

"Then you know better than anyone that He was a revolutionary. That He feared no opponent. The very message I have for your devout followers—"

"Followers of Jesus."

"—is that their salvation is in their intellect and that—"

"Even the Apostle Paul wrote that he would gladly be a fool for Christ."

"I deny Paul."

"That is why you have no place here."

"But I have been invited . . ."

"And you are welcome to sit quietly and listen. I am speaking today on—"

"A thousand pardons, rabbi," Ignatius said, "but am I not expected to teach today?"

"Excuse me," John said to Cerinthus, and he pulled Ignatius aside. "I am so sorry, Ignatius. Forgive me, but the Lord has just now impressed upon me that I should read from my gospel today, to counter this heresy head-on. I should have talked with you before announcing it to Cerinthus, and I hope I have not embarrassed or offended you."

"I am at your service, teacher. You know that."

"Would you be prepared, along with Polycarp and whomever else you choose, to escort Cerinthus and his men out, should the need arise?"

"Of course."

John turned back to Cerinthus. "Excuse my manners. I would ask that you sit in the back and not draw attention to yourself."

"I am willing to oblige, sir, but I feel compelled to tell you that many in your gathering will recognize me from the street. In fact, some seem quite interested in what I have to say."

John did not know how to respond. Was this man to be believed? Could he have already had an influence on newer believers? John prayed it wasn't so. But a few minutes later his worst fears were confirmed. As he and Ignatius and Polycarp found their places and prepared to begin a service of worship, singing, the Lord's Supper, and John's teaching, John was stunned to see Cerinthus being warmly greeted by many in the congregation, including at least one elder, who seemed to be speaking to him as an old friend.

John's next conundrum came when Cerinthus and his companions partook of the communion bread and wine. Paul had taught that people in churches died when some partook of the body and blood of Christ unworthily. Certainly Cerinthus was not a true believer, even if he considered himself one. John found himself praying earnestly for the safety of his own flock, and God granted him peace while also seeming to encourage him to be bold in his teaching.

He would tell the people, and in the process inform Cerinthus, what he had been doing during the time Ignatius spelled him. His flesh warned him against it, but God seemed to nudge him otherwise. As he finally stood to speak, warmed by the smiles from his own people, John was ready to plunge right in, to identify Cerinthus as a heretic, and to read from the papyrus he and Polycarp had been working on for so long.

He began by thanking Ignatius for standing in for him, but he was soon interrupted by some who insisted that he recognize and welcome "our most distinguished guest and his friends."

John hesitated.

"Cerinthus, the lauded thinker and follower of Christ," a man called out.

"Well, yes, he is here," John said, "and we have extended a welcome based on certain conditions. . . ."

"How rude!" someone called out. "Can we not fellowship with such a celebrated man of letters?"

John held up a hand. He would not be chastised into weakness by his own people. "Let me be forthright," he said. "It is the very teaching of this man, whose ideas I consider heretical, that have motivated me to write—with the able assistance of our own Polycarp—my version of the gospel of Jesus Christ. My purpose is not only to establish without question that Jesus was fully God while fully Man, but also to aver that He was God's own Son, deity in His own right, and that He claimed that very office Himself on many occasions.

"I was there. I knew Him. I heard Him. And my account is true."

John was aware of a hum of excitement and anticipation, but he was also vexed by people looking to Cerinthus, apparently to see what he made of all this. The man sat there with a condescending smile, shaking his head. And as John began reading his gospel aloud, Cerinthus grew only more animated in his disdain. John wanted to chastise him, to call him out, to have him removed, but now he dared not. He would be only giving the man permission to counter him, and then John would appear close-minded if he did not allow it.

Most gratifying, however, was that as John began his treatise and continued with the stories of the eight miracles he had recorded, he felt the blessing of God. The house fell silent and the people sat rapt, knowing they were hearing these accounts from a man who witnessed them firsthand. Many wept as the stories unfolded, and John could be grateful only that he had this unparalleled opportunity to drive home the best evidence he knew against the heresy of the Gnostics.

When the long service was over, people streamed to John, thanking him, encouraging him, exhorting him to spread this gospel far and wide. And yet many also crowded around Cerinthus, treating him with deference and respect. John would not have wanted that they be rude or unkind, but he was still troubled in his spirit that the enemy had sat at his feet in the very house of God.

As Cerinthus and his disciples made their way through the crowd to John, John overheard him saying, "Well, it was entertaining, even amusing at points. But when you get past the gifted storytelling, you are left with the imaginings of a well-intentioned but fading old man. It was less a historical account than a prejudiced treatise of his own particular viewpoint."

John wanted to call Cerinthus down right there, but he would not. Cerinthus finally reached him and said, "John, John! Most informative and uplifting. I reject most of it, of course, but—"

"But this is neither the time nor the place to debate

it," John said. "Let me put you on notice that I plan to cast as widely as possible the truths I expounded today."

Cerinthus's phony smile dissipated and he leaned close to John's ear. "I would advance cautiously, old man. Very cautiously. Your flock, as you call it, is not unanimous in its support of you or what you are teaching, as you will soon see."

Sadly, that proved true. Cerinthus succeeded in his efforts to further cripple the Ephesian church. Several faithful attenders left the house church over the next several weeks, and Cerinthus in fact began a small Gnostic church that began to grow. John redoubled his efforts to counter the blasphemy, especially after Ignatius had left for his tour of the other churches.

John rallied somewhat physically and believed God had given him, as it were, a second wind. If he was to exhaust his life, what better way than in defense of the truth of the gospel?

Shortly after, John received a message that might have changed the course of Polycarp's life. Ignatius had written that the church in Smyrna needed a new bishop, and he urged John to consider Polycarp for the post. It was perfect, a wonderful idea, but before John could even present the opportunity to his young charge, John's sleep chamber was invaded in the middle of the night.

PART TWO

THE
REVELATOR

TWENTY-TWO

Ephesus, A.D. 95
The Roman soldiers who rousted the old man from
his bed and hauled him to a local jail, while rough and
ruthless, seemed almost apologetic. "Guess this ends
your little gatherings," one of them said. John was
shoved into the back of a wood wagon and the door
slammed and locked.

John had to smile. His arrest would only empower
the church. While Polycarp would be unable to leave
for a high post as long as John was detained, this
might be the best thing that ever happened to the Ephesian body of believers. They would finally realize the
seriousness of their cause. They would step up the
work of copying and circulating John's gospel.

When word reached Rome that keeping John locked
up in Ephesus seemed only to spawn more house
churches, he was shipped to Rome for final sentencing. When the boiling in oil failed and he was sen-

tenced to Patmos, John worried he would never see or hear from his beloved brothers and sisters again. Few men sentenced to Patmos ever returned alive.

Old and feeble as he was, and as horrific as the trip from the capital had been, the first few days on the rocky isle found John so aglow from the miracle in Rome that he went about his backbreaking mining chores with gusto. Other prisoners needled him, badgering him to perform supernatural feats. The guards made him the target of their darkest vehemence, whipping and beating him for the slightest offense, ostensibly to make an example of him.

And while John reeled from the blows to the point of delirium and wondered, as did the others, why he had been spared the pain of the oil, not to mention death, and yet felt every sting of this torment, he continued to pray for grace. Once, when he had been beaten to where tears streamed, a guard bellowed, "Do you think we like this assignment any more than you do?"

John had replied quietly, "I can only imagine how hard this place must be for you."

That guard never touched him again.

Eventually the work—the breaking of rock virtually every waking hour to reveal marble—so wore on the old man that he could barely move. And yet he never complained. Every day had begun with the prayer his Lord had taught him and his giving of himself to God for His use. What that use was, John did not know. He saw the softening of the one guard and sensed perhaps the same in one or two others. And fellow prisoners started to give him a wide berth, eventually tiring of making him the object of their venom—or worse, their sport.

AFTER SEVERAL MONTHS, John resigned himself to the notion that God had allowed him to be sent to Patmos to die. Surely that was what the emperor had had in mind. Why Domitian thought physical labor would kill a man whom boiling oil could not harm, John had no idea. But killing him slowly it certainly was. He began to look forward to heaven.

John tried to keep track of the days of the week, and occasionally a guard would confirm that he was right. But eventually even the seemingly compassionate ones tired of his incessant worry over what day it was. He was the only inmate who cared when Sunday fell. Certainly no quarter was given to anyone's religious bent. Jewish prisoners were forced to work the entire Sabbath. And John, who soon determined he was the only Christ follower on Patmos—Domitian had taken great delight in parading the others before crowds in the Colosseum before their horrible deaths—had to play out any Lord's Day worship only in his mind.

It amused him to see the response of his fellow prisoners and the guards when he hummed the simple melodies of worship that had spread through the Asian churches under his charge. He prayed aloud, even smiled at times. Often he would simply softly recite a Psalm or a passage from the Pentateuch. He could even bring to mind the great theological treatises contained in letters to the churches from his martyred friend, the missionary Paul. Anyone within earshot seemed astounded at how much John remembered.

But then came the Lord's Day morning when the clanging of the guards' swords on the stone walls of the prisoners' barracks had a new effect on John. Normally he had to force himself to recite the daily prayer in the manner Jesus had taught him, and he had to fight off a terrible black cloud of despair to face another day in the mining caves. Yet this day he seemed to spring to his feet, his head full of ideas, warnings that must be communicated to the churches that had been under his care.

John knew this was of God. He wolfed down the meager breakfast slopped into his bowl, and he and the others tramped out to be allotted the tools for their merciless work. But all the while he toiled, God seemed to fill his mind with more exhortations to the churches, each with specifics that matched what he knew of the people. John had the feeling that every word was from the Lord Himself. The more the words came to him, the more desperate he became to record them.

Prisoners were not fed again until the end of the day, when they could barely move, but the evening meal seemed their only reward, the one thing to look forward to. It had larger portions than breakfast did, and while it consisted primarily of stale lentils shipped from Rome and old bread delivered from the Asian mainland—supplemented every other day by cast-off fish too small to market—everyone devoured every bite.

Every day, usually after the noon hour, a prisoner or two would drop from exhaustion or thirst, and that was the guards' signal to call the water break. Each prisoner was granted a generous measure of water and enough time to consume it while sitting briefly. That was when John, his mind swirling with messages from God, whispered the offer of his evening's ration of bread to a man he'd seen writing letters, in exchange for ink and an overused quill.

"They won't send your letters, you know," the man said. "Mine are merely stored for when I ever get off this godforsaken island."

"Oh, it is anything but godforsaken, sir," John said. "As long as God's children are here, He is here."

"He is *here?* You're a fool."

"Perhaps."

"I suppose you'll need papyrus too," the other prisoner said. "I had to bribe the guard for that."

"I'm afraid I need much," John said.

"That'll cost you your water."

Jesus had talked of being the Living Water. He would have to suffice. John pushed his cup to the man, who drank it fast while careful not to waste a drop. "Tonight," the man said.

John soon regretted giving up his water. Within minutes the men were forced back to work, John sent alone deep into a cave. Many a prisoner had been caught napping when assigned alone, but John was known to be trustworthy. As he worked, the messages to the churches seemed complete and of a piece in his mind. He bent to hammer at a huge rock. A cramp developed behind his thigh, and as he rose to relieve it, he felt lightheaded. He reached to steady himself and then turned and stared, having heard behind him a loud voice, as of a trumpet, saying, "I am the Alpha and the Omega, the First and the Last," and, "What you see, write in a book and send it to the seven churches which are in Asia: to Ephesus, to Smyrna, to Pergamos, to Thyatira, to Sardis, to Philadelphia, and to Laodicea."

It was Jesus! It had been so long since John had seen Him that he turned to see where the voice was coming from and saw seven golden lampstands, and in the midst of them One like the Son of Man, clothed with a garment down to the feet and girded about the chest with a golden band. His head and hair were white like wool, as white as snow, and His eyes like a flame of fire; His feet were like fine brass, as if refined in a furnace, and His voice as the sound of many waters; He had in His right hand seven stars, out of His mouth went a sharp two-edged sword, and His countenance was like the sun shining in its strength.

John fell at His feet as dead, and Jesus laid His right hand on him, saying, "Do not be afraid; I am the First and the Last. I am He who lives, and was dead, and behold, I am alive forevermore. Amen. And I have the keys of Hades and of Death. Write the things which you have seen, and the things which are, and the things which will take place after this.

"The mystery of the seven stars which you saw in My right hand, and the seven golden lampstands: the seven stars are the angels of the seven churches, and the seven lampstands which you saw are the seven churches."

John was overwhelmed and remained in the Spirit as he was shown all the wonders of heaven and of the future. Hours later he awakened in the barracks, where a guard told him, "When we found you we believed you dead and prepared a coffin to slide you into the sea. But still you breathed and your heart beat."

John sat up. "I am as alive as I have ever been."

"Then you will work as usual tomorrow."

"Of course."

"Can you make it to dinner?"

"I am famished."

John did not have to search for the prisoner to whom he had promised his loaf. "The quill and ink and papyrus are in your bed," the man said, grabbing the bread, and he was gone before John could thank him. As soon as John had eaten, he felt rejuvenated and rushed to his mat to find the writing tools. In the dim, flickering light of an oil-fueled torch, he sat scribbling all night, knowing he would pay for it the next day with fatigue. John wrote on and on through the night, feverishly recording everything the Lord had shown him that day.

The Revelation of Jesus Christ, which God gave Him to show His servants—things which must shortly take place. And He sent and signified it by His angel to His servant John, who bore witness to the word of God, and to the testimony of Jesus Christ, to all things that he saw.

Blessed is he who reads and those who hear the words of this prophecy, and keep those things which are written in it; for the time is near.

John, to the seven churches which are in Asia: Grace to you and peace from Him who is and who was and who is to come, and from the seven Spirits who are before His throne, and from Jesus Christ, the faithful witness, the firstborn from the dead, and the ruler over the kings of the earth. To Him who loved us and washed us from our sins in His own blood, and has made us kings and priests to His God and Father, to Him be glory and dominion forever and ever. Amen.

Behold, He is coming with clouds, and every eye will see Him, even they who pierced Him. And all the tribes of the earth will mourn because of Him. Even so, Amen.

"I am the Alpha and the Omega, the Beginning and the End," says the Lord, "who is and who was and who is to come, the Almighty."

I, John, both your brother and companion in the tribulation and kingdom and patience of Jesus Christ, was on the island that is called Patmos for the word of God and for the testimony of Jesus Christ. I was in the Spirit on the Lord's Day, and . . .

Following page after page of prophecies about Christ's return in the clouds and seven years of horrifying tribulation before his final glorious appearing on earth, John finished by documenting what God's angel had told him of heaven.

. . . There shall be no night there: They need no lamp nor light of the sun, for the Lord God gives them light. And they shall reign forever and ever.

Then he said to me, "These words are faithful and true." And the Lord God of the holy prophets sent His angel to show His servants the things which must shortly take place.

"Behold, I am coming quickly! Blessed is he who keeps the words of the prophecy of this book."

Now I, John, saw and heard these things. And when I heard and saw, I fell down to worship before the feet of the angel who showed me these things.

Then he said to me, "See that you do not do that. For I am your fellow servant, and of your brethren the prophets, and of those who keep the words of this book. Worship God."

And he said to me, "Do not seal the words of the prophecy of this book, for the time is at hand. He who is unjust, let him be unjust still; he who is filthy, let him be filthy still; he who is righteous, let him be righteous still; he who is holy, let him be holy still."

"And behold, I am coming quickly, and My reward is with Me, to give to every one according to his work. I am the Alpha and the Omega, the Beginning and the End, the First and the Last."

Blessed are those who do His commandments, that they may have the right to the tree of life, and may enter through the gates into the city. But outside are dogs and sorcerers and sexually immoral and murderers and idolaters, and whoever loves and practices a lie.

"I, Jesus, have sent My angel to testify to you these things in the churches. I am the Root and the Offspring of David, the Bright and Morning Star."

And the Spirit and the bride say, "Come!" And let him who hears say, "Come!" And let him who thirsts come. Whoever desires, let him take the water of life freely. For I testify to everyone who hears the words of the prophecy of this book: If anyone adds to these things, God will add to him the plagues that are written in this book; and if anyone takes away from the words of the book of this prophecy, God shall take away his part from the Book of Life, from the holy city, and from the things which are written in this book.

He who testifies to these things says, "Surely I am coming quickly." Amen. Even so, come, Lord Jesus!

The grace of our Lord Jesus Christ be with you all. Amen.

John finished just before dawn and rolled onto his mat on his back. He needed to try to recoup his energy after his collapse and his sleepless night, but he was so full of the images and prophecies he could barely remain prostrate, let alone close his eyes. Soon would come the clang of sword against rock, the cursing of his fellow prisoners, and the start of another relentless day. He had become convinced that enough days like that—even if he got his rest—would kill him. And yet the instructions from the Lord were clear. He was to send to the churches the message that had been entrusted to him. No one could do that for him. If the guards would not even send the personal letters of a prisoner to the supply ship, there was no way John could trust them to safeguard a message for Asia from the living God.

John began to believe he would survive Patmos after all.

LITTLE MORE THAN a year later, Caesar Augustus Domitian was assassinated in a palace coup, ending his reign of terror. He was replaced by Marcus Cocceius Nerva, who, though his sovereignty would last fewer than two years, made immediate changes, setting about to restore the image of the government in the eyes of the populace. He renamed Domitian's lavish dwelling the House of the People, personally resided elsewhere, pledged an oath to the Senate vowing he would execute none of its members (Domitian had killed eleven and exiled more), allowed no statues to be made of himself, and established economic measures to help the poor.

More significantly, Caesar Nerva released all those imprisoned by Domitian and freed exiles not found guilty of serious crimes.

John, the beloved apostle and disciple of Jesus the Christ, was free to return home.

TWENTY-THREE

Fall, A.D. *96*

John's decrepit body bore the ills of age and months of punishing labor, yet his mind was afire. While the memory of his miraculous deliverance from death in Rome was ever-present, his spiritual experience on the barren island in the Aegean surpassed even that escape.

He had worked to rags his one piece of attire, and upon his release had been issued a scratchy, cheap imitation of a Roman toga. He could not wait to burn it along with the memories it evoked and replace it with a silk undergarment covered by a common tunic.

The old man was puzzled at the seasickness that attacked him, despite his life on the Gennesaret as a fisherman until he was twenty-five years old. Even with all John knew of how to combat the malady, his belly churned and bile rose in his throat. He was grateful to be sailing on an empty stomach.

Ignoring his physical agony, John was giddy at the prospect of returning to his beloved home. He leaned this way and that, trying to peer through the cloudy horizon in hopes of a glimpse of the Ephesian harbor. He dragged his fingers through knotted hair, untangling but a few wispy white strands. John leaned over the side and caught a glimpse of his visage in the water, stunned to be reminded of his aged grandfather before he died.

Clutched to John's chest was a ragged leather bag containing the treasure of a lifetime: brittle papyrus bearing his shaky handwriting. He had had to grind black rock and mix it with water to fashion more ink he hoped would not fade before he could copy his work with better tools. The result of that furious scribbling represented the entirety of his earthly possessions, other than his garment.

Otherwise his bag was empty. John had not a copper coin to his name, never mind bronze or silver or gold. He didn't know how he would even get off the craft, not to mention make his way to the church or to his quarters. Surely his humble chamber had been appropriated for someone else by now. He had no idea whether the news of his survival of the oil cauldron in Rome had even reached Ephesus, so how could anyone know he had been released from Patmos? Surely his comrades assumed him dead.

John could pay for help getting him from the boat to

a surface conveyance and then for the price of his ride, provided those who aided him could wait for their fare until he reached his destination. But he would not beg, would not expect a workingman to count on a mere promise of recompense. He tried to stand, to test his legs, but knees and ankles would not cooperate, could not bear even his wasted frame. He feared he weighed less than he had as a twelve-year-old.

The boatman had gazed upon him with what appeared pity as he helped him aboard hours before. Had it been compassion he detected? Might the boatman at least help him to the pier? And even if so, what then? Perhaps God would grant him the strength to somehow make his way to the church, where the brethren might succor him until he regained some strength. There was so much to tell, so much to do. How John missed his cherished brothers and sisters in the faith, especially his young, devoted disciple, Polycarp.

In spite of John's eager anticipation, when clouds blocked his view of Ephesus, crushing fatigue overtook him, and he dozed. At the sound of the lowering of the sail and wood against wood as the oars were loosed to propel the boat into the harbor, he roused, relieved that even while unconscious he had kept the priceless package pressed against his bosom. And even under overcast skies, Ephesus assaulted his senses all at once, filling his heart.

Fishing boats were offloading. Gulls darted and dived. Men on the dock hurried about with heavy ropes, and what appeared to be a welcoming party awaited. People waved, bounced on their feet, and smiled, but John could not bring them into focus from that distance. Only when the craft nudged the pier did he realize the small band—a young man, an older man, and a middle-aged couple—were there for him.

It was Polycarp, his youthful longtime disciple and traveling companion, with three others from the church. John could not contain his sobs. *Thank you, Lord!*

As the boat docked, he rocked to try to stand, but he could not. The boatman was busy with the ropes and conferring with men on the pier. Polycarp rushed to ask if he could help the old man disembark, and the boatman waved him aboard. The apostle and the robust, red-bearded young disciple were soon embracing.

"Let me take your bag," Polycarp said.

"Please, dear friend," John said. "It is all I have, and I must not part with it. Just help me."

The strength of his protégé was a tonic, but Polycarp must have been as excited as he, because it was all John could do to keep up. He ached all over and begged to slow down.

"I apologize, teacher, but the news of your deliverance from Domitian thrilled the entire church, and word of your release from exile reached us days ago. We're all so eager to greet you."

"How did you know I was arriving today?"

"We didn't! We have come every day for more than

a week since we heard of the pardons, hoping you would soon be delivered, provided the banishment had not killed you."

"It nearly did," John said. He stopped and drew Polycarp close. "Tell me of the battle and of our adversary."

"Cerinthus? His little church has stalled. Most of our people have returned, seeing the error of their ways. Some took a copy of your gospel into that excuse for a church, and Cerinthus reacted with anger. Having accused you of fearing other ideas, he tried to legislate against your eyewitness account from even passing the threshold of his sanctuary. He was proved the charlatan. He still plans a school, but I daresay your gospel crippled him, sir."

And suddenly they were upon the others, who tearfully, shyly embraced the old man and helped him up into a horse-drawn cart. The woman produced a basket containing a bit of fish and bread she said "was warm two hours ago."

"Forgive me if I can tolerate but a few bites," John said, smiling weakly. He threaded an arm through the strap of his leather bag and ate tentatively as the wagon jostled slowly through the narrow stone streets.

John roused suddenly, embarrassed to find he had drifted off again, and dropped a heel of bread. "I'm so sorry," he told the woman as she retrieved it.

"Think nothing of it," she said. "It's clear you are not well. Your chambers are ready. Though dozens have begged to welcome you, we have urged them to give you a full day and night's rest first."

"And I have a plan," Polycarp said, "to have you revived by the Lord's Day to address the brothers and sisters."

John forced a smile. "I cannot imagine it. A greeting will be all I can manage."

"That will be sufficient," his young charge said. "I prepared a talk, not knowing whether you would be here."

Upon arrival at the former home of Aquila and Priscilla, Polycarp helped John down from the cart and led him to the vast courtyard in the midst of the three great wings of the house.

Polycarp bowed, kissed John on the cheek, and steered him to the guest room, where he removed the old man's sandals.

"You welcome me to my own home?" John said, smiling.

"You are our guest until you retire for the evening," Polycarp said, washing his feet and wiping them with a towel. "When you are up to it, you will again be master of the house and the host." He brought John a cup of water.

"I need new clothes," John said, sighing.

"You will find them in your quarters, when you are ready."

"Ready? I'm nearly faint."

"You look it."

"I know I must, friend. But I need you to tarry with me briefly. I must entrust you with a great mystery."

"I am at your service, teacher."

As the younger steered the older back outside and to his small room, John was overcome with gratitude to him and to God. His life had been spared, and perhaps, with the help of his friends and loved ones, he could regain some strength to match his enthusiasm. While that remained hard to fathom, seeing his old room encouraged him. An oil lamp, a pitcher of water, and a bowl awaited, along with a towel and fresh clothing. John was eager to bathe and stretch out on the bed. Yet this more urgent matter pressed.

"You are fading from me, rabbi," Polycarp said. "Do you not wish me to leave you?"

"Bear with me, please. I must show you something and entreat your help."

"Anything."

John handed his leather bag to Polycarp. "Don't open it until you are alone, and I beg you, treat it as my most treasured possession."

"What is it?"

"You will see. It will marvel and amaze you, but at first it may appear merely the ravings of an old man, perhaps a madman. But it is a gift from God Almighty. He entrusted me with the words herein, an exhortation to the churches, and then a vision of the future at once so glorious and horrifying that I scarcely know what to do with it."

"You're trembling."

"I am old and weak and tired."

"It's more than that, master. You are like a man possessed."

"Polycarp, the Lord gave me this in a rush. Indeed, it took me longer to record than to experience. This came to me on a Lord's Day, and I spent the rest of the day and the whole night scrawling it as fast as I could. Read it and tell me what you think, but share it with no one. God will tell us what to do with it. Perhaps he will tell you. At the very least it must be copied. Will you do it?"

"To again write what God has commended to you? My zeal to read it overwhelms me, but to undertake such an ambitious—"

"Oh, but you must, Polycarp!"

"I am at your service, of course, but my studies, my duties—"

"Believe me, all will pale next to this." John shook his head and pressed a palm on his young friend's shoulder. "You have more excuses than Moses, he of the uncertain tongue."

"Forgive me. I'll do whatever you ask."

"Read first. I will rest. And then you will tell me of your plan to restore me to full strength."

When Polycarp departed, John disrobed and bathed, dressing in the fresh undergarment laid out for him. Within minutes after he collapsed onto his bed, he yielded to the dreamless sleep of the free.

TWENTY-FOUR

E ager to test his seemingly renewed strength the next morning, John dressed quickly, but upon leaving his room he discovered a bountiful breakfast on a tray just outside the door. He had looked forward to eating with his friends, but perhaps this was their way of trying to protect him. The entire church had to know of his return by now, and he would soon be overwhelmed with well-wishers. That had its benefits and would be a balm to his soul. In the meantime, he would trust the judgment of his friends and enjoy breakfast alone.

Cheese, warm bread, fruit, a handful of olives, and even a bite of fish lay beautifully arranged, accompanied by a cup of wine. John had not seen a plate like this since before his arrest. He thanked God for it and asked Him to bless it, adding a request that he be granted the self-control necessary to leave half of it.

The day was already warming with the traverse of the sun, and John heard activity in the courtyard. A fire crackled. And the rasp of stone on stone told him the women were grinding grain. He soon heard the urgent voice of Polycarp.

"Is he up yet? Has he eaten?"

A woman laughed and suggested he check for himself.

"Oh, I must not! He will be along soon enough, will

he not? We must respect his privacy and his need for rest and rejuvenation. Have you seen him?"

"I left his breakfast as you instructed, sir," she said. "I expect he will be along when he is ready."

"I should watch for him. But I do not want to appear to be prying."

"Even though you are."

He laughed.

"Why is it so urgent that you see him early?" she said.

"I just don't want to miss him. He has always been an early riser."

"As have you."

"But I am a fourth his age. I have no reason to sleep the morning away."

"Oh, sir, the morning has just begun. The cock has just crowed. Leave an old man to his routine."

"I know. It's just that— There! There he is now! Master, how are you? Wait! Wait until I can assist you!"

Polycarp, red hair flopping, rushed to him, but John held up a hand. "Please," he said. "Please do not trouble yourself."

"It's no trouble! I just—"

"Then just take the tray and allow me to walk on my own. It will be good for me. And for you."

"If you're sure," Polycarp said, reaching him.

John gave him the tray and waved him off. He slid a hand along the wall as he walked.

"There, see? I will soon be trotting."

"You hardly ate, master. Finish the olives at least."

"I ate like a king. That should suffice until the evening meal. Polycarp, the papyrus . . ."

The young man handed the tray off to the woman and directed John to sit near the fire. "Right here," he said, reaching inside his mantle to under his leather girdle, from which he produced John's bag.

"And?" the old man said.

"Surely you had to know the effect this would have on me, rabbi. I have not slept. I read it through from beginning to end, and then again. I have even begun the copying, though I confess I was so unnerved that my handwriting is worse even than when I penned your gospel. I may have to do it again."

"The more you are exposed to the text, the more it will reach your heart."

"I cannot imagine it burning any more brightly inside me, teacher. What did the other prisoners and the guards think?"

"Oh, I dared not share it, Polycarp. What if it had been confiscated?"

"No one else has seen this? I feel so privileged."

"Never mind privilege, young one. What shall I do with it?"

Polycarp rose and paced. "How can there be even a question? Clearly our Lord gave you this for the churches."

"I know. That is clear. I must disseminate it. But what is the best way? I am not up to traveling anymore yet."

"Start with a copy right here in Ephesus, and then send it to the other churches."

"Copies, or just one manuscript that makes the rounds, entrusted anew to each gathering?"

"Eventually you would need several copies, sir, but this cannot wait. Unless you have a misgiving about what God has entrusted to you, He has hard things to say to every congregation."

John stood. "Misgivings? Hardly. Oh, son, the richness with which the vision came remains with me."

"It was more than a dream then."

"I was there, Polycarp. I was in heaven. Guards talked of finding me, saying that I had fallen as a dead man, but you can see from the writing that during that whole time, I was in the Spirit and God had an angel show me all that is to come."

Polycarp sat close to the bread oven. "Much of it is alarming, sir, as I'm sure you know. And much is difficult to understand."

John nodded. "And yet it all made perfect sense to me. God transported me, and when I write that 'I looked and I saw,' that is exactly what happened. He showed me wondrous things, frightening things. I knew when I committed it to the papyrus that only those to whom God speaks will be able to comprehend it."

Polycarp stood. "Are you up to walking?"

"I believe I am. Is this your scheme to restore my health?"

"Part of it, yes," Polycarp said, smiling. "What you eat, the air you breathe, how much you move, all of it will bring back the man of God we know and love."

As they slowly exited the compound, John said, "But no Roman baths."

Polycarp laughed. "No. Of course not. I believe I know your mind on that subject."

"And on the subject of the revelation, Polycarp. Did you comprehend it?"

"I should be a fool to say yes," he said, "but let me say this: I accept it as from God to you. I long to devote myself to the study of it. And I say again, it must be delivered to the churches. But first, I urge you to read it aloud to the people here yourself."

"I don't know that I have the strength. It is not a short document. And I have not formed an opinion as to whether each church should hear what has been intended for the others."

John quickly began to feel fatigue.

"Let me suggest this," Polycarp said. "You read up to the exhortation to us here at Ephesus, then allow me to read the vision."

John pondered this. "The entire vision would take most of the time allotted for the assembly."

"I have no doubt this will capture the people's attention. Now I see you are slowing, old man. Shall we race back to the house?"

John smiled. "I hope your foolishness amuses you."

"Because it does not amuse you?"

"Everything you do and say amuses me, Polycarp."

OVER THE NEXT SEVERAL DAYS, John was amazed at

how quickly his strength grew. His food was better than it had been in more than a year, and his daily walks with Polycarp through the city—not to mention interaction with old friends—invigorated and renewed him.

The evening of the Lord's Day, the house church in Ephesus was so full that those arriving late had to stand or sit in the windows. Word had spread that the revered John had returned, so the season of singing, sharing the Lord's Supper, and reading of Scripture seemed to carry a joy and anticipation the body had not enjoyed since the times of Paul and then Timothy.

Finally Polycarp stood in their midst.

"I greet you, my brothers and sisters, in the name of our living Lord and Savior, Jesus Christ. I bring you all good wishes from your compatriots at the other churches of Asia, based on messages that have been received here even this week. I believed, until several days ago, that I would continue standing in for our beloved former bishop, the last among us to personally walk with our God. My reunion with John here has been joyous. And for you who would rather hear from your apostle, let me say that the same is true of me and that we will all have our wish.

"I prayerfully considered what the Lord would have me say to you, and I believe He gave me a clear message. But I confess that in my preparations I had the feeling that He led me to only broad principles and seemed resistant to my pleas for further elucidation. I feared expanding on His leading and could pray only that anything I chose to add would be not of the flesh but of the spirit. As John has so often quoted John the Baptizer, the cousin and forerunner of Jesus, 'He must increase, but I must decrease.'

"Well, beloved, now I understand what was happening during my time of preparation. God gave me enough for only the time allotted me, because it happens that He gave my mentor more than enough to fill the rest of the time.

"I spent all of last night reading and rereading a recent revelation God bestowed on our bishop, and exhausted as I was, sleep was then impossible.

"Now that I have whetted your appetite to where you will only tolerate the lesser morsel I have to offer, let me cover it with dispatch. And then John himself will introduce the revelation, and I will help read you the rest. I assure you, while it is long and today allows us only enough time to read it to you in its entirety, the document itself will prove worthy of careful perusal and study for months and perhaps years."

Polycarp turned to his own notes.

"Beloved Ephesians, our church has found mercy in the transcendent majesty of the Most High Father and of Jesus Christ, His only Son. We, as do similar bodies of saints throughout the world, exist by the will of Him who willed all things that exist, beloved and illuminated through the faith and love of Jesus Christ our God. His is a church universal worthy of honor, worthy of felicitation, worthy of praise, worthy of success, worthy of sanctification, and presiding in love, maintaining the law of Christ, and bearing of the Father's name. I therefore salute you in the name of Jesus Christ, Son of the Father. I pray for your unimpaired joy in Jesus Christ our God, to those who are united in flesh and spirit by every commandment of His; who imperturbably enjoy the full measure of God's grace and have every foreign stain filtered out of them.

"The Prince of this world is resolved to abduct us and to corrupt our Godward aspirations. Let none of you assist him. Rather, side with me—that is, with God. Do not have Jesus Christ on your lips and the world in your hearts. Give envy no place among you. I am not on fire with the love of earthly things. But there is still in me a living water, which is eloquent and within me says, 'Come to the Father.' I have no taste for corruptible foods or for the delights of this life. Bread of God is what I desire; that is, the flesh of Jesus Christ, who was the seed of David; and for my drink I desire His blood, that is, incorruptible love."

John sat there astounded at the growth he saw in Polycarp. Why, the young man sounded like Ignatius! Indeed, Ignatius must have had a strong influence on Polycarp during his short visit. How good it had been to hear that Ignatius had enjoyed a profitable tour of the churches and returned to his own, emboldened by the seeming liberality of the new emperor. Now if John could find the strength to again assume his duties in charge of the Ephesian church, he would have to release Polycarp to take the vacant bishopry at

Smyrna, where, he was convinced, Polycarp could become as effective there as a bishop as Ignatius was. The young man's time had come.

Polycarp continued, "No longer should we wish to live after the manner of men. As you well know, an enemy of the truth remains within our city walls. Your bishop and I agree and humbly but forthrightly instruct you to continue to beware of him. Be not seduced by strange doctrines, neither by antiquated fables, which are profitless. For if even unto this day we live according to the law, we admit that we have not received grace: for the godly prophets lived after Christ Jesus. For this cause also they were persecuted, being inspired by His grace to the end that they who are disobedient might be fully persuaded that there is one God who manifested Himself through Jesus Christ His Son, who is His Word that proceeded from silence, who in all things was well pleasing unto His Father who sent Him.

"His death, which some men deny, is a mystery whereby we attained unto belief, and for this cause we endure patiently, that we may be found disciples of Jesus Christ, our only teacher. If this be so, how shall we be able to live apart from Him?"

Polycarp led in prayer. Then he said, "As we believe Jesus Christ is our only teacher, how blessed are we that we enjoy, in our midst, one who was His disciple, an eyewitness to His ministry, with Him when He performed His first miracle and several to follow. Our Lord has seen fit to teach us anew through His disciple via a divine revelation that will astound you as it has me. And while our revered mentor is still regaining his strength after his exile, I ask only that he introduce the text this evening, and I shall endeavor to read to you the rest."

A holy hush fell over the assembled as John slowly rose and was welcomed to the position of honor. In trembling hands he bore the missive he had carried across the sea from Patmos. After greeting the assembled and thanking them for their prayers and hospitality, he said, "The Lord has not granted me the freedom to speak of my predicament in Rome and how He delivered me. Perhaps another time."

There seemed a sigh of disappointment, to which John responded, "Verily, you will see that greater things than these are prophesied."

The old man told the story of his life on Patmos and what happened to him that fateful Lord's Day in the cave of marble. By the time he got to the papyrus, it was clear the people could wait no longer. He read the introduction and moved directly into the admonitions to the churches.

"To the angel of the church of Ephesus write, 'These things says He who holds the seven stars in His right hand, who walks in the midst of the seven golden lampstands: "I know your works, your labor, your patience, and that you cannot bear those who are evil. And you have tested those who say they are apostles and are not, and have found them liars; and you have persevered and have patience, and have labored for

My name's sake and have not become weary." ' "

At this John glanced up and saw smiles.

" ' "Nevertheless I have this against you, that you have left your first love. Remember therefore from where you have fallen; repent and do the first works, or else I will come to you quickly and remove your lampstand from its place—unless you repent.

" ' "But this you have, that you hate the deeds of the Nicolaitans, which I also hate.

" ' "He who has an ear, let him hear what the Spirit says to the churches. To him who overcomes I will give to eat from the tree of life, which is in the midst of the Paradise of God." ' "

"Beloved," John said, "as was made clear in the introduction, the seven stars are the angels—or leaders—of the seven churches in Asia, and the seven lampstands are the churches themselves. The Lord gave me similar exhortations to the six other churches that have been under my care. I have debated with my colleague whether to share those with you, and we have concluded that it would be instructive. But let us examine first what God is saying to us here. When He tells me to write to the angel of the church of Ephesus, you may wonder who that is, with Timothy now departed and my having been away from you so long. I believe He is referring to Polycarp. And though he is young and must follow in the footsteps of beloved predecessors like Paul, Timothy, and Tychicus—"

"Not to mention you!" Polycarp called out, and the people laughed.

"And while he is neither yet your pastor nor your bishop, we have conferred upon him the role of an elder. Regardless, the message to the angel of each church is in reality a message to the people as well. It is to be conferred upon the leaders so they can reveal it to those under their charge.

"Now, when the Lord refers to this body's ability to discern between the real and the deceitful, I believe He is recognizing your fearlessness in testing those who have falsely claimed authority they did not have. And in the four decades since the founding of this church, you have endured and been found faithful to your original purpose, to lift up the name of Christ and His reputation.

"But the Lord says He has *this* against us, and so it behooves us to know what *this* is. He is referring to the dimming of our first love of Christ. Our zeal and our service cannot cover that our passion for the risen Christ has grown stale.

"He does give us this, however, for which we must be grateful: that we resisted the Nicolaitans. Only those new to us would be unaware of the apostasy that invaded when we once made a deacon of a false believer. Nicolas led us into sin, immorality, and sensual temptation. As believers and saints, we enjoy grace and liberty from the law, but Nicolas would have had us pervert this as license to act as we pleased. Praise God He recognizes that we hated such heresy as He does.

"And when the Lord promises, 'To him who overcomes I will give to eat from the tree of life, which is in the midst of the Paradise of God,' I trust you see this immediately as His promise that believers will one day join him in heaven.

"And now let me read to you what He revealed to me for the six other churches:

"'And to the angel of the church in Smyrna write, "These things says the First and the Last, who was dead, and came to life . . ."'"

Suddenly it seemed as if the years had melted away from the beloved disciple. He was doing what he had been born to do—preach and teach and exhort. He grew animated, began to move about, looking this and that one in the eye, asking that his listeners interact with him aloud. "The 'angel' at the church in Smyrna is?" he said.

"The pastor or the bishop," someone called out.

"Excellent, yes. And that is who currently?"

The people laughed, for everyone was aware that the position was vacant and that John had long sought someone to fill it. He could not tell them whom he had in mind for the role, for it would have vexed them and drawn their attention from the important matter at hand.

"All right, who is the 'first and last'? Come, come, you know this. We have studied the ancient texts."

"God," a man called out.

"Yes, of course. The Holy Scriptures refer to Him in just that way. And so who is He 'who was dead, and came to life'?"

A long pause.

"Jesus?" one suggested timidly.

"Why did you not all cry out His name in unison? For years I have taught you that Jesus, the One who died for our sins and arose on the third day *is* the Son of God and is God Himself! Listen now to what He says to the church at Smyrna:

" 'I know your works, tribulation, and poverty (but you are rich); and I know the blasphemy of those who say they are Jews and are not, but are a synagogue of Satan.' "

"What is Jesus saying here, people? The believers in the beautiful port city of Smyrna work tirelessly for the kingdom of God despite tribulation from Rome. The rest of the city worships the emperor and even offers annual sacrifices, which believers in the Lord Christ must not and cannot do. For this reason they are labeled blasphemers and rebels. They are in poverty materially—indeed, many are slaves—but Jesus reminds them they are rich in the spiritual realm.

"Now, who are these who say they are Jews really of Satan? Those who inform Rome of the disobedience of the church of Christ. A true Jew would recognize his Messiah, but these rather attempt to destroy His followers.

"Jesus goes on to say:

" 'Do not fear any of those things which you are about to suffer. Indeed, the devil is about to throw some of you into prison, that you may be tested, and you will have tribulation ten days. Be faithful until death, and I will give you the crown of life.'

"Oh, beloved!" John said, his mind fixed on Polycarp. "Martyrdom will surely come for some in Smyrna. Now you know why my heart is so heavy and I am troubled about whom I dare send to lead that flock. And yet our Lord tells us not to fear, for even such victims will one day receive the crown of life from the Master Himself."

John continued, reading the letter to the church in Pergamos, whom He told to repent of their acceptance of false teaching "or else I will come to you quickly and will fight against them with the sword of My mouth. He who has an ear, let him hear what the Spirit says to the churches. To him who overcomes I will give some of the hidden manna to eat. And I will give him a white stone, and on the stone a new name written which no one knows except him who receives it."

John looked up from his writings. "When God refers to the 'sword of My mouth,' He is speaking of judgment and the words Jesus will use to pronounce it. The hidden manna is Jesus, who called Himself the Bread of Life. And as we award victors in athletic contests a white stone, so the Lord will reward us, also giving us a new name."

After reading the letters of warning to the church at Thyatira, which tolerated sin, and to Sardis (the dead church), John came to the church at Philadelphia. To this faithful church Jesus promised, "Because you have kept My command to persevere, I also will keep you from the hour of trial which shall come upon the whole world, to test those who dwell on the earth.

"Behold, I am coming quickly! Hold fast what you have, that no one may take your crown. He who overcomes, I will make him a pillar in the temple of My God, and he shall go out no more. And I will write on him the name of My God and the name of the city of My God, the New Jerusalem, which comes down out of heaven from My God. And I will write on him My new name."

John asked for a chair and a cup of water. Polycarp approached, concern on his face, but John waved him off. "I can continue a few more minutes," he said. "Thank you." After a sip, he stood again. "Finally we come to the sad letter from the living Christ to the church at wealthy Laodicea.

"And to the angel of the church of the Laodiceans write, 'These things says the Amen, the Faithful and True Witness, the Beginning of the creation of God: "I know your works, that you are neither cold nor hot. I could wish you were cold or hot. So then, because you are lukewarm, and neither cold nor hot, I will vomit you out of My mouth.

" ' "Because you say, 'I am rich, have become wealthy, and have need of nothing'—and do not know that you are wretched, miserable, poor, blind, and naked—I counsel you to buy from Me gold refined in the fire, that you may be rich; and white garments, that you may be clothed, that the shame of your nakedness may not be revealed; and anoint your eyes with eye salve, that you may see.

" ' "As many as I love, I rebuke and chasten. Therefore be zealous and repent. Behold, I stand at the door and knock. If anyone hears My voice and opens the door, I will come in to him and dine with him, and he with Me. To him who overcomes I will grant to sit with Me on My throne, as I also overcame and sat down with My Father on His throne.

" ' "He who has an ear, let him hear what the Spirit says to the churches." ' "

John carefully handed the manuscript to Polycarp. "I shall sit now, if you will indulge me," the old man said to the assembled. "But I know that some of the language the Lord gave me needs clarification. Allow me to explain some of it as my colleague reads the revelation.

"As you can see, dear children, there is much here that is rich and deep and worthy of intense study over several months. You will find this even more so with what Elder Polycarp reads, and I dare say the scope and supernaturalness of it will astound you."

TWENTY-FIVE

John sat directly behind Polycarp, where he could judge the response of the Ephesian church while the young man read from the revelation God gave John in the cave of marble on the Isle of Patmos. He knew that for the rest of the evening he would relive the most profound experience of his life, since seeing for himself the resurrected Christ on that Lord's Day so long before and living through his own intended execution so recently.

John believed the people would respond in much the way he had, as if they too were transported to heaven with an angel of God as their guide.

Polycarp began:

"After these things I looked, and behold, a door standing open in heaven. And the first voice which I heard was like a trumpet speaking with me, saying, 'Come up here, and I will show you things which must take place after this.'

"Immediately I was in the Spirit; and behold, a throne set in heaven, and One sat on the throne. And He who sat there was like a jasper and a sardius stone in appearance; and there was a rainbow around the throne, in appearance like an emerald.

"Around the throne were twenty-four thrones, and on the thrones I saw twenty-four elders sitting, clothed in white robes; and they had crowns of gold on their heads. And from the throne proceeded lightnings, thunderings, and voices. Seven lamps of fire were burning before the throne, which are the seven Spirits of God."

The images cascaded over the Ephesians until they appeared overwhelmed.

"What does it mean?" a woman cried out, and several shushed her.

"No!" John said. "It is all right. I too was puzzled, and I was there. I should say, in the Spirit I was there. What troubles you most?"

"All of it!" she said. "Who are the twenty-four elders?"

"I believe they represent the church, and a little later you will see that they sing songs of worship to the Lamb, who is, of course, the risen Christ."

"And the seven spirits?"

"The sevenfold ministry of the Holy Spirit," John said.

Polycarp said, "Isaiah prophesied of this. He writes, 'There shall come forth a Rod from the stem of Jesse'—that's David's father—'and a Branch shall grow out of his roots.' That's Jesus. 'The spirit of the Lord shall rest upon Him,'—and here are the seven-fold manifestations of the Spirit—'the Spirit of wisdom and understanding, the Spirit of counsel and might, the spirit of knowledge and the fear of the Lord.' So, wisdom, understanding, counsel, strength, knowledge, reverence, and deity."

"Forgive me," the woman whispered.

"Do not apologize, dear one," John said. "If you have found this much curious, you can only imagine what is coming. It concerns a great evil one, an enemy of Christ. Polycarp and I will attempt to explain it all in time to come."

Polycarp did wonders with the text, despite his lack of sleep, because, John decided, the young man had read and reread John's scribbling and had himself begun to understand the import of the message.

As Polycarp continued, the church heard the majestic and terrifying language of God Himself, as He revealed to John what was to come. They sat rapt, gasping, moaning, weeping, sometimes sliding from their seats to kneel or even to lie prostrate as the spectacular, otherworldly words filled the room. At times John could not contain himself and rose to summarize. "Not long after the reappearance of Jesus in the clouds will come a seven-year period of tribulations so devastating that twenty-one curses and plagues will be hurled from heaven. Finally will come the glorious reappearing of Jesus on the earth to set up a millennial kingdom of peace."

Polycarp continued:

"Before the throne there was a sea of glass, like crystal. And in the midst of the throne, and around the throne, were four living creatures full of eyes in front and in back.

"The first living creature was like a lion, the second living creature like a calf, the third living creature had a face like a man, and the fourth living creature was like a flying eagle.

"The four living creatures, each having six wings, were full of eyes around and within. And they do not rest day or night, saying:

'Holy, holy, holy,
Lord God Almighty,
Who was and is and is to come!' "

A man stood, causing John to lay a hand on Polycarp's shoulder. "Yes, sir," John said. "A question?"

"This is all so thrilling," the man said, near tears. "But I fear I am not understanding. Who are these creatures? What do they represent?"

"They are angels," John said. "I know this not only because I saw them. The great prophet Ezekiel called them cherubim. Their many eyes allow them to miss nothing, and that they have faces like a lion, a calf, a man, and an eagle makes me conclude that they represent wild beasts, passive beasts, human beings, and flying creatures."

"And why six wings?" the man said.

"Isaiah," John said, "writes that with two they covered their eyes, with two they covered their feet, and with two they flew. So four of their wings have to do with worship, covering their eyes from looking at Almighty God in His glory, and covering their feet because they, as Moses, stand on holy ground."

The man nodded and sat, and Polycarp continued.

"Whenever the living creatures give glory and honor and thanks to Him who sits on the throne, who lives forever and ever, the twenty-four elders fall down before Him who sits on the throne and worship Him who lives forever and ever, and cast their crowns before the throne, saying:

'You are worthy, O Lord,
To receive glory and honor and power;
For You created all things,

And by Your will they exist and were created.'

"And I saw in the right hand of Him who sat on the throne a scroll written inside and on the back, sealed with seven seals. Then I saw a strong angel proclaiming with a loud voice, 'Who is worthy to open the scroll and to loose its seals?'

"And no one in heaven or on the earth or under the earth was able to open the scroll, or to look at it. So I wept much, because no one was found worthy to open and read the scroll, or to look at it. But one of the elders said to me, 'Do not weep. Behold, the Lion of the tribe of Judah, the Root of David, has prevailed to open the scroll and to loose its seven seals.'

"And I looked, and behold, in the midst of the throne and of the four living creatures, and in the midst of the elders, stood a Lamb as though it had been slain, having seven horns and seven eyes, which are the seven Spirits of God sent out into all the earth. Then He came and took the scroll out of the right hand of Him who sat on the throne.

"Now when He had taken the scroll, the four living creatures and the twenty-four elders fell down before the Lamb, each having a harp, and golden bowls full of incense, which are the prayers of the saints. And they sang a new song, saying:

'You are worthy to take the scroll,
And to open its seals;
For You were slain,

And have redeemed us to God by Your blood
Out of every tribe and tongue and people and
  nation,
And have made us kings and priests to our God;
And we shall reign on the earth.'"

Here Polycarp paused and looked to John. "Master, may we assume the scroll is a contract of some sort, or a will?"

John stood. "No, though that is a logical conclusion. I believe God is giving Jesus here the title deed to the earth. Once the search was over for the worthy One to open the scroll, the heavens rejoiced. Please read on."

Polycarp did.

"Then I looked, and I heard the voice of many angels around the throne, the living creatures, and the elders; and the number of them was ten thousand times ten thousand, and thousands of thousands, saying with a loud voice:

'Worthy is the Lamb who was slain
To receive power and riches and wisdom,
And strength and honor and glory and blessing!'

"And every creature which is in heaven and on the earth and under the earth and such as are in the sea, and all that are in them, I heard saying:

'Blessing and honor and glory and power
Be to Him who sits on the throne,

And to the Lamb, forever and ever!'

"Then the four living creatures said, 'Amen!' And the twenty-four elders fell down and worshiped Him who lives forever and ever."

By now most in the house were on their faces on the floor, praising God and crying out in prayer. Polycarp paused and let this continue several minutes. When people began returning to their chairs and benches, he said, "Now hear me. I am reluctant to press on, given the myriad questions that can arise over every phrase. However, we must. Let us get the entire revelation read aloud so it is in your ears and in your hearts. I have told John that I will supervise the making of copies of this so that while we are working out all the richness of doctrine contained herein—probably over the next several months, if not years—your brothers and sisters everywhere will be able to do the same."

"Now I saw when the Lamb opened one of the seals; and I heard one of the four living creatures saying with a voice like thunder, 'Come and see.' And I looked, and behold, a white horse. He who sat on it had a bow; and a crown was given to him, and he went out conquering and to conquer.

"When He opened the second seal, I heard the second living creature saying, 'Come and see.'

"Another horse, fiery red, went out. And it was granted to the one who sat on it to take peace from the earth, and that people should kill one another; and there was given to him a great sword.

"When He opened the third seal, I heard the third living creature say, 'Come and see.' So I looked, and behold, a black horse, and he who sat on it had a pair of scales in his hand.

"And I heard a voice in the midst of the four living creatures saying, 'A quart of wheat for a denarius, and three quarts of barley for a denarius; and do not harm the oil and the wine.'

"When He opened the fourth seal, I heard the voice of the fourth living creature saying, 'Come and see.' So I looked, and behold, a pale horse. And the name of him who sat on it was Death, and Hades followed with him. And power was given to them over a fourth of the earth, to kill with sword, with hunger, with death, and by the beasts of the earth."

"Excuse me," came the voice of a young man John knew was still in his teens. "I know you wish to press on, but plainly we must understand these four horsemen."

Polycarp looked to John, who stood again.

"When I saw the rider of the white horse with a bow, there is a reason I did not add that he had arrows, for he did not. This is a proclaimer of peace, but it is a false peace. Someone has crowned him and he goes out to conquer, but his battles will be bloodless and true peace only artificial. He will be honored and given a place of high authority, but his peace and his reign shall not last.

"The second rider, on the red horse of war, is, you will notice, granted the ability to take peace from the earth. God remains in control. Nothing happens without His granting it. The false peace will end. War will ensue.

"The black horse represents the famine that results from war. The scales indicate the required rationing of food. And notice the exorbitant price of food. An entire day's wage for barely enough wheat to feed one person. So do not let your oil and wine go bad. You will need them.

"War and famine lead to death, and God told me the fourth rider, mounted on the pale horse, was named Death."

Polycarp asked the people whether they had absorbed enough for one night. As one they urged him to continue. He turned to John, who cocked his head and nodded.

"When He opened the fifth seal, I saw under the altar the souls of those who had been slain for the word of God and for the testimony which they held. And they cried with a loud voice, saying, 'How long, O Lord, holy and true, until You judge and avenge our blood on those who dwell on the earth?'

"Then a white robe was given to each of them; and it was said to them that they should rest a little while longer, until both the number of their fellow servants and their brethren, who would be killed as they were, was completed.

"I looked when He opened the sixth seal, and behold, there was a great earthquake; and the sun became black as sackcloth of hair, and the moon became like blood. And the stars of heaven fell to the earth, as a fig tree drops its late figs when it is shaken by a mighty wind.

"Then the sky receded as a scroll when it is rolled up, and every mountain and island was moved out of its place. And the kings of the earth, the great men, the rich men, the commanders, the mighty men, every slave, and every free man, hid themselves in the caves and in the rocks of the mountains, and said to the mountains and rocks, 'Fall on us and hide us from the face of Him who sits on the throne and from the wrath of the Lamb! For the great day of His wrath has come, and who is able to stand?' "

Polycarp read passage after passage as the night skies grew black and breezes chilled the listeners. Many sat holding each other, comforting each other as the strange, terrifying images filled the air. The bulk of the passages covered a long treatise on the three separate sets of seven curses from heaven—the seal judgments, the trumpet judgments, and the bowl judgments. John noticed many wide eyes and ashen faces as Polycarp read of hail and fire and blood from heaven, the sea turning to blood, a great star falling, the sun dimmed, the earth overrun by locusts, and a horde of two hundred million demonic horsemen that kill millions.

Polycarp soon reached a most triumphant portion that drove even John to his knees.

"After these things I looked, and behold, a great multitude which no one could number, of all nations, tribes, peoples, and tongues, standing before the throne and before the Lamb, clothed with white robes, with palm branches in their hands, and crying out with a loud voice, saying, 'Salvation belongs to our God who sits on the throne, and to the Lamb!'

"All the angels stood around the throne and the elders and the four living creatures, and fell on their faces before the throne and worshiped God, saying:

'Amen! Blessing and glory and wisdom,
Thanksgiving and honor and power and might,
Be to our God forever and ever.
Amen.'

"Then one of the elders answered, saying to me, 'Who are these arrayed in white robes, and where did they come from?'

"And I said to him, 'Sir, you know.'

"So he said to me, 'These are the ones who come out of the great tribulation, and washed their robes and made them white in the blood of the Lamb. Therefore they are before the throne of God, and serve Him day and night in His temple. And He who sits on the throne will dwell among them. They shall neither hunger anymore nor thirst anymore; the sun shall not strike them, nor any heat; for the Lamb who is in the midst of the throne will shepherd them and lead them to living fountains of waters. And God will wipe away every tear from their eyes.'"

John sensed a sigh of relief as the faithful took in this

godly promise. He knew more evidence of bloodshed and mayhem was to come, but he was amazed anew at the fear and wonder it instilled. Sores were prophesied that would afflict unbelievers and make them wish they were dead, people would be scorched by a devastating sun, darkness would descend so black that it caused pain, the Euphrates River would dry up, and an earthquake would strike the entire world.

But John also looked forward to the great finish of the revelation, from which he knew his beloved brothers and sisters in Christ could take deep encouragement. Finally, finally, Polycarp neared the end.

"Now I saw heaven opened, and behold, a white horse. And He who sat on him was called Faithful and True, and in righteousness He judges and makes war. His eyes were like a flame of fire, and on His head were many crowns. He had a name written that no one knew except Himself. He was clothed with a robe dipped in blood, and His name is called The Word of God. And the armies in heaven, clothed in fine linen, white and clean, followed Him on white horses.

"Now out of His mouth goes a sharp sword, that with it He should strike the nations. And He Himself will rule them with a rod of iron. He Himself treads the winepress of the fierceness and wrath of Almighty God. And He has on His robe and on His thigh a name written:

KING OF KINGS
AND LORD OF LORDS.

"Then I saw an angel standing in the sun; and he cried with a loud voice, saying to all the birds that fly in the midst of heaven, 'Come and gather together for the supper of the great God, that you may eat the flesh of kings, the flesh of captains, the flesh of mighty men, the flesh of horses and of those who sit on them, and the flesh of all people, free and slave, both small and great.'

"And I saw the beast, the kings of the earth, and their armies, gathered together to make war against Him who sat on the horse and against His army.

"Then the beast was captured, and with him the false prophet who worked signs in his presence, by which he deceived those who received the mark of the beast and those who worshiped his image. These two were cast alive into the lake of fire burning with brimstone. And the rest were killed with the sword which proceeded from the mouth of Him who sat on the horse. And all the birds were filled with their flesh.

"Then I saw an angel coming down from heaven, having the key to the bottomless pit and a great chain in his hand. He laid hold of the dragon, that serpent of old, who is the Devil and Satan, and bound him for a thousand years; and he cast him into the bottomless pit, and shut him up, and set a seal on him, so that he should deceive the nations no more till the thousand years were finished. But after these things he must be released for a little while.

"And I saw thrones, and they sat on them, and judgment was committed to them. Then I saw the souls of those who had been beheaded for their witness to Jesus and for the word of God, who had not worshiped the beast or his image, and had not received his mark on their foreheads or on their hands. And they lived and reigned with Christ for a thousand years. But the rest of the dead did not live again until the thousand years were finished. This is the first resurrection.

"Blessed and holy is he who has part in the first resurrection. Over such the second death has no power, but they shall be priests of God and of Christ, and shall reign with Him a thousand years. Now when the thousand years have expired, Satan will be released from his prison and will go out to deceive the nations which are in the four corners of the earth, Gog and Magog, to gather them together to battle, whose number is as the sand of the sea.

"They went up on the breadth of the earth and surrounded the camp of the saints and the beloved city. And fire came down from God out of heaven and devoured them. The devil, who deceived them, was cast into the lake of fire and brimstone where the beast and the false prophet are. And they will be tormented day and night forever and ever.

"Then I saw a great white throne and Him who sat on it, from whose face the earth and the heaven fled away. And there was found no place for them. And I saw the dead, small and great, standing before God, and books were opened. And another book was opened, which is the Book of Life. And the dead were judged according to their works, by the things which were written in the books.

"The sea gave up the dead who were in it, and Death and Hades delivered up the dead who were in them. And they were judged, each one according to his works. Then Death and Hades were cast into the lake of fire. This is the second death.

"And anyone not found written in the Book of Life was cast into the lake of fire.

"Now I saw a new heaven and a new earth, for the first heaven and the first earth had passed away. Also there was no more sea.

"Then I, John, saw the holy city, New Jerusalem, coming down out of heaven from God, prepared as a bride adorned for her husband. And I heard a loud voice from heaven saying, 'Behold, the tabernacle of God is with men, and He will dwell with them, and they shall be His people. God Himself will be with them and be their God. And God will wipe away every tear from their eyes; there shall be no more death, nor sorrow, nor crying. There shall be no more pain, for the former things have passed away.'

"Then He who sat on the throne said, 'Behold, I make all things new.' And He said to me, 'Write, for these words are true and faithful.' And He said to me, 'It is done! I am the Alpha and the Omega, the Beginning and the End. I will give of the fountain of the water of life freely to him who thirsts. He who overcomes shall inherit all things, and I will be his God and he shall be My son. But the cowardly, unbelieving, abominable, murderers, sexually immoral, sorcerers, idolaters, and all liars shall have their part in the lake which burns with fire and brimstone, which is the second death.'

"Then one of the seven angels who had the seven bowls filled with the seven last plagues came to me and talked with me, saying, 'Come, I will show you the bride, the Lamb's wife.' And he carried me away in the Spirit to a great and high mountain, and showed me the great city, the holy Jerusalem, descending out of heaven from God, having the glory of God. Her light was like a most precious stone, like a jasper stone, clear as crystal. Also she had a great and high wall with twelve gates, and twelve angels at the gates, and names written on them, which are the names of the twelve tribes of the children of Israel: three gates on the east, three gates on the north, three gates on the south, and three gates on the west.

"Now the wall of the city had twelve foundations, and on them were the names of the twelve apostles of the Lamb. And he who talked with me had a gold reed to measure the city, its gates, and its wall. The city is laid out as a square; its length is as great as its breadth. And he measured the city with the reed: twelve thousand furlongs. Its length, breadth, and height are equal. Then he measured its wall: one hundred and forty-four cubits, according to the measure of a man, that is, of an angel. The construction of its wall was of jasper; and the city was pure gold, like clear glass.

"The foundations of the wall of the city were

adorned with all kinds of precious stones: the first foundation was jasper, the second sapphire, the third chalcedony, the fourth emerald, the fifth sardonyx, the sixth sardius, the seventh chrysolite, the eighth beryl, the ninth topaz, the tenth chrysoprase, the eleventh jacinth, and the twelfth amethyst.

"The twelve gates were twelve pearls: each individual gate was of one pearl. And the street of the city was pure gold, like transparent glass. But I saw no temple in it, for the Lord God Almighty and the Lamb are its temple. The city had no need of the sun or of the moon to shine in it, for the glory of God illuminated it. The Lamb is its light.

"And the nations of those who are saved shall walk in its light, and the kings of the earth bring their glory and honor into it. Its gates shall not be shut at all by day (there shall be no night there). And they shall bring the glory and the honor of the nations into it. But there shall by no means enter it anything that defiles, or causes an abomination or a lie, but only those who are written in the Lamb's Book of Life.

"And he showed me a pure river of water of life, clear as crystal, proceeding from the throne of God and of the Lamb. In the middle of its street, and on either side of the river, was the tree of life, which bore twelve fruits, each tree yielding its fruit every month. The leaves of the tree were for the healing of the nations. And there shall be no more curse, but the throne of God and of the Lamb shall be in it, and His servants shall serve Him. They shall see His face, and

His name shall be on their foreheads.

"There shall be no night there: They need no lamp nor light of the sun, for the Lord God gives them light. And they shall reign forever and ever."

John realized exactly where Polycarp was in the text, and so he stood. Several around him noticed and stood with him. Polycarp stopped and said, "Rabbi, would you care to finish this yourself?"

John moved forward and the entire assembly came to its feet. Polycarp stepped behind him as the old man tilted the papyrus to the light. Quivering, his voice thick with emotion, he read:

"Then he said to me, 'These words are faithful and true.' And the Lord God of the holy prophets sent His angel to show His servants the things which must shortly take place. 'Behold, I am coming quickly! Blessed is he who keeps the words of the prophecy of this book.'

"Now I, John, saw and heard these things. And when I heard and saw, I fell down to worship before the feet of the angel who showed me these things. Then he said to me, 'See that you do not do that. For I am your fellow servant, and of your brethren the prophets, and of those who keep the words of this book. Worship God.'

"And he said to me, 'Do not seal the words of the prophecy of this book, for the time is at hand. He who is unjust, let him be unjust still; he who is filthy, let him be filthy still; he who is righteous, let him be righteous still; he who is holy, let him be holy still.'"

"Forgive me," a man said. "I know you are nearly finished, but I am confused. What was God telling you there?"

Others tried to quiet him, scowling, apparently eager to have John finish. But the elderly revelator raised a hand. "I believe he is simply saying that once this has come to pass, the sinners and the forgiven will have sealed their own fates. If you have been unjust and filthy, that you shall remain. And if you have been righteous and holy, that you shall remain."

The man nodded, and John continued:

" 'And behold, I am coming quickly, and My reward is with Me, to give to every one according to his work. I am the Alpha and the Omega, the Beginning and the End, the First and the Last.'

"Blessed are those who do His commandments, that they may have the right to the tree of life, and may enter through the gates into the city. But outside are dogs and sorcerers and sexually immoral and murderers and idolaters, and whoever loves and practices a lie.

" 'I, Jesus, have sent My angel to testify to you these things in the churches. I am the Root and the Offspring of David, the Bright and Morning Star.'

"And the Spirit and the bride say, 'Come!' And let him who hears say, 'Come!' And let him who thirsts come. Whoever desires, let him take the water of life freely.

"For I testify to everyone who hears the words of the prophecy of this book: If anyone adds to these things,

God will add to him the plagues that are written in this book; and if anyone takes away from the words of the book of this prophecy, God shall take away his part from the Book of Life, from the holy city, and from the things which are written in this book.

"He who testifies to these things says, 'Surely I am coming quickly.' Amen. Even so, come, Lord Jesus!

"The grace of our Lord Jesus Christ be with you all. Amen."

IT WAS AFTER MIDNIGHT, and John was as weary as he had been at the end of any day on Patmos. He sat on the pallet in his chamber. Polycarp sat in the chair at the table, facing him.

"When you must sleep, dismiss me," Polycarp said, elbows on his knees, resting his red-bearded chin on his fists. "I am as exhausted as you look. And yet I won't sleep. Not after that."

"I do not know why my eyes remain open," John said. "But I would not sleep either. The tasks related to the revelation weigh heavy upon me."

"We already have many volunteers," Polycarp said. "And I will supervise them. The work will not fall to you."

"Do you know," John said, smiling, "that I feared this was too much for the people when the reading was only half done?"

Polycarp threw his head back and laughed heartily. "I had the same concern! That they would be so dumbstruck with fear that they would not want to go home. That we would spend the rest of the night comforting them and praying with them."

As it was, people had lingered for hours, raising questions, praying, talking among themselves.

Finally Polycarp rose. "I must let you sleep, master, or at least try to sleep. But let me also tell you before I take my leave that today was one of the most fulfilling of my life. Having come to faith in Christ, having the privilege of serving under you, penning your gospel, and now reading the revelation Jesus Himself gave you . . . nothing else can compare."

"Just one more moment," John said, motioning that Polycarp should sit again. "I need tell you of an assignment I wish for you to prayerfully consider, as soon as your work with the copying of the revelation is complete. You need take it first to the church at Smyrna."

"With great joy," Polycarp said.

"And there you must stay, as they have need of a bishop."

"I know of that vacancy, rabbi. You wish me to fill in, teaching them the revelation, until a bishop is appointed?"

John shook his head. "A bishop has been appointed, son. You are the man."

EPILOGUE

F ollowing this, John, failing rapidly, dictated to Polycarp the three epistles that would become known as First, Second, and Third John. Less than a month later the beloved apostle John died in his sleep—the only one of Jesus' twelve disciples to die a natural death. His eyewitness account of the miracles of Jesus, his three epistles, and the revelation he received on the Isle of Patmos became five of the twenty-seven books of the New Testament. His gospel has become known as the Gospel of Belief and is considered by many the cornerstone of the first four books of the New Testament, establishing Jesus as the Son of God and Savior of the world.

In the early years of the second century, Caesar Trajan decreed that Christians must unite with their pagan neighbors and worship their gods. So resolute was Ignatius in his opposition that he boldly spoke against Rome, even while Trajan was sojourning in Antioch.

Ignatius was dragged before the emperor to answer charges of violating the imperial edict and inciting others to do the same. Ignatius saw this as his opportunity to give his very life for Christ, as he had long desired. So he was not only forthright in his response, but also showed a spirit of exultation.

Frustrated with him, Trajan had Ignatius bound and

delivered to Rome to be fed to beasts in the Flavian amphitheater for the entertainment of the people. During the trip Ignatius wrote to the churches of Asia, exhorting the people to obey their bishops and beware of heresy. But primarily he pleaded with them to not interfere or in any way hamper the designs of the empire on his life. He did not want to be deprived of his opportunity for martyrdom. And he was granted his heart's deepest desire.

Polycarp served more than fifty years as Bishop of Smyrna and became known as a steadfast witness of truth.

Legend says that when he was arrested he warmly greeted the Roman soldiers and offered them food. They granted his request that he be allowed to pray before they hauled him to Rome, and for two hours he prayed aloud. Many of the soldiers repented.

Facing death in the Colosseum, Polycarp was urged by one of the judges to renounce his faith and save himself. "Reverence thy old age," the judge said. "Swear by Caesar's Fortune . . . and I will set thee at liberty; reproach Christ!"

Polycarp responded, "Eighty and six years have I now served Christ, and He has never done me the least wrong: how then can I blaspheme my King and my Savior?"

The judge said, "I have wild beasts ready; to those I will cast you unless you repent."

"Call for them then," Polycarp said. "For we Christians are fixed in our minds not to change from good to evil; but for me it will be good to be changed from evil to good."

Furious, the judge said, "Seeing that you despise the wild beasts, I will cause you to be devoured by fire, unless you repent."

"You threaten me with fire, which burns for an hour and is then extinguished; but do you not know of the fire of the future judgment of that eternal punishment which is reserved for the ungodly? But why tarry? Bring forth what you will!"

They took Polycarp to the stake to nail him there, but he said, "He who has given me strength to endure the fire will also enable me, without your securing me by nails, to stand without moving in the pile." And so he was merely tied to the stake.

After Polycarp had prayed and thanked God for "bringing me to this day, and to this hour; that I should have a part in the number of your martyrs," the executioner lit the fire. However, the flames arched around Polycarp like a sail of a ship, and he would not burn. Finally the executioner was commanded to stab him with a sword. So much blood flowed that it extinguished the fire. The fire had to be rekindled to burn Polycarp's body to ashes.

THE WORDS
OF JOHN

JOHN

The Eternal Word

1 In the beginning was the Word, and the Word was with God, and the Word was God. [2]He was in the beginning with God. [3]All things were made through Him, and without Him nothing was made that was made. [4]In Him was life, and the life was the light of men. [5]And the light shines in the darkness, and the darkness did not comprehend[a] it.

John's Witness:
The True Light

[6]There was a man sent from God, whose name *was* John. [7]This man came for a witness, to bear witness of the Light, that all through him might believe. [8]He was not that Light, but *was sent* to bear witness of that Light. [9]That was the true Light which gives light to every man coming into the world.[a]

[10]He was in the world, and the world was made through Him, and the world did not know Him. [11]He came to His own,[a] and His own[b] did not receive Him.

¹²But as many as received Him, to them He gave the right to become children of God, to those who believe in His name: ¹³who were born, not of blood, nor of the will of the flesh, nor of the will of man, but of God.

The Word Becomes Flesh

¹⁴And the Word became flesh and dwelt among us, and we beheld His glory, the glory as of the only begotten of the Father, full of grace and truth.

¹⁵John bore witness of Him and cried out, saying, "This was He of whom I said, 'He who comes after me is preferred before me, for He was before me.' "

¹⁶And[a] of His fullness we have all received, and grace for grace. ¹⁷For the law was given through Moses, *but* grace and truth came through Jesus Christ. ¹⁸No one has seen God at any time. The only begotten Son,[a] who is in the bosom of the Father, He has declared *Him.*

A Voice in the Wilderness

¹⁹Now this is the testimony of John, when the Jews sent priests and Levites from Jerusalem to ask him, "Who are you?"

²⁰He confessed, and did not deny, but confessed, "I am not the Christ."

²¹And they asked him, "What then? Are you Elijah?" He said, "I am not."

"Are you the Prophet?"

And he answered, "No."

²²Then they said to him, "Who are you, that we may

give an answer to those who sent us? What do you say about yourself?"

²³He said: "I *am*

'The voice of one crying in the wilderness:
"Make straight the way of the LORD," 'ᵃ

As the prophet Isaiah said."

²⁴Now those who were sent were from the Pharisees. ²⁵And they asked him, saying, "Why then do you baptize if you are not the Christ, nor Elijah, nor the Prophet?"

²⁶John answered them, saying, "I baptize with water, but there stands One among you whom you do not know. ²⁷It is He who, coming after me, is preferred before me, whose sandal strap I am not worthy to loose."

²⁸These things were done in Bethabaraᵃ beyond the Jordan, where John was baptizing.

The Lamb of God

²⁹The next day John saw Jesus coming toward him, and said, "Behold! The Lamb of God who takes away the sin of the world! ³⁰This is He of whom I said, 'After me comes a Man who is preferred before me, for He was before me.' ³¹I did not know Him; but that He should be revealed to Israel, therefore I came baptizing with water."

³²And John bore witness, saying, "I saw the Spirit descending from heaven like a dove, and He remained

upon Him. [33]I did not know Him, but He who sent me to baptize with water said to me, 'Upon whom you see the Spirit descending, and remaining on Him, this is He who baptizes with the Holy Spirit.' [34]And I have seen and testified that this is the Son of God."

The First Disciples

[35]Again, the next day, John stood with two of his disciples. [36]And looking at Jesus as He walked, he said, "Behold the Lamb of God!"

[37]The two disciples heard him speak, and they followed Jesus. [38]Then Jesus turned, and seeing them following, said to them, "What do you seek?"

They said to Him, "Rabbi" (which is to say, when translated, Teacher), "where are You staying?"

[39]He said to them, "Come and see." They came and saw where He was staying, and remained with Him that day (now it was about the tenth hour).

[40]One of the two who heard John *speak,* and followed Him, was Andrew, Simon Peter's brother. [41]He first found his own brother Simon, and said to him, "We have found the Messiah" (which is translated, the Christ). [42]And he brought him to Jesus.

Now when Jesus looked at him, He said, "You are Simon the son of Jonah.[a] You shall be called Cephas" (which is translated, A Stone).

Philip and Nathanael

[43]The following day Jesus wanted to go to Galilee, and He found Philip and said to him, "Follow Me."

[44]Now Philip was from Bethsaida, the city of Andrew and Peter. [45]Philip found Nathanael and said to him, "We have found Him of whom Moses in the law, and also the prophets, wrote—Jesus of Nazareth, the son of Joseph."

[46]And Nathanael said to him, "Can anything good come out of Nazareth?"

Philip said to him, "Come and see."

[47]Jesus saw Nathanael coming toward Him, and said of him, "Behold, an Israelite indeed, in whom is no deceit!"

[48]Nathanael said to Him, "How do You know me?"

Jesus answered and said to him, "Before Philip called you, when you were under the fig tree, I saw you."

[49]Nathanael answered and said to Him, "Rabbi, You are the Son of God! You are the King of Israel!"

[50]Jesus answered and said to him, "Because I said to you, 'I saw you under the fig tree,' do you believe? You will see greater things than these." [51]And He said to him, "Most assuredly, I say to you, hereafter[a] you shall see heaven open, and the angels of God ascending and descending upon the Son of Man."

Water Turned to Wine

2 On the third day there was a wedding in Cana of Galilee, and the mother of Jesus was there. [2]Now both Jesus and His disciples were invited to the wedding. [3]And when they ran out of wine, the mother of Jesus said to Him, "They have no wine."

⁴Jesus said to her, "Woman, what does your concern have to do with Me? My hour has not yet come."

⁵His mother said to the servants, "Whatever He says to you, do *it*."

⁶Now there were set there six waterpots of stone, according to the manner of purification of the Jews, containing twenty or thirty gallons apiece. ⁷Jesus said to them, "Fill the waterpots with water." And they filled them up to the brim. ⁸And He said to them, "Draw *some* out now, and take *it* to the master of the feast." And they took *it*. ⁹When the master of the feast had tasted the water that was made wine, and did not know where it came from (but the servants who had drawn the water knew), the master of the feast called the bridegroom. ¹⁰And he said to him, "Every man at the beginning sets out the good wine, and when the *guests* have well drunk, then the inferior. You have kept the good wine until now!"

¹¹This beginning of signs Jesus did in Cana of Galilee, and manifested His glory; and His disciples believed in Him.

¹²After this He went down to Capernaum, He, His mother, His brothers, and His disciples; and they did not stay there many days.

Jesus Cleanses the Temple

¹³Now the Passover of the Jews was at hand, and Jesus went up to Jerusalem. ¹⁴And He found in the temple those who sold oxen and sheep and doves, and the money changers doing business. ¹⁵When He had

made a whip of cords, He drove them all out of the temple, with the sheep and the oxen, and poured out the changers' money and overturned the tables. ¹⁶And He said to those who sold doves, "Take these things away! Do not make My Father's house a house of merchandise!" ¹⁷Then His disciples remembered that it was written, *"Zeal for Your house has eaten*[a] *Me up."*[b]

¹⁸So the Jews answered and said to Him, "What sign do You show to us, since You do these things?"

¹⁹Jesus answered and said to them, "Destroy this temple, and in three days I will raise it up."

²⁰Then the Jews said, "It has taken forty-six years to build this temple, and will You raise it up in three days?"

²¹But He was speaking of the temple of His body. ²²Therefore, when He had risen from the dead, His disciples remembered that He had said this to them;[a] and they believed the Scripture and the word which Jesus had said.

The Discerner of Hearts

²³Now when He was in Jerusalem at the Passover, during the feast, many believed in His name when they saw the signs which He did. ²⁴But Jesus did not commit Himself to them, because He knew all *men,* ²⁵and had no need that anyone should testify of man, for He knew what was in man.

The New Birth

3 There was a man of the Pharisees named Nicodemus, a ruler of the Jews. ²This man came to Jesus by night and said to Him, "Rabbi, we know that You are a teacher come from God; for no one can do these signs that You do unless God is with him."

³Jesus answered and said to him, "Most assuredly, I say to you, unless one is born again, he cannot see the kingdom of God."

⁴Nicodemus said to Him, "How can a man be born when he is old? Can he enter a second time into his mother's womb and be born?"

⁵Jesus answered, "Most assuredly, I say to you, unless one is born of water and the Spirit, he cannot enter the kingdom of God. ⁶That which is born of the flesh is flesh, and that which is born of the Spirit is spirit. ⁷Do not marvel that I said to you, 'You must be born again.' ⁸The wind blows where it wishes, and you hear the sound of it, but cannot tell where it comes from and where it goes. So is everyone who is born of the Spirit."

⁹Nicodemus answered and said to Him, "How can these things be?"

¹⁰Jesus answered and said to him, "Are you the teacher of Israel, and do not know these things? ¹¹Most assuredly, I say to you, We speak what We know and testify what We have seen, and you do not receive Our witness. ¹²If I have told you earthly things and you do not believe, how will you believe if I tell you heavenly

things? [13]No one has ascended to heaven but He who came down from heaven, *that is,* the Son of Man who is in heaven.[a] [14]And as Moses lifted up the serpent in the wilderness, even so must the Son of Man be lifted up, [15]that whoever believes in Him should not perish but[a] have eternal life. [16]For God so loved the world that He gave His only begotten Son, that whoever believes in Him should not perish but have everlasting life. [17]For God did not send His Son into the world to condemn the world, but that the world through Him might be saved.

[18]"He who believes in Him is not condemned; but he who does not believe is condemned already, because he has not believed in the name of the only begotten Son of God. [19]And this is the condemnation, that the light has come into the world, and men loved darkness rather than light, because their deeds were evil. [20]For everyone practicing evil hates the light and does not come to the light, lest his deeds should be exposed. [21]But he who does the truth comes to the light, that his deeds may be clearly seen, that they have been done in God."

John the Baptist Exalts Christ
[22]After these things Jesus and His disciples came into the land of Judea, and there He remained with them and baptized. [23]Now John also was baptizing in Aenon near Salim, because there was much water there. And they came and were baptized. [24]For John had not yet been thrown into prison.

²⁵Then there arose a dispute between *some* of John's disciples and the Jews about purification. ²⁶And they came to John and said to him, "Rabbi, He who was with you beyond the Jordan, to whom you have testified—behold, He is baptizing, and all are coming to Him!"

²⁷John answered and said, "A man can receive nothing unless it has been given to him from heaven. ²⁸You yourselves bear me witness, that I said, 'I am not the Christ,' but, 'I have been sent before Him.' ²⁹He who has the bride is the bridegroom; but the friend of the bridegroom, who stands and hears him, rejoices greatly because of the bridegroom's voice. Therefore this joy of mine is fulfilled. ³⁰He must increase, but I *must* decrease. ³¹He who comes from above is above all; he who is of the earth is earthly and speaks of the earth. He who comes from heaven is above all. ³²And what He has seen and heard, that He testifies; and no one receives His testimony. ³³He who has received His testimony has certified that God is true. ³⁴For He whom God has sent speaks the words of God, for God does not give the Spirit by measure. ³⁵The Father loves the Son, and has given all things into His hand. ³⁶He who believes in the Son has everlasting life; and he who does not believe the Son shall not see life, but the wrath of God abides on him."

A Samaritan Woman
Meets Her Messiah

4 Therefore, when the Lord knew that the Pharisees had heard that Jesus made and baptized more disciples than John ²(though Jesus Himself did not baptize, but His disciples), ³He left Judea and departed again to Galilee. ⁴But He needed to go through Samaria.

⁵So He came to a city of Samaria which is called Sychar, near the plot of ground that Jacob gave to his son Joseph. ⁶Now Jacob's well was there. Jesus therefore, being wearied from *His* journey, sat thus by the well. It was about the sixth hour.

⁷A woman of Samaria came to draw water. Jesus said to her, "Give Me a drink." ⁸For His disciples had gone away into the city to buy food.

⁹Then the woman of Samaria said to Him, "How is it that You, being a Jew, ask a drink from me, a Samaritan woman?" For Jews have no dealings with Samaritans.

¹⁰Jesus answered and said to her, "If you knew the gift of God, and who it is who says to you, 'Give Me a drink,' you would have asked Him, and He would have given you living water."

¹¹The woman said to Him, "Sir, You have nothing to draw with, and the well is deep. Where then do You get that living water? ¹²Are You greater than our father Jacob, who gave us the well, and drank from it himself, as well as his sons and his livestock?"

¹³Jesus answered and said to her, "Whoever drinks of this water will thirst again, ¹⁴but whoever drinks of the water that I shall give him will never thirst. But the water that I shall give him will become in him a fountain of water springing up into everlasting life."

¹⁵The woman said to Him, "Sir, give me this water, that I may not thirst, nor come here to draw."

¹⁶Jesus said to her, "Go, call your husband, and come here."

¹⁷The woman answered and said, "I have no husband."

Jesus said to her, "You have well said, 'I have no husband,' ¹⁸for you have had five husbands, and the one whom you now have is not your husband; in that you spoke truly."

¹⁹The woman said to Him, "Sir, I perceive that You are a prophet. ²⁰Our fathers worshiped on this mountain, and you *Jews* say that in Jerusalem is the place where one ought to worship."

²¹Jesus said to her, "Woman, believe Me, the hour is coming when you will neither on this mountain, nor in Jerusalem, worship the Father. ²²You worship what you do not know; we know what we worship, for salvation is of the Jews. ²³But the hour is coming, and now is, when the true worshipers will worship the Father in spirit and truth; for the Father is seeking such to worship Him. ²⁴God *is* Spirit, and those who worship Him must worship in spirit and truth."

²⁵The woman said to Him, "I know that Messiah is

coming" (who is called Christ). "When He comes, He will tell us all things."

²⁶Jesus said to her, "I who speak to you am *He.*"

The Whitened Harvest

²⁷And at this *point* His disciples came, and they marveled that He talked with a woman; yet no one said, "What do You seek?" or, "Why are You talking with her?"

²⁸The woman then left her waterpot, went her way into the city, and said to the men, ²⁹"Come, see a Man who told me all things that I ever did. Could this be the Christ?" ³⁰Then they went out of the city and came to Him.

³¹In the meantime His disciples urged Him, saying, "Rabbi, eat."

³²But He said to them, "I have food to eat of which you do not know."

³³Therefore the disciples said to one another, "Has anyone brought Him *anything* to eat?"

³⁴Jesus said to them, "My food is to do the will of Him who sent Me, and to finish His work. ³⁵Do you not say, 'There are still four months and *then* comes the harvest'? Behold, I say to you, lift up your eyes and look at the fields, for they are already white for harvest! ³⁶And he who reaps receives wages, and gathers fruit for eternal life, that both he who sows and he who reaps may rejoice together. ³⁷For in this the saying is true: 'One sows and another reaps.' ³⁸I sent you to reap that for which you have not labored;

others have labored, and you have entered into their labors."

The Savior of the World

[39]And many of the Samaritans of that city believed in Him because of the word of the woman who testified, "He told me all that I *ever* did." [40]So when the Samaritans had come to Him, they urged Him to stay with them; and He stayed there two days. [41]And many more believed because of His own word.

[42]Then they said to the woman, "Now we believe, not because of what you said, for we ourselves have heard *Him* and we know that this is indeed the Christ,[a] the Savior of the world."

Welcome at Galilee

[43]Now after the two days He departed from there and went to Galilee. [44]For Jesus Himself testified that a prophet has no honor in his own country. [45]So when He came to Galilee, the Galileans received Him, having seen all the things He did in Jerusalem at the feast; for they also had gone to the feast.

A Nobleman's Son Healed

[46]So Jesus came again to Cana of Galilee where He had made the water wine. And there was a certain nobleman whose son was sick at Capernaum. [47]When he heard that Jesus had come out of Judea into Galilee, he went to Him and implored Him to come down and heal his son, for he was at the point of death. [48]Then

Jesus said to him, "Unless you *people* see signs and wonders, you will by no means believe."

⁴⁹The nobleman said to Him, "Sir, come down before my child dies!"

⁵⁰Jesus said to him, "Go your way; your son lives." So the man believed the word that Jesus spoke to him, and he went his way. ⁵¹And as he was now going down, his servants met him and told *him,* saying, "Your son lives!"

⁵²Then he inquired of them the hour when he got better. And they said to him, "Yesterday at the seventh hour the fever left him." ⁵³So the father knew that *it was* at the same hour in which Jesus said to him, "Your son lives." And he himself believed, and his whole household.

⁵⁴This again *is* the second sign Jesus did when He had come out of Judea into Galilee.

A Man Healed
at the Pool of Bethesda

5 After this there was a feast of the Jews, and Jesus went up to Jerusalem. ²Now there is in Jerusalem by the Sheep *Gate* a pool, which is called in Hebrew, Bethesda,ᵃ having five porches. ³In these lay a great multitude of sick people, blind, lame, paralyzed, waiting for the moving of the water. ⁴For an angel went down at a certain time into the pool and stirred up the water; then whoever stepped in first, after the stirring of the water, was made well of whatever disease he had.ᵃ ⁵Now a certain man was there who had

an infirmity thirty-eight years. ⁶When Jesus saw him lying there, and knew that he already had been *in that condition* a long time, He said to him, "Do you want to be made well?"

⁷The sick man answered Him, "Sir, I have no man to put me into the pool when the water is stirred up; but while I am coming, another steps down before me."

⁸Jesus said to him, "Rise, take up your bed and walk." ⁹And immediately the man was made well, took up his bed, and walked.

And that day was the Sabbath. ¹⁰The Jews therefore said to him who was cured, "It is the Sabbath; it is not lawful for you to carry your bed."

¹¹He answered them, "He who made me well said to me, 'Take up your bed and walk.' "

¹²Then they asked him, "Who is the Man who said to you, 'Take up your bed and walk'?" ¹³But the one who was healed did not know who it was, for Jesus had withdrawn, a multitude being in *that* place. ¹⁴Afterward Jesus found him in the temple, and said to him, "See, you have been made well. Sin no more, lest a worse thing come upon you."

¹⁵The man departed and told the Jews that it was Jesus who had made him well.

Honor the Father and the Son

¹⁶For this reason the Jews persecuted Jesus, and sought to kill Him,ᵃ because He had done these things on the Sabbath. ¹⁷But Jesus answered them, "My

Father has been working until now, and I have been working."

¹⁸Therefore the Jews sought all the more to kill Him, because He not only broke the Sabbath, but also said that God was His Father, making Himself equal with God. ¹⁹Then Jesus answered and said to them, "Most assuredly, I say to you, the Son can do nothing of Himself, but what He sees the Father do; for whatever He does, the Son also does in like manner. ²⁰For the Father loves the Son, and shows Him all things that He Himself does; and He will show Him greater works than these, that you may marvel. ²¹For as the Father raises the dead and gives life to *them,* even so the Son gives life to whom He will. ²²For the Father judges no one, but has committed all judgment to the Son, ²³that all should honor the Son just as they honor the Father. He who does not honor the Son does not honor the Father who sent Him.

Life and Judgment
Are Through the Son

²⁴"Most assuredly, I say to you, he who hears My word and believes in Him who sent Me has everlasting life, and shall not come into judgment, but has passed from death into life. ²⁵Most assuredly, I say to you, the hour is coming, and now is, when the dead will hear the voice of the Son of God; and those who hear will live. ²⁶For as the Father has life in Himself, so He has granted the Son to have life in Himself, ²⁷and has given Him authority to execute judgment

also, because He is the Son of Man. ²⁸Do not marvel at this; for the hour is coming in which all who are in the graves will hear His voice ²⁹and come forth—those who have done good, to the resurrection of life, and those who have done evil, to the resurrection of condemnation. ³⁰I can of Myself do nothing. As I hear, I judge; and My judgment is righteous, because I do not seek My own will but the will of the Father who sent Me.

The Fourfold Witness

³¹"If I bear witness of Myself, My witness is not true. ³²There is another who bears witness of Me, and I know that the witness which He witnesses of Me is true. ³³You have sent to John, and he has borne witness to the truth. ³⁴Yet I do not receive testimony from man, but I say these things that you may be saved. ³⁵He was the burning and shining lamp, and you were willing for a time to rejoice in his light. ³⁶But I have a greater witness than John's; for the works which the Father has given Me to finish—the very works that I do—bear witness of Me, that the Father has sent Me. ³⁷And the Father Himself, who sent Me, has testified of Me. You have neither heard His voice at any time, nor seen His form. ³⁸But you do not have His word abiding in you, because whom He sent, Him you do not believe. ³⁹You search the Scriptures, for in them you think you have eternal life; and these are they which testify of Me. ⁴⁰But you are not willing to come to Me that you may have life.

⁴¹"I do not receive honor from men. ⁴²But I know you, that you do not have the love of God in you. ⁴³I have come in My Father's name, and you do not receive Me; if another comes in his own name, him you will receive. ⁴⁴How can you believe, who receive honor from one another, and do not seek the honor that *comes* from the only God? ⁴⁵Do not think that I shall accuse you to the Father; there is *one* who accuses you—Moses, in whom you trust. ⁴⁶For if you believed Moses, you would believe Me; for he wrote about Me. ⁴⁷But if you do not believe his writings, how will you believe My words?"

Feeding the Five Thousand

6 After these things Jesus went over the Sea of Galilee, which is *the Sea* of Tiberias. ²Then a great multitude followed Him, because they saw His signs which He performed on those who were diseased. ³And Jesus went up on the mountain, and there He sat with His disciples.

⁴Now the Passover, a feast of the Jews, was near. ⁵Then Jesus lifted up *His* eyes, and seeing a great multitude coming toward Him, He said to Philip, "Where shall we buy bread, that these may eat?" ⁶But this He said to test him, for He Himself knew what He would do.

⁷Philip answered Him, "Two hundred denarii worth of bread is not sufficient for them, that every one of them may have a little."

⁸One of His disciples, Andrew, Simon Peter's

brother, said to Him, [9]"There is a lad here who has five barley loaves and two small fish, but what are they among so many?"

[10]Then Jesus said, "Make the people sit down." Now there was much grass in the place. So the men sat down, in number about five thousand. [11]And Jesus took the loaves, and when He had given thanks He distributed *them* to the disciples, and the disciples[a] to those sitting down; and likewise of the fish, as much as they wanted. [12]So when they were filled, He said to His disciples, "Gather up the fragments that remain, so that nothing is lost." [13]Therefore they gathered *them* up, and filled twelve baskets with the fragments of the five barley loaves which were left over by those who had eaten. [14]Then those men, when they had seen the sign that Jesus did, said, "This is truly the Prophet who is to come into the world."

Jesus Walks on the Sea

[15]Therefore when Jesus perceived that they were about to come and take Him by force to make Him king, He departed again to the mountain by Himself alone.

[16]Now when evening came, His disciples went down to the sea, [17]got into the boat, and went over the sea toward Capernaum. And it was already dark, and Jesus had not come to them. [18]Then the sea arose because a great wind was blowing. [19]So when they had rowed about three or four miles,[a] they saw Jesus walking on the sea and drawing near the boat; and they were

afraid. [20]But He said to them, "It is I; do not be afraid." [21]Then they willingly received Him into the boat, and immediately the boat was at the land where they were going.

The Bread from Heaven

[22]On the following day, when the people who were standing on the other side of the sea saw that there was no other boat there, except that one which His disciples had entered,[a] and that Jesus had not entered the boat with His disciples, but His disciples had gone away alone—[23]however, other boats came from Tiberias, near the place where they ate bread after the Lord had given thanks—[24]when the people therefore saw that Jesus was not there, nor His disciples, they also got into boats and came to Capernaum, seeking Jesus. [25]And when they found Him on the other side of the sea, they said to Him, "Rabbi, when did You come here?"

[26]Jesus answered them and said, "Most assuredly, I say to you, you seek Me, not because you saw the signs, but because you ate of the loaves and were filled. [27]Do not labor for the food which perishes, but for the food which endures to everlasting life, which the Son of Man will give you, because God the Father has set His seal on Him."

[28]Then they said to Him, "What shall we do, that we may work the works of God?"

[29]Jesus answered and said to them, "This is the work of God, that you believe in Him whom He sent."

[30]Therefore they said to Him, "What sign will You perform then, that we may see it and believe You? What work will You do? [31]Our fathers ate the manna in the desert; as it is written, *'He gave them bread from heaven to eat.'*"[a]

[32]Then Jesus said to them, "Most assuredly, I say to you, Moses did not give you the bread from heaven, but My Father gives you the true bread from heaven. [33]For the bread of God is He who comes down from heaven and gives life to the world."

[34]Then they said to Him, "Lord, give us this bread always."

[35]And Jesus said to them, "I am the bread of life. He who comes to Me shall never hunger, and he who believes in Me shall never thirst. [36]But I said to you that you have seen Me and yet do not believe. [37]All that the Father gives Me will come to Me, and the one who comes to Me I will by no means cast out. [38]For I have come down from heaven, not to do My own will, but the will of Him who sent Me. [39]This is the will of the Father who sent Me, that of all He has given Me I should lose nothing, but should raise it up at the last day. [40]And this is the will of Him who sent Me, that everyone who sees the Son and believes in Him may have everlasting life; and I will raise him up at the last day."

Rejected by His Own

[41]The Jews then complained about Him, because He said, "I am the bread which came down from heaven."

⁴²And they said, "Is not this Jesus, the son of Joseph, whose father and mother we know? How is it then that He says, 'I have come down from heaven'?"

⁴³Jesus therefore answered and said to them, "Do not murmur among yourselves. ⁴⁴No one can come to Me unless the Father who sent Me draws him; and I will raise him up at the last day. ⁴⁵It is written in the prophets, *'And they shall all be taught by God.'*ᵃ Therefore everyone who has heard and learnedᵇ from the Father comes to Me. ⁴⁶Not that anyone has seen the Father, except He who is from God; He has seen the Father. ⁴⁷Most assuredly, I say to you, he who believes in Meᵃ has everlasting life. ⁴⁸I am the bread of life. ⁴⁹Your fathers ate the manna in the wilderness, and are dead. ⁵⁰This is the bread which comes down from heaven, that one may eat of it and not die. ⁵¹I am the living bread which came down from heaven. If anyone eats of this bread, he will live forever; and the bread that I shall give is My flesh, which I shall give for the life of the world."

⁵²The Jews therefore quarreled among themselves, saying, "How can this Man give us *His* flesh to eat?"

⁵³Then Jesus said to them, "Most assuredly, I say to you, unless you eat the flesh of the Son of Man and drink His blood, you have no life in you. ⁵⁴Whoever eats My flesh and drinks My blood has eternal life, and I will raise him up at the last day. ⁵⁵For My flesh is food indeed,ᵃ and My blood is drink indeed. ⁵⁶He who eats My flesh and drinks My blood abides in Me, and I in him. ⁵⁷As the living Father sent Me, and I live

because of the Father, so he who feeds on Me will live because of Me. [58]This is the bread which came down from heaven—not as your fathers ate the manna, and are dead. He who eats this bread will live forever."

[59]These things He said in the synagogue as He taught in Capernaum.

Many Disciples Turn Away

[60]Therefore many of His disciples, when they heard *this,* said, "This is a hard saying; who can understand it?"

[61]When Jesus knew in Himself that His disciples complained about this, He said to them, "Does this offend you? [62]*What* then if you should see the Son of Man ascend where He was before? [63]It is the Spirit who gives life; the flesh profits nothing. The words that I speak to you are spirit, and *they* are life. [64]But there are some of you who do not believe." For Jesus knew from the beginning who they were who did not believe, and who would betray Him. [65]And He said, "Therefore I have said to you that no one can come to Me unless it has been granted to him by My Father."

[66]From that *time* many of His disciples went back and walked with Him no more. [67]Then Jesus said to the twelve, "Do you also want to go away?"

[68]But Simon Peter answered Him, "Lord, to whom shall we go? You have the words of eternal life. [69]Also we have come to believe and know that You are the Christ, the Son of the living God."[a]

[70]Jesus answered them, "Did I not choose you, the

twelve, and one of you is a devil?" ⁷¹He spoke of Judas Iscariot, *the son* of Simon, for it was he who would betray Him, being one of the twelve.

Jesus' Brothers Disbelieve

7 After these things Jesus walked in Galilee; for He did not want to walk in Judea, because the Jews^a sought to kill Him. ²Now the Jews' Feast of Tabernacles was at hand. ³His brothers therefore said to Him, "Depart from here and go into Judea, that Your disciples also may see the works that You are doing. ⁴For no one does anything in secret while he himself seeks to be known openly. If You do these things, show Yourself to the world." ⁵For even His brothers did not believe in Him.

⁶Then Jesus said to them, "My time has not yet come, but your time is always ready. ⁷The world cannot hate you, but it hates Me because I testify of it that its works are evil. ⁸You go up to this feast. I am not yet^a going up to this feast, for My time has not yet fully come." ⁹When He had said these things to them, He remained in Galilee.

The Heavenly Scholar

¹⁰But when His brothers had gone up, then He also went up to the feast, not openly, but as it were in secret. ¹¹Then the Jews sought Him at the feast, and said, "Where is He?" ¹²And there was much complaining among the people concerning Him. Some said, "He is good"; others said, "No, on the contrary,

He deceives the people." [13]However, no one spoke openly of Him for fear of the Jews.

[14]Now about the middle of the feast Jesus went up into the temple and taught. [15]And the Jews marveled, saying, "How does this Man know letters, having never studied?"

[16]Jesus[a] answered them and said, "My doctrine is not Mine, but His who sent Me. [17]If anyone wills to do His will, he shall know concerning the doctrine, whether it is from God or *whether* I speak on My own *authority.* [18]He who speaks from himself seeks his own glory; but He who seeks the glory of the One who sent Him is true, and no unrighteousness is in Him. [19]Did not Moses give you the law, yet none of you keeps the law? Why do you seek to kill Me?"

[20]The people answered and said, "You have a demon. Who is seeking to kill You?"

[21]Jesus answered and said to them, "I did one work, and you all marvel. [22]Moses therefore gave you circumcision (not that it is from Moses, but from the fathers), and you circumcise a man on the Sabbath. [23]If a man receives circumcision on the Sabbath, so that the law of Moses should not be broken, are you angry with Me because I made a man completely well on the Sabbath? [24]Do not judge according to appearance, but judge with righteous judgment."

Could This Be the Christ?

[25]Now some of them from Jerusalem said, "Is this not He whom they seek to kill? [26]But look! He speaks

boldly, and they say nothing to Him. Do the rulers know indeed that this is truly[a] the Christ? [27]However, we know where this Man is from; but when the Christ comes, no one knows where He is from."

[28]Then Jesus cried out, as He taught in the temple, saying, "You both know Me, and you know where I am from; and I have not come of Myself, but He who sent Me is true, whom you do not know. [29]But[a] I know Him, for I am from Him, and He sent Me."

[30]Therefore they sought to take Him; but no one laid a hand on Him, because His hour had not yet come. [31]And many of the people believed in Him, and said, "When the Christ comes, will He do more signs than these which this *Man* has done?"

Jesus and the Religious Leaders

[32]The Pharisees heard the crowd murmuring these things concerning Him, and the Pharisees and the chief priests sent officers to take Him. [33]Then Jesus said to them,[a] "I shall be with you a little while longer, and *then* I go to Him who sent Me. [34]You will seek Me and not find *Me,* and where I am you cannot come."

[35]Then the Jews said among themselves, "Where does He intend to go that we shall not find Him? Does He intend to go to the Dispersion among the Greeks and teach the Greeks? [36]What is this thing that He said, 'You will seek Me and not find Me, and where I am you cannot come'?"

The Promise of the Holy Spirit

[37]On the last day, that great *day* of the feast, Jesus stood and cried out, saying, "If anyone thirsts, let him come to Me and drink. [38]He who believes in Me, as the Scripture has said, out of his heart will flow rivers of living water." [39]But this He spoke concerning the Spirit, whom those believing[a] in Him would receive; for the Holy[b] Spirit was not yet *given,* because Jesus was not yet glorified.

Who Is He?

[40]Therefore many[a] from the crowd, when they heard this saying, said, "Truly this is the Prophet." [41]Others said, "This is the Christ."

But some said, "Will the Christ come out of Galilee? [42]Has not the Scripture said that the Christ comes from the seed of David and from the town of Bethlehem, where David was?" [43]So there was a division among the people because of Him. [44]Now some of them wanted to take Him, but no one laid hands on Him.

Rejected by the Authorities

[45]Then the officers came to the chief priests and Pharisees, who said to them, "Why have you not brought Him?"

[46]The officers answered, "No man ever spoke like this Man!"

[47]Then the Pharisees answered them, "Are you also deceived? [48]Have any of the rulers or the Pharisees

believed in Him? [49]But this crowd that does not know the law is accursed."

[50]Nicodemus (he who came to Jesus by night,[a] being one of them) said to them, [51]"Does our law judge a man before it hears him and knows what he is doing?"

[52]They answered and said to him, "Are you also from Galilee? Search and look, for no prophet has arisen[a] out of Galilee."

An Adulteress Faces
the Light of the World

[53]And everyone went to his *own* house.[a]

8 But Jesus went to the Mount of Olives. [2]Now early[a] in the morning He came again into the temple, and all the people came to Him; and He sat down and taught them. [3]Then the scribes and Pharisees brought to Him a woman caught in adultery. And when they had set her in the midst, [4]they said to Him, "Teacher, this woman was caught[a] in adultery, in the very act. [5]Now Moses, in the law, commanded[a] us that such should be stoned.[b] But what do You say?"[c] [6]This they said, testing Him, that they might have *something* of which to accuse Him. But Jesus stooped down and wrote on the ground with *His* finger, as though He did not hear.[a]

[7]So when they continued asking Him, He raised Himself up[a] and said to them, "He who is without sin among you, let him throw a stone at her first." [8]And again He stooped down and wrote on the ground. [9]Then those who heard *it,* being convicted by *their*

conscience,[a] went out one by one, beginning with the oldest *even* to the last. And Jesus was left alone, and the woman standing in the midst. [10]When Jesus had raised Himself up and saw no one but the woman, He said to her,[a] "Woman, where are those accusers of yours?[a] Has no one condemned you?"

[11]She said, "No one, Lord."

And Jesus said to her, "Neither do I condemn you; go and[a] sin no more."

[12]Then Jesus spoke to them again, saying, "I am the light of the world. He who follows Me shall not walk in darkness, but have the light of life."

Jesus Defends His Self-Witness

[13]The Pharisees therefore said to Him, "You bear witness of Yourself; Your witness is not true."

[14]Jesus answered and said to them, "Even if I bear witness of Myself, My witness is true, for I know where I came from and where I am going; but you do not know where I come from and where I am going. [15]You judge according to the flesh; I judge no one. [16]And yet if I do judge, My judgment is true; for I am not alone, but I *am* with the Father who sent Me. [17]It is also written in your law that the testimony of two men is true. [18]I am One who bears witness of Myself, and the Father who sent Me bears witness of Me."

[19]Then they said to Him, "Where is Your Father?"

Jesus answered, "You know neither Me nor My Father. If you had known Me, you would have known My Father also."

20These words Jesus spoke in the treasury, as He taught in the temple; and no one laid hands on Him, for His hour had not yet come.

Jesus Predicts His Departure

21Then Jesus said to them again, "I am going away, and you will seek Me, and will die in your sin. Where I go you cannot come."

22So the Jews said, "Will He kill Himself, because He says, 'Where I go you cannot come'?"

23And He said to them, "You are from beneath; I am from above. You are of this world; I am not of this world. 24Therefore I said to you that you will die in your sins; for if you do not believe that I am *He,* you will die in your sins."

25Then they said to Him, "Who are You?"

And Jesus said to them, "Just what I have been saying to you from the beginning. 26I have many things to say and to judge concerning you, but He who sent Me is true; and I speak to the world those things which I heard from Him."

27They did not understand that He spoke to them of the Father.

28Then Jesus said to them, "When you lift up the Son of Man, then you will know that I am *He,* and *that* I do nothing of Myself; but as My Father taught Me, I speak these things. 29And He who sent Me is with Me. The Father has not left Me alone, for I always do those things that please Him." 30As He spoke these words, many believed in Him.

The Truth Shall Make You Free

[31]Then Jesus said to those Jews who believed Him, "If you abide in My word, you are My disciples indeed. [32]And you shall know the truth, and the truth shall make you free."

[33]They answered Him, "We are Abraham's descendants, and have never been in bondage to anyone. How *can* You say, 'You will be made free'?"

[34]Jesus answered them, "Most assuredly, I say to you, whoever commits sin is a slave of sin. [35]And a slave does not abide in the house forever, *but* a son abides forever. [36]Therefore if the Son makes you free, you shall be free indeed.

Abraham's Seed and Satan's

[37]"I know that you are Abraham's descendants, but you seek to kill Me, because My word has no place in you. [38]I speak what I have seen with My Father, and you do what you have seen with[a] your father."

[39]They answered and said to Him, "Abraham is our father."

Jesus said to them, "If you were Abraham's children, you would do the works of Abraham. [40]But now you seek to kill Me, a Man who has told you the truth which I heard from God. Abraham did not do this. [41]You do the deeds of your father."

Then they said to Him, "We were not born of fornication; we have one Father—God."

[42]Jesus said to them, "If God were your Father, you

would love Me, for I proceeded forth and came from God; nor have I come of Myself, but He sent Me. ⁴³Why do you not understand My speech? Because you are not able to listen to My word. ⁴⁴You are of *your* father the devil, and the desires of your father you want to do. He was a murderer from the beginning, and does not stand in the truth, because there is no truth in him. When he speaks a lie, he speaks from his own *resources,* for he is a liar and the father of it. ⁴⁵But because I tell the truth, you do not believe Me. ⁴⁶Which of you convicts Me of sin? And if I tell the truth, why do you not believe Me? ⁴⁷He who is of God hears God's words; therefore you do not hear, because you are not of God."

Before Abraham Was, I AM

⁴⁸Then the Jews answered and said to Him, "Do we not say rightly that You are a Samaritan and have a demon?"

⁴⁹Jesus answered, "I do not have a demon; but I honor My Father, and you dishonor Me. ⁵⁰And I do not seek My *own* glory; there is One who seeks and judges. ⁵¹Most assuredly, I say to you, if anyone keeps My word he shall never see death."

⁵²Then the Jews said to Him, "Now we know that You have a demon! Abraham is dead, and the prophets; and You say, 'If anyone keeps My word he shall never taste death.' ⁵³Are You greater than our father Abraham, who is dead? And the prophets are dead. Who do You make Yourself out to be?"

⁵⁴Jesus answered, "If I honor Myself, My honor is nothing. It is My Father who honors Me, of whom you say that He is your^a God. ⁵⁵Yet you have not known Him, but I know Him. And if I say, 'I do not know Him,' I shall be a liar like you; but I do know Him and keep His word. ⁵⁶Your father Abraham rejoiced to see My day, and he saw *it* and was glad."

⁵⁷Then the Jews said to Him, "You are not yet fifty years old, and have You seen Abraham?"

⁵⁸Jesus said to them, "Most assuredly, I say to you, before Abraham was, I AM."

⁵⁹Then they took up stones to throw at Him; but Jesus hid Himself and went out of the temple,^a going through the midst of them, and so passed by.

A Man Born Blind
Receives Sight

9 Now as *Jesus* passed by, He saw a man who was blind from birth. ²And His disciples asked Him, saying, "Rabbi, who sinned, this man or his parents, that he was born blind?"

³Jesus answered, "Neither this man nor his parents sinned, but that the works of God should be revealed in him. ⁴I^a must work the works of Him who sent Me while it is day; *the* night is coming when no one can work. ⁵As long as I am in the world, I am the light of the world."

⁶When He had said these things, He spat on the ground and made clay with the saliva; and He anointed the eyes of the blind man with the clay. ⁷And

He said to him, "Go, wash in the pool of Siloam" (which is translated, Sent). So he went and washed, and came back seeing.

[8]Therefore the neighbors and those who previously had seen that he was blind[a] said, "Is not this he who sat and begged?"

[9]Some said, "This is he." Others *said,* "He is like him."[a]

He said, "I am *he.*"

[10]Therefore they said to him, "How were your eyes opened?"

[11]He answered and said, "A Man called Jesus made clay and anointed my eyes and said to me, 'Go to the pool of[a] Siloam and wash.' So I went and washed, and I received sight."

[12]Then they said to him, "Where is He?"

He said, "I do not know."

The Pharisees Excommunicate the Healed Man

[13]They brought him who formerly was blind to the Pharisees. [14]Now it was a Sabbath when Jesus made the clay and opened his eyes. [15]Then the Pharisees also asked him again how he had received his sight. He said to them, "He put clay on my eyes, and I washed, and I see."

[16]Therefore some of the Pharisees said, "This Man is not from God, because He does not keep the Sabbath."

Others said, "How can a man who is a sinner do such signs?" And there was a division among them.

¹⁷They said to the blind man again, "What do you say about Him because He opened your eyes?"

He said, "He is a prophet."

¹⁸But the Jews did not believe concerning him, that he had been blind and received his sight, until they called the parents of him who had received his sight. ¹⁹And they asked them, saying, "Is this your son, who you say was born blind? How then does he now see?"

²⁰His parents answered them and said, "We know that this is our son, and that he was born blind; ²¹but by what means he now sees we do not know, or who opened his eyes we do not know. He is of age; ask him. He will speak for himself." ²²His parents said these *things* because they feared the Jews, for the Jews had agreed already that if anyone confessed *that* He *was* Christ, he would be put out of the synagogue. ²³Therefore his parents said, "He is of age; ask him."

²⁴So they again called the man who was blind, and said to him, "Give God the glory! We know that this Man is a sinner."

²⁵He answered and said, "Whether He is a sinner *or not* I do not know. One thing I know: that though I was blind, now I see."

²⁶Then they said to him again, "What did He do to you? How did He open your eyes?"

²⁷He answered them, "I told you already, and you did not listen. Why do you want to hear *it* again? Do you also want to become His disciples?"

²⁸Then they reviled him and said, "You are His disciple, but we are Moses' disciples. ²⁹We know that

God spoke to Moses; *as for* this *fellow,* we do not know where He is from."

³⁰The man answered and said to them, "Why, this is a marvelous thing, that you do not know where He is from; yet He has opened my eyes! ³¹Now we know that God does not hear sinners; but if anyone is a worshiper of God and does His will, He hears him. ³²Since the world began it has been unheard of that anyone opened the eyes of one who was born blind. ³³If this Man were not from God, He could do nothing."

³⁴They answered and said to him, "You were completely born in sins, and are you teaching us?" And they cast him out.

True Vision and True Blindness

³⁵Jesus heard that they had cast him out; and when He had found him, He said to him, "Do you believe in the Son of God?"ᵃ

³⁶He answered and said, "Who is He, Lord, that I may believe in Him?"

³⁷And Jesus said to him, "You have both seen Him and it is He who is talking with you."

³⁸Then he said, "Lord, I believe!" And he worshiped Him.

³⁹And Jesus said, "For judgment I have come into this world, that those who do not see may see, and that those who see may be made blind."

⁴⁰Then *some* of the Pharisees who were with Him heard these words, and said to Him, "Are we blind also?"

311

⁴¹Jesus said to them, "If you were blind, you would have no sin; but now you say, 'We see.' Therefore your sin remains.

Jesus the True Shepherd

10 "Most assuredly, I say to you, he who does not enter the sheepfold by the door, but climbs up some other way, the same is a thief and a robber. ²But he who enters by the door is the shepherd of the sheep. ³To him the doorkeeper opens, and the sheep hear his voice; and he calls his own sheep by name and leads them out. ⁴And when he brings out his own sheep, he goes before them; and the sheep follow him, for they know his voice. ⁵Yet they will by no means follow a stranger, but will flee from him, for they do not know the voice of strangers." ⁶Jesus used this illustration, but they did not understand the things which He spoke to them.

Jesus the Good Shepherd

⁷Then Jesus said to them again, "Most assuredly, I say to you, I am the door of the sheep. ⁸All who *ever* came before Me[a] are thieves and robbers, but the sheep did not hear them. ⁹I am the door. If anyone enters by Me, he will be saved, and will go in and out and find pasture. ¹⁰The thief does not come except to steal, and to kill, and to destroy. I have come that they may have life, and that they may have *it* more abundantly.

¹¹"I am the good shepherd. The good shepherd gives

His life for the sheep. ¹²But a hireling, *he who is* not the shepherd, one who does not own the sheep, sees the wolf coming and leaves the sheep and flees; and the wolf catches the sheep and scatters them. ¹³The hireling flees because he is a hireling and does not care about the sheep. ¹⁴I am the good shepherd; and I know My *sheep,* and am known by My own. ¹⁵As the Father knows Me, even so I know the Father; and I lay down My life for the sheep. ¹⁶And other sheep I have which are not of this fold; them also I must bring, and they will hear My voice; and there will be one flock *and* one shepherd.

¹⁷"Therefore My Father loves Me, because I lay down My life that I may take it again. ¹⁸No one takes it from Me, but I lay it down of Myself. I have power to lay it down, and I have power to take it again. This command I have received from My Father."

¹⁹Therefore there was a division again among the Jews because of these sayings. ²⁰And many of them said, "He has a demon and is mad. Why do you listen to Him?"

²¹Others said, "These are not the words of one who has a demon. Can a demon open the eyes of the blind?"

The Shepherd Knows His Sheep

²²Now it was the Feast of Dedication in Jerusalem, and it was winter. ²³And Jesus walked in the temple, in Solomon's porch. ²⁴Then the Jews surrounded Him

and said to Him, "How long do You keep us in doubt? If You are the Christ, tell us plainly."

²⁵Jesus answered them, "I told you, and you do not believe. The works that I do in My Father's name, they bear witness of Me. ²⁶But you do not believe, because you are not of My sheep, as I said to you.^a ²⁷My sheep hear My voice, and I know them, and they follow Me. ²⁸And I give them eternal life, and they shall never perish; neither shall anyone snatch them out of My hand. ²⁹My Father, who has given *them* to Me, is greater than all; and no one is able to snatch *them* out of My Father's hand. ³⁰I and *My* Father are one."

Renewed Efforts
to Stone Jesus

³¹Then the Jews took up stones again to stone Him. ³²Jesus answered them, "Many good works I have shown you from My Father. For which of those works do you stone Me?"

³³The Jews answered Him, saying, "For a good work we do not stone You, but for blasphemy, and because You, being a Man, make Yourself God."

³⁴Jesus answered them, "Is it not written in your law, *'I said, "You are gods" '*?^a ³⁵If He called them gods, to whom the word of God came (and the Scripture cannot be broken), ³⁶do you say of Him whom the Father sanctified and sent into the world, 'You are blaspheming,' because I said, 'I am the Son of God'? ³⁷If I do not do the works of My Father, do not believe Me;

³⁸but if I do, though you do not believe Me, believe the works, that you may know and believe[a] that the Father *is* in Me, and I in Him." ³⁹Therefore they sought again to seize Him, but He escaped out of their hand.

The Believers Beyond Jordan

⁴⁰And He went away again beyond the Jordan to the place where John was baptizing at first, and there He stayed. ⁴¹Then many came to Him and said, "John performed no sign, but all the things that John spoke about this Man were true." ⁴²And many believed in Him there.

The Death of Lazarus

11 Now a certain *man* was sick, Lazarus of Bethany, the town of Mary and her sister Martha. ²It was *that* Mary who anointed the Lord with fragrant oil and wiped His feet with her hair, whose brother Lazarus was sick. ³Therefore the sisters sent to Him, saying, "Lord, behold, he whom You love is sick."

⁴When Jesus heard *that,* He said, "This sickness is not unto death, but for the glory of God, that the Son of God may be glorified through it."

⁵Now Jesus loved Martha and her sister and Lazarus. ⁶So, when He heard that he was sick, He stayed two more days in the place where He was. ⁷Then after this He said to *the* disciples, "Let us go to Judea again."

⁸*The* disciples said to Him, "Rabbi, lately the Jews

sought to stone You, and are You going there again?"

⁹Jesus answered, "Are there not twelve hours in the day? If anyone walks in the day, he does not stumble, because he sees the light of this world. ¹⁰But if one walks in the night, he stumbles, because the light is not in him." ¹¹These things He said, and after that He said to them, "Our friend Lazarus sleeps, but I go that I may wake him up."

¹²Then His disciples said, "Lord, if he sleeps he will get well." ¹³However, Jesus spoke of his death, but they thought that He was speaking about taking rest in sleep.

¹⁴Then Jesus said to them plainly, "Lazarus is dead. ¹⁵And I am glad for your sakes that I was not there, that you may believe. Nevertheless let us go to him."

¹⁶Then Thomas, who is called the Twin, said to his fellow disciples, "Let us also go, that we may die with Him."

I Am the Resurrection and the Life

¹⁷So when Jesus came, He found that he had already been in the tomb four days. ¹⁸Now Bethany was near Jerusalem, about two miles[a] away. ¹⁹And many of the Jews had joined the women around Martha and Mary, to comfort them concerning their brother.

²⁰Now Martha, as soon as she heard that Jesus was coming, went and met Him, but Mary was sitting in the house. ²¹Now Martha said to Jesus, "Lord, if You had been here, my brother would not have died. ²²But

even now I know that whatever You ask of God, God will give You."

²³Jesus said to her, "Your brother will rise again."

²⁴Martha said to Him, "I know that he will rise again in the resurrection at the last day."

²⁵Jesus said to her, "I am the resurrection and the life. He who believes in Me, though he may die, he shall live. ²⁶And whoever lives and believes in Me shall never die. Do you believe this?"

²⁷She said to Him, "Yes, Lord, I believe that You are the Christ, the Son of God, who is to come into the world."

Jesus and Death, the Last Enemy

²⁸And when she had said these things, she went her way and secretly called Mary her sister, saying, "The Teacher has come and is calling for you." ²⁹As soon as she heard *that,* she arose quickly and came to Him. ³⁰Now Jesus had not yet come into the town, but wasᵃ in the place where Martha met Him. ³¹Then the Jews who were with her in the house, and comforting her, when they saw that Mary rose up quickly and went out, followed her, saying, "She is going to the tomb to weep there."ᵃ

³²Then, when Mary came where Jesus was, and saw Him, she fell down at His feet, saying to Him, "Lord, if You had been here, my brother would not have died."

³³Therefore, when Jesus saw her weeping, and the

317

Jews who came with her weeping, He groaned in the spirit and was troubled. ³⁴And He said, "Where have you laid him?"

They said to Him, "Lord, come and see."

³⁵Jesus wept. ³⁶Then the Jews said, "See how He loved him!"

³⁷And some of them said, "Could not this Man, who opened the eyes of the blind, also have kept this man from dying?"

Lazarus Raised from the Dead

³⁸Then Jesus, again groaning in Himself, came to the tomb. It was a cave, and a stone lay against it. ³⁹Jesus said, "Take away the stone."

Martha, the sister of him who was dead, said to Him, "Lord, by this time there is a stench, for he has been *dead* four days."

⁴⁰Jesus said to her, "Did I not say to you that if you would believe you would see the glory of God?" ⁴¹Then they took away the stone *from the place* where the dead man was lying.ᵃ And Jesus lifted up *His* eyes and said, "Father, I thank You that You have heard Me. ⁴²And I know that You always hear Me, but because of the people who are standing by I said *this,* that they may believe that You sent Me." ⁴³Now when He had said these things, He cried with a loud voice, "Lazarus, come forth!" ⁴⁴And he who had died came out bound hand and foot with graveclothes, and his face was wrapped with a cloth. Jesus said to them, "Loose him, and let him go."

The Plot to Kill Jesus

⁴⁵Then many of the Jews who had come to Mary, and had seen the things Jesus did, believed in Him. ⁴⁶But some of them went away to the Pharisees and told them the things Jesus did. ⁴⁷Then the chief priests and the Pharisees gathered a council and said, "What shall we do? For this Man works many signs. ⁴⁸If we let Him alone like this, everyone will believe in Him, and the Romans will come and take away both our place and nation."

⁴⁹And one of them, Caiaphas, being high priest that year, said to them, "You know nothing at all, ⁵⁰nor do you consider that it is expedient for us[a] that one man should die for the people, and not that the whole nation should perish." ⁵¹Now this he did not say on his own *authority;* but being high priest that year he prophesied that Jesus would die for the nation, ⁵²and not for that nation only, but also that He would gather together in one the children of God who were scattered abroad.

⁵³Then, from that day on, they plotted to put Him to death. ⁵⁴Therefore Jesus no longer walked openly among the Jews, but went from there into the country near the wilderness, to a city called Ephraim, and there remained with His disciples.

⁵⁵And the Passover of the Jews was near, and many went from the country up to Jerusalem before the Passover, to purify themselves. ⁵⁶Then they sought Jesus, and spoke among themselves as they stood in the

temple, "What do you think—that He will not come to the feast?" [57]Now both the chief priests and the Pharisees had given a command, that if anyone knew where He was, he should report *it,* that they might seize Him.

The Anointing at Bethany

12 Then, six days before the Passover, Jesus came to Bethany, where Lazarus was who had been dead,[a] whom He had raised from the dead. [2]There they made Him a supper; and Martha served, but Lazarus was one of those who sat at the table with Him. [3]Then Mary took a pound of very costly oil of spikenard, anointed the feet of Jesus, and wiped His feet with her hair. And the house was filled with the fragrance of the oil.

[4]But one of His disciples, Judas Iscariot, Simon's *son,* who would betray Him, said, [5]"Why was this fragrant oil not sold for three hundred denarii[a] and given to the poor?" [6]This he said, not that he cared for the poor, but because he was a thief, and had the money box; and he used to take what was put in it.

[7]But Jesus said, "Let her alone; she has kept[a] this for the day of My burial. [8]For the poor you have with you always, but Me you do not have always."

The Plot to Kill Lazarus

[9]Now a great many of the Jews knew that He was there; and they came, not for Jesus' sake only, but that they might also see Lazarus, whom He had raised from the dead. [10]But the chief priests plotted to put

Lazarus to death also, ¹¹because on account of him many of the Jews went away and believed in Jesus.

The Triumphal Entry

¹²The next day a great multitude that had come to the feast, when they heard that Jesus was coming to Jerusalem, ¹³took branches of palm trees and went out to meet Him, and cried out:

"Hosanna!
'Blessed is He who comes in the name of the
*LORD!'*ᵃ
The King of Israel!"

¹⁴Then Jesus, when He had found a young donkey, sat on it; as it is written:

¹⁵"Fear not, daughter of Zion;
Behold, your King is coming,
*Sitting on a donkey's colt."*ᵃ

¹⁶His disciples did not understand these things at first; but when Jesus was glorified, then they remembered that these things were written about Him and *that* they had done these things to Him. ¹⁷Therefore the people, who were with Him when He called Lazarus out of his tomb and raised him from the dead, bore witness. ¹⁸For this reason the people also met Him, because they heard that He had done this sign. ¹⁹The Pharisees therefore said among them-

selves, "You see that you are accomplishing nothing. Look, the world has gone after Him!"

The Fruitful Grain of Wheat

²⁰Now there were certain Greeks among those who came up to worship at the feast. ²¹Then they came to Philip, who was from Bethsaida of Galilee, and asked him, saying, "Sir, we wish to see Jesus."

²²Philip came and told Andrew, and in turn Andrew and Philip told Jesus.

²³But Jesus answered them, saying, "The hour has come that the Son of Man should be glorified. ²⁴Most assuredly, I say to you, unless a grain of wheat falls into the ground and dies, it remains alone; but if it dies, it produces much grain. ²⁵He who loves his life will lose it, and he who hates his life in this world will keep it for eternal life. ²⁶If anyone serves Me, let him follow Me; and where I am, there My servant will be also. If anyone serves Me, him *My* Father will honor.

Jesus Predicts His Death
on the Cross

²⁷"Now My soul is troubled, and what shall I say? 'Father, save Me from this hour'? But for this purpose I came to this hour. ²⁸Father, glorify Your name."

Then a voice came from heaven, *saying,* "I have both glorified *it* and will glorify *it* again."

²⁹Therefore the people who stood by and heard *it* said that it had thundered. Others said, "An angel has spoken to Him."

[30]Jesus answered and said, "This voice did not come because of Me, but for your sake. [31]Now is the judgment of this world; now the ruler of this world will be cast out. [32]And I, if I am lifted up from the earth, will draw all *peoples* to Myself." [33]This He said, signifying by what death He would die.

[34]The people answered Him, "We have heard from the law that the Christ remains forever; and how *can* You say, 'The Son of Man must be lifted up'? Who is this Son of Man?"

[35]Then Jesus said to them, "A little while longer the light is with you. Walk while you have the light, lest darkness overtake you; he who walks in darkness does not know where he is going. [36]While you have the light, believe in the light, that you may become sons of light." These things Jesus spoke, and departed, and was hidden from them.

Who Has Believed Our Report?

[37]But although He had done so many signs before them, they did not believe in Him, [38]that the word of Isaiah the prophet might be fulfilled, which he spoke:

"Lord, who has believed our report?
And to whom has the arm of the LORD been
  revealed?"[a]

[39]Therefore they could not believe, because Isaiah said again:

40 *"He has blinded their eyes and hardened their*
 hearts,
Lest they should see with their eyes,
Lest they should understand with their hearts and
 turn,
So that I should heal them. "[a]

41These things Isaiah said when[a] he saw His glory and
spoke of Him.

Walk in the Light

42Nevertheless even among the rulers many believed
in Him, but because of the Pharisees they did not confess *Him,* lest they should be put out of the synagogue;
43for they loved the praise of men more than the praise
of God.

44Then Jesus cried out and said, "He who believes
in Me, believes not in Me but in Him who sent Me.
45And he who sees Me sees Him who sent Me. 46I
have come *as* a light into the world, that whoever
believes in Me should not abide in darkness. 47And if
anyone hears My words and does not believe,[a] I do
not judge him; for I did not come to judge the world
but to save the world. 48He who rejects Me, and does
not receive My words, has that which judges him—
the word that I have spoken will judge him in the last
day. 49For I have not spoken on My own *authority;*
but the Father who sent Me gave Me a command,
what I should say and what I should speak. 50And I
know that His command is everlasting life. There-

fore, whatever I speak, just as the Father has told Me, so I speak."

Jesus Washes
the Disciples' Feet

13 Now before the Feast of the Passover, when Jesus knew that His hour had come that He should depart from this world to the Father, having loved His own who were in the world, He loved them to the end. [2]And supper being ended,[a] the devil having already put it into the heart of Judas Iscariot, Simon's *son,* to betray Him, [3]Jesus, knowing that the Father had given all things into His hands, and that He had come from God and was going to God, [4]rose from supper and laid aside His garments, took a towel and girded Himself. [5]After that, He poured water into a basin and began to wash the disciples' feet, and to wipe *them* with the towel with which He was girded. [6]Then He came to Simon Peter. And *Peter* said to Him, "Lord, are You washing my feet?"

[7]Jesus answered and said to him, "What I am doing you do not understand now, but you will know after this."

[8]Peter said to Him, "You shall never wash my feet!"

Jesus answered him, "If I do not wash you, you have no part with Me."

[9]Simon Peter said to Him, "Lord, not my feet only, but also *my* hands and *my* head!"

[10]Jesus said to him, "He who is bathed needs only to

wash *his* feet, but is completely clean; and you are clean, but not all of you." [11]For He knew who would betray Him; therefore He said, "You are not all clean."

[12]So when He had washed their feet, taken His garments, and sat down again, He said to them, "Do you know what I have done to you? [13]You call Me Teacher and Lord, and you say well, for *so* I am. [14]If I then, *your* Lord and Teacher, have washed your feet, you also ought to wash one another's feet. [15]For I have given you an example, that you should do as I have done to you. [16]Most assuredly, I say to you, a servant is not greater than his master; nor is he who is sent greater than he who sent him. [17]If you know these things, blessed are you if you do them.

Jesus Identifies His Betrayer

[18]"I do not speak concerning all of you. I know whom I have chosen; but that the Scripture may be fulfilled, *'He who eats bread with Me*[a] *has lifted up his heel against Me.'*[b] [19]Now I tell you before it comes, that when it does come to pass, you may believe that I am *He.* [20]Most assuredly, I say to you, he who receives whomever I send receives Me; and he who receives Me receives Him who sent Me."

[21]When Jesus had said these things, He was troubled in spirit, and testified and said, "Most assuredly, I say to you, one of you will betray Me." [22]Then the disciples looked at one another, perplexed about whom He spoke.

[23]Now there was leaning on Jesus' bosom one of His

disciples, whom Jesus loved. [24]Simon Peter therefore motioned to him to ask who it was of whom He spoke.

[25]Then, leaning back[a] on Jesus' breast, he said to Him, "Lord, who is it?"

[26]Jesus answered, "It is he to whom I shall give a piece of bread when I have dipped *it*." And having dipped the bread, He gave *it* to Judas Iscariot, *the son* of Simon. [27]Now after the piece of bread, Satan entered him. Then Jesus said to him, "What you do, do quickly." [28]But no one at the table knew for what reason He said this to him. [29]For some thought, because Judas had the money box, that Jesus had said to him, "Buy *those things* we need for the feast," or that he should give something to the poor.

[30]Having received the piece of bread, he then went out immediately. And it was night.

The New Commandment

[31]So, when he had gone out, Jesus said, "Now the Son of Man is glorified, and God is glorified in Him. [32]If God is glorified in Him, God will also glorify Him in Himself, and glorify Him immediately. [33]Little children, I shall be with you a little while longer. You will seek Me; and as I said to the Jews, 'Where I am going, you cannot come,' so now I say to you. [34]A new commandment I give to you, that you love one another; as I have loved you, that you also love one another. [35]By this all will know that you are My disciples, if you have love for one another."

Jesus Predicts Peter's Denial

[36]Simon Peter said to Him, "Lord, where are You going?"

Jesus answered him, "Where I am going you cannot follow Me now, but you shall follow Me afterward."

[37]Peter said to Him, "Lord, why can I not follow You now? I will lay down my life for Your sake."

[38]Jesus answered him, "Will you lay down your life for My sake? Most assuredly, I say to you, the rooster shall not crow till you have denied Me three times.

The Way, the Truth, and the Life

14 "Let not your heart be troubled; you believe in God, believe also in Me. [2]In My Father's house are many mansions;[a] if *it were* not *so,* I would have told you. I go to prepare a place for you.[b] [3]And if I go and prepare a place for you, I will come again and receive you to Myself; that where I am, *there* you may be also. [4]And where I go you know, and the way you know."

[5]Thomas said to Him, "Lord, we do not know where You are going, and how can we know the way?"

[6]Jesus said to him, "I am the way, the truth, and the life. No one comes to the Father except through Me.

The Father Revealed

[7]"If you had known Me, you would have known My

Father also; and from now on you know Him and have seen Him."

⁸Philip said to Him, "Lord, show us the Father, and it is sufficient for us."

⁹Jesus said to him, "Have I been with you so long, and yet you have not known Me, Philip? He who has seen Me has seen the Father; so how can you say, 'Show us the Father'? ¹⁰Do you not believe that I am in the Father, and the Father in Me? The words that I speak to you I do not speak on My own *authority;* but the Father who dwells in Me does the works. ¹¹Believe Me that I *am* in the Father and the Father in Me, or else believe Me for the sake of the works themselves.

The Answered Prayer

¹²"Most assuredly, I say to you, he who believes in Me, the works that I do he will do also; and greater *works* than these he will do, because I go to My Father. ¹³And whatever you ask in My name, that I will do, that the Father may be glorified in the Son. ¹⁴If you askᵃ anything in My name, I will do *it.*

Jesus Promises Another Helper

¹⁵"If you love Me, keepᵃ My commandments. ¹⁶And I will pray the Father, and He will give you another Helper, that He may abide with you forever—¹⁷the Spirit of truth, whom the world cannot receive, because it neither sees Him nor knows Him; but you know Him, for He dwells with you and will be in you. ¹⁸I will not leave you orphans; I will come to you.

Indwelling of the Father
and the Son

¹⁹"A little while longer and the world will see Me no more, but you will see Me. Because I live, you will live also. ²⁰At that day you will know that I *am* in My Father, and you in Me, and I in you. ²¹He who has My commandments and keeps them, it is he who loves Me. And he who loves Me will be loved by My Father, and I will love him and manifest Myself to him."

²²Judas (not Iscariot) said to Him, "Lord, how is it that You will manifest Yourself to us, and not to the world?"

²³Jesus answered and said to him, "If anyone loves Me, he will keep My word; and My Father will love him, and We will come to him and make Our home with him. ²⁴He who does not love Me does not keep My words; and the word which you hear is not Mine but the Father's who sent Me.

The Gift of His Peace

²⁵"These things I have spoken to you while being present with you. ²⁶But the Helper, the Holy Spirit, whom the Father will send in My name, He will teach you all things, and bring to your remembrance all things that I said to you. ²⁷Peace I leave with you, My peace I give to you; not as the world gives do I give to you. Let not your heart be troubled, neither let it be afraid. ²⁸You have heard Me say to you, 'I am going away and coming *back* to you.' If you loved Me, you

would rejoice because I said,[a] 'I am going to the Father,' for My Father is greater than I.

[29]"And now I have told you before it comes, that when it does come to pass, you may believe. [30]I will no longer talk much with you, for the ruler of this world is coming, and he has nothing in Me. [31]But that the world may know that I love the Father, and as the Father gave Me commandment, so I do. Arise, let us go from here.

The True Vine

15 "I am the true vine, and My Father is the vinedresser. [2]Every branch in Me that does not bear fruit He takes away;[a] and every *branch* that bears fruit He prunes, that it may bear more fruit. [3]You are already clean because of the word which I have spoken to you. [4]Abide in Me, and I in you. As the branch cannot bear fruit of itself, unless it abides in the vine, neither can you, unless you abide in Me.

[5]"I am the vine, you *are* the branches. He who abides in Me, and I in him, bears much fruit; for without Me you can do nothing. [6]If anyone does not abide in Me, he is cast out as a branch and is withered; and they gather them and throw *them* into the fire, and they are burned. [7]If you abide in Me, and My words abide in you, you will[a] ask what you desire, and it shall be done for you. [8]By this My Father is glorified, that you bear much fruit; so you will be My disciples.

Love and Joy Perfected

⁹"As the Father loved Me, I also have loved you; abide in My love. ¹⁰If you keep My commandments, you will abide in My love, just as I have kept My Father's commandments and abide in His love.

¹¹"These things I have spoken to you, that My joy may remain in you, and *that* your joy may be full. ¹²This is My commandment, that you love one another as I have loved you. ¹³Greater love has no one than this, than to lay down one's life for his friends. ¹⁴You are My friends if you do whatever I command you. ¹⁵No longer do I call you servants, for a servant does not know what his master is doing; but I have called you friends, for all things that I heard from My Father I have made known to you. ¹⁶You did not choose Me, but I chose you and appointed you that you should go and bear fruit, and *that* your fruit should remain, that whatever you ask the Father in My name He may give you. ¹⁷These things I command you, that you love one another.

The World's Hatred

¹⁸"If the world hates you, you know that it hated Me before *it hated* you. ¹⁹If you were of the world, the world would love its own. Yet because you are not of the world, but I chose you out of the world, therefore the world hates you. ²⁰Remember the word that I said to you, 'A servant is not greater than his master.' If they persecuted Me, they will also persecute you. If

they kept My word, they will keep yours also. [21]But all these things they will do to you for My name's sake, because they do not know Him who sent Me. [22]If I had not come and spoken to them, they would have no sin, but now they have no excuse for their sin. [23]He who hates Me hates My Father also. [24]If I had not done among them the works which no one else did, they would have no sin; but now they have seen and also hated both Me and My Father. [25]But *this happened* that the word might be fulfilled which is written in their law, *'They hated Me without a cause.'*[a]

The Coming Rejection

[26]"But when the Helper comes, whom I shall send to you from the Father, the Spirit of truth who proceeds from the Father, He will testify of Me. [27]And you also will bear witness, because you have been with Me from the beginning.

16 "These things I have spoken to you, that you should not be made to stumble. [2]They will put you out of the synagogues; yes, the time is coming that whoever kills you will think that he offers God service. [3]And these things they will do to you[a] because they have not known the Father nor Me. [4]But these things I have told you, that when the[a] time comes, you may remember that I told you of them.

"And these things I did not say to you at the beginning, because I was with you.

The Work of the Holy Spirit

[5]"But now I go away to Him who sent Me, and none of you asks Me, 'Where are You going?' [6]But because I have said these things to you, sorrow has filled your heart. [7]Nevertheless I tell you the truth. It is to your advantage that I go away; for if I do not go away, the Helper will not come to you; but if I depart, I will send Him to you. [8]And when He has come, He will convict the world of sin, and of righteousness, and of judgment: [9]of sin, because they do not believe in Me; [10]of righteousness, because I go to My Father and you see Me no more; [11]of judgment, because the ruler of this world is judged.

[12]"I still have many things to say to you, but you cannot bear *them* now. [13]However, when He, the Spirit of truth, has come, He will guide you into all truth; for He will not speak on His own *authority,* but whatever He hears He will speak; and He will tell you things to come. [14]He will glorify Me, for He will take of what is Mine and declare *it* to you. [15]All things that the Father has are Mine. Therefore I said that He will take of Mine and declare *it* to you.[a]

Sorrow Will Turn to Joy

[16]"A little while, and you will not see Me; and again a little while, and you will see Me, because I go to the Father."

[17]Then *some* of His disciples said among themselves, "What is this that He says to us, 'A little while, and

you will not see Me; and again a little while, and you will see Me'; and, 'because I go to the Father'?" [18]They said therefore, "What is this that He says, 'A little while'? We do not know what He is saying."

[19]Now Jesus knew that they desired to ask Him, and He said to them, "Are you inquiring among yourselves about what I said, 'A little while, and you will not see Me; and again a little while, and you will see Me'? [20]Most assuredly, I say to you that you will weep and lament, but the world will rejoice; and you will be sorrowful, but your sorrow will be turned into joy. [21]A woman, when she is in labor, has sorrow because her hour has come; but as soon as she has given birth to the child, she no longer remembers the anguish, for joy that a human being has been born into the world. [22]Therefore you now have sorrow; but I will see you again and your heart will rejoice, and your joy no one will take from you.

[23]"And in that day you will ask Me nothing. Most assuredly, I say to you, whatever you ask the Father in My name He will give you. [24]Until now you have asked nothing in My name. Ask, and you will receive, that your joy may be full.

Jesus Christ Has Overcome
the World

[25]"These things I have spoken to you in figurative language; but the time is coming when I will no longer speak to you in figurative language, but I will tell you plainly about the Father. [26]In that day you will ask in

My name, and I do not say to you that I shall pray the Father for you; [27]for the Father Himself loves you, because you have loved Me, and have believed that I came forth from God. [28]I came forth from the Father and have come into the world. Again, I leave the world and go to the Father."

[29]His disciples said to Him, "See, now You are speaking plainly, and using no figure of speech! [30]Now we are sure that You know all things, and have no need that anyone should question You. By this we believe that You came forth from God."

[31]Jesus answered them, "Do you now believe? [32]Indeed the hour is coming, yes, has now come, that you will be scattered, each to his own, and will leave Me alone. And yet I am not alone, because the Father is with Me. [33]These things I have spoken to you, that in Me you may have peace. In the world you will[a] have tribulation; but be of good cheer, I have overcome the world."

Jesus Prays for Himself

17 Jesus spoke these words, lifted up His eyes to heaven, and said: "Father, the hour has come. Glorify Your Son, that Your Son also may glorify You, [2]as You have given Him authority over all flesh, that He should[a] give eternal life to as many as You have given Him. [3]And this is eternal life, that they may know You, the only true God, and Jesus Christ whom You have sent. [4]I have glorified You on the earth. I have finished the work which You have given Me to

do. [5]And now, O Father, glorify Me together with Yourself, with the glory which I had with You before the world was.

Jesus Prays for His Disciples

[6]"I have manifested Your name to the men whom You have given Me out of the world. They were Yours, You gave them to Me, and they have kept Your word. [7]Now they have known that all things which You have given Me are from You. [8]For I have given to them the words which You have given Me; and they have received *them,* and have known surely that I came forth from You; and they have believed that You sent Me.

[9]"I pray for them. I do not pray for the world but for those whom You have given Me, for they are Yours. [10]And all Mine are Yours, and Yours are Mine, and I am glorified in them. [11]Now I am no longer in the world, but these are in the world, and I come to You. Holy Father, keep through Your name those whom You have given Me,[a] that they may be one as We *are.* [12]While I was with them in the world,[a] I kept them in Your name. Those whom You gave Me I have kept;[b] and none of them is lost except the son of perdition, that the Scripture might be fulfilled. [13]But now I come to You, and these things I speak in the world, that they may have My joy fulfilled in themselves. [14]I have given them Your word; and the world has hated them because they are not of the world, just as I am not of the world. [15]I do not pray that You should take them

out of the world, but that You should keep them from the evil one. [16]They are not of the world, just as I am not of the world. [17]Sanctify them by Your truth. Your word is truth. [18]As You sent Me into the world, I also have sent them into the world. [19]And for their sakes I sanctify Myself, that they also may be sanctified by the truth.

Jesus Prays for All Believers

[20]"I do not pray for these alone, but also for those who will[a] believe in Me through their word; [21]that they all may be one, as You, Father, *are* in Me, and I in You; that they also may be one in Us, that the world may believe that You sent Me. [22]And the glory which You gave Me I have given them, that they may be one just as We are one: [23]I in them, and You in Me; that they may be made perfect in one, and that the world may know that You have sent Me, and have loved them as You have loved Me.

[24]"Father, I desire that they also whom You gave Me may be with Me where I am, that they may behold My glory which You have given Me; for You loved Me before the foundation of the world. [25]O righteous Father! The world has not known You, but I have known You; and these have known that You sent Me. [26]And I have declared to them Your name, and will declare *it,* that the love with which You loved Me may be in them, and I in them."

Betrayal and Arrest
in Gethsemane

18 When Jesus had spoken these words, He went out with His disciples over the Brook Kidron, where there was a garden, which He and His disciples entered. ²And Judas, who betrayed Him, also knew the place; for Jesus often met there with His disciples. ³Then Judas, having received a detachment *of troops,* and officers from the chief priests and Pharisees, came there with lanterns, torches, and weapons. ⁴Jesus therefore, knowing all things that would come upon Him, went forward and said to them, "Whom are you seeking?"

⁵They answered Him, "Jesus of Nazareth."

Jesus said to them, "I am *He.*" And Judas, who betrayed Him, also stood with them. ⁶Now when He said to them, "I am *He,*" they drew back and fell to the ground.

⁷Then He asked them again, "Whom are you seeking?"

And they said, "Jesus of Nazareth."

⁸Jesus answered, "I have told you that I am *He.* Therefore, if you seek Me, let these go their way," ⁹that the saying might be fulfilled which He spoke, "Of those whom You gave Me I have lost none."

¹⁰Then Simon Peter, having a sword, drew it and struck the high priest's servant, and cut off his right ear. The servant's name was Malchus.

¹¹So Jesus said to Peter, "Put your sword into the

sheath. Shall I not drink the cup which My Father has given Me?"

Before the High Priest

[12]Then the detachment *of troops* and the captain and the officers of the Jews arrested Jesus and bound Him. [13]And they led Him away to Annas first, for he was the father-in-law of Caiaphas who was high priest that year. [14]Now it was Caiaphas who advised the Jews that it was expedient that one man should die for the people.

Peter Denies Jesus

[15]And Simon Peter followed Jesus, and so *did* another[a] disciple. Now that disciple was known to the high priest, and went with Jesus into the courtyard of the high priest. [16]But Peter stood at the door outside. Then the other disciple, who was known to the high priest, went out and spoke to her who kept the door, and brought Peter in. [17]Then the servant girl who kept the door said to Peter, "You are not also *one* of this Man's disciples, are you?"

He said, "I am not."

[18]Now the servants and officers who had made a fire of coals stood there, for it was cold, and they warmed themselves. And Peter stood with them and warmed himself.

Jesus Questioned
by the High Priest

[19]The high priest then asked Jesus about His disciples and His doctrine.

[20]Jesus answered him, "I spoke openly to the world. I always taught in synagogues and in the temple, where the Jews always meet,[a] and in secret I have said nothing. [21]Why do you ask Me? Ask those who have heard Me what I said to them. Indeed they know what I said."

[22]And when He had said these things, one of the officers who stood by struck Jesus with the palm of his hand, saying, "Do You answer the high priest like that?"

[23]Jesus answered him, "If I have spoken evil, bear witness of the evil; but if well, why do you strike Me?"

[24]Then Annas sent Him bound to Caiaphas the high priest.

Peter Denies Twice More

[25]Now Simon Peter stood and warmed himself. Therefore they said to him, "You are not also *one* of His disciples, are you?"

He denied *it* and said, "I am not!"

[26]One of the servants of the high priest, a relative *of him* whose ear Peter cut off, said, "Did I not see you in the garden with Him?" [27]Peter then denied again; and immediately a rooster crowed.

In Pilate's Court

²⁸Then they led Jesus from Caiaphas to the Praetorium, and it was early morning. But they themselves did not go into the Praetorium, lest they should be defiled, but that they might eat the Passover. ²⁹Pilate then went out to them and said, "What accusation do you bring against this Man?"

³⁰They answered and said to him, "If He were not an evildoer, we would not have delivered Him up to you."

³¹Then Pilate said to them, "You take Him and judge Him according to your law."

Therefore the Jews said to him, "It is not lawful for us to put anyone to death," ³²that the saying of Jesus might be fulfilled which He spoke, signifying by what death He would die.

³³Then Pilate entered the Praetorium again, called Jesus, and said to Him, "Are You the King of the Jews?"

³⁴Jesus answered him, "Are you speaking for yourself about this, or did others tell you this concerning Me?"

³⁵Pilate answered, "Am I a Jew? Your own nation and the chief priests have delivered You to me. What have You done?"

³⁶Jesus answered, "My kingdom is not of this world. If My kingdom were of this world, My servants would fight, so that I should not be delivered to the Jews; but now My kingdom is not from here."

³⁷Pilate therefore said to Him, "Are You a king then?"

Jesus answered, "You say *rightly* that I am a king. For this cause I was born, and for this cause I have come into the world, that I should bear witness to the truth. Everyone who is of the truth hears My voice."

³⁸Pilate said to Him, "What is truth?" And when he had said this, he went out again to the Jews, and said to them, "I find no fault in Him at all.

Taking the Place of Barabbas

³⁹"But you have a custom that I should release someone to you at the Passover. Do you therefore want me to release to you the King of the Jews?"

⁴⁰Then they all cried again, saying, "Not this Man, but Barabbas!" Now Barabbas was a robber.

The Soldiers Mock Jesus

19 So then Pilate took Jesus and scourged *Him.* ²And the soldiers twisted a crown of thorns and put *it* on His head, and they put on Him a purple robe. ³Then they said,[a] "Hail, King of the Jews!" And they struck Him with their hands.

⁴Pilate then went out again, and said to them, "Behold, I am bringing Him out to you, that you may know that I find no fault in Him."

Pilate's Decision

⁵Then Jesus came out, wearing the crown of thorns

and the purple robe. And *Pilate* said to them, "Behold the Man!"

⁶Therefore, when the chief priests and officers saw Him, they cried out, saying, "Crucify *Him,* crucify *Him!*"

Pilate said to them, "You take Him and crucify *Him,* for I find no fault in Him."

⁷The Jews answered him, "We have a law, and according to ourᵃ law He ought to die, because He made Himself the Son of God."

⁸Therefore, when Pilate heard that saying, he was the more afraid, ⁹and went again into the Praetorium, and said to Jesus, "Where are You from?" But Jesus gave him no answer.

¹⁰Then Pilate said to Him, "Are You not speaking to me? Do You not know that I have power to crucify You, and power to release You?"

¹¹Jesus answered, "You could have no power at all against Me unless it had been given you from above. Therefore the one who delivered Me to you has the greater sin."

¹²From then on Pilate sought to release Him, but the Jews cried out, saying, "If you let this Man go, you are not Caesar's friend. Whoever makes himself a king speaks against Caesar."

¹³When Pilate therefore heard that saying, he brought Jesus out and sat down in the judgment seat in a place that is called *The* Pavement, but in Hebrew, Gabbatha. ¹⁴Now it was the Preparation Day of the Passover, and about the sixth hour. And he said to the

Jews, "Behold your King!"

¹⁵But they cried out, "Away with *Him,* away with *Him!* Crucify Him!"

Pilate said to them, "Shall I crucify your King?"

The chief priests answered, "We have no king but Caesar!"

¹⁶Then he delivered Him to them to be crucified. Then they took Jesus and led *Him* away.ᵃ

The King on a Cross

¹⁷And He, bearing His cross, went out to a place called *the Place* of a Skull, which is called in Hebrew, Golgotha, ¹⁸where they crucified Him, and two others with Him, one on either side, and Jesus in the center. ¹⁹Now Pilate wrote a title and put *it* on the cross. And the writing was:

JESUS OF NAZARETH,
THE KING OF THE JEWS.

²⁰Then many of the Jews read this title, for the place where Jesus was crucified was near the city; and it was written in Hebrew, Greek, *and* Latin.

²¹Therefore the chief priests of the Jews said to Pilate, "Do not write, 'The King of the Jews,' but, 'He said, "I am the King of the Jews."'"

²²Pilate answered, "What I have written, I have written."

²³Then the soldiers, when they had crucified Jesus, took His garments and made four parts, to each soldier

a part, and also the tunic. Now the tunic was without seam, woven from the top in one piece. [24]They said therefore among themselves, "Let us not tear it, but cast lots for it, whose it shall be," that the Scripture might be fulfilled which says:

"They divided My garments among them,
And for My clothing they cast lots."[a]

Therefore the soldiers did these things.

Behold Your Mother
[25]Now there stood by the cross of Jesus His mother, and His mother's sister, Mary the *wife* of Clopas, and Mary Magdalene. [26]When Jesus therefore saw His mother, and the disciple whom He loved standing by, He said to His mother, "Woman, behold your son!" [27]Then He said to the disciple, "Behold your mother!" And from that hour that disciple took her to his own *home.*

It Is Finished
[28]After this, Jesus, knowing[a] that all things were now accomplished, that the Scripture might be fulfilled, said, "I thirst!" [29]Now a vessel full of sour wine was sitting there; and they filled a sponge with sour wine, put *it* on hyssop, and put *it* to His mouth. [30]So when Jesus had received the sour wine, He said, "It is finished!" And bowing His head, He gave up His spirit.

Jesus' Side Is Pierced

³¹Therefore, because it was the Preparation *Day,* that the bodies should not remain on the cross on the Sabbath (for that Sabbath was a high day), the Jews asked Pilate that their legs might be broken, and *that* they might be taken away. ³²Then the soldiers came and broke the legs of the first and of the other who was crucified with Him. ³³But when they came to Jesus and saw that He was already dead, they did not break His legs. ³⁴But one of the soldiers pierced His side with a spear, and immediately blood and water came out. ³⁵And he who has seen has testified, and his testimony is true; and he knows that he is telling the truth, so that you may believe. ³⁶For these things were done that the Scripture should be fulfilled, *"Not one of His bones shall be broken."*ᵃ ³⁷And again another Scripture says, *"They shall look on Him whom they pierced."*ᵃ

Jesus Buried in Joseph's Tomb

³⁸After this, Joseph of Arimathea, being a disciple of Jesus, but secretly, for fear of the Jews, asked Pilate that he might take away the body of Jesus; and Pilate gave *him* permission. So he came and took the body of Jesus. ³⁹And Nicodemus, who at first came to Jesus by night, also came, bringing a mixture of myrrh and aloes, about a hundred pounds. ⁴⁰Then they took the body of Jesus, and bound it in strips of linen with the spices, as the custom of the Jews is to bury. ⁴¹Now in the place where He was crucified there was a garden,

and in the garden a new tomb in which no one had yet been laid. ⁴²So there they laid Jesus, because of the Jews' Preparation *Day,* for the tomb was nearby.

The Empty Tomb

20 Now the first *day* of the week Mary Magdalene went to the tomb early, while it was still dark, and saw *that* the stone had been taken away from the tomb. ²Then she ran and came to Simon Peter, and to the other disciple, whom Jesus loved, and said to them, "They have taken away the Lord out of the tomb, and we do not know where they have laid Him."

³Peter therefore went out, and the other disciple, and were going to the tomb. ⁴So they both ran together, and the other disciple outran Peter and came to the tomb first. ⁵And he, stooping down and looking in, saw the linen cloths lying *there;* yet he did not go in. ⁶Then Simon Peter came, following him, and went into the tomb; and he saw the linen cloths lying *there,* ⁷and the handkerchief that had been around His head, not lying with the linen cloths, but folded together in a place by itself. ⁸Then the other disciple, who came to the tomb first, went in also; and he saw and believed. ⁹For as yet they did not know the Scripture, that He must rise again from the dead. ¹⁰Then the disciples went away again to their own homes.

Mary Magdalene Sees
the Risen Lord

¹¹But Mary stood outside by the tomb weeping, and

as she wept she stooped down *and looked* into the tomb. [12]And she saw two angels in white sitting, one at the head and the other at the feet, where the body of Jesus had lain. [13]Then they said to her, "Woman, why are you weeping?"

She said to them, "Because they have taken away my Lord, and I do not know where they have laid Him."

[14]Now when she had said this, she turned around and saw Jesus standing *there,* and did not know that it was Jesus. [15]Jesus said to her, "Woman, why are you weeping? Whom are you seeking?"

She, supposing Him to be the gardener, said to Him, "Sir, if You have carried Him away, tell me where You have laid Him, and I will take Him away."

[16]Jesus said to her, "Mary!"

She turned and said to Him,[a] "Rabboni!" (which is to say, Teacher).

[17]Jesus said to her, "Do not cling to Me, for I have not yet ascended to My Father; but go to My brethren and say to them, 'I am ascending to My Father and your Father, and *to* My God and your God.' "

[18]Mary Magdalene came and told the disciples that she had seen the Lord,[a] and *that* He had spoken these things to her.

The Apostles Commissioned

[19]Then, the same day at evening, being the first *day* of the week, when the doors were shut where the dis-

ciples were assembled,[a] for fear of the Jews, Jesus came and stood in the midst, and said to them, "Peace *be* with you." [20]When He had said this, He showed them *His* hands and His side. Then the disciples were glad when they saw the Lord.

[21]So Jesus said to them again, "Peace to you! As the Father has sent Me, I also send you." [22]And when He had said this, He breathed on *them,* and said to them, "Receive the Holy Spirit. [23]If you forgive the sins of any, they are forgiven them; if you retain the *sins* of any, they are retained."

Seeing and Believing

[24]Now Thomas, called the Twin, one of the twelve, was not with them when Jesus came. [25]The other disciples therefore said to him, "We have seen the Lord."

So he said to them, "Unless I see in His hands the print of the nails, and put my finger into the print of the nails, and put my hand into His side, I will not believe."

[26]And after eight days His disciples were again inside, and Thomas with them. Jesus came, the doors being shut, and stood in the midst, and said, "Peace to you!" [27]Then He said to Thomas, "Reach your finger here, and look at My hands; and reach your hand *here,* and put *it* into My side. Do not be unbelieving, but believing."

[28]And Thomas answered and said to Him, "My Lord and my God!"

[29]Jesus said to him, "Thomas,[a] because you have seen Me, you have believed. Blessed *are* those who have not seen and *yet* have believed."

That You May Believe

[30]And truly Jesus did many other signs in the presence of His disciples, which are not written in this book; [31]but these are written that you may believe that Jesus is the Christ, the Son of God, and that believing you may have life in His name.

Breakfast by the Sea

21 After these things Jesus showed Himself again to the disciples at the Sea of Tiberias, and in this way He showed *Himself:* [2]Simon Peter, Thomas called the Twin, Nathanael of Cana in Galilee, the *sons* of Zebedee, and two others of His disciples were together. [3]Simon Peter said to them, "I am going fishing."

They said to him, "We are going with you also." They went out and immediately[a] got into the boat, and that night they caught nothing. [4]But when the morning had now come, Jesus stood on the shore; yet the disciples did not know that it was Jesus. [5]Then Jesus said to them, "Children, have you any food?"

They answered Him, "No."

[6]And He said to them, "Cast the net on the right side of the boat, and you will find *some.*" So they cast, and now they were not able to draw it in because of the multitude of fish.

⁷Therefore that disciple whom Jesus loved said to Peter, "It is the Lord!" Now when Simon Peter heard that it was the Lord, he put on *his* outer garment (for he had removed it), and plunged into the sea. ⁸But the other disciples came in the little boat (for they were not far from land, but about two hundred cubits), dragging the net with fish. ⁹Then, as soon as they had come to land, they saw a fire of coals there, and fish laid on it, and bread. ¹⁰Jesus said to them, "Bring some of the fish which you have just caught."

¹¹Simon Peter went up and dragged the net to land, full of large fish, one hundred and fifty-three; and although there were so many, the net was not broken. ¹²Jesus said to them, "Come *and* eat breakfast." Yet none of the disciples dared ask Him, "Who are You?"—knowing that it was the Lord. ¹³Jesus then came and took the bread and gave it to them, and likewise the fish.

¹⁴This *is* now the third time Jesus showed Himself to His disciples after He was raised from the dead.

Jesus Restores Peter

¹⁵So when they had eaten breakfast, Jesus said to Simon Peter, "Simon, *son* of Jonah,ᵃ do you love Me more than these?"

He said to Him, "Yes, Lord; You know that I love You."

He said to him, "Feed My lambs."

¹⁶He said to him again a second time, "Simon, *son* of Jonah,ᵃ do you love Me?"

He said to Him, "Yes, Lord; You know that I love You."

He said to him, "Tend My sheep."

[17]He said to him the third time, "Simon, *son* of Jonah,[a] do you love Me?" Peter was grieved because He said to him the third time, "Do you love Me?"

And he said to Him, "Lord, You know all things; You know that I love You."

Jesus said to him, "Feed My sheep. [18]Most assuredly, I say to you, when you were younger, you girded yourself and walked where you wished; but when you are old, you will stretch out your hands, and another will gird you and carry *you* where you do not wish." [19]This He spoke, signifying by what death he would glorify God. And when He had spoken this, He said to him, "Follow Me."

The Beloved Disciple
and His Book

[20]Then Peter, turning around, saw the disciple whom Jesus loved following, who also had leaned on His breast at the supper, and said, "Lord, who is the one who betrays You?" [21]Peter, seeing him, said to Jesus, "But Lord, what *about* this man?"

[22]Jesus said to him, "If I will that he remain till I come, what *is that* to you? You follow Me."

[23]Then this saying went out among the brethren that this disciple would not die. Yet Jesus did not say to him that he would not die, but, "If I will that he remain till I come, what *is that* to you?"

²⁴This is the disciple who testifies of these things, and wrote these things; and we know that his testimony is true.

²⁵And there are also many other things that Jesus did, which if they were written one by one, I suppose that even the world itself could not contain the books that would be written. Amen.

1 JOHN

What Was Heard, Seen, and Touched

1 That which was from the beginning, which we have heard, which we have seen with our eyes, which we have looked upon, and our hands have handled, concerning the Word of life—²the life was manifested, and we have seen, and bear witness, and declare to you that eternal life which was with the Father and was manifested to us—³that which we have seen and heard we declare to you, that you also may have fellowship with us; and truly our fellowship *is* with the Father and with His Son Jesus Christ. ⁴And these things we write to you that your^a joy may be full.

Fellowship with Him and One Another

⁵This is the message which we have heard from Him and declare to you, that God is light and in Him is no darkness at all. ⁶If we say that we have fellowship with Him, and walk in darkness, we lie and do not practice the truth. ⁷But if we walk in the light as He is in the light, we have fellowship with one another, and the blood of Jesus Christ His Son cleanses us from all sin.

⁸If we say that we have no sin, we deceive ourselves,

and the truth is not in us. ⁹If we confess our sins, He is faithful and just to forgive us *our* sins and to cleanse us from all unrighteousness. ¹⁰If we say that we have not sinned, we make Him a liar, and His word is not in us.

2 My little children, these things I write to you, so that you may not sin. And if anyone sins, we have an Advocate with the Father, Jesus Christ the righteous. ²And He Himself is the propitiation for our sins, and not for ours only but also for the whole world.

The Test of Knowing Him

³Now by this we know that we know Him, if we keep His commandments. ⁴He who says, "I know Him," and does not keep His commandments, is a liar, and the truth is not in him. ⁵But whoever keeps His word, truly the love of God is perfected in him. By this we know that we are in Him. ⁶He who says he abides in Him ought himself also to walk just as He walked.

⁷Brethren,[a] I write no new commandment to you, but an old commandment which you have had from the beginning. The old commandment is the word which you heard from the beginning.[b] ⁸Again, a new commandment I write to you, which thing is true in Him and in you, because the darkness is passing away, and the true light is already shining.

⁹He who says he is in the light, and hates his brother, is in darkness until now. ¹⁰He who loves his brother abides in the light, and there is no cause for stumbling in him. ¹¹But he who hates his brother is in darkness

and walks in darkness, and does not know where he is going, because the darkness has blinded his eyes.

Their Spiritual State

¹² I write to you, little children,
  Because your sins are forgiven you
    for His name's sake.
¹³ I write to you, fathers,
  Because you have known Him *who is*
    from the beginning.
I write to you, young men,
  Because you have overcome the wicked one.
I write to you, little children,
  Because you have known the Father.
¹⁴ I have written to you, fathers,
  Because you have known Him *who is*
    from the beginning.
I have written to you, young men,
  Because you are strong, and the word
    of God abides in you,
  And you have overcome the wicked one.

Do Not Love the World

¹⁵Do not love the world or the things in the world. If anyone loves the world, the love of the Father is not in him. ¹⁶For all that *is* in the world—the lust of the flesh, the lust of the eyes, and the pride of life—is not of the Father but is of the world. ¹⁷And the world is passing away, and the lust of it; but he who does the will of God abides forever.

Deceptions of the Last Hour

[18]Little children, it is the last hour; and as you have heard that the[a] Antichrist is coming, even now many antichrists have come, by which we know that it is the last hour. [19]They went out from us, but they were not of us; for if they had been of us, they would have continued with us; but *they went out* that they might be made manifest, that none of them were of us.

[20]But you have an anointing from the Holy One, and you know all things.[a] [21]I have not written to you because you do not know the truth, but because you know it, and that no lie is of the truth.

[22]Who is a liar but he who denies that Jesus is the Christ? He is antichrist who denies the Father and the Son. [23]Whoever denies the Son does not have the Father either; he who acknowledges the Son has the Father also.

Let Truth Abide in You

[24]Therefore let that abide in you which you heard from the beginning. If what you heard from the beginning abides in you, you also will abide in the Son and in the Father. [25]And this is the promise that He has promised us—eternal life.

[26]These things I have written to you concerning those who *try to* deceive you. [27]But the anointing which you have received from Him abides in you, and you do not need that anyone teach you; but as the same anointing teaches you concerning all things, and

is true, and is not a lie, and just as it has taught you, you will[a] abide in Him.

The Children of God

[28]And now, little children, abide in Him, that when[a] He appears, we may have confidence and not be ashamed before Him at His coming. [29]If you know that He is righteous, you know that everyone who practices righteousness is born of Him.

3 Behold what manner of love the Father has bestowed on us, that we should be called children of God![a] Therefore the world does not know us,[b] because it did not know Him. [2]Beloved, now we are children of God; and it has not yet been revealed what we shall be, but we know that when He is revealed, we shall be like Him, for we shall see Him as He is. [3]And everyone who has this hope in Him purifies himself, just as He is pure.

Sin and the Child of God

[4]Whoever commits sin also commits lawlessness, and sin is lawlessness. [5]And you know that He was manifested to take away our sins, and in Him there is no sin. [6]Whoever abides in Him does not sin. Whoever sins has neither seen Him nor known Him.

[7]Little children, let no one deceive you. He who practices righteousness is righteous, just as He is righteous. [8]He who sins is of the devil, for the devil has sinned from the beginning. For this purpose the Son of God was manifested, that He might destroy the

works of the devil. [9]Whoever has been born of God does not sin, for His seed remains in him; and he cannot sin, because he has been born of God.

The Imperative of Love

[10]In this the children of God and the children of the devil are manifest: Whoever does not practice right-eousness is not of God, nor *is* he who does not love his brother. [11]For this is the message that you heard from the beginning, that we should love one another, [12]not as Cain *who* was of the wicked one and murdered his brother. And why did he murder him? Because his works were evil and his brother's righteous.

[13]Do not marvel, my brethren, if the world hates you. [14]We know that we have passed from death to life, because we love the brethren. He who does not love *his* brother[a] abides in death. [15]Whoever hates his brother is a murderer, and you know that no murderer has eternal life abiding in him.

The Outworking of Love

[16]By this we know love, because He laid down His life for us. And we also ought to lay down *our* lives for the brethren. [17]But whoever has this world's goods, and sees his brother in need, and shuts up his heart from him, how does the love of God abide in him?

[18]My little children, let us not love in word or in tongue, but in deed and in truth. [19]And by this we know[a] that we are of the truth, and shall assure our hearts before Him. [20]For if our heart condemns us,

God is greater than our heart, and knows all things. [21]Beloved, if our heart does not condemn us, we have confidence toward God. [22]And whatever we ask we receive from Him, because we keep His commandments and do those things that are pleasing in His sight. [23]And this is His commandment: that we should believe on the name of His Son Jesus Christ and love one another, as He gave us[a] commandment.

The Spirit of Truth and
the Spirit of Error

[24]Now he who keeps His commandments abides in Him, and He in him. And by this we know that He abides in us, by the Spirit whom He has given us.

4 Beloved, do not believe every spirit, but test the spirits, whether they are of God; because many false prophets have gone out into the world. [2]By this you know the Spirit of God: Every spirit that confesses that Jesus Christ has come in the flesh is of God, [3]and every spirit that does not confess that[a] Jesus Christ has come in the flesh is not of God. And this is the *spirit* of the Antichrist, which you have heard was coming, and is now already in the world.

[4]You are of God, little children, and have overcome them, because He who is in you is greater than he who is in the world. [5]They are of the world. Therefore they speak *as* of the world, and the world hears them. [6]We are of God. He who knows God hears us; he who is not of God does not hear us. By this we know the spirit of truth and the spirit of error.

Knowing God Through Love

[7]Beloved, let us love one another, for love is of God; and everyone who loves is born of God and knows God. [8]He who does not love does not know God, for God is love. [9]In this the love of God was manifested toward us, that God has sent His only begotten Son into the world, that we might live through Him. [10]In this is love, not that we loved God, but that He loved us and sent His Son *to be* the propitiation for our sins. [11]Beloved, if God so loved us, we also ought to love one another.

Seeing God Through Love

[12]No one has seen God at any time. If we love one another, God abides in us, and His love has been perfected in us. [13]By this we know that we abide in Him, and He in us, because He has given us of His Spirit. [14]And we have seen and testify that the Father has sent the Son *as* Savior of the world. [15]Whoever confesses that Jesus is the Son of God, God abides in him, and he in God. [16]And we have known and believed the love that God has for us. God is love, and he who abides in love abides in God, and God in him.

The Consummation of Love

[17]Love has been perfected among us in this: that we may have boldness in the day of judgment; because as He is, so are we in this world. [18]There is no fear in love; but perfect love casts out fear, because fear

involves torment. But he who fears has not been made perfect in love. [19]We love Him[a] because He first loved us.

Obedience by Faith

[20]If someone says, "I love God," and hates his brother, he is a liar; for he who does not love his brother whom he has seen, how can[a] he love God whom he has not seen? [21]And this commandment we have from Him: that he who loves God *must* love his brother also.

5 Whoever believes that Jesus is the Christ is born of God, and everyone who loves Him who begot also loves him who is begotten of Him. [2]By this we know that we love the children of God, when we love God and keep His commandments. [3]For this is the love of God, that we keep His commandments. And His commandments are not burdensome. [4]For whatever is born of God overcomes the world. And this is the victory that has overcome the world—our[a] faith. [5]Who is he who overcomes the world, but he who believes that Jesus is the Son of God?

The Certainty of God's Witness

[6]This is He who came by water and blood—Jesus Christ; not only by water, but by water and blood. And it is the Spirit who bears witness, because the Spirit is truth. [7]For there are three that bear witness in heaven: the Father, the Word, and the Holy Spirit; and these three are one. [8]And there are three that bear witness on

earth:[a] the Spirit, the water, and the blood; and these three agree as one.

[9]If we receive the witness of men, the witness of God is greater; for this is the witness of God which[a] He has testified of His Son. [10]He who believes in the Son of God has the witness in himself; he who does not believe God has made Him a liar, because he has not believed the testimony that God has given of His Son. [11]And this is the testimony: that God has given us eternal life, and this life is in His Son. [12]He who has the Son has life; he who does not have the Son of God does not have life. [13]These things I have written to you who believe in the name of the Son of God, that you may know that you have eternal life,[a] and that you may *continue to* believe in the name of the Son of God.

Confidence and Compassion
in Prayer

[14]Now this is the confidence that we have in Him, that if we ask anything according to His will, He hears us. [15]And if we know that He hears us, whatever we ask, we know that we have the petitions that we have asked of Him.

[16]If anyone sees his brother sinning a sin *which does* not *lead* to death, he will ask, and He will give him life for those who commit sin not *leading* to death. There is sin *leading* to death. I do not say that he should pray about that. [17]All unrighteousness is sin, and there is sin not *leading* to death.

Knowing the True—
Rejecting the False

[18]We know that whoever is born of God does not sin; but he who has been born of God keeps himself,[a] and the wicked one does not touch him.

[19]We know that we are of God, and the whole world lies *under the sway of* the wicked one.

[20]And we know that the Son of God has come and has given us an understanding, that we may know Him who is true; and we are in Him who is true, in His Son Jesus Christ. This is the true God and eternal life.

[21]Little children, keep yourselves from idols. Amen.

2 JOHN

Greeting the Elect Lady

The Elder,

To the elect lady and her children, whom I love in truth, and not only I, but also all those who have known the truth, ²because of the truth which abides in us and will be with us forever:

³Grace, mercy, *and* peace will be with you[a] from God the Father and from the Lord Jesus Christ, the Son of the Father, in truth and love.

Walk in Christ's Commandments

⁴I rejoiced greatly that I have found *some* of your children walking in truth, as we received commandment from the Father. ⁵And now I plead with you, lady, not as though I wrote a new commandment to you, but that which we have had from the beginning: that we love one another. ⁶This is love, that we walk according to His commandments. This is the commandment, that as you have heard from the beginning, you should walk in it.

Beware of
Antichrist Deceivers

[7]For many deceivers have gone out into the world who do not confess Jesus Christ *as* coming in the flesh. This is a deceiver and an antichrist. [8]Look to yourselves, that we[a] do not lose those things we worked for, but *that* we[b] may receive a full reward.

[9]Whoever transgresses[a] and does not abide in the doctrine of Christ does not have God. He who abides in the doctrine of Christ has both the Father and the Son. [10]If anyone comes to you and does not bring this doctrine, do not receive him into your house nor greet him; [11]for he who greets him shares in his evil deeds.

John's Farewell Greeting

[12]Having many things to write to you, I did not wish *to do so* with paper and ink; but I hope to come to you and speak face to face, that our joy may be full.

[13]The children of your elect sister greet you. Amen.

3 JOHN

Greeting to Gaius

The Elder,

To the beloved Gaius, whom I love in truth:

[2]Beloved, I pray that you may prosper in all things and be in health, just as your soul prospers. [3]For I rejoiced greatly when brethren came and testified of the truth *that is* in you, just as you walk in the truth. [4]I have no greater joy than to hear that my children walk in truth.[a]

Gaius Commended for Generosity

[5]Beloved, you do faithfully whatever you do for the brethren and[a] for strangers, [6]who have borne witness of your love before the church. *If* you send them forward on their journey in a manner worthy of God, you will do well, [7]because they went forth for His name's sake, taking nothing from the Gentiles. [8]We therefore ought to receive[a] such, that we may become fellow workers for the truth.

Diotrephes and Demetrius

[9]I wrote to the church, but Diotrephes, who loves to

have the preeminence among them, does not receive us. [10]Therefore, if I come, I will call to mind his deeds which he does, prating against us with malicious words. And not content with that, he himself does not receive the brethren, and forbids those who wish to, putting *them* out of the church.

[11]Beloved, do not imitate what is evil, but what is good. He who does good is of God, but[a] he who does evil has not seen God.

[12]Demetrius has a *good* testimony from all, and from the truth itself. And we also bear witness, and you know that our testimony is true.

Farewell Greeting

[13]I had many things to write, but I do not wish to write to you with pen and ink; [14]but I hope to see you shortly, and we shall speak face to face.

Peace to you. Our friends greet you. Greet the friends by name.

REVELATION

Introduction and Benediction

1 The Revelation of Jesus Christ, which God gave Him to show His servants—things which must shortly take place. And He sent and signified *it* by His angel to His servant John, ²who bore witness to the word of God, and to the testimony of Jesus Christ, to all things that he saw. ³Blessed *is* he who reads and those who hear the words of this prophecy, and keep those things which are written in it; for the time *is* near.

Greeting the Seven Churches

⁴John, to the seven churches which are in Asia:

Grace to you and peace from Him who is and who was and who is to come, and from the seven Spirits who are before His throne, ⁵and from Jesus Christ, the faithful witness, the firstborn from the dead, and the ruler over the kings of the earth.

To Him who loved us and washed[a] us from our sins in His own blood, ⁶and has made us kings[a] and priests to His God and Father, to Him *be* glory and dominion forever and ever. Amen.

⁷Behold, He is coming with clouds, and every eye will see Him, even they who pierced Him. And all the tribes of the earth will mourn because of Him. Even so, Amen.

[8]"I am the Alpha and the Omega, *the* Beginning and *the* End,"[a] says the Lord,[b] "who is and who was and who is to come, the Almighty."

Vision of the Son of Man

[9]I, John, both[a] your brother and companion in the tribulation and kingdom and patience of Jesus Christ, was on the island that is called Patmos for the word of God and for the testimony of Jesus Christ. [10]I was in the Spirit on the Lord's Day, and I heard behind me a loud voice, as of a trumpet, [11]saying, "I am the Alpha and the Omega, the First and the Last,"[a] and, "What you see, write in a book and send *it* to the seven churches which are in Asia:[b] to Ephesus, to Smyrna, to Pergamos, to Thyatira, to Sardis, to Philadelphia, and to Laodicea."

[12]Then I turned to see the voice that spoke with me. And having turned I saw seven golden lampstands, [13]and in the midst of the seven lampstands *One* like the Son of Man, clothed with a garment down to the feet and girded about the chest with a golden band. [14]His head and hair *were* white like wool, as white as snow, and His eyes like a flame of fire; [15]His feet *were* like fine brass, as if refined in a furnace, and His voice as the sound of many waters; [16]He had in His right hand seven stars, out of His mouth went a sharp two-edged sword, and His countenance *was* like the sun shining in its strength. [17]And when I saw Him, I fell at His feet as dead. But He laid His right hand on me, saying to me,[a] "Do not be afraid; I am the First and the Last. [18]I

am He who lives, and was dead, and behold, I am alive forevermore. Amen. And I have the keys of Hades and of Death. [19]Write[a] the things which you have seen, and the things which are, and the things which will take place after this. [20]The mystery of the seven stars which you saw in My right hand, and the seven golden lampstands: The seven stars are the angels of the seven churches, and the seven lampstands which you saw[a] are the seven churches.

The Loveless Church

2 "To the angel of the church of Ephesus write, 'These things says He who holds the seven stars in His right hand, who walks in the midst of the seven golden lampstands: [2]"I know your works, your labor, your patience, and that you cannot bear those who are evil. And you have tested those who say they are apostles and are not, and have found them liars; [3]and you have persevered and have patience, and have labored for My name's sake and have not become weary. [4]Nevertheless I have *this* against you, that you have left your first love. [5]Remember therefore from where you have fallen; repent and do the first works, or else I will come to you quickly and remove your lampstand from its place—unless you repent. [6]But this you have, that you hate the deeds of the Nicolaitans, which I also hate.

[7]"He who has an ear, let him hear what the Spirit says to the churches. To him who overcomes I will give to eat from the tree of life, which is in the midst of the Paradise of God."'

The Persecuted Church

[8]"And to the angel of the church in Smyrna write,

'These things says the First and the Last, who was dead, and came to life: [9]"I know your works, tribulation, and poverty (but you are rich); and *I know* the blasphemy of those who say they are Jews and are not, but *are* a synagogue of Satan. [10]Do not fear any of those things which you are about to suffer. Indeed, the devil is about to throw *some* of you into prison, that you may be tested, and you will have tribulation ten days. Be faithful until death, and I will give you the crown of life.

[11]"He who has an ear, let him hear what the Spirit says to the churches. He who overcomes shall not be hurt by the second death." '

The Compromising Church

[12]"And to the angel of the church in Pergamos write,

'These things says He who has the sharp two-edged sword: [13]"I know your works, and where you dwell, where Satan's throne *is*. And you hold fast to My name, and did not deny My faith even in the days in which Antipas *was* My faithful martyr, who was killed among you, where Satan dwells. [14]But I have a few things against you, because you have there those who hold the doctrine of Balaam, who taught Balak to put a stumbling block before the children of Israel, to eat things sacrificed to idols, and to commit sexual immorality. [15]Thus you also have those who hold the

doctrine of the Nicolaitans, which thing I hate.[a]
[16]Repent, or else I will come to you quickly and will fight against them with the sword of My mouth.

[17]"He who has an ear, let him hear what the Spirit says to the churches. To him who overcomes I will give some of the hidden manna to eat. And I will give him a white stone, and on the stone a new name written which no one knows except him who receives *it.*" '

The Corrupt Church

[18]"And to the angel of the church in Thyatira write,

'These things says the Son of God, who has eyes like a flame of fire, and His feet like fine brass: [19]"I know your works, love, service, faith,[a] and your patience; and *as* for your works, the last *are* more than the first. [20]Nevertheless I have a few things against you, because you allow[a] that woman[b] Jezebel, who calls herself a prophetess, to teach and seduce[c] My servants to commit sexual immorality and eat things sacrificed to idols. [21]And I gave her time to repent of her sexual immorality, and she did not repent.[a] [22]Indeed I will cast her into a sickbed, and those who commit adultery with her into great tribulation, unless they repent of their[a] deeds. [23]I will kill her children with death, and all the churches shall know that I am He who searches the minds and hearts. And I will give to each one of you according to your works.

[24]"Now to you I say, and[a] to the rest in Thyatira, as many as do not have this doctrine, who have not

known the depths of Satan, as they say, I will[b] put on you no other burden. [25]But hold fast what you have till I come. [26]And he who overcomes, and keeps My works until the end, to him I will give power over the nations—

[27] *'He shall rule them with a rod of iron;*
They shall be dashed to pieces like the potter's
vessels '[a]—

as I also have received from My Father; [28]and I will give him the morning star.

[29]"He who has an ear, let him hear what the Spirit says to the churches." '

The Dead Church

3 "And to the angel of the church in Sardis write, 'These things says He who has the seven Spirits of God and the seven stars: "I know your works, that you have a name that you are alive, but you are dead. [2]Be watchful, and strengthen the things which remain, that are ready to die, for I have not found your works perfect before God.[a] [3]Remember therefore how you have received and heard; hold fast and repent. Therefore if you will not watch, I will come upon you as a thief, and you will not know what hour I will come upon you. [4]You[a] have a few names even in Sardis who have not defiled their garments; and they shall walk with Me in white, for they are worthy. [5]He who overcomes shall be clothed in white garments, and I will not blot out his name from the Book of Life; but I will confess his name before My Father and before His angels.

[6]"He who has an ear, let him hear what the Spirit says to the churches." '

The Faithful Church

[7]"And to the angel of the church in Philadelphia write,

'These things says He who is holy, He who is true, *"He who has the key of David, He who opens and no one shuts, and shuts and no one opens"*:[a] [8]"I know your works. See, I have set before you an open door, and no one can shut it;[a] for you have a little strength, have kept My word, and have not denied My name. [9]Indeed I will make *those* of the synagogue of Satan, who say they are Jews and are not, but lie—indeed I will make them come and worship before your feet, and to know that I have loved you. [10]Because you have kept My command to persevere, I also will keep you from the hour of trial which shall come upon the whole world, to test those who dwell on the earth. [11]Behold,[a] I am coming quickly! Hold fast what you have, that no one may take your crown. [12]He who overcomes, I will make him a pillar in the temple of My God, and he shall go out no more. I will write on him the name of My God and the name of the city of My God, the New Jerusalem, which comes down out of heaven from My God. And *I will write on him* My new name.

[13]"He who has an ear, let him hear what the Spirit says to the churches." '

The Lukewarm Church

[14]"And to the angel of the church of the Laodiceans[a] write,

'These things says the Amen, the Faithful and True Witness, the Beginning of the creation of God: [15]"I know your works, that you are neither cold nor hot. I could wish you were cold or hot. [16]So then, because you are lukewarm, and neither cold nor hot,[a] I will vomit you out of My mouth. [17]Because you say, 'I am rich, have become wealthy, and have need of nothing'—and do not know that you are wretched, miserable, poor, blind, and naked—[18]I counsel you to buy from Me gold refined in the fire, that you may be rich; and white garments, that you may be clothed, *that* the shame of your nakedness may not be revealed; and anoint your eyes with eye salve, that you may see. [19]As many as I love, I rebuke and chasten. Therefore be zealous and repent. [20]Behold, I stand at the door and knock. If anyone hears My voice and opens the door, I will come in to him and dine with him, and he with Me. [21]To him who overcomes I will grant to sit with Me on My throne, as I also over- came and sat down with My Father on His throne.

[22]"He who has an ear, let him hear what the Spirit says to the churches." ' "

The Throne Room of Heaven

4 After these things I looked, and behold, a door *standing* open in heaven. And the first voice which I heard *was* like a trumpet speaking with me, saying, "Come up here, and I will show you things which must take place after this."

[2]Immediately I was in the Spirit; and behold, a throne set in heaven, and *One* sat on the throne. [3]And He who sat there was[a] like a jasper and a sardius stone in appearance; and *there was* a rainbow around the throne, in appearance like an emerald. [4]Around the throne *were* twenty-four thrones, and on the thrones I saw twenty-four elders sitting, clothed in white robes; and they had crowns[a] of gold on their heads. [5]And from the throne proceeded lightnings, thunderings, and voices.[a] Seven lamps of fire *were* burning before the throne, which are the[b] seven Spirits of God.

[6]Before the throne *there was*[a] a sea of glass, like crystal. And in the midst of the throne, and around the throne, *were* four living creatures full of eyes in front and in back. [7]The first living creature *was* like a lion, the second living creature like a calf, the third living creature had a face like a man, and the fourth living creature *was* like a flying eagle. [8]*The* four living creatures, each having six wings, were full of eyes around and within. And they do not rest day or night, saying:

"Holy, holy, holy,[a]
Lord God Almighty,

Who was and is and is to come!"

⁹Whenever the living creatures give glory and honor and thanks to Him who sits on the throne, who lives forever and ever, ¹⁰the twenty-four elders fall down before Him who sits on the throne and worship Him who lives forever and ever, and cast their crowns before the throne, saying:

¹¹"You are worthy, O Lord,ᵃ
To receive glory and honor and power;
For You created all things,
And by Your will they existᵇ and were created."

The Lamb Takes the Scroll

5 And I saw in the right *hand* of Him who sat on the throne a scroll written inside and on the back, sealed with seven seals. ²Then I saw a strong angel proclaiming with a loud voice, "Who is worthy to open the scroll and to loose its seals?" ³And no one in heaven or on the earth or under the earth was able to open the scroll, or to look at it.

⁴So I wept much, because no one was found worthy to open and readᵃ the scroll, or to look at it. ⁵But one of the elders said to me, "Do not weep. Behold, the Lion of the tribe of Judah, the Root of David, has prevailed to open the scroll and to looseᵃ its seven seals."

⁶And I looked, and behold,ᵃ in the midst of the throne and of the four living creatures, and in the midst of the elders, stood a Lamb as though it had

been slain, having seven horns and seven eyes, which are the seven Spirits of God sent out into all the earth. ⁷Then He came and took the scroll out of the right hand of Him who sat on the throne.

Worthy Is the Lamb

⁸Now when He had taken the scroll, the four living creatures and the twenty-four elders fell down before the Lamb, each having a harp, and golden bowls full of incense, which are the prayers of the saints. ⁹And they sang a new song, saying:

"You are worthy to take the scroll,
And to open its seals;
For You were slain,
And have redeemed us to God by Your blood
Out of every tribe and tongue and people and
    nation,
¹⁰And have made us[a] kings[b] and priests to our
    God;
And we[c] shall reign on the earth."

¹¹Then I looked, and I heard the voice of many angels around the throne, the living creatures, and the elders; and the number of them was ten thousand times ten thousand, and thousands of thousands, ¹²saying with a loud voice:

"Worthy is the Lamb who was slain
To receive power and riches and wisdom,

And strength and honor and glory and blessing!"

[13]And every creature which is in heaven and on the earth and under the earth and such as are in the sea, and all that are in them, I heard saying:

"Blessing and honor and glory and power
Be to Him who sits on the throne,
And to the Lamb, forever and ever!"[a]

[14]Then the four living creatures said, "Amen!" And the twenty-four[a] elders fell down and worshiped Him who lives forever and ever.[b]

First Seal: The Conqueror

6 Now I saw when the Lamb opened one of the seals;[a] and I heard one of the four living creatures saying with a voice like thunder, "Come and see." [2]And I looked, and behold, a white horse. He who sat on it had a bow; and a crown was given to him, and he went out conquering and to conquer.

Second Seal:
Conflict on Earth

[3]When He opened the second seal, I heard the second living creature saying, "Come and see."[a] [4]Another horse, fiery red, went out. And it was granted to the one who sat on it to take peace from the earth, and that *people* should kill one another; and there was given to him a great sword.

Third Seal: Scarcity on Earth

⁵When He opened the third seal, I heard the third living creature say, "Come and see." So I looked, and behold, a black horse, and he who sat on it had a pair of scales in his hand. ⁶And I heard a voice in the midst of the four living creatures saying, "A quart^a of wheat for a denarius,^{b} and three quarts of barley for a denarius; and do not harm the oil and the wine."

Fourth Seal:
Widespread Death on Earth

⁷When He opened the fourth seal, I heard the voice of the fourth living creature saying, "Come and see." ⁸So I looked, and behold, a pale horse. And the name of him who sat on it was Death, and Hades followed with him. And power was given to them over a fourth of the earth, to kill with sword, with hunger, with death, and by the beasts of the earth.

Fifth Seal:
The Cry of the Martyrs

⁹When He opened the fifth seal, I saw under the altar the souls of those who had been slain for the word of God and for the testimony which they held. ¹⁰And they cried with a loud voice, saying, "How long, O Lord, holy and true, until You judge and avenge our blood on those who dwell on the earth?" ¹¹Then a white robe was given to each of them; and it was said to them that they should rest a little while longer, until both *the*

number of their fellow servants and their brethren, who would be killed as they *were,* was completed.

Sixth Seal:
Cosmic Disturbances

[12]I looked when He opened the sixth seal, and behold,[a] there was a great earthquake; and the sun became black as sackcloth of hair, and the moon[b] became like blood. [13]And the stars of heaven fell to the earth, as a fig tree drops its late figs when it is shaken by a mighty wind. [14]Then the sky receded as a scroll when it is rolled up, and every mountain and island was moved out of its place. [15]And the kings of the earth, the great men, the rich men, the commanders,[a] the mighty men, every slave and every free man, hid themselves in the caves and in the rocks of the mountains, [16]and said to the mountains and rocks, "Fall on us and hide us from the face of Him who sits on the throne and from the wrath of the Lamb! [17]For the great day of His wrath has come, and who is able to stand?"

The Sealed of Israel

7 After these things I saw four angels standing at the four corners of the earth, holding the four winds of the earth, that the wind should not blow on the earth, on the sea, or on any tree. [2]Then I saw another angel ascending from the east, having the seal of the living God. And he cried with a loud voice to the four angels to whom it was granted to harm the earth and the sea, [3]saying, "Do not harm the earth, the sea, or the trees

till we have sealed the servants of our God on their foreheads." [4]And I heard the number of those who were sealed. One hundred *and* forty-four thousand of all the tribes of the children of Israel *were* sealed:

[5] of the tribe of Judah twelve thousand
    were sealed;[a]
of the tribe of Reuben twelve thousand
    were sealed;
of the tribe of Gad twelve thousand
    were sealed;
[6] of the tribe of Asher twelve thousand
    were sealed;
of the tribe of Naphtali twelve thousand
    were sealed;
of the tribe of Manasseh twelve thousand
    were sealed;
[7] of the tribe of Simeon twelve thousand
    were sealed;
of the tribe of Levi twelve thousand
    were sealed;
of the tribe of Issachar twelve thousand
    were sealed;
[8] of the tribe of Zebulun twelve thousand
    were sealed;
of the tribe of Joseph twelve thousand
    were sealed;
of the tribe of Benjamin twelve thousand
    were sealed.

A Multitude from the Great Tribulation

⁹After these things I looked, and behold, a great multitude which no one could number, of all nations, tribes, peoples, and tongues, standing before the throne and before the Lamb, clothed with white robes, with palm branches in their hands, ¹⁰and crying out with a loud voice, saying, "Salvation *belongs* to our God who sits on the throne, and to the Lamb!" ¹¹All the angels stood around the throne and the elders and the four living creatures, and fell on their faces before the throne and worshiped God, ¹²saying:

"Amen! Blessing and glory and wisdom,
Thanksgiving and honor and power and might,
Be to our God forever and ever.
Amen."

¹³Then one of the elders answered, saying to me, "Who are these arrayed in white robes, and where did they come from?"

¹⁴And I said to him, "Sir,ᵃ you know."

So he said to me, "These are the ones who come out of the great tribulation, and washed their robes and made them white in the blood of the Lamb. ¹⁵Therefore they are before the throne of God, and serve Him day and night in His temple. And He who sits on the throne will dwell among them. ¹⁶They shall neither hunger anymore nor thirst anymore; the sun shall not strike them, nor any heat; ¹⁷for the Lamb who is in the midst of the throne will shepherd them and lead them to living fountains of waters.[a] And God will wipe away every tear from their eyes."

Seventh Seal: Prelude to
the Seven Trumpets

8 When He opened the seventh seal, there was silence in heaven for about half an hour. [2]And I saw the seven angels who stand before God, and to them were given seven trumpets. [3]Then another angel, having a golden censer, came and stood at the altar. He was given much incense, that he should offer *it* with the prayers of all the saints upon the golden altar which was before the throne. [4]And the smoke of the incense, with the prayers of the saints, ascended before God from the angel's hand. [5]Then the angel took the censer, filled it with fire from the altar, and threw *it* to the earth. And there were noises, thunderings, lightnings, and an earthquake.

[6]So the seven angels who had the seven trumpets prepared themselves to sound.

First Trumpet: Vegetation Struck

[7]The first angel sounded: And hail and fire followed, mingled with blood, and they were thrown to the earth.[a] And a third of the trees were burned up, and all green grass was burned up.

Second Trumpet:
The Seas Struck

[8]Then the second angel sounded: And *something* like a great mountain burning with fire was thrown into the sea, and a third of the sea became blood. [9]And a third of the living creatures in the sea died, and a third of the ships were destroyed.

Third Trumpet:
The Waters Struck

[10]Then the third angel sounded: And a great star fell from heaven, burning like a torch, and it fell on a third of the rivers and on the springs of water. [11]The name of the star is Wormwood. A third of the waters became wormwood, and many men died from the water, because it was made bitter.

Fourth Trumpet:
The Heavens Struck

[12]Then the fourth angel sounded: And a third of the sun was struck, a third of the moon, and a third of the stars, so that a third of them were darkened. A third of the day did not shine, and likewise the night.

[13]And I looked, and I heard an angel[a] flying through the midst of heaven, saying with a loud voice, "Woe, woe, woe to the inhabitants of the earth, because of the remaining blasts of the trumpet of the three angels who are about to sound!"

Fifth Trumpet:
The Locusts from the Bottomless Pit

9 Then the fifth angel sounded: And I saw a star fallen from heaven to the earth. To him was given the key to the bottomless pit. ²And he opened the bottomless pit, and smoke arose out of the pit like the smoke of a great furnace. So the sun and the air were darkened because of the smoke of the pit. ³Then out of the smoke locusts came upon the earth. And to them was given power, as the scorpions of the earth have power. ⁴They were commanded not to harm the grass of the earth, or any green thing, or any tree, but only those men who do not have the seal of God on their foreheads. ⁵And they were not given *authority* to kill them, but to torment them *for* five months. Their torment *was* like the torment of a scorpion when it strikes a man. ⁶In those days men will seek death and will not find it; they will desire to die, and death will flee from them.

⁷The shape of the locusts was like horses prepared for battle. On their heads were crowns of something like gold, and their faces *were* like the faces of men. ⁸They had hair like women's hair, and their teeth were like lions' *teeth.* ⁹And they had breastplates like breastplates of iron, and the sound of their wings *was* like the sound of chariots with many horses running into battle. ¹⁰They had tails like scorpions, and there were stings in their tails. Their power *was* to hurt men five months. ¹¹And they had as king over them the

angel of the bottomless pit, whose name in Hebrew *is* Abaddon, but in Greek he has the name Apollyon.

¹²One woe is past. Behold, still two more woes are coming after these things.

Sixth Trumpet:
The Angels from the Euphrates

¹³Then the sixth angel sounded: And I heard a voice from the four horns of the golden altar which is before God, ¹⁴saying to the sixth angel who had the trumpet, "Release the four angels who are bound at the great river Euphrates." ¹⁵So the four angels, who had been prepared for the hour and day and month and year, were released to kill a third of mankind. ¹⁶Now the number of the army of the horsemen *was* two hundred million; I heard the number of them. ¹⁷And thus I saw the horses in the vision: those who sat on them had breastplates of fiery red, hyacinth blue, and sulfur yellow; and the heads of the horses *were* like the heads of lions; and out of their mouths came fire, smoke, and brimstone. ¹⁸By these three *plagues* a third of mankind was killed—by the fire and the smoke and the brimstone which came out of their mouths. ¹⁹For their power[a] is in their mouth and in their tails; for their tails *are* like serpents, having heads; and with them they do harm.

²⁰But the rest of mankind, who were not killed by these plagues, did not repent of the works of their hands, that they should not worship demons, and idols of gold, silver, brass, stone, and wood, which can nei-

ther see nor hear nor walk. ²¹And they did not repent of their murders or their sorceries^a or their sexual immorality or their thefts.

The Mighty Angel with the Little Book

10 I saw still another mighty angel coming down from heaven, clothed with a cloud. And a rainbow *was* on his head, his face *was* like the sun, and his feet like pillars of fire. ²He had a little book open in his hand. And he set his right foot on the sea and *his* left *foot* on the land, ³and cried with a loud voice, as *when* a lion roars. When he cried out, seven thunders uttered their voices. ⁴Now when the seven thunders uttered their voices,^a I was about to write; but I heard a voice from heaven saying to me,^b "Seal up the things which the seven thunders uttered, and do not write them."

⁵The angel whom I saw standing on the sea and on the land raised up his hand^a to heaven ⁶and swore by Him who lives forever and ever, who created heaven and the things that are in it, the earth and the things that are in it, and the sea and the things that are in it, that there should be delay no longer, ⁷but in the days of the sounding of the seventh angel, when he is about to sound, the mystery of God would be finished, as He declared to His servants the prophets.

John Eats the Little Book

⁸Then the voice which I heard from heaven spoke to

me again and said, "Go, take the little book which is open in the hand of the angel who stands on the sea and on the earth."

⁹So I went to the angel and said to him, "Give me the little book."

And he said to me, "Take and eat it; and it will make your stomach bitter, but it will be as sweet as honey in your mouth."

¹⁰Then I took the little book out of the angel's hand and ate it, and it was as sweet as honey in my mouth. But when I had eaten it, my stomach became bitter. ¹¹And he[a] said to me, "You must prophesy again about many peoples, nations, tongues, and kings."

The Two Witnesses

11 Then I was given a reed like a measuring rod. And the angel stood,[a] saying, "Rise and measure the temple of God, the altar, and those who worship there. ²But leave out the court which is outside the temple, and do not measure it, for it has been given to the Gentiles. And they will tread the holy city underfoot *for* forty-two months. ³And I will give *power* to my two witnesses, and they will prophesy one thousand two hundred and sixty days, clothed in sackcloth."

⁴These are the two olive trees and the two lampstands standing before the God[a] of the earth. ⁵And if anyone wants to harm them, fire proceeds from their mouth and devours their enemies. And if anyone wants to harm them, he must be killed in this manner.

⁶These have power to shut heaven, so that no rain falls in the days of their prophecy; and they have power over waters to turn them to blood, and to strike the earth with all plagues, as often as they desire.

The Witnesses Killed

⁷When they finish their testimony, the beast that ascends out of the bottomless pit will make war against them, overcome them, and kill them. ⁸And their dead bodies *will lie* in the street of the great city which spiritually is called Sodom and Egypt, where also our[a] Lord was crucified. ⁹Then *those* from the peoples, tribes, tongues, and nations will see their dead bodies three-and-a-half days, and not allow[a] their dead bodies to be put into graves. ¹⁰And those who dwell on the earth will rejoice over them, make merry, and send gifts to one another, because these two prophets tormented those who dwell on the earth.

The Witnesses Resurrected

¹¹Now after the three-and-a-half days the breath of life from God entered them, and they stood on their feet, and great fear fell on those who saw them. ¹²And they[a] heard a loud voice from heaven saying to them, "Come up here." And they ascended to heaven in a cloud, and their enemies saw them. ¹³In the same hour there was a great earthquake, and a tenth of the city fell. In the earthquake seven thousand people were killed, and the rest were afraid and gave glory to the God of heaven.

¹⁴The second woe is past. Behold, the third woe is coming quickly.

Seventh Trumpet: The Kingdom Proclaimed

¹⁵Then the seventh angel sounded: And there were loud voices in heaven, saying, "The kingdomsᵃ of this world have become *the kingdoms* of our Lord and of His Christ, and He shall reign forever and ever!" ¹⁶And the twenty-four elders who sat before God on their thrones fell on their faces and worshiped God, ¹⁷saying:

"We give You thanks, O Lord God Almighty,
The One who is and who was and who is to
 come,ᵃ
Because You have taken Your great power and
 reigned.
¹⁸The nations were angry, and Your wrath has
 come,
And the time of the dead, that they should be
 judged,
And that You should reward Your servants the
 prophets and the saints,
And those who fear Your name, small and great,
And should destroy those who destroy the earth."

¹⁹Then the temple of God was opened in heaven, and the ark of His covenantᵃ was seen in His temple. And there were lightnings, noises, thunderings, an earthquake, and great hail.

The Woman, the Child, and the Dragon

12 Now a great sign appeared in heaven: a woman clothed with the sun, with the moon under her feet, and on her head a garland of twelve stars. ²Then being with child, she cried out in labor and in pain to give birth.

³And another sign appeared in heaven: behold, a great, fiery red dragon having seven heads and ten horns, and seven diadems on his heads. ⁴His tail drew a third of the stars of heaven and threw them to the earth. And the dragon stood before the woman who was ready to give birth, to devour her Child as soon as it was born. ⁵She bore a male Child who was to rule all nations with a rod of iron. And her Child was caught up to God and His throne. ⁶Then the woman fled into the wilderness, where she has a place prepared by God, that they should feed her there one thousand two hundred and sixty days.

Satan Thrown Out of Heaven

⁷And war broke out in heaven: Michael and his angels fought with the dragon; and the dragon and his angels fought, ⁸but they did not prevail, nor was a place found for them[a] in heaven any longer. ⁹So the great dragon was cast out, that serpent of old, called the Devil and Satan, who deceives the whole world; he was cast to the earth, and his angels were cast out with him.

¹⁰Then I heard a loud voice saying in heaven, "Now salvation, and strength, and the kingdom of our God, and the power of His Christ have come, for the accuser of our brethren, who accused them before our God day and night, has been cast down. ¹¹And they overcame him by the blood of the Lamb and by the word of their testimony, and they did not love their lives to the death. ¹²Therefore rejoice, O heavens, and you who dwell in them! Woe to the inhabitants of the earth and the sea! For the devil has come down to you, having great wrath, because he knows that he has a short time."

The Woman Persecuted

¹³Now when the dragon saw that he had been cast to the earth, he persecuted the woman who gave birth to the male *Child.* ¹⁴But the woman was given two wings of a great eagle, that she might fly into the wilderness to her place, where she is nourished for a time and times and half a time, from the presence of the serpent. ¹⁵So the serpent spewed water out of his mouth like a flood after the woman, that he might cause her to be carried away by the flood. ¹⁶But the earth helped the woman, and the earth opened its mouth and swallowed up the flood which the dragon had spewed out of his mouth. ¹⁷And the dragon was enraged with the woman, and he went to make war with the rest of her offspring, who keep the commandments of God and have the testimony of Jesus Christ.[a]

The Beast from the Sea

13 Then I[a] stood on the sand of the sea. And I saw a beast rising up out of the sea, having seven heads and ten horns,[b] and on his horns ten crowns, and on his heads a blasphemous name. [2]Now the beast which I saw was like a leopard, his feet were like *the feet of* a bear, and his mouth like the mouth of a lion. The dragon gave him his power, his throne, and great authority. [3]And I saw one of his heads as if it had been mortally wounded, and his deadly wound was healed. And all the world marveled and followed the beast. [4]So they worshiped the dragon who gave authority to the beast; and they worshiped the beast, saying, "Who *is* like the beast? Who is able to make war with him?"

[5]And he was given a mouth speaking great things and blasphemies, and he was given authority to continue[a] for forty-two months. [6]Then he opened his mouth in blasphemy against God, to blaspheme His name, His tabernacle, and those who dwell in heaven. [7]It was granted to him to make war with the saints and to overcome them. And authority was given him over every tribe,[a] tongue, and nation. [8]All who dwell on the earth will worship him, whose names have not been written in the Book of Life of the Lamb slain from the foundation of the world.

[9]If anyone has an ear, let him hear. [10]He who leads into captivity shall go into captivity; he who kills with the sword must be killed with the sword. Here is the patience and the faith of the saints.

The Beast from the Earth

[11]Then I saw another beast coming up out of the earth, and he had two horns like a lamb and spoke like a dragon. [12]And he exercises all the authority of the first beast in his presence, and causes the earth and those who dwell in it to worship the first beast, whose deadly wound was healed. [13]He performs great signs, so that he even makes fire come down from heaven on the earth in the sight of men. [14]And he deceives those[a] who dwell on the earth by those signs which he was granted to do in the sight of the beast, telling those who dwell on the earth to make an image to the beast who was wounded by the sword and lived. [15]He was granted *power* to give breath to the image of the beast, that the image of the beast should both speak and cause as many as would not worship the image of the beast to be killed. [16]He causes all, both small and great, rich and poor, free and slave, to receive a mark on their right hand or on their foreheads, [17]and that no one may buy or sell except one who has the mark or[a] the name of the beast, or the number of his name.

[18]Here is wisdom. Let him who has understanding calculate the number of the beast, for it is the number of a man: His number *is* 666.

The Lamb and the 144,000

14 Then I looked, and behold, a[a] Lamb standing on Mount Zion, and with Him one hundred *and* forty-four thousand, having[b] His Father's name

written on their foreheads. ²And I heard a voice from heaven, like the voice of many waters, and like the voice of loud thunder. And I heard the sound of harpists playing their harps. ³They sang as it were a new song before the throne, before the four living creatures, and the elders; and no one could learn that song except the hundred *and* forty-four thousand who were redeemed from the earth. ⁴These are the ones who were not defiled with women, for they are virgins. These are the ones who follow the Lamb wherever He goes. These were redeemed[a] from *among* men, *being* firstfruits to God and to the Lamb. ⁵And in their mouth was found no deceit,[a] for they are without fault before the throne of God.[b]

The Proclamations
of Three Angels

⁶Then I saw another angel flying in the midst of heaven, having the everlasting gospel to preach to those who dwell on the earth—to every nation, tribe, tongue, and people—⁷saying with a loud voice, "Fear God and give glory to Him, for the hour of His judgment has come; and worship Him who made heaven and earth, the sea and springs of water."

⁸And another angel followed, saying, "Babylon[a] is fallen, is fallen, that great city, because she has made all nations drink of the wine of the wrath of her fornication."

⁹Then a third angel followed them, saying with a loud voice, "If anyone worships the beast and his

image, and receives *his* mark on his forehead or on his hand, [10]he himself shall also drink of the wine of the wrath of God, which is poured out full strength into the cup of His indignation. He shall be tormented with fire and brimstone in the presence of the holy angels and in the presence of the Lamb. [11]And the smoke of their torment ascends forever and ever; and they have no rest day or night, who worship the beast and his image, and whoever receives the mark of his name."

[12]Here is the patience of the saints; here *are* those[a] who keep the commandments of God and the faith of Jesus.

[13]Then I heard a voice from heaven saying to me,[a] "Write: 'Blessed *are* the dead who die in the Lord from now on.'"

"Yes," says the Spirit, "that they may rest from their labors, and their works follow them."

Reaping the Earth's Harvest

[14]Then I looked, and behold, a white cloud, and on the cloud sat *One* like the Son of Man, having on His head a golden crown, and in His hand a sharp sickle. [15]And another angel came out of the temple, crying with a loud voice to Him who sat on the cloud, "Thrust in Your sickle and reap, for the time has come for You[a] to reap, for the harvest of the earth is ripe." [16]So He who sat on the cloud thrust in His sickle on the earth, and the earth was reaped.

Reaping the Grapes of Wrath

[17]Then another angel came out of the temple which is in heaven, he also having a sharp sickle.

[18]And another angel came out from the altar, who had power over fire, and he cried with a loud cry to him who had the sharp sickle, saying, "Thrust in your sharp sickle and gather the clusters of the vine of the earth, for her grapes are fully ripe." [19]So the angel thrust his sickle into the earth and gathered the vine of the earth, and threw *it* into the great winepress of the wrath of God. [20]And the winepress was trampled outside the city, and blood came out of the winepress, up to the horses' bridles, for one thousand six hundred furlongs.

Prelude to the Bowl Judgments

15 Then I saw another sign in heaven, great and marvelous: seven angels having the seven last plagues, for in them the wrath of God is complete.

[2]And I saw *something* like a sea of glass mingled with fire, and those who have the victory over the beast, over his image and over his mark[a] *and* over the number of his name, standing on the sea of glass, having harps of God. [3]They sing the song of Moses, the servant of God, and the song of the Lamb, saying:

"Great and marvelous *are* Your works,
Lord God Almighty!
Just and true *are* Your ways,

O King of the saints!^a

⁴Who shall not fear You, O Lord, and glorify
Your name?
For *You* alone *are* holy.
For all nations shall come and worship before
You,
For Your judgments have been manifested."

⁵After these things I looked, and behold,^a the temple of the tabernacle of the testimony in heaven was opened. ⁶And out of the temple came the seven angels having the seven plagues, clothed in pure bright linen, and having their chests girded with golden bands. ⁷Then one of the four living creatures gave to the seven angels seven golden bowls full of the wrath of God who lives forever and ever. ⁸The temple was filled with smoke from the glory of God and from His power, and no one was able to enter the temple till the seven plagues of the seven angels were completed.

16 Then I heard a loud voice from the temple saying to the seven angels, "Go and pour out the bowls^a of the wrath of God on the earth."

First Bowl: Loathsome Sores

²So the first went and poured out his bowl upon the earth, and a foul and loathsome sore came upon the men who had the mark of the beast and those who worshiped his image.

Second Bowl:
The Sea Turns to Blood

³Then the second angel poured out his bowl on the sea, and it became blood as of a dead *man;* and every living creature in the sea died.

Third Bowl:
The Waters Turn to Blood

⁴Then the third angel poured out his bowl on the rivers and springs of water, and they became blood. ⁵And I heard the angel of the waters saying:

"You are righteous, O Lord,ᵃ
The One who is and who was and who is to be,ᵇ
Because You have judged these things.
⁶For they have shed the blood of saints and
    prophets,
And You have given them blood to drink.
Forᵃ it is their just due."

⁷And I heard another fromᵃ the altar saying, "Even so, Lord God Almighty, true and righteous *are* Your judgments."

Fourth Bowl:
Men Are Scorched

⁸Then the fourth angel poured out his bowl on the sun, and power was given to him to scorch men with fire. ⁹And men were scorched with great heat, and

they blasphemed the name of God who has power over these plagues; and they did not repent and give Him glory.

Fifth Bowl: Darkness and Pain

[10]Then the fifth angel poured out his bowl on the throne of the beast, and his kingdom became full of darkness; and they gnawed their tongues because of the pain. [11]They blasphemed the God of heaven because of their pains and their sores, and did not repent of their deeds.

Sixth Bowl:
Euphrates Dried Up

[12]Then the sixth angel poured out his bowl on the great river Euphrates, and its water was dried up, so that the way of the kings from the east might be prepared. [13]And I saw three unclean spirits like frogs *coming* out of the mouth of the dragon, out of the mouth of the beast, and out of the mouth of the false prophet. [14]For they are spirits of demons, performing signs, *which* go out to the kings of the earth and[a] of the whole world, to gather them to the battle of that great day of God Almighty.

[15]"Behold, I am coming as a thief. Blessed *is* he who watches, and keeps his garments, lest he walk naked and they see his shame."

[16]And they gathered them together to the place called in Hebrew, Armageddon.[a]

Seventh Bowl:
The Earth Utterly Shaken

[17]Then the seventh angel poured out his bowl into the air, and a loud voice came out of the temple of heaven, from the throne, saying, "It is done!" [18]And there were noises and thunderings and lightnings; and there was a great earthquake, such a mighty and great earthquake as had not occurred since men were on the earth. [19]Now the great city was divided into three parts, and the cities of the nations fell. And great Babylon was remembered before God, to give her the cup of the wine of the fierceness of His wrath. [20]Then every island fled away, and the mountains were not found. [21]And great hail from heaven fell upon men, *each hailstone* about the weight of a talent. Men blasphemed God because of the plague of the hail, since that plague was exceedingly great.

The Scarlet Woman and
the Scarlet Beast

17 Then one of the seven angels who had the seven bowls came and talked with me, saying to me,[a] "Come, I will show you the judgment of the great harlot who sits on many waters, [2]with whom the kings of the earth committed fornication, and the inhabitants of the earth were made drunk with the wine of her fornication."

[3]So he carried me away in the Spirit into the wilderness. And I saw a woman sitting on a scarlet beast

which was full of names of blasphemy, having seven heads and ten horns. [4]The woman was arrayed in purple and scarlet, and adorned with gold and precious stones and pearls, having in her hand a golden cup full of abominations and the filthiness of her fornication.[a] [5]And on her forehead a name *was* written:

MYSTERY, BABYLON THE GREAT,
THE MOTHER OF HARLOTS AND OF
THE ABOMINATIONS OF THE EARTH.

[6]I saw the woman, drunk with the blood of the saints and with the blood of the martyrs of Jesus. And when I saw her, I marveled with great amazement.

The Meaning of the Woman and the Beast

[7]But the angel said to me, "Why did you marvel? I will tell you the mystery of the woman and of the beast that carries her, which has the seven heads and the ten horns. [8]The beast that you saw was, and is not, and will ascend out of the bottomless pit and go to perdition. And those who dwell on the earth will marvel, whose names are not written in the Book of Life from the foundation of the world, when they see the beast that was, and is not, and yet is.[a]

[9]"Here *is* the mind which has wisdom: The seven heads are seven mountains on which the woman sits. [10]There are also seven kings. Five have fallen, one is, *and* the other has not yet come. And when he comes,

he must continue a short time. [11]The beast that was, and is not, is himself also the eighth, and is of the seven, and is going to perdition.

[12]"The ten horns which you saw are ten kings who have received no kingdom as yet, but they receive authority for one hour as kings with the beast. [13]These are of one mind, and they will give their power and authority to the beast. [14]These will make war with the Lamb, and the Lamb will overcome them, for He is Lord of lords and King of kings; and those *who are* with Him *are* called, chosen, and faithful."

[15]Then he said to me, "The waters which you saw, where the harlot sits, are peoples, multitudes, nations, and tongues. [16]And the ten horns which you saw on[a] the beast, these will hate the harlot, make her desolate and naked, eat her flesh and burn her with fire. [17]For God has put it into their hearts to fulfill His purpose, to be of one mind, and to give their kingdom to the beast, until the words of God are fulfilled. [18]And the woman whom you saw is that great city which reigns over the kings of the earth."

The Fall of Babylon the Great

18 After these things I saw another angel coming down from heaven, having great authority, and the earth was illuminated with his glory. [2]And he cried mightily[a] with a loud voice, saying, "Babylon the great is fallen, is fallen, and has become a dwelling place of demons, a prison for every foul spirit, and a cage for every unclean and hated bird! [3]For all the

nations have drunk of the wine of the wrath of her fornication, the kings of the earth have committed fornication with her, and the merchants of the earth have become rich through the abundance of her luxury."

⁴And I heard another voice from heaven saying, "Come out of her, my people, lest you share in her sins, and lest you receive of her plagues. ⁵For her sins have reached[a] to heaven, and God has remembered her iniquities. ⁶Render to her just as she rendered to you,[a] and repay her double according to her works; in the cup which she has mixed, mix double for her. ⁷In the measure that she glorified herself and lived luxuriously, in the same measure give her torment and sorrow; for she says in her heart, 'I sit *as* queen, and am no widow, and will not see sorrow.' ⁸Therefore her plagues will come in one day—death and mourning and famine. And she will be utterly burned with fire, for strong *is* the Lord God who judges[a] her.

The World Mourns
Babylon's Fall

⁹"The kings of the earth who committed fornication and lived luxuriously with her will weep and lament for her, when they see the smoke of her burning, ¹⁰standing at a distance for fear of her torment, saying, 'Alas, alas, that great city Babylon, that mighty city! For in one hour your judgment has come.'

¹¹"And the merchants of the earth will weep and mourn over her, for no one buys their merchandise anymore: ¹²merchandise of gold and silver, precious

stones and pearls, fine linen and purple, silk and scarlet, every kind of citron wood, every kind of object of ivory, every kind of object of most precious wood, bronze, iron, and marble; [13]and cinnamon and incense, fragrant oil and frankincense, wine and oil, fine flour and wheat, cattle and sheep, horses and chariots, and bodies and souls of men. [14]The fruit that your soul longed for has gone from you, and all the things which are rich and splendid have gone from you,[a] and you shall find them no more at all. [15]The merchants of these things, who became rich by her, will stand at a distance for fear of her torment, weeping and wailing, [16]and saying, 'Alas, alas, that great city that was clothed in fine linen, purple, and scarlet, and adorned with gold and precious stones and pearls! [17]For in one hour such great riches came to nothing.' Every shipmaster, all who travel by ship, sailors, and as many as trade on the sea, stood at a distance [18]and cried out when they saw the smoke of her burning, saying, 'What *is* like this great city?'

[19]"They threw dust on their heads and cried out, weeping and wailing, and saying, 'Alas, alas, that great city, in which all who had ships on the sea became rich by her wealth! For in one hour she is made desolate.'

[20]"Rejoice over her, O heaven, and *you* holy apostles[a] and prophets, for God has avenged you on her!"

Finality of Babylon's Fall

[21]Then a mighty angel took up a stone like a great

millstone and threw *it* into the sea, saying, "Thus with violence the great city Babylon shall be thrown down, and shall not be found anymore. [22]The sound of harpists, musicians, flutists, and trumpeters shall not be heard in you anymore. No craftsman of any craft shall be found in you anymore, and the sound of a millstone shall not be heard in you anymore. [23]The light of a lamp shall not shine in you anymore, and the voice of bridegroom and bride shall not be heard in you anymore. For your merchants were the great men of the earth, for by your sorcery all the nations were deceived. [24]And in her was found the blood of prophets and saints, and of all who were slain on the earth."

Heaven Exults over Babylon

19 After these things I heard[a] a loud voice of a great multitude in heaven, saying, "Alleluia! Salvation and glory and honor and power *belong* to the Lord[b] our God! [2]For true and righteous *are* His judgments, because He has judged the great harlot who corrupted the earth with her fornication; and He has avenged on her the blood of His servants *shed* by her." [3]Again they said, "Alleluia! Her smoke rises up forever and ever!" [4]And the twenty-four elders and the four living creatures fell down and worshiped God who sat on the throne, saying, "Amen! Alleluia!" [5]Then a voice came from the throne, saying, "Praise our God, all you His servants and those who fear Him, both[a] small and great!"

⁶And I heard, as it were, the voice of a great multitude, as the sound of many waters and as the sound of mighty thunderings, saying, "Alleluia! For theᵃ Lord God Omnipotent reigns! ⁷Let us be glad and rejoice and give Him glory, for the marriage of the Lamb has come, and His wife has made herself ready." ⁸And to her it was granted to be arrayed in fine linen, clean and bright, for the fine linen is the righteous acts of the saints.

⁹Then he said to me, "Write: 'Blessed *are* those who are called to the marriage supper of the Lamb!'" And he said to me, "These are the true sayings of God." ¹⁰And I fell at his feet to worship him. But he said to me, "See *that you do* not *do that!* I am your fellow servant, and of your brethren who have the testimony of Jesus. Worship God! For the testimony of Jesus is the spirit of prophecy."

Christ on a White Horse

¹¹Now I saw heaven opened, and behold, a white horse. And He who sat on him *was* called Faithful and True, and in righteousness He judges and makes war. ¹²His eyes *were* like a flame of fire, and on His head *were* many crowns. He hadᵃ a name written that no one knew except Himself. ¹³He *was* clothed with a robe dipped in blood, and His name is called The Word of God. ¹⁴And the armies in heaven, clothed in fine linen, white and clean,ᵃ followed Him on white horses. ¹⁵Now out of His mouth goes a sharpᵃ sword, that with it He should strike the nations. And He Him-

self will rule them with a rod of iron. He Himself treads the winepress of the fierceness and wrath of Almighty God. ¹⁶And He has on *His* robe and on His thigh a name written:

KING OF KINGS
AND LORD OF LORDS.

The Beast and His Armies Defeated

¹⁷Then I saw an angel standing in the sun; and he cried with a loud voice, saying to all the birds that fly in the midst of heaven, "Come and gather together for the supper of the great God,[a] ¹⁸that you may eat the flesh of kings, the flesh of captains, the flesh of mighty men, the flesh of horses and of those who sit on them, and the flesh of all *people,* free[a] and slave, both small and great."

¹⁹And I saw the beast, the kings of the earth, and their armies, gathered together to make war against Him who sat on the horse and against His army. ²⁰Then the beast was captured, and with him the false prophet who worked signs in his presence, by which he deceived those who received the mark of the beast and those who worshiped his image. These two were cast alive into the lake of fire burning with brimstone. ²¹And the rest were killed with the sword which proceeded from the mouth of Him who sat on the horse. And all the birds were filled with their flesh.

Satan Bound 1000 Years

20 Then I saw an angel coming down from heaven, having the key to the bottomless pit and a great chain in his hand. ²He laid hold of the dragon, that serpent of old, who is *the* Devil and Satan, and bound him for a thousand years; ³and he cast him into the bottomless pit, and shut him up, and set a seal on him, so that he should deceive the nations no more till the thousand years were finished. But after these things he must be released for a little while.

The Saints Reign with Christ 1000 Years

⁴And I saw thrones, and they sat on them, and judgment was committed to them. Then *I saw* the souls of those who had been beheaded for their witness to Jesus and for the word of God, who had not worshiped the beast or his image, and had not received *his* mark on their foreheads or on their hands. And they lived and reigned with Christ for a^a thousand years. ⁵But the rest of the dead did not live again until the thousand years were finished. This *is* the first resurrection. ⁶Blessed and holy *is* he who has part in the first resurrection. Over such the second death has no power, but they shall be priests of God and of Christ, and shall reign with Him a thousand years.

Satanic Rebellion Crushed

⁷Now when the thousand years have expired, Satan will be released from his prison ⁸and will go out to

deceive the nations which are in the four corners of the earth, Gog and Magog, to gather them together to battle, whose number *is* as the sand of the sea. ⁹They went up on the breadth of the earth and surrounded the camp of the saints and the beloved city. And fire came down from God out of heaven and devoured them. ¹⁰The devil, who deceived them, was cast into the lake of fire and brimstone where[a] the beast and the false prophet *are*. And they will be tormented day and night forever and ever.

The Great White Throne Judgment

¹¹Then I saw a great white throne and Him who sat on it, from whose face the earth and the heaven fled away. And there was found no place for them. ¹²And I saw the dead, small and great, standing before God,[a] and books were opened. And another book was opened, which is *the Book* of Life. And the dead were judged according to their works, by the things which were written in the books. ¹³The sea gave up the dead who were in it, and Death and Hades delivered up the dead who were in them. And they were judged, each one according to his works. ¹⁴Then Death and Hades were cast into the lake of fire. This is the second death.[a] ¹⁵And anyone not found written in the Book of Life was cast into the lake of fire.

All Things Made New

21 Now I saw a new heaven and a new earth, for the first heaven and the first earth had passed

away. Also there was no more sea. [2]Then I, John,[a] saw the holy city, New Jerusalem, coming down out of heaven from God, prepared as a bride adorned for her husband. [3]And I heard a loud voice from heaven saying, "Behold, the tabernacle of God *is* with men, and He will dwell with them, and they shall be His people. God Himself will be with them *and be* their God. [4]And God will wipe away every tear from their eyes; there shall be no more death, nor sorrow, nor crying. There shall be no more pain, for the former things have passed away."

[5]Then He who sat on the throne said, "Behold, I make all things new." And He said to me,[a] "Write, for these words are true and faithful."

[6]And He said to me, "It is done![a] I am the Alpha and the Omega, the Beginning and the End. I will give of the fountain of the water of life freely to him who thirsts. [7]He who overcomes shall inherit all things,[a] and I will be his God and he shall be My son. [8]But the cowardly, unbelieving,[a] abominable, murderers, sexually immoral, sorcerers, idolaters, and all liars shall have their part in the lake which burns with fire and brimstone, which is the second death."

The New Jerusalem

[9]Then one of the seven angels who had the seven bowls filled with the seven last plagues came to me[a] and talked with me, saying, "Come, I will show you the bride, the Lamb's wife."[b] [10]And he carried me away in the Spirit to a great and high mountain, and

showed me the great city, the holy[a] Jerusalem, descending out of heaven from God, [11]having the glory of God. Her light *was* like a most precious stone, like a jasper stone, clear as crystal. [12]Also she had a great and high wall with twelve gates, and twelve angels at the gates, and names written on them, which are *the names* of the twelve tribes of the children of Israel: [13]three gates on the east, three gates on the north, three gates on the south, and three gates on the west.

[14]Now the wall of the city had twelve foundations, and on them were the names[a] of the twelve apostles of the Lamb. [15]And he who talked with me had a gold reed to measure the city, its gates, and its wall. [16]The city is laid out as a square; its length is as great as its breadth. And he measured the city with the reed: twelve thousand furlongs. Its length, breadth, and height are equal. [17]Then he measured its wall: one hundred *and* forty-four cubits, *according* to the measure of a man, that is, of an angel. [18]The construction of its wall was *of* jasper; and the city *was* pure gold, like clear glass. [19]The foundations of the wall of the city *were* adorned with all kinds of precious stones: the first foundation *was* jasper, the second sapphire, the third chalcedony, the fourth emerald, [20]the fifth sardonyx, the sixth sardius, the seventh chrysolite, the eighth beryl, the ninth topaz, the tenth chrysoprase, the eleventh jacinth, and the twelfth amethyst. [21]The twelve gates *were* twelve pearls: each individual gate was of one pearl. And the street of the city *was* pure gold, like transparent glass.

The Glory of the New Jerusalem

²²But I saw no temple in it, for the Lord God Almighty and the Lamb are its temple. ²³The city had no need of the sun or of the moon to shine in it,^a for the glory^b of God illuminated it. The Lamb *is* its light. ²⁴And the nations of those who are saved^a shall walk in its light, and the kings of the earth bring their glory and honor into it.^b ²⁵Its gates shall not be shut at all by day (there shall be no night there). ²⁶And they shall bring the glory and the honor of the nations into it.^a ²⁷But there shall by no means enter it anything that defiles, or causes^a an abomination or a lie, but only those who are written in the Lamb's Book of Life.

The River of Life

22 And he showed me a pure^a river of water of life, clear as crystal, proceeding from the throne of God and of the Lamb. ²In the middle of its street, and on either side of the river, *was* the tree of life, which bore twelve fruits, each *tree* yielding its fruit every month. The leaves of the tree *were* for the healing of the nations. ³And there shall be no more curse, but the throne of God and of the Lamb shall be in it, and His servants shall serve Him. ⁴They shall see His face, and His name *shall be* on their foreheads. ⁵There shall be no night there: They need no lamp nor light of the sun, for the Lord God gives them light. And they shall reign forever and ever.

The Time Is Near

⁶Then he said to me, "These words *are* faithful and true." And the Lord God of the holy^a prophets sent His angel to show His servants the things which must shortly take place.

⁷"Behold, I am coming quickly! Blessed *is* he who keeps the words of the prophecy of this book."

⁸Now I, John, saw and heard^a these things. And when I heard and saw, I fell down to worship before the feet of the angel who showed me these things.

⁹Then he said to me, "See *that you do* not *do that.* For^a I am your fellow servant, and of your brethren the prophets, and of those who keep the words of this book. Worship God." ¹⁰And he said to me, "Do not seal the words of the prophecy of this book, for the time is at hand. ¹¹He who is unjust, let him be unjust still; he who is filthy, let him be filthy still; he who is righteous, let him be righteous^a still; he who is holy, let him be holy still."

Jesus Testifies to the Churches

¹²"And behold, I am coming quickly, and My reward *is* with Me, to give to every one according to his work. ¹³I am the Alpha and the Omega, *the* Beginning and *the* End, the First and the Last."^a

¹⁴Blessed *are* those who do His commandments,^a that they may have the right to the tree of life, and may enter through the gates into the city. ¹⁵But^a outside *are* dogs and sorcerers and sexually immoral and

murderers and idolaters, and whoever loves and practices a lie.

[16]"I, Jesus, have sent My angel to testify to you these things in the churches. I am the Root and the Offspring of David, the Bright and Morning Star."

[17]And the Spirit and the bride say, "Come!" And let him who hears say, "Come!" And let him who thirsts come. Whoever desires, let him take the water of life freely.

A Warning

[18]For[a] I testify to everyone who hears the words of the prophecy of this book: If anyone adds to these things, God will add[b] to him the plagues that are written in this book; [19]and if anyone takes away from the words of the book of this prophecy, God shall take away[a] his part from the Book[b] of Life, from the holy city, and *from* the things which are written in this book.

I Am Coming Quickly

[20]He who testifies to these things says, "Surely I am coming quickly."

Amen. Even so, come, Lord Jesus!

[21]The grace of our Lord Jesus Christ *be* with you all.[a] Amen.

NOTES

JOHN

1:5 [a]Or *overcome*

1:9 [a]Or *That was the true Light which, coming into the world, gives light to every man.*

1:11 [a]That is, His own things or domain [b]That is, His own people

1:16 [a]NU-Text reads *For.*

1:18 [a]NU-Text reads *only begotten God.*

1:23 [a]Isaiah 40:3

1:28 [a]NU-Text and M-Text read *Bethany.*

1:42 [a]NU-Text reads *John.*

1:51 [a]NU-Text omits *hereafter.*

2:17 [a]NU-Text and M-Text read *will eat.* [b]Psalm 69:9

2:22 [a]NU-Text and M-Text omit *to them.*

3:13 [a]NU-Text omits *who is in heaven.*

3:15 [a]NU-Text omits *not perish but.*

4:42 [a]NU-Text omits *the Christ.*

5:2 [a]NU-Text reads *Bethzatha.*

5:4 [a]NU-Text omits *waiting for the moving of the water* at the end of verse 3, and all of verse 4.

5:16 [a]NU-Text omits *and sought to kill Him.*

6:11 [a]NU-Text omits *to the disciples, and the disciples.*

6:19 aLiterally *twenty-five or thirty stadia*

6:22 aNU-Text omits *that* and *which His disciples had entered.*

6:31 aExodus 16:4; Nehemiah 9:15; Psalm 78:24

6:45 aIsaiah 54:13   bM-Text reads *hears and has learned.*

6:47 aNU-Text omits *in Me.*

6:55 aNU-Text reads *true food* and *true drink.*

6:69 aNU-Text reads *You are the Holy One of God.*

7:1 aThat is, the ruling authorities

7:8 aNU-Text omits *yet.*

7:16 aNU-Text and M-Text read *So Jesus.*

7:26 aNU-Text omits *truly.*

7:29 aNU-Text and M-Text omit *But.*

7:33 aNU-Text and M-Text omit *to them.*

7:39 aNU-Text reads *who believed.*   bNU-Text omits *Holy.*

7:40 aNU-Text reads *some.*

7:50 aNU-Text reads *before.*

7:52 aNU-Text reads *is to rise.*

7:53 aThe words *And everyone* through *sin no more* (8:11) are bracketed by NU-Text as not original. They are present in over 900 manuscripts.

8:2 aM-Text reads *very early.*

8:4 aM-Text reads *we found this woman.*

8:5 aM-Text reads *in our law Moses commanded.* bNU-Text and M-Text read *to stone such.*   cM-Text adds *about her.*

8:6 aNU-Text and M-Text omit *as though He did not hear.*

8:7 [a]M-Text reads *He looked up.*

8:9 [a]NU-Text and M-Text omit *being convicted by their conscience.*

8:10 [a]NU-Text omits *and saw no one but the woman;* M-Text reads *He saw her and said.* [a]NU-Text and M-Text omit *of yours.*

8:11 [a]NU-Text and M-Text add *from now on.*

8:38 [a]NU-Text reads *heard from.*

8:54 [a]NU-Text and M-Text read *our.*

8:59 [a]NU-Text omits the rest of this verse.

9:4 [a]NU-Text reads *We.*

9:8 [a]NU-Text reads *a beggar.*

9:9 [a]NU-Text reads *"No, but he is like him."*

9:11 [a]NU-Text omits *the pool of.*

9:35 [a]NU-Text reads *Son of Man.*

10:8 [a]M-Text omits *before Me.*

10:26 [a]NU-Text omits *as I said to you.*

10:34 [a]Psalm 82:6

10:38 [a]NU-Text reads *understand.*

11:18 [a]Literally *fifteen stadia*

11:30 [a]NU-Text adds *still.*

11:31 [a]NU-Text reads *supposing that she was going to the tomb to weep there.*

11:41 [a]NU-Text omits *from the place where the dead man was lying.*

11:50 [a]NU-Text reads *you.*

12:1 [a]NU-Text omits *who had been dead.*

12:5 [a]About one year's wages for a worker

12:7 [a]NU-Text reads *that she may keep.*

12:13 [a]Psalm 118:26

12:15 ^aZechariah 9:9

12:38 ^aIsaiah 53:1

12:40 ^aIsaiah 6:10

12:41 ^aNU-Text reads *because.*

12:47 ^aNU-Text reads *keep them.*

13:2 ^aNU-Text reads *And during supper.*

13:18 ^aNU-Text reads *My bread.*   ^bPsalm 41:9

13:25 ^aNU-Text and M-Text add *thus.*

14:2 ^aLiterally *dwellings*   ^bNU-Text adds a word which would cause the text to read either *if it were not so, would I have told you that I go to prepare a place for you?* or *if it were not so I would have told you; for I go to prepare a place for you.*

14:14 ^aNU-Text adds *Me.*

14:15 ^aNU-Text reads *you will keep.*

14:28 ^aNU-Text omits *I said.*

15:2 ^aOr *lifts up*

15:7 ^aNU-Text omits *you will.*

15:25 ^aPsalm 69:4

16:3 ^aNU-Text and M-Text omit *to you.*

16:4 ^aNU-Text reads *their.*

16:15 ^aNU-Text and M-Text read *He takes of Mine and will declare it to you.*

16:33 ^aNU-Text and M-Text omit *will.*

17:2 ^aM-Text reads *shall.*

17:11 ^aNU-Text and M-Text read *keep them through Your name which You have given Me.*

17:12 ^aNU-Text omits *in the world.*   ^bNU-Text reads *in Your name which You gave Me. And I guarded them;* (or *it;*).

17:20 [a]NU-Text and M-Text omit *will.*

18:15 [a]M-Text reads *the other.*

18:20 [a]NU-Text reads *where all the Jews meet.*

19:3 [a]NU-Text reads *And they came up to Him and said.*

19:7 [a]NU-Text reads *the law.*

19:16 [a]NU-Text omits *and led Him away.*

19:24 [a]Psalm 22:18

19:28 [a]M-Text reads *seeing.*

19:36 [a]Exodus 12:46; Numbers 9:12; Psalm 34:20

19:37 [a]Zechariah 12:10

20:16 [a]NU-Text adds *in Hebrew.*

20:18 [a]NU-Text reads *disciples, "I have seen the Lord," . . .*

20:19 [a]NU-Text omits *assembled.*

20:29 [a]NU-Text and M-Text omit *Thomas.*

21:3 [a]NU-Text omits *immediately.*

21:15 [a]NU-Text reads *John.*

21:16 [a]NU-Text reads *John.*

21:17 [a]NU-Text reads *John.*

1 JOHN

1:4 [a]NU-Text and M-Text read *our.*

2:7 [a]NU-Text reads *Beloved.*   [b]NU-Text omits *from the beginning.*

2:18 [a]NU-Text omits *the.*

2:20 [a]NU-Text reads *you all know.*

2:27 [a]NU-Text reads *you abide.*

2:28 [a]NU-Text reads *if.*
3:1 [a]NU-Text adds *And we are.*   [b]M-Text reads *you.*
3:14 [a]NU-Text omits *his brother.*
3:19 [a]NU-Text reads *we shall know.*
3:23 [a]M-Text omits *us.*
4:3 [a]NU-Text omits *that* and *Christ has come in the flesh.*
4:19 [a]NU-Text omits *Him.*
4:20 [a]NU-Text reads *he cannot.*
5:4 [a]M-Text reads *your.*
5:8 [a]NU-Text and M-Text omit the words from *in heaven* (verse 7) through *on earth* (verse 8). Only four or five very late manuscripts contain these words in Greek.
5:9 [a]NU-Text reads *God, that.*
5:13 [a]NU-Text omits the rest of this verse.
5:18 [a]NU-Text reads *him.*

2 JOHN

3 [a]NU-Text and M-Text read *us.*
8 [a]NU-Text reads *you.*   [b]NU-Text reads *you.*
9 [a]NU-Text reads *goes ahead.*

3 JOHN

4 [a]NU-Text reads *the truth.*
5 [a]NU-Text adds *especially.*

8 [a]NU-Text reads *support.*
11 [a]NU-Text and M-Text omit *but.*

REVELATION

1:5 [a]NU-Text reads *loves us and freed;* M-Text reads *loves us and washed.*

1:6 [a]NU-Text and M-Text read *a kingdom.*

1:8 [a]NU-Text and M-Text omit *the Beginning and the End.* [b]NU-Text and M-Text add *God.*

1:9 [a]NU-Text and M-Text omit *both.*

1:11 [a]NU-Text and M-Text omit *I am* through *third and.* [b]NU-Text and M-Text omit *which are in Asia.*

1:17 [a]NU-Text and M-Text omit *to me.*

1:19 [a]NU-Text and M-Text read *Therefore, write.*

1:20 [a]NU-Text and M-Text omit *which you saw.*

2:15 [a]NU-Text and M-Text read *likewise* for *which thing I hate.*

2:19 [a]NU-Text and M-Text read *faith, service.*

2:20 [a]NU-Text and M-Text read *I have against you that you tolerate.* [b]M-Text reads *your wife Jezebel.* [c]NU-Text and M-Text read *and teaches and seduces.*

2:21 [a]NU-Text and M-Text read *time to repent, and she does not want to repent of her sexual immorality.*

2:22 [a]NU-Text and M-Text read *her.*

2:24 [a]NU-Text and M-Text omit *and.* [b]NU-Text and

M-Text omit *will.*

2:27 [a]Psalm 2:9

3:2 [a]NU-Text and M-Text read *My God.*

3:4 [a]NU-Text and M-Text read *Nevertheless you have a few names in Sardis.*

3:7 [a]Isaiah 22:22

3:8 [a]NU-Text and M-Text read *which no one can shut.*

3:11 [a]NU-Text and M-Text omit *Behold.*

3:14 [a]NU-Text and M-Text read *in Laodicea.*

3:16 [a]NU-Text and M-Text read *hot nor cold.*

4:3 [a]M-Text omits *And He who sat there was* (which makes the description in verse 3 modify the throne rather than God).

4:4 [a]NU-Text and M-Text read *robes, with crowns.*

4:5 [a]NU-Text and M-Text read *voices, and thunderings.* [b]M-Text omits *the.*

4:6 [a]NU-Text and M-Text add *something like.*

4:8 [a]M-Text has *holy* nine times.

4:11 [a]NU-Text and M-Text read *our Lord and God.* [b]NU-Text and M-Text read *existed.*

5:4 [a]NU-Text and M-Text omit *and read.*

5:5 [a]NU-Text and M-Text omit *to loose.*

5:6 [a]NU-Text and M-Text read *I saw in the midst . . . a Lamb standing.*

5:10 [a]NU-Text and M-Text read *them.* [b]NU-Text reads *a kingdom.* [c]NU-Text and M-Text read *they.*

5:13 [a]M-Text adds *Amen.*

5:14 [a]NU-Text and M-Text omit *twenty-four.* [b]NU-Text and M-Text omit *Him who lives forever and ever.*

6:1 [a]NU-Text and M-Text read *seven seals.*

6:3 [a]NU-Text and M-Text omit *and see.*

6:6 [a]Greek *choinix;* that is, approximately one quart [b]This was approximately one day's wage for a worker.

6:12 [a]NU-Text and M-Text omit *behold.* [b]NU-Text and M-Text read *the whole moon.*

6:15 [a]NU-Text and M-Text read *the commanders, the rich men.*

7:5 [a]In NU-Text and M-Text *were sealed* is stated only in verses 5a and 8c; the words are understood in the remainder of the passage.

7:14 [a]NU-Text and M-Text read *My lord.*

7:17 [a]NU-Text and M-Text read *to fountains of the waters of life.*

8:7 [a]NU-Text and M-Text add *and a third of the earth was burned up.*

8:13 [a]NU-Text and M-Text read *eagle.*

9:19 [a]NU-Text and M-Text read *the power of the horses.*

9:21 [a]NU-Text and M-Text read *drugs.*

10:4 [a]NU-Text and M-Text read *sounded.* [b]NU-Text and M-Text omit *to me.*

10:5 [a]NU-Text and M-Text read *right hand.*

10:11 [a]NU-Text and M-Text read *they.*

11:1 [a]NU-Text and M-Text omit *And the angel stood.*

11:4 [a]NU-Text and M-Text read *Lord.*

11:8 [a]NU-Text and M-Text read *their.*

11:9 [a]NU-Text and M-Text read *nations see . . . and will not allow.*

11:12 [a]M-Text reads *I.*

11:15 [a]NU-Text and M-Text read *kingdom . . . has become.*

11:17 [a]NU-Text and M-Text omit *and who is to come.*

11:19 [a]M-Text reads *the covenant of the Lord.*

12:8 [a]M-Text reads *him.*

12:17 [a]NU-Text and M-Text omit *Christ.*

13:1 [a]NU-Text reads *he.*   [b]NU-Text and M-Text read *ten horns and seven heads.*

13:5 [a]M-Text reads *make war.*

13:7 [a]NU-Text and M-Text add *and people.*

   13:14 [a]M-Text reads *my own people.*

13:17 [a]NU-Text and M-Text omit *or.*

14:1 [a]NU-Text and M-Text read *the.*   [b]NU-Text and M-Text add *His name and.*

14:4 [a]M-Text adds *by Jesus.*

14:5 [a]NU-Text and M-Text read *falsehood.*   [b]NU-Text and M-Text omit *before the throne of God.*

14:8 [a]NU-Text reads *Babylon the great is fallen, is fallen, which has made;* M-Text reads *Babylon the great is fallen. She has made.*

14:12 [a]NU-Text and M-Text omit *here are those.*

14:13 [a]NU-Text and M-Text omit *to me.*

14:15 [a]NU-Text and M-Text omit *for You.*

15:2 [a]NU-Text and M-Text omit *over his mark.*

15:3 [a]NU-Text and M-Text read *nations.*

15:5 [a]NU-Text and M-Text omit *behold.*

16:1 [a]NU-Text and M-Text read *seven bowls.*

16:5 [a]NU-Text and M-Text omit *O Lord.*   [b]NU-Text and M-Text read *who was, the Holy One.*

16:6 ªNU-Text and M-Text omit *For.*

16:7 ªNU-Text and M-Text omit *another from.*

16:14 ªNU-Text and M-Text omit *of the earth and.*

16:16 ªM-Text reads *Megiddo.*

17:1 ªNU-Text and M-Text omit *to me.*

17:4 ªM-Text reads *the filthiness of the fornication of the earth.*

17:8 ªNU-Text and M-Text read *and shall be present.*

17:16 ªNU-Text and M-Text read *saw, and the beast.*

18:2 ªNU-Text and M-Text omit *mightily.*

18:5 ªNU-Text and M-Text read *have been heaped up.*

18:6 ªNU-Text and M-Text omit *to you.*

18:8 ªNU-Text and M-Text read *has judged.*

18:14 ªNU-Text and M-Text read *been lost to you.*

18:20 ªNU-Text and M-Text read *saints and apostles.*

19:1 ªNU-Text and M-Text add *something like.* ᵇNU-Text and M-Text omit *the Lord.*

19:5 ªNU-Text and M-Text omit *both.*

19:6 ªNU-Text and M-Text read *our.*

19:12 ªM-Text adds *names written, and.*

19:14 ªNU-Text and M-Text read *pure white linen.*

19:15 ªM-Text adds *two-edged.*

19:17 ªNU-Text and M-Text read *the great supper of God.*

19:18 ªNU-Text and M-Text read *both free.*

20:4 ªM-Text reads *the.*

20:10 ªNU-Text and M-Text add *also.*

20:12 ªNU-Text and M-Text read *the throne.*

20:14 ªNU-Text and M-Text add *the lake of fire.*

21:2 ªNU-Text and M-Text omit *John.*

21:5 ^aNU-Text and M-Text omit *to me.*

21:6 ^aM-Text omits *It is done.*

21:7 ^aM-Text reads *overcomes, I shall give him these things.*

21:8 ^aM-Text adds *and sinners.*

21:9 ^aNU-Text and M-Text omit *to me.* ^bM-Text reads *I will show you the woman, the Lamb's bride.*

21:10 ^aNU-Text and M-Text omit *the great* and read *the holy city, Jerusalem.*

21:14 ^aNU-Text and M-Text read *twelve names.*

21:23 ^aNU-Text and M-Text omit *in it.* ^bM-Text reads *the very glory.*

21:24 ^aNU-Text and M-Text omit *of those who are saved.* ^bM-Text reads *the glory and honor of the nations to Him.*

21:26 ^aM-Text adds *that they may enter in.*

21:27 ^aNU-Text and M-Text read *anything profane, nor one who causes.* **22:1** ^aNU-Text and M-Text omit *pure.*

22:6 ^aNU-Text and M-Text read *spirits of the prophets.*

22:8 ^aNU-Text and M-Text read *am the one who heard and saw.*

22:9 ^aNU-Text and M-Text omit *For.*

22:11 ^aNU-Text and M-Text read *do right.*

22:13 ^aNU-Text and M-Text read *the First and the Last, the Beginning and the End.*

22:14 ^aNU-Text reads *wash their robes.*

22:15 ^aNU-Text and M-Text omit *But.*

22:18 ^aNU-Text and M-Text omit *For.*

22:18 ^bM-Text reads *may God add.*

22:19 ^aM-Text reads *may God take away.*   ^bNU-Text and M-Text read *tree of life.*

22:21 ^aNU-Text reads *with all;* M-Text reads *with all the saints.*

Center Point Publishing
600 Brooks Road ● PO Box 1
Thorndike ME 04986-0001 USA

(207) 568-3717

US & Canada:
1 800 929-9108